Praise for Morgan McCarthy:

'Gripping and atmospheric, this is a cracking read' *Sun*

'This is an accomplished debut novel which captures every tear and smile of the two enthralling main characters as they grapple with life and McCarthy's exquisite storytelling points to a promising literary career' *Edinburgh Evening News*

'Gorgeously written' *Heat*

'A beautiful, brooding novel of siblings growing up half-wild in a grand Welsh manor house. . . Darkly lush, filled with an irresistibly sad glamour, this is a memorable debut' *Kirkus*

'[A] moving debut' *Woman's Weekly*

'*Brideshead Revisited* meets *Dynasty* in this enthralling family saga' *You*

'[An] evocative debut. . . culminating in a tear-jerking conclusion' *Publishers Weekly*

'[An] accomplished first novel' *Booklist*

'Exquisitely written. . . a gripping tale of the burden of legacy and secrets' We Love This Book

'Dark,   *an*

Also by Morgan McCarthy

The Other Half of Me
The Outline of Love

Strange
GIRLS
and
ORDINARY
Women

MORGAN
McCARTHY

TINDER
PRESS

First published in Great Britain in 2014 by Tinder Press
An imprint of HEADLINE PUBLISHING GROUP

First published in paperback in 2014 by Tinder Press
An imprint of HEADLINE PUBLISHING GROUP

1

Cataloguing in Publication Data is available from the British Library

ISBN 978 1 47220 581 0

Typeset in Dante MT by Palimpsest Book Production Ltd, Falkirk, Stirlingshire
Printed and bound in Great Britain by Clays Ltd, St Ives plc

Headline's policy is to use papers that are natural, renewable and recyclable
products and made from wood grown in sustainable forests. The logging and
manufacturing processes are expected to conform to the environmental regulations
of the country of origin.

HEADLINE PUBLISHING GROUP
An Hachette UK Company
338 Euston Road
London NW1 3BH

www.tinderpress.co.uk
www.headline.co.uk
www.hachette.co.uk

For Cian

ACKNOWLEDGEMENTS

I would like to thank Diane for her advice, Jon and Hannah for help with research, Cian for making it all possible, and my friends and family for their general love and support. Huge thanks as always to Jo, and to Leah, Claire, Emily and the team at Tinder Press, for all their time, insight and hard work.

PART ONE

PART ONE

ALICE

Alice Rooke, the doctor's wife, is preparing dinner for six. She is the only person in the kitchen full of fireless yellow light, flameless oven heat, though the mirror facing the window tricks her occasionally into glancing up in the belief that someone else is standing outside the window, looking in. But it is only ever her reflected self, following her usual routes across the large room. The Victorian tiles of the floor, a strict kaleidoscopic pattern of ochre, white, blue and red, have been perceptibly worn down into their most used paths over the years, and Alice likes to think of the women of previous centuries doing what she is doing; though the former pantry doorway is a ghost in the wall, the great old table's place is taken by a marble-topped breakfast bar, and the Belfast sink at which she washes the invisible chemicals off her vegetables is an expensive reproduction.

Alice doesn't know quite why it reassures her to call up an entirely imagined connection to the history of the house, but it does: the idea of standing not alone, but at the end of a queue, stretching right back into the beginning of things. It gives her a sense of *sense;* of the possibility that there is nothing so very catastrophic in having bought the wrong thing for dinner, with no idea of how to cook it.

Alice has never been an ambitious cook, so she isn't sure why today she found herself abruptly sick of her usual variations on chicken breasts and purchased a whole salmon, which she has no idea what to do with. She hefts the weight of it in both hands, its cold slippery muscle, the solidity of it. The eye fixes on her with the flatness of pyrrhic victory. She repacks the eviscerated body with lemon slices, embalms it in salt and white wine, then wraps it in silver foil, neat as a dead pharaoh. The Egyptians, she remembers from a trip to the British Museum with Ben, preserved not only their kings but also various animals, their god-pets, ready for the afterlife. Though, in the end, it was not quite the afterlife they had intended: discovery, excavation, and a display case at the museum. A painted zoo behind glass: hawks, baboons, cats, fish.

Ben was startled by the display. He was eight then, and easily surprised by life. Even now he lacks the protective casing of his friends, their clumsy displays of intellectual superiority, their rowdy physical prowess. Alice has always worried about him. When he began walking home from school by himself, she used to look out for him approaching up the hill, trailing blue-blazered in a small group of boys, moving messily, uneconomically, along low garden walls and kerbs like animals pushing at the outer edges of their pens. She watched for the signs of betrayal in the faces of his companions. Though she still looks with concern at his slenderness – his skin undented, without the cuts and scabs of the others, but seeming conversely more damageable – she has relaxed more these

days; let go of the need to locate herself in the sitting room
at half past three, to watch him turn in at the drive.

Alice puts the silver-bandaged fish into the oven and goes to
the sitting room to look out of the window, without real
purpose: neither Ben nor Jasper is due home yet. The road
beyond the house is January-dark, as settled a dark as if it has
always been night-time on this tree-studded hill, the dim
gold of the streetlights extending partway into the long drives
of the Victorian houses muffled by their conifers and fence
panels, met by the lights of each house now that most people
are home, now that the nocturnal life of the road has begun.

Alone in the house, Alice can feel the uneasy boundary
between interior and exterior. She senses it with her skin, her
hairs rising in a shiver. The night chill is close; the English winter,
dripping and penetrating, draws in with a claustrophobic intent,
pushing at the windows as if it might find one open, and pour
inside like ink. And the house is too large for one person: she
doesn't have the personal vitality to animate it, to be anything
more than a small sound, flitting between rooms.

Alice tries not to think too much about the approaching
evening, which is headed with absolute certainty towards
disaster; the only question being what scale of disaster: tsunami
or school bus crash. She stops herself there, guiltily. She remembers a poem of her school days in which Sylvia Plath compared
her own pains to those of the Holocaust. A tasteless move – and
one she can't approve – but a bold one, nonetheless. As an

assertion it has its own loud grandeur. Her own territory is that of hesitancy, the small gesture. Raised eyebrows, sighs, a ceaseless wondering of 'perhaps' and 'are you sure?'.

Tonight their guests are a strange collection: pieces from very different puzzles. She and Jasper have chosen a couple each; Alice's selected partly in the hope that they will ease the awkward edges and gaps of Jasper's couple. She hasn't met Jasper's colleague Robert before, but the stories, when Jasper tells them, aren't encouraging. Accustomed to hearing only about 'Bloody Robert', she hadn't expected the arrival of Bloody Robert in her home, like some legend of a Scottish chieftain, post-massacre, swathed in gore and tartan.

'I thought you didn't like Robert?' she said to Jasper.

'What gave you that idea?' Jasper was surprised.

'You said he was an idiot.'

'That was when I first arrived at the practice. We play golf together now.' He contemplates this, then adds, 'He's still an idiot.'

About Robert's wife, Amelia, Alice hasn't heard anything at all.

Then there is her couple, Oliver and Maya. Oliver is an old friend of hers from university, part of a circle that used to include his now ex-wife, Sophia. Sophia was always the beauty of the group, a blonde with a charming way of receiving compliments, her appetite for which led her into several affairs. After the last of these, Oliver spent a few months drinking too much, then moved to Australia and took up surfing, then finally came back looking, if not exactly happy, at least tanned. Alice was surprised to see him when he came back: not only his body but his face visibly hardened, as if the salt water had eroded all soft tissue matter, leaving only the polished elements of a man. Oliver's new frame has been predictably attractive to women; Maya being the latest to fall under its spell, almost three months ago.

'I thought three months shows commitment. Seriousness,' she explained to Jasper.

'Pity about him and Sophia,' Jasper said, blandly. 'She was always good company.'

'I'm sure Maya will be very nice.'

Jasper raised his eyebrows. He isn't enthusiastic about meeting new people. He says he has enough friends, enough protection against solitude, and can't see the point beyond that.

Alice reacts immediately and predictably when she hears Jasper's arrival. She knows her own involuntary motions: the jump of the heart, the quiver of the hands, moving up to her hair, obsessively smoothing. Even after so many years together, she still hasn't quite got used to Jasper. She doesn't feel the luxury – the laziness – of ownership. She watches him secretly like a girl watches a handsome teacher, his ghostly frown, his downturned mouth when he is reading a journal, or even watching television, investing the most trivial of his activities with a grave solemnity, so that she finds herself worrying about interrupting him. She admires his height, his dark hair – still thick – and his near-black eyes, hung around with their heavy lashes. She is incapable of laughing about him to her friends, or teasing him to his face, which is just as well, because Jasper doesn't like to be the subject of a joke.

'Fucking traffic,' Jasper says, coming in and administering a brisk kiss to her cheek, 'Where's Ben – upstairs? How's everything?'

'He got in ten minutes ago; he's playing computer games in his room. Everything's fine, though we might have to eat a little later. I made an error of judgement –' she laughs, hearing it as a thin sound, a flutter of apology – 'I bought a whole salmon. I had to look up some recipes for sauces, and I realised it'll take longer to cook. Not too much longer. Just half an hour.'

'Why did you buy it?' Jasper enquires, eyebrows elevated.

'Oh, I don't know. A silly moment, I suppose. Sorry.'

'It's fine.' He takes off his coat, speckled with rain, and starts to go upstairs. He turns at the top and calls back down, 'I'll just book a restaurant next time. Easier for everyone.'

Alice stands at the foot of the stairs for a little while, leaning on the banister, head turned upwards, as if Jasper will reappear. Only his sounds travel down to her; the clunk of the stiff bedroom door, the noise of two shoes falling, the rattle of clothes hangers. Then she goes back to the kitchen to check on the fish.

Looking around the dinner table, reflecting the imprecise ovals of the faces above it like a pool, Alice considers the various ways a gathering of people might fail to connect. You can push people together like a heap of sticks, soak them in alcohol, wave a match over them, and yet something refuses to ignite. A few difficult guests stall the conversation. The reliable entertainers start looking at their watches and wondering when they can escape. And yet the dinner must limp on, until everyone can go, gratefully, to bed.

To her right, Oliver has been grounded by Bloody Robert's impenetrable politics. Opposite, Jasper is tolerating Robert's wife, Amelia, with nothing to indicate his discomfort except a longer, narrower stare. Alice is half relieved to see that Amelia – her laugh bordering on the wild, her hand shaking as it closes on her wine glass ('Robert thinks I drink too much, don't you, Robert?') – is something of a liability; she hopes that Jasper's complaints, later, will focus on that, and not his irritation at the late dinner. Oliver's new girlfriend Maya (as Alice will probably think of her for the next few years, or at least until the memory of Sophia's sexual devastation has faded) is beautiful but silent. Whether out of shyness or boredom, she has said very little since arriving, confining herself to keenly nodding and smiling in the way of someone who doesn't speak much English, which isn't the case.

After a few bottles of wine, Robert and Jasper begin to debate something or other, and Oliver turns to talk to Alice, telling her a story that makes her laugh: laughter that – for the first time that evening – is not decided upon, but shaken into sound; an involuntary upwards movement. Oliver smiles at her in the settling warmth of it, moving his hand across to hers, as if to touch or tap it, but at the last moment laying it on the table instead, where it forms a neighbourly companionship with her own. She glances at the corded infrastructure of it, brown and round nailed. Then her own: white – too white – allowing the blue trails of veins to leach through. Thinning skin. She has noticed that when she pinches the skin on the back of her hand, it keeps its shape for a moment, before subsiding. She moves her hand into her lap.

'Oh, why don't we play charades?' Amelia calls suddenly, her face alight, tense and clenched with fun.

Robert looks over and frowns. 'No,' he says.

Amelia shrugs and turns to Jasper, saying (in the distinct, high voice she apparently uses for asides): 'Robert's in a bad mood because our son's been expelled from school.'

'Oh, really?' Jasper says, becoming interested in this misfortune.

'You ought to keep an eye on yours,' Amelia says. 'One minute they're quiet and well behaved and well – just your little boy. The next—'

'Amelia,' Robert interrupts, low-browed with suppressed rage. 'Nobody wants to hear about this.'

There is a moment of violence in the air, a crackable, brilliant tension, until Alice brightly announces that she's going to check on the pudding, and everyone starts talking overenthusiastically about how much they are looking forward to it.

Outside the dining room she feels a change in pressure, like a diver coming up to the surface. Instead of going to the kitchen she goes up the stairs to Ben's room. She finds him asleep, lying on top of the bed sheets in his pyjamas, a dropped video game controller next to his hand. His slight body is lit by the blue-flickering sun of the television screen, the only light in the room, showing his arms up: pale, too delicate.

She unfolds and refolds Ben in the duvet, as he shifts and murmurs something; the slurred language of sleep, untranslatable. He wouldn't allow this tucking in if he were fully conscious: he is fierce about his autonomies. Perhaps she could take advantage of his docility now to sing something to him; read a story, perhaps. But that might be pushing it, and she needs to go back to the party, make sure it hasn't clattered to a total halt. She strokes Ben's warm forehead for a moment, brushing the fine hair back from it, then turns off the television and goes back downstairs.

Alice arrives with the plum tart as Robert is saying loudly to Jasper: 'I can safely say I know patients. I know which of them are drugs types and which aren't. I know when they're trying to pull the wool over my eyes.'

Jasper brings his eyebrows up and together, an expression that has always looked attractively wolfish to Alice, though in the past it has occasionally been taken for arrogance.

'Someone really clever could pull the wool over any doctor's eyes,' he says. 'And too solid a belief in one's own infallible judgement might, in fact, help them to do so.'

'Someone really clever doesn't get addicted to drugs,' Robert says, with an air of coup de grâce.

'Now...' Oliver begins, but the protest is lost in the ensuing tussle between Robert and Jasper, playing their famous addicts as if in a strange game of top trumps.

Alice can tell that Jasper thinks he is wiser than Robert – pompous Robert, telling them about methamphetamine through a mouthful of fragmented pastry – but it strikes her for the first time that neither of them are as wise as they believe themselves to be. They don't feel the need to preface their opinions with 'I think'; presenting their own conclusions as unalterable fact. They talk about disciplines – writing, sport, economics – as if they could have mastered any of them, but didn't bother. And in this, their artificially tightened circle of society, so far from either the bottom or the top, they can argue; two big fish lording it over their small pond.

Not hungry, Alice levers a glossy plum from its sugary bed and eats it thoughtfully. She contemplates her disloyal thought: new and untested, floating in on a tide of wine, coming to rest on the empty shore. She isn't sure what she will do with it when tomorrow comes, if it is still there.

'The fact is,' Robert says loudly, as if speaking over dissenters, '*The fact is*, we are responsible for ourselves. We can choose whether to do drugs or not. We have free will.'

'According to Spinoza there is no free will,' Jasper says. 'We are shaped by our circumstances, limited by our own innate abilities, limited by our own bodies. Someone who isn't born really clever, for example, is handicapped by that. Their free will is limited.'

'Let's not get into philosophy,' Robert says, irritated.

'No, let's not,' Amelia says. 'This is far too highbrow for me. I never understand what Robert's talking about half the time.'

At this point Alice catches Oliver's eye, having avoided it so far, and they exchange a near-smile, a moment of smuggled amusement.

When she clears the plates away later, she thinks of the fish, which turned out perfectly. Not that it will be remembered, when people look back on tonight. They will remember the claustrophobic feel of the conversation, the intimation of cruelty, of boredom. They will remember the press of winter at the glass dividing inside from outside, where the rain and blown leaves whirl savagely in the night, the comparative quietness of the table under its refined lamplight. Not a simple division. Not without the possibility of breach.

Alice takes her make-up off sitting on the edge of the bed, facing away from Jasper. It seems a bit much for him to have to watch the beauty wiped from her, stroke by stroke. At forty-two, she doesn't like to watch it herself; avoiding mirrors at the end of the night, the glimpses of the skin concertinaing around her eyes, the slippage around the jaw, the beginnings of the disappearance of the substrata of fat that she never even knew about when she was young; has learned to worry about in the same way that she was warned about lakes shrinking, polar caps melting, the ozone layer wearing thin.

'At a certain age,' Alice's mother used to say, before she reached that age herself, 'everyone starts to look like their own caricature.'

Jasper, behind her, yawns. 'You're not going to be much longer, are you?' he asks. 'I'm exhausted.'

'Just one more minute. Sorry.' Then, to hear the worst – 'Did you have a good night?'

'I think we both know it was a bit of a disaster, wasn't it?'

She laughs, relieved, before she realises that he isn't

including her as a fellow survivor, but as the irresponsible captain of their stricken ship.

'It was a bad start with the late dinner,' he carries on. 'And what on earth was wrong with Maya? She barely said a word.'

Alice gets into bed next to him, his ceiling-facing, straight-nosed profile emerging sternly from its dark hair.

'Light out?'

'Yes, thank you.' Jasper pauses for a moment, then continues, more gently, 'Robert made a bit of a fool of himself on a few things, I thought.'

'I thought so too.'

'What was that about the death penalty? He sounded like a *Daily Mail* editorial.'

'Death for rioters,' says Alice, sliding down to meet the sleep that flows up from the pillowy bed, the dense white sheets.

'Bloody Robert,' says Jasper, laughing softly, then turns and resettles himself in the bed and, before long, she hears the sounds of him moving off into unconsciousness; arrhythmic breathing, slight movements of his lips, the occasional chuffing in his throat. She remembers when they were first sharing beds: her rolling like a raindrop into the gully between his arm and chest, to put her head in the yielding well of his neck. After a while it would begin to feel uncomfortable and they would move apart, the while getting shorter and shorter over the years, sustained by less and less patience, until it vanished altogether.

The next morning, Alice is the last person in the house to wake up. Ben is in the kitchen pouring himself a bowl of brightly coloured cereal. She watches him for a moment; his oversized hands and feet, milk-stained red T-shirt, eyes the same blue as her own, with her own expression of faint uncertainty. Jasper is in his study with the door closed; a faint smell of coffee marking his progress from the kitchen like a smoke trail.

'Sleep well?' she asks Ben.

'Yeah.'

'I tucked you in,' she says playfully. 'I haven't done that for a while. You were fast asleep.'

Ben is immediately outraged. '*Mum...*'

'It serves you right for playing computer games until you pass out. Next time you'll remember you're leaving yourself vulnerable to acts of maternal love.'

'Whatever,' says Ben. 'Can I go to the park?'

'Not today, sweetie. We're going to Granny's for lunch, remember.' She fetches a cloth to wipe up the milk splashes on the black marble, a constellation of cereal hoops; the small galaxies of housewifery.

'Okay,' Ben says, leaving reluctantly to get ready, to Alice's relief. It is only at the last minute that he makes his plea, turning halfway through the trudge to find his shoes: 'If Dad isn't going, why do I have to go?'

Alice tries not to cast a reproachful look in the direction of the sitting room, in which Jasper has settled down to watch cricket. He rarely visits her mother, and doesn't see why she should either.

('Why do you put yourself through it?' he asks, reasonably. 'Guilt? Duty?'

'She's alone in the country,' is Alice's reply.

'She could move. She just likes to demonstrate her power by making people drive out to see her'.)

'Because Granny likes to see you,' Alice tells Ben now. 'And Dad has work to do.'

'But she doesn't like me,' Ben says. 'She said I was dozy. And she always goes on about the time I broke her cup and saucer. She always says "*and* the saucer", like it was on purpose that I broke both, but if she hadn't been making me hold them both, I wouldn't have dropped them both, would I, when the dog jumped at me –' he pauses, frowning, collecting new sorrows – 'I don't *like* those dogs.'

At this point Jasper calls from the sitting room, 'Alice, if he doesn't want to go, let him stay. I'll look after him', at which Ben turns such a shining look of gratitude in his father's direction that Alice is tempted to inform him that Jasper isn't, in fact, helping Ben, but scoring a point against his old enemy, Tamara; but she swallows it, bulky in her throat, and leaves them both at home.

The gravelled drive at Pembers, Tamara's large grey manor house, has always been a problem for Alice. She would prefer to sit in the stilled car and gather herself and her thoughts for a moment in preparation for her mother, who might otherwise catch at a loose end and unravel her, but the sonic rockslide that announces her arrival makes this moment of quiet time impossible. Already, as she turns off the engine, she can hear the barking of the dogs. As Alice gets out of the car, Tamara appears in the doorway, erect and formidable as a general, if there ever was a general with a wind-blown silver bob and a lavender cardigan. She always puts on her war paint, even for Alice; her eyes dark, her mouth pearly pink. The two large white poodles jump around her, snapping their long, many-toothed snouts like crocodiles.

'Oh goodness me, Alice, they're only playing,' Tamara cries merrily, as one feints at Alice's dangling fingers. 'You always look so *nervous*.' Tamara leads Alice into the house, talking about deadlines in a way that implies she is inconvenienced by Alice's visit, which she had coerced Alice into the week before by reminding her that she was alone in the country. Tamara writes a column for a national paper, called *Pastoral Living* ('Out to Pasture,' Jasper calls it), in which she tells charming little stories about chaffinches and dispenses lifestyle advice: 'The farmhouse kitchen need not become a stale idea. Add a twist with these perspex chairs.' 'The asparagus is poking its divine green spears up to the sky. To keep asparagus blight at bay use a natural and age-old trick – sprinkle lemon juice on the soil.'

In the kitchen of hanging copper pans and Spode-crowded dressers, Tamara opens several cupboards looking for the teapot.

'Isn't the housekeeper here today?' Alice asks.

'Housekeeper?' birdcalls Tamara. '*Some* of us live a simple existence where we don't rely on staff. Don't you ever read my column?' Alice blinks, silenced by the shamelessness of this, and puzzled by the insinuation that she herself has staff.

'So, where is Ben today?' Tamara, discovering the teapot, turns sharply with it and raises her eyebrows at Alice.

'Oh, he had a birthday party I'd forgotten about. I'm so disorganised these days.'

'I suppose birthday parties are more fun than grandmothers,' Tamara says, unconvincingly. 'I certainly wouldn't want Ben to be forced to visit me.'

'He loves visiting you.'

'Yes, well,' Tamara says, looking reprovingly at the teacups as if they might tell a different story, 'I always used to make sure you visited your grandparents when you were young. I didn't want you to turn to me one day, after their death, and say, "Mummy, why didn't I see more of them, when I had the chance?" . . . do you still take sugar?'

Alice, trying to decide which of the problems with this faulty reminiscence to address first – the most obvious being that she has no memory of ever visiting her maternal grandparents, the most unexpected being that Tamara has always hated being called Mummy – hesitates too long over her answer, so that Tamara begins tapping her spoon impatiently against the teapot, as if demanding a speech, until Alice says finally, lamely, 'No sugar, thank you.'

She looks out into the long garden, dimmed and greyed by the arrival of rain. The lawn is as smooth and flat as a murky pool, rhododendron bushes floating stately across its calm surface. She remembers sitting on the grass as a child, her dolls arranged around her, having an awkward picnic. Even when she was doing all the voices her parties were not a success.

'So, how is Jasper?' Tamara asks.

'He has work. He's got a lot of work at the moment,' Alice says.

'I read in the papers the other day that GPs are cutting their opening hours,' Tamara says. 'It's causing all sorts of problems. People have to go to A and E instead. Waiting weeks for appointments.'

'I don't think that's happened at Jasper's surgery,' Alice says mildly.

'Oh, give it time,' Tamara says, with her rattled-chandelier laugh. 'Everyone wants to do the minimum. That's the problem with society these days.'

Driving away from the house, Alice tries to picture her father, Edward, whom she saw very little of before he died of a stroke when she was eleven. She remembers his arrivals at home, late evening; a truncated black shape forming in the glass of the front door. He sometimes asked her a few questions; about her schoolwork mostly, though his vague blue eyes didn't really look at her, and he'd become irritable if she was left out before him too long, like a dirty dinner plate. He and Tamara didn't seem to like each other: in the short periods of time when they were both at home they would only occasionally come face to face in the hall or on the landing, where they would manage to quickly and comprehensively disagree with each other, before disappearing in different directions.

According to Spinoza there is no free will, Jasper said. Alice is familiar with this answer of his, plucked from its original setting (*University Challenge,* possibly, or a newspaper) almost word for word; deposited with a flourish into a conversation, to confound the more easily confounded of his opponents. But she has thought about it, and she thinks of it now; of herself growing up in empty room after empty room, occasionally feeling the movement of the air, the entrance of tension, or disappointment, but not love. Has she been shaped by circumstance? What sort of shape might these circumstances make? Something attenuated, something lean. A bowl shape, a waiting vessel. Or a figurine, china-faced, with its interior vacancy.

But, she thinks. But. She does have love. This is what she should have explained to Jasper, when he asks why she visits her mother when it clearly upsets her. She does it because she can do it. She can be upset for a little while because there is a clear end to it these days; signalled by the closing of the car door, settling heavy and neat into its socket. Her mother, whether she cares or not, is loved by nobody but Alice. But Alice has Jasper, and that means something, when someone like him could have so many other options. She has Ben, who is nothing if not a distillation of love, unreasonable and complete. Whatever forces acted on her young, mouldable shape, whatever her childhood taught her to expect, she has won – and clung on to – much more than that.

That night Jasper is out for an old school friend's birthday so Alice makes dinner for Ben and herself, the oddly opal light of the evening melting through the kitchen window over them: Alice assembling an uninspired salad, Ben sitting at the table, parrying her enquiries about his day.

'Did you have fun?'

'Yeah.'

'Who was there?'

'Oh . . . James. Mark. George.'

'George is new, isn't he? You only mentioned him last week.'

Ben mutters something.

'What's that?'

'I said George is a *girl*.'

'Oh!' She turns away to raise her eyebrows. 'Well, if you want to invite her over here, just let me know. It'd be nice to have another girl around, if only briefly.'

'What's wrong with us?' Ben asks. 'What's wrong with boys?'

Alice hesitates. Despite his studied mumbling, his attitude of being unbothered, Ben is a boy of small but sharply felt hurts. 'Boys are very nice,' she says. 'But girls are nice too.'

Ben nods, contented with this neutrality, a statement of nothing much. The worry visibly slips off his face, replaced in turn with a new thought, a signalling blink, a small frown.

'Why aren't you going out tonight?' he asks.

'Oh, they aren't my friends. There's no need for me to be there. And I wanted to stay home tonight.'

'Why?'

'Why? Well . . . to watch a film.'

Then because of this, Alice has to find a DVD – *Brief Encounter* – put it on, and settle herself with a glass of wine and every appearance of enjoyment on the sofa. By the time Ben has gone to bed and she is alone, the cold movement of the wine stinging her throat into pleasurable life, watching the dark train go hooting into the fog, she has subsided into an odd form of contentment: calmly solitary, as if she has always been like this, the sort of woman who can give her attention over to a film and a glass of wine, without feeling the pull, the pressure, of human connection.

Alice has redecorated the whole house, but the sitting room is the place in which her taste has reached its radiant apotheosis, in which the observation that she 'really ought to take up interior design – professionally, I mean' is most often heard. The room is gold and brown like a tiger's eye; the same spectrum rising and falling in the heavy drop of the curtains, the sheen of the gold sofa, the honey walls, the varnished floorboards glowing like brandy, the twin chiffoniers like coffee.

She thought once, while studying archaeology at university, that she might be an interior designer. She used to tell people that whenever she was drunk. She probably mentioned it in her first conversation with Jasper, now sadly stricken from the records, written as it was in alcohol; disappearing ink.

When she first met Jasper, it was the final year of both their courses. She had slept with more people than she should have by that time: she didn't see the point in saying no. She never minded seeing a boy sidle out of her room late at night, or the next morning, with sometimes only a wave – a sheepish salute – because neither of them could remember each other's names. On occasion, she'd be surprised by someone coming back to her, asking if she wanted a drink or something. The night she met Jasper she was being busily harassed by one of these returning sexual partners; a boy she had no attraction to, not even now that she was drunk again, and who was beginning to piss her off.

She was hiding from him on the landing of the party – worn carpet, bare Victorian bannister, open window letting in a small shower of rain from the black sky – when she overheard the conversation next to her. A dark-haired boy talking to a blonde girl, holding both her hands in a way that suggested not intimacy but prevention, keeping her at bay. The blonde girl, her face cloaked by hair, was trying to stop crying.

'Sorry,' Alice heard the boy say. 'I didn't realise that's what you wanted.'

'Yes, you did,' the girl said. 'I'm going home.'

'Sorry,' the boy said again. His voice sounded muted, respectful, like someone working at a funeral home. It also sounded dishonest. Alice didn't think he was very sorry.

The girl rushed past Alice and downstairs, so that for a brief moment she and the dark-haired boy were the only two people on the landing. In the sudden drop of silence they exchanged a look, which was – oddly – not awkward, but something else: a kind of complicity. The moment was interrupted by the appearance of Alice's admirer (what was his name? She doesn't know now. She may not even have known back then) and so she exited, pursued by anon. As she left, she knew the dark-haired boy was still watching her, feeling it rather than seeing it, in the way one does.

The night after that there was another party and when she walked in, already unsteady, there was Jasper, standing in the hall as if he was waiting for her. His eyes had a heat in them, and a changeability, like a dark road melting in the sun, or freshly poured tar, ready to take shape. She went to him, smiling, as if he had been waiting for her, as if she knew him well.

In the early days, before their roles were silently settled, Alice had the brief, strange experience of being the one who is most wanted. Her previous admirer had put it about that she was a type of succubus, a bewitching devil woman who had kicked him out of bed as quickly as she allowed him into it, leaving him broken hearted and ball-less. Jasper had heard the rumour, saw evidence of it in Alice's habitually vague, half-smiling manner -and it made her magnetic to him. He called often, arrived at her door with flowers, which, surprised, she laughed at. He went away excited, baffled and determined. By the time they graduated, they were already discussing one-bedroom flats.

She agreed to his proposals, she thinks, later in bed. It is past three in the morning and she has been woken by the mournful cry of the front door, un-oiled metal on metal. She agreed to be won. Since then, all the asking has been carried out by Alice herself ('*What would you like for dinner?*' '*What time will you be home?*'): many, many small questions, now that the big questions have been settled.

The stairs sigh one by one, the penultimate step with its familiar creak, then she hears the soft disturbance of the landing carpet, yielding under pressure, before the bedroom door opens. Jasper stands at his side of the bed undressing awkwardly; strenuously quiet, wrestling with his socks and sleeves. She guesses he must be drunk. Finally, he slips like a cat into the sheets beside her, finding his own spot, curling reflexively, before vanishing into the solid coma of his sleep.

On Sunday, Alice gets out of bed with cau
wake Jasper. She takes Ben to the supermar
they join with the currents of day-time shoppers,
lished routes, following the drift of the usual. Alice n
straying off-course, an old woman in a coat with a
collar. Beneath the colours of her heavily layered face
powder and salmon pink rouge – her skin is dead white,
veined. As she passes, Alice can make out what the woman
muttering. 'Gone,' she says, 'gone, gone, gone, gone, gone.' She
picks things up, carries them about, drops them onto other shelves.
She puts a lemon, absently, in her pocket, followed by a bottle of
whisky. The staff watch her, raise their eyebrows and shrug.

'What is she doing?' Ben asks. 'Is she stealing stuff?'

'Sssh,' Alice says. 'She's probably not very well.'

She remembers a night of her childhood; a dark globe with
a small, bright picture at its centre, like a spark in the pupil
of an eye. Stage lights blazing, yellow-lit boards, a heavy red
velvet curtain. A row of small girls tap dancing, hair in butter-
smooth ringlets, feet rattling on the boards like machine-gun
fire. One little girl at the end (Alice) dancing slightly out of
time. She ran up to her mother afterwards, wearing her showy
white dress with red polka dots, holding out the skirt with
both hands, and an old woman turned, looked at her and said
in a loud and ominous voice: 'Blood and bandages.'

Tamara glanced at her and drew Alice away, as if the old
woman might be about to grab or bite, though really there
was nothing threatening about her, standing with a plain
canvas bag and large glasses with pink rims, a smell of drying
raincoats and old cigarettes and an air of defiance.

children from the estate,'
ising her eyebrows. 'Not

ned her head around to
ed the hall to the table
her own enchanted
ice, not directed at
of sound. Tamara
polyester' or 'instant coffee',
stood that these things were conditions
she did not know why. She herself had mixed feel-
gs about the interloper: a yearning, and an equal repulsion.
She watched her in fascination until it was time to leave.

At home she tells Jasper about the shoplifting woman.

'I worry about these people. So much for care in the community,' she finishes.

'It's a disgrace,' Jasper agrees. He is sitting holding a cup of coffee with both hands.

'So what happened to you last night?' Alice asks, when it appears the information won't be volunteered.

'I can't even remember.' Jasper shrugs with exaggerated confusion, a gesture so unlike him that Alice feels her skin tighten, as if drawing in around her. Lucky not to be an animal at these times, to be made obvious by the turn of an ear, a lifted lip, such visible rearrangements. 'We went to some late-opening bar, then I remember a taxi home. Completely overcharged me. I'm probably too old for this.'

'Probably,' Alice agrees. He frowns. A quick appearance of wrinkles gathers around his eyebrows, folding the smooth, untanned skin. Jasper has always looked younger than he is. Though he would never admit to it, she knows he is pleased by his evasion of the downward forces of time, pulling the rest of his peers into the grave, one jowl, one eye bag at a time. The year he turned forty he hid his birthday cards and announced that, instead of a party, he, Alice and Ben would be spending the fortnight in Croatia.

'I tried not to wake you when I came home. I don't even know what time it was.'

Now Alice shrugs. 'I didn't hear you get in.'

On Monday, Alice collects Ben from football practice; standing by the open car door and making small talk with a couple of other parents as their mud-slicked sons tease each other and kick aimlessly at the wet leaves. The boys and their parents are tired, as wiped clean of energy as the pale grey sky, the desolate licks of wind that stir them too faintly to move them finally home.

When Ben gets into the car, crusted crocodilian with mud from the knees downwards, Alice says, 'Hey, James's mum just told me you were invited to sleep over at theirs on Saturday, but apparently you told them you had a family party – which obviously we didn't. Don't worry, I didn't drop you in it. But why didn't you want to go?'

'Oh,' Ben says, flatly. She looks over at him, his face turned to the window, luminous in the white grey that falls on him. She wonders whether his studied lack of expression at these times has been learned from Jasper, or from his school friends.

The round sweep of his cheek now is as impermeable and blank as a plate.

'I'm not cross,' Alice says. 'Just wondering . . .?'

She has read too many stories about bullied children, no doubt, their photo-smiles scattered across the pages of newspapers, already looking like the past, like years ago. Found in bedrooms or under trees, suspended by cords as friendly and everyday as dressing gown ties, skipping ropes, the wires of games controllers.

She remembers watching a younger Ben trying to shoo a bluebottle out of the window. The fly ducked and wove, looped out of range of his waved magazine, resisting guidance. Eventually, Jasper, annoyed at the buzzing, took the magazine and swatted the fly.

'It's dead,' Ben said, as if surprised.

'Don't worry,' Alice said quickly, 'it's not the same sort of dead as people-dead.'

'Why?' Ben said. Jasper picked him up, jostling him gently in mid-air. 'Because, Buddha, it doesn't have consciousness or a central nervous system. By which I mean, it doesn't know it's alive, and it doesn't know it's dead. Cheer up. They only live for a few days anyway.'

This is the problem: Ben is gentle. His gentleness is visible even when he is running howling through the wet grass, or glaring down the length of a sniper rifle in his CGI warzones. She hopes it isn't so visible to everyone as it is to Alice: herself another exposed heart, another soft-centre.

'Are you getting on with everyone?' she pushes. 'Is anyone bothering you, in any way?'

'No,' Ben says, scratching his head.

'Then why spend a night at home with me?' Alice says. 'I didn't even watch a film you liked.'

'I didn't want you to be by yourself,' Ben says.

Alice is startled. 'What? You didn't want me to . . . why?'

'I don't know,' he says. She is only able to watch him in her peripheral vision: slouching in his seat, the uncertain shrug, the resolutely turned-away face. 'It seemed like you were sad. I thought I'd keep you company.'

'Oh, Ben,' Alice says. She doesn't know what else to say.

A few weeks later, Alice is feeling not sadness, exactly, but something approaching it, something wilder and looser than the inertia of sadness, its soft, paralysing weight. She has been carrying out calculations, counting her worry out into neat rows of numbers. In the past week, Jasper has been home more than two hours late on three days out of five; blaming traffic, workloads, drinks with friends. Plus he didn't come home at all last night, claiming that he went to Windsor and by 9 p.m. had drunk more than four pints, which necessitated a stay with a former colleague, before he could drive to work at seven. Number of times he has deliberated over his appearance: seven. Expressed as a percentage of days this week: 100 per cent. Alice hovers over the equals.

Equals what?

Abandoning her maths, she carries on as usual. Three days a week she walks down from the hill to the small charity shop in town where she volunteers. The walk is short and familiar – counting off the oak trees that heave up the pavements, the large Victorian houses, their criss-crossed and checkerboarded brick, bay windows, the occasional turret – and doesn't allow her enough time to sink too deeply, too irreversibly, into her own thoughts. Her shifts at the charity shop are often sweetly companionable, talking about the other volunteers' grown-up children (some of which are Alice's age, giving her the pleasing sense of being the younger generation; one of the kids).

Afterwards Alice walks home again and makes dinner, usually only for herself and Ben. Then, before he is allowed to watch TV, she helps him with homework; smiling a lot, teasing him, to reassure him that she isn't sad. Sometimes she thinks she is overdoing it, and he will remember this years later, talking with his wife or psychologist: the manic cheer of his mother, hanging over him with her bottle of glue. Or perhaps the smell of felt-tips in the early evening, the tarry, grassy scent of rain outside, will make him vaguely anxious, and he won't know why. She avoids confronting Jasper over his absences, until one Saturday afternoon he arrives home from his morning at the surgery, wearing a fresh shirt and trousers.

'You had a change of clothes with you?' Alice asks.

'I always have them in the car,' Jasper says. 'In case something happens to the first lot. Patients have thrown up on me before. Or worse.' He takes out the cafetière and fills the kettle. 'Coffee?'

'Not for me. You know, if you didn't stay up so late, you wouldn't be dependent on coffee.' Jasper gives her a look of comprehension, knowing no reply is necessary, and sits down at the table. He moves his eyes over the kitchen without looking at it. Jasper accepts the kitchen as it is, not really caring about it one way or another, while Alice inspects it like a child, checking for smudges and smears on its smooth cream face, noticing the notches in the paint of the door frame, the wine-glass circles, the slight warp of the sash window, which makes it harder and harder to lift as the air outside turns silver-grey and dense, suffused with cold water. She is attuned to its daylight cycles; the sun tracking across from the steel front of the oven to end at the pristinely unused pasta maker, like a slow search beam, high and full of gold and green patterning in summer, low and skulking in the winter, peering over the facing roofs.

Jasper doesn't even look quite right in the kitchen: he seems oddly placed, as if in a mocked-up photograph. It may as well be the Taj Mahal in the background, the Eiffel Tower. His own body seems to have an awareness of this; its expressions carrying a faint sense of the ironic, even down to the way his coffee cup nests egglike in his hands. His fingers are elegant: he used to play the piano when he was younger, and once thought he might be a surgeon. He talks about it as if being a surgeon was something that had been offered to him, like a flyer on the street. He considered it; shook his head: *nah*. Alice is one of the few people who know that he wasn't good enough, despite the elegance and cleverness of his long, neat-nailed fingers. She knows that his skim of the topic, the shrug and the smile, the hint at dismissal, are the reflexive motions of pride. She doesn't mind it. Better a proud man who is still making an effort, surely, than the collapsed man, the stalled man, who better understands his own essential ridiculousness.

Who could blame Jasper, anyway, for his certainty that his inside must distinguish him in the same way as his outside? Looking at his mobile phone now, he has the resting grandeur of a panther; dark, eyes low but still points of brightness, drawing focus. Straight nose, steeply built cheekbones. He looks like a man who could govern a company, or a country. He could be a spy, or a detective. This is why his manner is ironic, this is why his smile hints at various, mysterious things. He might be wasted as a GP in a small suburban practice, but he is gracious about it. His loosely regal gestures say: *Yes, I could do more than this. But I'm needed here.*

Alice runs out of pretend things to do around the kitchen and says, finally, 'You might have let me know sooner that you weren't coming home last night.'

'I didn't know at first that I wasn't coming home,' Jasper says, glancing up with the beginnings of weariness, a raised eyebrow, at this predictable henpeckery.

'You didn't let me know until twelve,' Alice says. 'Surely you could have worked it out before then.'

'I apologise,' Jasper says. 'I was drunk. I didn't make the decision until then.'

'I would have liked us to spend some time together,' she persists. 'Is that important to you at all?'

'Of course it is. I didn't have to come home today, but I'm here.'

'Is that all I'm allowed? Saturday afternoon?'

'And Sunday,' he says, with irritation. 'And I don't see the point of spoiling the time we do have, with a pointless row.'

'I'm not rowing,' Alice says, levelling out her voice, trying to flatten its needy peaks, its sad valleys. 'But if we don't see much of each other, it's reasonable to have a conversation about whether this is a problem or not.'

'It seems as if you've already decided it's a problem.'

'Maybe it is when I haven't seen you at all this week!' Her voice has risen and tears fill her eyes: a mistake. Jasper picks up his cup and phone and stands up. 'Look, Alice, I've had a very stressful week and I don't need an argument. We can come back to this when you're calmer.'

He exits, frowning, and a few moments later, above the distant bleeps and booms of Ben and his friend playing a video game in Ben's bedroom, she hears the noise of the study door being closed.

VIC

'Please God,' Victoria Robinson (known to everybody except her parents as Vic) begins, rather unceremoniously, because she is short on time and is – out of necessity – praying under the fringed umbrella of a large palm, visible to anyone who might be passing by, 'Please let me be more tolerant towards others, particularly Lawrence. Please let me find the compassion in my heart to better understand his stupid, petty behaviour. Amen.'

Vic isn't sure if this is too perfunctory to pass muster as a prayer. She doesn't want to treat God like Twitter; something she was warned about only last week by a copy of *Catholicism Today* she had been leafing through while waiting for Father Antonio. (Vic spends rather a lot of time waiting for Father Antonio, who likes to say; 'Travel with the Lord', without really considering whether the Lord might like to travel with Father Antonio, stopping as he did to chat to everybody whose eye he manages to catch, dawdling in doorways and at shop windows, wheeling his capricious darling of a bicycle alongside him like a pedigree dog).

She coughs and glances around the Quinta Verde's gardens;

jungles of fancifully varied trees, which – even late in the morning – submerge the paths and courtyards in an absolute shade, the cool green of a lagoon, through which small birds float, silenced by the late arrival of the day. Hotel guests, lost and in search of the pool, will intermittently wander by, and mindful of this, she ducks out hurriedly from under her palm and starts making her own circuitous route back towards the hotel.

As Vic passes the pool, struck violently with sunlight so that the scattered figures around it appear to move through a brilliant white haze, she notices a slender red-haired girl sitting on the edge, dawdling her legs through the water. She pauses to fix the girl in her vision: the hair wet at the ends, the narrow back, propped on her elbows to watch a teenage boy perform a forbidden backflip. The girl's profile is so strangely like Kate's that even when she looks up, feeling herself watched, Vic doesn't look away immediately. Only when she realises the girl's nose is entirely different and her jaw is wrong – all wrong – can she pull herself free of the irresistible, heavy downwardness of memory, turn away, and walk on.

Kate was actually blonde when Vic knew her; she only saw her once with red hair (one of the times she caught sight of her in Funchal, and quickly looked away), and then it was dyed a near purple. Moreover, sitting and watching had never been Kate's style. She would have been executing the backflip herself, with some added showmanship for the sake of the boys; dropping a towel and showing herself suddenly naked, before running, becoming an indistinct, thin body, legs snapping like willow switches. Or maybe she'd have been in a mood for one of her jokes, in which case she would have been leading boys to the sea cliffs, to backflip onto the rocks.

The moment of false recognition – the sudden arrival of the dead into new, strange bodies – disturbs Vic, and to delay the inevitability of social contact she turns and takes a roundabout route back to the hotel, around the leaf-patterned pathways of its borders, arriving finally at the main entrance where the red and gold doorman, Rafael, is sitting on the edge of the step inspecting his phone. Not at all surprised to see her, he salutes as she goes past, without turning his eyes away from the screen.

Ana, the receptionist, says, 'What a strange day. You have arrived for work twice. And that poia Lawrence is here today, when he's not meant to be.'

'He swapped our shifts this morning,' Vic says, remaining professional. 'He's taking Saturday off.'

'Isn't that your day off?'

'It was meant to be,' Vic replies neutrally.

Lawrence and Vic uneasily co-manage the Quinta Verde, the eighteenth-century manor hotel once owned by her parents, now owned by David Berry of Regent Thames Hotels. Lawrence, a trainee manager at the company, was sent over from England to work with Vic. David Berry has never given any more than the vaguest explanation for this arrangement, but Lawrence and Vic have been aware from the beginning of the truth of their relationship – that Vic is raising her replacement rather like a bee's body nourishes the wasp parasite that, in time, will eat up the bee – and this awareness has, not unexpectedly, led to tension between the two managers.

Vic looks over the lobby now without really seeing it; visiting instead some remembered Vic, playing on the floor under the revolving ceiling fans, the gaze of the large marble nymph. If she wanted to, she could reassemble the entire room from memory, the desultory balloon-backed chairs circling each other at intervals on the black and white chequered floor, the precise location of the potted palms.

After only one holiday in Madeira, Jim and Bernie Robinson had sold their Peterborough pub and bought the Quinta Verde. Without a second thought they ditched England for Azenhas do Mar, a small village with neat borders enforced by the mountains behind and the sea cliffs before it, its beauty always striking; languorous and purple-lit in the evening, lazy in the afternoon, sharpest in the early morning, with the early stir of the wind bringing the scent of the sea in, drifting vaporous through the date palms, the ferocious brightness of the bougainvillea. They bought a house in one of the secretive streets of terracotta-roofed houses with their white faces and black-outlined windows like stark geisha masks, explained to the six-year-old Vic that they were all going to paradise (Vic, always literal, thought death was imminent and set about an appropriate wailing), and emigrated, leaving their friends to either admire their guts or prophesy doom at the leaving party they held in their former pub.

Ultimately, it was the doubting friends who were proved right when, thirteen years, later Jim and Bernie sat down with their accounts and a bottle of wine and admitted that the financial workings of the Quinta Verde were slightly beyond them. Without ever being unpopular the hotel failed to make enough money; without being understaffed there was always too much to do. They had given it their savings and their Sundays for thirteen years – they had given it their teenage daughter, for God's sake, a sacrificial virgin working in the cocktail bar – and enough was enough. The Quinta Verde, with its marble floors, palms and ornamental gardens, the cooled glamour of the grand era of hotels, of the time when Madeira was the jewel of the colonial classes, was passed at a loss to David Berry, and as suddenly as they had once left England, the Robinsons left Madeira.

Vic stayed behind. Though she never quite succeeded as the Portuguese-speaking Catholic girl she tried so hard to be indistinguishable from, Madeira was still more home to her than 'home', as her parents always called it. Her memories of England were dim: a brown sofa, baked beans, rain on an aluminium-framed window. Even the word 'England' was at once strange and dull. The land of Eng. It sounded like someone swallowing; short and curt. So she rented the family home from her parents, with the warning that it would need to be sold once they retired, and kept her job as hotel manager at the Quinta Verde, not knowing where else to go.

Later that evening, Vic walks back to her house, with her usual glance up at the Quinta do Rosal, standing with lonely dignity above the village, its face turned amber in the late sun casting its long shadows across the mountain. The house belongs to John Worth, an American property developer, and his wife Paula, formerly Dona Paula Bonifacio, whose family have owned the house for the last couple of centuries. About a month ago the Worths left Azenhas do Mar to care for John's elderly mother in Boston. (They didn't say how long they would live with her: the unspoken understanding was that they would be back when she was dead.)

The loss of the Worths has been deeply felt by Vic. Longstanding friends of her parents, John and Paula have been like family to her, drinking cocktails in the eighties with the Robinsons as a young Vic and their son Michael – a noisy little boy with pale blond hair overhanging his eyes and small ears – played together under the table. Since then, Michael has come and gone – to boarding school in England, university in America, engineering projects in various countries – each time coming back jarringly changed, as if Vic is turning the pages of a flickbook too many at a time; his hair darkening as if tanned by the sun, his height lagging behind hers, then suddenly overtaking. These absences, along with his parents' wealth and his unarguable good looks, have given Michael the status of local celebrity, a favourite figure in the mythology of the village: the lucky boy, the wandering son, the young prince. When he came home from university, the teenage girls of Azenhas do Mar sought him out in packs, loitering in the white jeans they considered to be the height of chic, jutting one hip forward, whisking their hands through their hair, biting on their varnished nails.

One comfort to Vic (though it is a far-off and unreliable comfort, conveyed by John Worth on the phone; his voice tiny, as if half his sound had got lost across the Atlantic) has been the news that Michael is expected to return to Madeira.

'I don't think he would have remembered to tell us if I hadn't heard it from an old local government friend in Funchal,' said John. 'He's been offered a contract at a civil engineering firm. I think he's planning to take it. It's a small island but the engineering is big, as they say. Big enough for Michael to be tempted.'

'Oh, that would be wonderful,' Vic said. 'To have Michael back.'

'Really, you two ought to marry,' John said. He paused to consider it, apparently charmed by the idea. 'Yes! You would keep in touch with your parents-in-law. Michael might stay in one place. You'd be a good influence in general.'

'Michael? No way!' Vic said, reminding herself of an uncomfortable teenager. (It occurred to her, distantly, that in situations like this she – someone destined always to behave like an uncomfortable teenager – might have an advantage over other, more socially adept people). 'He's like a brother. It would be weird.'

John laughed and, not being a man overly attached to his ideas, let it go.

Vic is trying not to hope too much for Michael to come back, but it is difficult when so much of herself seems to be staked on it. The departure of first her parents and then the Worths has not just been the loss of the people closest to her but the removal of something of Vic herself; her much-treasured sociability – a laugher, an inexpert joke-maker, who may now be frightened off, not to be easily coaxed out again.

As a young child, Vic was cheerfully and loudly rude. Her parents used to enjoy repeating the things she said: 'Are you having a baby?' to a fat woman, 'What's a fuck?' over dinner. She swooped eagle-like and unerring on faults of nature:

port-wine stains, baldness, wheelchairs; none of these escaped her. Awkwardness trailed around the young Vic like a slip-stream; she was usually to be found in the middle of a general hush, mouth half open, wondering what she had said. Only at school did she learn to shut up. Instead of saying something stupid, she stayed quiet; a technique she still favours. When she does have to speak, she still frequently says the wrong thing, only understanding the wrongness of her contribution by the way it lands, like a stone dropping into water: a solid plunk, leaving ripples of uneasy silence.

The Worths, however, know Vic well enough not to be disconcerted by her social ineptitude, and Vic in turn is more comfortable with them; a confidence that comes only from having known them for so long that she can't remember an actual *meeting* (meetings usually bringing out the worst in Vic). It makes her queasy to imagine what impression she'd make if she were introduced to them now, or to Michael, whose bright light she has grown used to from prolonged exposure. If she had met him as an adult – fully formed, good-looking, at absolute ease with himself – she would prob-ably have been too nervous to speak to him.

Vic tries to explain her sadness about the Worths' absence to her mother and father when they call, but – as she had expected – they don't quite understand.

'John and Paula will be back eventually,' Bernie says. 'And even if they did decide to stay, they'd visit you. You'd visit them. We could all go! Make a family holiday of it. I haven't been to America in years. You had such screaming fits on aeroplanes when you were little that we got out of the habit of family holidays.'

'I just don't like looking up at the house and seeing it empty,' she says, knowing this sounds stupid. 'It seems wrong.'

Bernie isn't really listening. 'Jim! Vic's on the phone!' she calls; presumably beckoning Vic's father over towards the phone, which she has on speaker mode. Vic hates speaker mode. She can't tell how loud or silly her voice sounds, echoing through her parents' sitting room like a ghost at a séance.

'Your dad's built a shed. Haven't you, Jim?'

'Bloody mice got in it within a week,' says Jim, 'chewed through the deck chairs. Made a stripy nest for themselves.'

'It did make us laugh a bit, didn't it? We got those humane traps. You put some peanut butter in and then when you find them there's a mouse inside.'

'And of course your mother says we have to find them a new home, but not so close they can find their way back, so we've been driving mice all around the bloody area like some sort of shuttlebus service.'

'I can't bear to be killing them—'

'They probably die anyway, once they've been relocated. You've put them in some other mouse's territory. Or they get confused, and a cat gets them.'

'Oh, shut up, Jim. He says this to wind me up.'

Later in the conversation, her parents tell her they won't be coming to Madeira for their annual visit this year. They explain that the holiday fund has been eaten by a new bathroom, with a floating lavatory and mixer taps. But they are cagey, and she suspects the real reason isn't the money. Jim and Bernie's last visit was a short one, and their enthusiasm for the walks and the cafés had something of the reproduction about it, a clever, nearly seamless imitation of the real thing. At one point Jim looked out over a sea cliff at the blue inferno below him, its white smoke, flaring sparks, and sighed.

'You're bored of Madeira,' Vic says now, realising it.

'Oh, no,' Bernie protests.

'We are,' says Jim. 'Sorry, love, but we've lived in Madeira for years. We've *seen* Madeira. We want to go to Spain next year. You could meet us in Spain. Eh?'

'Or in the UK?' Bernie says hopefully. 'See some of the relatives.'

Vic reminds them of her fear of flying.

'Can't God get you over?' her father jokes. 'If you ask him nicely. You and he are still great pals, aren't you?'

'*Jim*,' says Bernie. 'But really, Victoria, you could think about it. Coming back, I mean. If you feel like there's nobody left and you're fed up with those blooming Thames Regent people. I'm just not sure why you want to stay. It's not like it's all good memories – you know, that business with your school friend Kate—'

Vic cuts her off. 'Actually, Michael's coming back.'

'Really? Permanently?'

'I don't know. Maybe.'

Bernie pauses; her silence sounds doubting. 'Well, all right then, love. But at least think about it. There's always a home here for you. Anyway, we've got to go now. Sainsbury's is closing soon. Look after yourself. Don't be down about the Worths. And send our love to Michael, won't you?'

A month later, Vic is waiting for Michael at Funchal airport, worrying that his plane will crash. Her failure to say a novena for him weighs on her mind. She always says one for flights, but Michael had only given her eight days' notice of his departure (a jaunty, one-line email: 'Vic, I'm back next Monday! . . . will get taxi, don't be ridiculous x') and she didn't think it would be quite *on* to just miss out a day, as if God mightn't notice.

By the time Michael arrives, an hour late, Vic has passed from impatience to forced calm to impatience, so that when she finally spots him, blond and brown and loose of movement, confident even in a concertinaed shirt (arms open, a casual, 'Vic! Hello! What's up?'), she can't help mentioning how long she has waited, and how bad the traffic had been around Funchal, wanting her efforts to be fully understood. She feels ashamed of herself when Michael is immediately apologetic.

'Though I did tell you I'd get a taxi,' he adds.

'I said I wouldn't hear of it. Taxis are for people with no friends or family.'

'My parents made their peace with me taking public transport long ago,' he says, then adds, with surprise, 'You look smart.'

Vic has actually bought a new dress, and is a little surprised by it herself. On one of her rare visits to Funchal she strayed into a boutique and promptly fell prey to an experienced saleswoman who slid out like a shark from behind her counter, displaying all her teeth. The saleswoman told Vic that with her beautiful complexion she could carry off cream, and that the cut of this dress would narrow her waist, sculpt her bottom, and generally *transform* her, as if understanding what Vic herself saw as they both gazed at the girl in the mirror.

Vic has never been sure how, when she spends a significant part of each day rushing from one end of the Quinta Verde to another to calm squabbles amongst the staff, inspect leaking taps, and placate the guests who try from the moment of their arrival to recreate the discontent of home, she is still overweight; or how her parents' lean genes combined to produce this monument of placid, pale flesh, not what anybody would call fat – but not thin, either. There is an implacability about her body: the refusal of her legs and waist to vacillate in and out, the stern thickness of her wrists, the sensible flatness of her feet. Her face is a regular oval, as pleasant and featureless as the smiling face of a pill. She feels like a marble statue that hasn't quite been finished; waiting for someone to come and make the necessary refinements. She isn't entirely sure that this dress is up to the job.

'It *is* a special occasion,' she says now, self-conscious, 'and anyway, it's not as if you need a special occasion to look nice.'

'And you do look very nice,' Michael says agreeably.

Vic and Michael travel back through the high roads in her parents' old car, a winded estate that coughs like a smoker as it follows the stepped slopes. From time to time they vanish into one of the long snake holes that thread the island's rocky interior, passing through its volcanic heart. The tunnels and viaducts of the *autoestradas* are the reason Michael has come back. 'I'm going to be part of a very bad idea,' he explains, not uncheerfully. 'Madeira's in an insane amount of debt, but it's still building.'

'We're in debt?'

'As a country we've been downgraded for bad governance. Didn't you hear about that?'

'Probably,' Vic says. It seems that Michael – who can take or leave his former home, dropping back in to visit as if the island is an elderly relative, to be placated for years of absence with a bunch of flowers and a kiss on the cheek – can still apparently refer to the island as 'we'. Vic, on behalf of Madeira, feels faintly affronted by this. At the same time she herself has no interest in its debt or national economics. The life of the hotel and the tricky negotiations of volunteering at the church keep her up at night, not the abstract billions being wheedled out of Portugal and the far-off EU to build Madeira's astonishing roads. Michael sighs with enjoyment now and peers up through his window at the banana plantations bordering the road; the waterfalls and the ravines, the dripping greenness and the extravagant flowers. 'It's good to be back,' he says.

'How long is it for this time?'

'I don't know. This engineering spending spree is on borrowed time. It could be years or it could all be over tomorrow.'

'Years!' marvels Vic.

'Well, *I* won't be here for years,' Michael says. 'I'd want a change by then, I expect.'

'Right.' There is a brief pause as the car passes in and out of a darkly lit tunnel, emerging through a shower of water into the stinging sunlight.

'How do you feel about your parents not being here?' Vic asks. 'It must be upsetting.'

'It's been a while since I was at home and they weren't there. I feel like a teenager again,' he says. 'I keep thinking I ought to call everyone and shout "house party!" But if I did, I'd only be worried about people breaking and spilling things. See what age has done to me.'

'Aren't you sad?'

'No . . . should I be? My grandmother's fine, really. Just some mobility issues. I saw her a couple of weeks ago and she didn't see the point in my parents coming at all. She's always been stubborn. Not as stubborn as my mother, though. Duty calls and all that, and nothing is going to stand between Paula Bonifacio and duty.'

'I mean, sad about your parents not being home. Your house being empty when you get back to it. Aren't you going to be . . .' Here she hesitates, because 'lonely' doesn't seem like quite the right word. She is looking for something between lonely and melancholy and unsettled, the peculiar shade of wrongness that comes from other people's left-behind possessions; of not knowing whether to move into your parents' old bedroom or to stay in your own, smaller space; living in a home of infinite silences, the outlines of family members cut through each room.

'Not really. I spend so little time in one place it doesn't make much difference to me whether I visit them in Madeira or America. So, what did you get up to while I was away?' Vic – not a confident enough driver to turn her eyes away from the road – can only see him in her peripheral vision, looking at her with an interest that makes her feel uncomfortable, as any interest usually does. He continues, 'I left you a to-do list. Did you get through it?'

'I can't even remember it,' she says.

'Rubbish – it was only two things: One – Get a new job; Two – Get some action.'

'That wasn't a joke?'

'Not in the least. God definitely won't mind the first one, and I doubt he gives a shit about the second.'

Vic laughs. 'Oh well, that's fine, then. Never mind the Bible: Michael thinks it's probably OK. Look, I know you think it's all nonsense, but, really, it's common sense, mostly. Like if everyone were just to have *sex* all the time, without caring about who they have sex with, there'll be cheating and lying and disease everywhere and nobody will know whose children are whose.'

'Sounds like a perfect Saturday night,' Michael says. 'So you didn't do either?'

'No. Sorry. I do know I ought to leave the hotel. There just aren't many other opportunities here.'

'So leave Madeira.'

He isn't joking now. This is Michael's favourite subject: adventuring. Michael, who has more blood here than she does, but has shunned the torpor of the Mediterranean; throwing himself instead into colder, wilder waters. For, despite the flurry of ostentatious construction, Madeira itself is like the island of the lotus-eaters, suspended and beautiful. Its lava hardened thousands of years ago, its primeval laurel forests are under preservation order; the tiled streets of its capital, Funchal, are maintained in a stately calm. It is the floating garden, the island of no-time: Atlantis, if Atlantis were open to tourists. Everything big that has happened to Madeira has happened long ago, and now nothing will ever change. Sometimes she feels as if she will never change either; not enough to leave, anyway. And so it is Vic who has the uneasy, overly close relationship with the island, a slow-formed resentment and familiarity, while Michael can love it from a distance, and with more enthusiasm, because he is in no danger of succumbing to its stasis.

'Go somewhere where there *are* opportunities,' Michael continues. 'Keep moving. Keep your enthusiasm. It can't be good for you to stay here, living a compromised version of your old life, your old memories.'

For an unpleasant moment Vic thinks he is referring to Kate, before she realises that he means her family, and the hotel. She supposes Kate is on her mind because her mother brought it up, or perhaps because of a dream she had a couple of nights ago, in which she had a picture of Kate that was talking to her. In the photo Kate was a child again, blonde and small, but her eyes were oddly cognisant of the viewer, her mouth moving in an adult way. Vic listened but could make out only a small sound, like a bee; nothing at all of what Kate was saying, and in the end she became upset by the photo, and tore it into pieces.

But then, it doesn't take much to bring Kate into her mind. At times she can go for a week without tripping up on any associations, but at other times it seems as if Kate is back, right next to her ear, and she can hear her this time. Kate has her legs crossed and the Bible on her lap and wears her usual expression – half scornful, half watchful, assessing Vic's reactions. She is saying, 'So, right, Lot was just going to give his two virgin daughters up for all those guys to have sex with them? So that he could be a good host? He didn't even know those guests were angels! Then he gets saved and rewarded! He should have offered himself to the men. Don't even get me started on how unfair it is that his wife got turned to salt just because she looked back. The whole thing's a set-up, if you ask me.'

'Are you OK?' Michael asks.

'Yes. Sorry.'

'You went quiet. Is it because of the flying thing?'

'Yes,' Vic lies, and then regrets it, because Michael begins talking about conditioning and desensitisation techniques – adding emphasis with one sternly pointed finger – as if they were a course of antibiotics, to quickly clear up her fear of flying, while Vic tries not to be hurt that he has mentally packed her bags and waved her onto the nearest plane, without so much as a prayer, presumably: no novenas to be said for Vic, strapped in and heading for the sky, hurtling off into her new life.

After dropping Michael home to unpack his bags and – perhaps – reflect on the absence of his parents, Vic parks at her own house and walks down to the Church of Santa Maria in the village. Its white walls reflect the light with something like the glare of a snowy Swiss slope (something Vic has only ever seen on the television) and its chequered clock tower is almost swallowed by the blaze of the sun, dissolved in light.

She enters the sudden dim, scented faintly with wood, decayed velvet, and the ghost of incense, sits in a pew and closes her eyes. Nobody else is inside: Father Antonio spends most of his time out in the village wheeling his bicycle from conversation to conversation (Vic tries – and frequently fails – not to compare him unfavourably with Father Blanca, her old school chaplain), and the rest of the congregation will arrive later in the evening for Vespers. She can hear the rustle of the date palms beyond the door; the voices of passers-by growing and shrinking. She opens her eyes again and looks for inspiration in the figure of the Virgin Mary, cradling an infant Jesus; the paintings of Christ enclosed within their wreaths of baroque gilding; an ornate scrollwork that garlands the pillars, ceilings and altar like gold bougainvillea, unrepressed, slightly camp. But after so many years, the interior of Santa Maria has become too familiar: more familiar than her own, and her eyes slip over the serene face of the Madonna, the upturned smile of her divine baby, not finding anything beyond them.

Recently Vic – unbeknownst to Father Antonio – has been suffering not exactly a crisis of faith, which would imply some drama, or decisive conflict, but something much quieter and slower. Gradually, she has realised herself to be standing apart from her own belief, as if at some time she left the room, and the door blew shut behind her. She is still able to see everything that goes on inside the room, but isn't part of it, for a reason she can't understand. She isn't sure how she got outside, or how long ago it happened. Sitting in the shade cut into slices by the windows and pillars, in a space that ought to be filled with peace and enlightenment, she feels neither peaceful nor enlightened. She is stung by worries moving too quickly to catch and examine; she is busy with anxiety. She begins a rosary, but – not for the first time – can't reach through the recitation to any sense of God.

Vic first found God at her Catholic secondary school in Funchal, though it was not the school but Kate Clare who was to be her erratic Tenzing Norgay. As an eleven-year-old, still learning Portuguese, and not quite at home in English either, Vic had trouble finding words in either language to describe herself. She was not ugly, not pretty; not slender, not curvy. She slipped through the cracks of playground slang, resisting either insults or endearments. Kate, in contrast, was distinctive, an English girl – another ex-pat – with blond hair and unexpectedly dark eyes. Vic already knew who she was before Kate accosted her outside class and said, 'So, do you want to join my club?' as if she had already been waiting weeks for an answer.

Vic looked at Kate, both unmarked white socks pulled neatly up to her knees, the sun rebounding off her glittering blond hair. She was chewing gum, which was strictly forbidden.

'What club?'

'Bible Club,' Kate said triumphantly. (Vic had no idea why she might sound this way, having, at the time, no idea of Kate's history with clubs. Later on she found out that Kate had become famous at her primary school for running Sports Club – forcibly dissolved after one girl broke her leg – and Adventure Club, none of the former members of which would speak to each other, or talk to anyone else about exactly what had happened. The nuns at their new school had been made aware of this and had already given Kate a list of clubs they considered acceptable for her to start).

'Bible Club . . .' Vic said, uncertainly.

'You *are* a Catholic, aren't you?' Kate asked. In her very dark eyes Vic thought she could make out the beginnings of doubt, coming closer to the iris, like an approaching ghost.

Vic hesitated only a moment longer. 'Yes,' she lied. And that was how she became a member of Bible Club.

Bible Club consisted of Kate, Vic and Beatriz, a nervy Madeiran girl with a lazy right eye and a habit of chewing her fingernails. It surprised Vic to discover that they would actually be studying the Bible. Kate was quite strict on this point. However, Vic wasn't sure that Kate approached the Bible in quite the same spirit as the nuns. Kate read them bits of the Bible they never knew existed.

'The Bible can be pretty shady,' she said.

'No, it's not,' said Beatriz.

'Yes it is. Listen to this.' Kate began leafing showily through her Bible as if to find the page – the location of which she had already marked – looking as earnest and outraged as a prosecutor in an American legal drama. 'Ezekiel twenty-three. It's saying Jerusalem is a woman called Oholibah. It says here that she "was a prostitute in Egypt. There she lusted after her lovers, whose genitals were like those of donkeys and whose emission was like that of horses –" Wait, there's more . . . "So you longed for the lewdness of your youth, when in Egypt your bosom was caressed and your young breasts fondled."'

'It doesn't say that!'

'Does too.' Kate displayed the page.

'What's emission?' Vic asked.

'Testicles,' Kate said confidently. 'Genitals are the penis and emission is the testicles. Now, if we read this out in class we'd be expelled. But we're supposed to be here learning the Bible, aren't we? I asked Sister Maria about Bible Club and she said she was glad to see I was finally channelling my energies into something appropriate. Something appropriate!' She waved the book fiercely. 'Have they even read it? That's what I want to know. I bet they haven't. They're all pretending. Or is it something more sinister?'

'Like what?'

'The *Da Vinci Code*. For example. It's probably much worse than that.'

'That's just a film,' Beatriz said, uncertainly.

'Either way,' Kate concludes, 'people should know the truth. The nuns . . . *are not to be trusted*.' And, on the available evidence, neither Vic nor Beatriz knew quite how to argue with her.

Having looked forward to Michael's return, Vic has been disappointed not to see much of him since he started his new job. He has been working in Funchal for the past few weeks and, it seems, staying there too. His black car appears outside the Quinta do Rosal at odd times, and rarely overnight. She has sent him a few messages and received only one reply, apologetic but maddeningly cheery too, and not answering any of her questions. The next she hears of him is the sound of his laughter in the hotel reception, before she rounds the corner and sees him there, one elbow on the desk, listening to one of Ana's stories, of which there are many, mostly characterised by the absurdity of their events and their significant structural flaws.

'My mother said, "Ana, you silly bitch, what possessed you? We can't eat it. Look at its little ears." And so it lived in the garden until it died of mysterious causes. I believe poisoning.'

'Who would poison a pig?' Michael asks.

'Our neighbours. It was a murder. They hated that pig because it ate their flowers. I will not speak to them to this day.'

Vic is fond of Ana; she admires her humour, her prettiness – those bright white teeth, one a little crooked, and those black curls – but professionally it doesn't look good to have the hotel receptionist leaning forward over the desk, breasts resting on the guestbook, giggling up at Michael. One of Ana's feet is toying with the slingback strap of the other in a way that makes Vic uncomfortable. She heads over to them as quickly as she can without seeming to hurry. Ana, catching sight of her, reluctantly straightens up.

'Michael is here, Vic,' she says, still looking amused, enjoying the afterglow of her laughter.

'I can see that,' Vic says. 'Thank you.'

This is meant to dismiss Ana but she stays where she is, smiling and looking from Vic to Michael, as if the three of them are all good friends and she hasn't just met Michael for the first time that day.

'Busy morning?' Michael asks. 'You look stressed.'

'Not particularly. No more than usual, anyway.'

'Lawrence is being a fucker more than usual,' Ana puts in. Vic frowns at her, 'Careful not to be heard saying that.'

'Oh, it's only you here,' Ana says. 'And Michael can keep a secret.'

Michael winks at her to confirm this.

'Why are you here?' Vic asks him, then realises she sounds curt. Ana raises her eyebrows but Michael, who is used to it, only smiles.

'Well, before I began to doubt whether it was a good idea,' he says, 'I was going to ask if you wanted to do something for lunch later. We could have ice cream. Loiter in the square. Cause trouble.'

'I . . .' Vic hesitates, but not for very long. Happiness is Michael's special power; few can resist it. His good mood takes her irresistibly up with it, like an outstretched arm in a dance, the string of a balloon. 'You know what, Ana? When you see Lawrence, can you tell him something came up, and I'll be taking today off. I've been working the past few weekends, so I'm sure he won't mind.'

'Really?' Ana says, visibly enlivened. 'I can certainly do that. Hehe. I'll like to do that. Enjoy your ice creams, you two.' And they leave the hotel, Ana waving energetically, as if holding the flag of the revolution, Rafael the doorman glancing up from his phone with lazy curiosity, and all the little birds of the bowered courtyard breaking together into song.

Later, sitting with Michael in a café, under the redundant shade of a striped parasol already shaded by the enormous chestnut tree that squats imperially in the east corner of the square, Vic reflects on how much better it felt simply to do something wrong, like walking out of work, than to do the right thing, stay on, and try to forgive Lawrence later for changing their shifts.

The square constitutes the heart of Azenhas do Mar, the sun around which the straw-hatted villagers revolve, eternally to-ing and fro-ing. Its cobbles are tattooed with abstract designs in grey basalt, its boundaries elegantly hemmed with a long ornately pillared balustrade, banked flowers, nodding palms. Michael watches a white and brown dog trot across the stones. When the dog reaches the shade of the chestnut tree it stops and drops languidly to the ground. Its eyes close in apparent enjoyment.

'It's like you,' Vic says.

'Lazy?'

Vic shakes her head, trying to think of some way of explaining the impression that struck her without sounding silly, or rude, but from long experience she knows that expressing her thoughts in the way they sound in her head usually fails, like taking a photograph of a sunset, and so she says, 'It's the same colours as you.'

'Nice save,' Michael says. He is wearing a white shirt with an open neck and short sleeves. His upper arms are hard-looking; brown skin, edged off crisply with white. 'So, who's Lawrence?'

'I *have* told you about Lawrence,' Vic says. 'He's the other manager at the hotel.'

'Oh. Well, you probably spoke about him nicely and insincerely and so, quite reasonably, I lost interest and forgot all about him. Ana gave me a better picture.'

'It's not insincere to try to see the good in someone and not allow yourself to just be . . . horrible about them.'

Michael shrugs. 'Perhaps. But if you don't call a fucker a fucker every now and again you'll give yourself an ulcer.'

The café is owned by a widow named Trinidade, who appears now to collect their empty glasses. Vic's glass isn't empty, but Trinidade hasn't noticed this. She has been waiting for Michael to finish his glass so that she can come out and talk to him again, lingering as she tidies; sweeping imaginary crumbs off the table, readjusting imaginary wrinkles in the tablecloth.

'Sorry, but I haven't finished,' Vic says. Trinidade puts her glass back down without looking at her, asking instead, 'Would you like anything else, Mika?' Like many women of Azenhas do Mar, Trinidade has a long-running crush on Michael and doesn't appear to know who Vic is, though Michael is away for months at a time and Vic is reliably *around*; passing in the streets, shopping, working, visible almost every day of the year.

When Trinidade has been prised from Michael by the banging of glasses from another table, occupied by a couple of humorous old men, he says 'So, anyway, I'm sorry I've been useless', without attaching any particular weight to the words, as if he hasn't expected her to even notice his uselessness. 'How are you? What's been going on?'

Vic, having confessed to and yet having failed to shake off her hurt at his unreliability, is reminded of her grievance and says, stiffly, 'Lots of things, but I can't remember them all to tell you just like that.'

'Oh, no, Vic!' Michael cries. 'Are you genuinely pissed off? Please don't be. I'll make you dinner – to say sorry. Shit. I'm a terrible friend.'

'It's fine. Don't be silly,' Vic says, gratified.

'It's not all my fault. This new job has been ridiculous. Basically, they're still recruiting but they've decided to start anyway. I'm doing the work of two people in the meantime. Everyone there is running about trying to do different jobs. My manager's been doing admin because the admin people are doing the health and safety training. I thought I might have to go out and pour concrete at one point.'

'It could be fun. Pouring concrete. Have you tried it?'

'Actually the job *is* quite fun. The people are fun. We've all got to know each other because nobody knows what's going on and everyone's rushing and working late. It's like a hothouse. Intensive friendship building.'

'Oh. Well, that's good.'

'So, yeah – about this dinner. Let's do it soon. What are you doing on Friday? Are you working?'

'No.'

'Then let's have dinner at mine. I thought—'

'Hang on,' Vic interrupts. 'I said I wasn't working. That doesn't mean I don't have other plans. Social plans.'

'Humblest apologies,' he says. 'Do you have any social engagements planned for Friday evening?'

'No.'

'OK.'

'I might have had, though. You shouldn't assume things.'

'Come over at seven,' Michael says, laughing. 'We'll have soup, then fish, then lemon tart, so dress accordingly. I want you to meet one of my hothouse friends. She's called Estella. You'll love her.'

KAYA

Kaya's earliest memory is of sitting on a beach with her mother, sifting pebbles through her fingers, looking for one that is perfectly round. When she finds it, she plans to take it home and keep it under her pillow. The reasons for this, now, are mysterious to her. Another problem with this memory is that Kaya's mother Louise claims not to be able to remember it, and – indeed – to hate beaches, and it's true that they haven't been to the seaside since. Kaya isn't sure if she has made the whole thing up.

But, still, she remembers it so clearly: the seagulls eyeing her ice cream, the towels laid out on the sand, a stinging array of blue, red and green, the glare of the light off her mother's white-rimmed sunglasses. She can't remember anything below the sunglasses. A bikini? A sun dress? The memory starts to break up the tighter she grips it, until, finally, it is sand filtering away through her clenched fingers, ebbing like an overturned hourglass, and she gives up and agrees with Louise that she must be remembering something she heard somewhere, or maybe saw on the TV.

'I'll need a photocopy of your birth certificate to prove you're over eighteen,' Paul tells Kaya. 'The police check us regularly – CCTV footage, paperwork, everything.' He notes her look of surprise. 'The industry's not what it used to be. You can't invite the local coppers in for a free dance. We're under closer watch than the blimmin' . . .' Apparently unable to think of something under a notoriously close watch, he tails off. 'Anyway, love, why don't you get on? Chloe's told you how it goes, right? You pick a song. Get up on the stage and take your clothes off. Leave your knickers on. Dance a bit. Simple as that.'

He struggles with the sound system ('The DJ normally does this . . . it's a blimmin' mystery to me') as Kaya takes the couple of purple-carpeted steps up onto the round stage. There is a pole in its centre, layered with fingerprints. It is late afternoon and she and Paul are the only people inside the Purple Tiger. The room is dim, but its shabbiness is in evidence: speared by the bolts of light that enter through the drawn-down shutters. The stage circled by booths upholstered in plum-coloured leatherette, slightly worn; the sticky floor, too dark to see properly, holding onto the soles of her feet as if reluctant to let her go. On the walls are mirrors with curlicued silver frames; herself reflected in every one of them, her panoramic uncertainty.

'What song?' Paul asks her. He is about forty and wears a pair of jeans too high at the waist, dividing his paunch neatly in half. Neither predatory nor paternal, his manner is tired but patient, utterly everyday, as if he is waiting for a train or for a sandwich, not for his (or anybody's) first sight of Kaya naked. She is unable to think of any music at first. 'Anything. Whatever you usually play.'

'R&B it is,' says Paul. 'It all sounds the same to me. I'm a Dire Straits man myself.'

When the music starts – an unfamiliar song but a familiar beat, a cajoling male voice – Kaya moves to it in a stony daze, sealed closed by nerves, as Paul watches without a glimmer of sexual interest from his table in the corner. From time to time he drinks from a bottle of water or glances down at his phone. She doesn't look at the mirrors, at Paul, or at her own body gradually appearing pale and chilly underneath her; like an apple being peeled, a vivid white blur in the darkness. This leaves her with the middle distance, at which she gazes seriously, hoping it will be taken for a stare of abstracted lust. She nearly loses her balance when she tries to get her jeans down and he calls, 'Don't worry, love, you won't be starting in jeans', intending it as reassurance.

In the end, Kaya has just managed to get all her clothes off before the song finishes, leaving her time only for a few uptight rotations of her body. Afterwards she stands awkwardly, feeling as if she would like to cover herself with her hands, but understanding the ridiculousness of doing so.

'Don't wait about – get dressed quick,' Paul says. 'Too cold for this really. It's snowing later this week, I hear.'

'Oh, is it?'

'Yep. Another freezing winter. Don't suppose we'll get the sun to make up for it though, come July.'

'No, I guess not.'

'Now,' he says, becoming more brisk, 'I probably don't need to tell you that you're a beautiful girl. You'd be the prettiest girl here but you're not strong on the dancing end of things. Not sure whether that's nerves or what, but you seem shy. You need to get Chloe to show you the way she dances. Because all the girls take their turns doing a stage show – nothing elaborate, but you do need to fill the time and you've got to be sexy. Nobody's going to pay for a private dance if you can't dance and can't talk to them. A lot of this business is charm. You understand me?'

Kaya nods. She finishes dressing and comes down the steps into the dark pool of the club. Paul gestures for her to sit down on one of the velvet-covered stools.

'Chloe's probably told you about the money, but I'll tell you again anyway. Basically, we charge you forty pounds to be here for the night. Think of it like a market stall. You get to sell your stuff, but you have to rent the space from the market. It's about half the rate of London clubs and we don't take commission off your dances like they would. You keep all your money. How does that sound to you?' He sits back beneficently, disappearing up to his shoulders in the purple gloom of the corner, and Kaya, realising that appreciation is called for, smiles and thanks him.

He walks out with her – their progress tracked by more silver mirrors – through the bar area, which is crowned with a silver chandelier hung with black glass droplets, winking like animal eyes.

'I'll tell you one thing, to help with the shyness: most of the customers find the whole thing awkward too. They have to get drunk to enjoy it. I always say: they're more scared of you than you are of them. Sometimes, though, you get a real creep, or some guy showing off, being a cocky prick, you know. If they offend you, you don't have to be around them. If they cross a line, you get them thrown out.'

'OK,' Kaya says. She smiles again. 'That's reassuring.'

They have reached the door and stand in the coloured light dyed by the stained glass, a cold pouring in of the winter. Kaya is reminded of the slightly scruffy entrance of her local church, a place she only visited at Christmas, when Louise would have one of her moments of repentance and go along to sit in one of the aisles, Kaya's mittened hand closed in her own, singing carols with tears standing in her eyes. Both the entrance to the club and the church were provisional places; cold with the draft from the door, forgotten signs curling up at the edges, things stacked and forgotten.

Paul continues, warming to his subject; 'I always say, who's really more vulnerable? The girl taking her clothes off or the lonely guy spending his whole pay cheque on her because he thinks she actually likes him. Who's taking advantage of whom here? Anyway, I'll leave you with that.'

Kaya realises she hasn't asked what to wear, or what time to come, but she thinks he might be put out if she doesn't allow the meeting to end here, with her in contemplation of this wisdom, so she nods solemnly, puts her hood up, and steps outside, into the abrupt iciness of the afternoon.

Chloe is walking up the street to meet her, an ersatz Eskimo in her parka; thin featureless legs ending in synthetic fur boots, a cheerful trail of smoke emerging from the hood pulled around her ears.

'Fucking cold out here, eh? Thought you'd be longer than that,' she says when she reaches Kaya. 'Guess he liked you. Let's stop by the garage on the way home and get some drinks to celebrate!'

They walk under the railway bridge away from the centre of town, circled with green-glassed office blocks that remind Kaya of Oz, if she looks from the right angle, and squints. Towards Chloe's flat, the buildings begin to tumble and peel, their faces growing ever more disconsolate.

'Dave's not home tonight,' Chloe says, with a careful off-handedness, letting Kaya know that this will be a good night, in the flat lined like a mouse hole with the hoardings of its occupants: piles of magazines and clothing, leaking car parts in newspaper in the sitting room, boxes of crisps stolen by Dave from outside the corner shop; that the two of them will put MTV on and drink some vodka and coke, and be silly and lighthearted. On the nights Dave is home Kaya mostly stays in her room; trying to fall asleep on her airbed to the aural rise and fall of Dave's soliloquys on Chloe's lack of effort, the state of the place, the empty fridge and the need for more money and the continued presence (voice slightly lowered) of that *fucking friend of yours Kaya Doherty*.

Chloe, a friend of Kaya's since infant school (their closeness owing mainly to this long acquaintance), is a girl with a metal-lised, plastinated exterior – dyed red hair interwoven with glassy acrylic extensions, long silver nails, fake tan – and a painfully tender heart. Chloe's heart was the subject of most of her long laments; its propensity to be broken, stolen, stabbed, trodden on and shat all over, but also, at times, delighting her with its leaps and skipped beats. She discussed her heart in the sentimental language of greetings cards and pop music, but she said it all so passionately that when she would tell Kaya her heart had been broken into a million pieces by something or other, it seemed both moving and true.

'Once you get over the whole *nudity* thing,' Chloe is saying now, 'it's just like any other job. It's funny how it happens. You get used to it. You have your clothes off and they all have theirs on and it gets normal. You know, you look down at your own tits and they look boring to you, like they're clothes too. And we always have a few drinks.'

'But you can't get drunk?'

'You can't be *seen* drunk,' Chloe says, giving her a meaningful, slow nod. 'It's like when you're thirteen or whatever and you're starting to go down the park and start drinking and then you get home and your parents are like, "Where've you been," and you have to chew gum and stand up straight and act sober. Think of it like that.'

Kaya tries and fails to imagine this scene, with Louise and herself in the mother and daughter roles. 'OK,' she says.

'It'll be good to be earning properly, though, yeah?'

'I can give you the rent I owe you for the last couple of weeks, as soon as I get paid.'

'Nah, man, don't worry about that,' Chloe cries, hitting her arm affectionately. 'Nobody's bothered about that. It's the recession, isn't it? I saw you looking for work. Going round all those fucking clothes shops. No rush.' But the absent Dave is at their shoulders, and they face forward, and walk on, carrying their vodka and coke, faces sheltering in their furry hoods, pulled in against the long, low wind.

Kaya grew up not far from here, about half an hour's walk away from the town centre, beyond the down-at-heel rows of Victorian terraces where she lives now. She and Louise lived, back then ('back then' meaning 'up until three weeks ago', but feeling further back, somehow), in the littered terrain of a sixties housing estate, as wide and alienated as a moon landscape or an abandoned factory, nestling in the shelter of mostly forgotten industrial buildings estate, watched over by a disused, satellite-covered tower. The word *regeneration* is used a lot about this estate, but not by its residents. It is of a type: chain-link fences with concrete posts, garage blocks, scuffed grass verges overgrown with dandelions, dogs chained in the small, square gardens. An underpass beloved by glue sniffers, the navigation of which used to take guile and cunning, as in the story of the Billy Goats Gruff. The houses were small, huddled grey cuboids or large grey cuboids parcelled into flats. Some boarded, awaiting the regeneration.

To Kaya the estate had the flat, emptied-out feel of the post-war Eastern Bloc countries seen on television. She always half expected to see signs of conflict – bullet holes in concrete, corrugated iron flowering in new shapes. Though the unhappiness there was more of an everyday variety, she wondered if it might feel any different – how similar the shock of great horror might be to the shock of the usual, moving stunned and defeated, under the vacant bowls of the satellite tower.

Kaya and her mother Louise lived in one of the flat blocks, a two-bedroom space with its windows overlooking a graffitied wall opposite. When Kaya was six, she leaned on the sill of her bedroom window one morning and spelt out the words on the wall: 'Fuck off Paki Scum'. These were erased by the council, but other words and pictures came to fill their place, mostly confusing, scrubbed off and rewritten, as if on a blackboard, or in the sand, endlessly washed out by the tide.

Louise didn't usually leave the flat, or look out of the window at the mutable words of the wall. Kaya walked to school with Satvinder, a girl from the floor below her, and Satvinder's mother Sudhana did the Dohertys' weekly shopping along with her own. Sudhana believed – as did most people, including the council's disability benefit assessor – that Louise suffered from ME, and would often drop by to press food on her, or offer to take Kaya to the park.

Louise may or may not have had ME – Kaya was never quite sure, even as she grew up – but she did like to drink. Nobody suspected her of being a drunk because she looked classically, tragically ill, with a lissom Victorian sort of enervation. Her skin was very white, her legs thin under the soft fabric of her tracksuit, her eyes as beautifully pale and pained as those of a consumptive. She started the day with a vodka, continued with gin, and finished with whatever was to hand by the time the gin and vodka were gone. Kaya was never even sure where all the alcohol came from, because Sudhana didn't bring it over.

Kaya didn't have any idea who her father was ('a cunt,' was

all Louise would say) and so it was frequently her job to wake Louise up in the morning, to shepherd her to the bathroom when she needed to be sick, and to try to put her to bed at night. While Kaya was at school – a holy place to her, made special by the goldfish in their tank, the rasp of the coloured sugar paper, the smell of powdered paint, gravy, wet coats – Louise would sit on the green velvety sofa in the sitting room, with its wallpaper bleached on the wall facing the window, watching television. There wasn't much else to do in the sitting room: aside from the television and the chairs it contained a fold-out table to eat on – never used – a gilt clock, and one, small shelf, on which stood a porcelain figure of a woman in a ball gown. This had been given to Louise by her dead mother and Kaya wasn't allowed to touch it. Instead, she stood on her toes to see the woman on the shelf, her face glinting in the light from the window, her pink lips and cheeks, the real-gold necklace painted onto her throat, the frozen lacy foam of her dress.

When Kaya got home, Louise would look up and hold her arms out.

'How's your day been, cherub cheeks?' she would ask, and Kaya would go to her and put her face in her mother's neck and smell the sweetness of her perfume, mingled with the slightly stale odour of her skin, the thin, sharp smell of alcohol. Louise varied the greeting each day, miraculously able to never repeat an endearment – angel cloud, little bunny, sugar cake – even when she could barely focus her own eyes, half shuttered and regretful, on Kaya's face.

'What did you do today?' Louise would ask. 'What did the teachers give you?'

To which Kaya would say something like, 'A smiley face for my painting, and one for my subtraction,' and then later, 'Ten out of ten,' and later still, 'A-plus', and to all of this Louise would smile her dreamy, guilty smile, and tell her she was very proud, and that Kaya was going to be very special. At least once a day she made Kaya promise that she would not turn out anything like Louise.

Quiet and dormant during the day, the Purple Tiger wakes into a strange kind of life at night; the neon sign above the door casting a pink light over the faces of the two doormen, the music within filtering into the empty road outside. Standing alone under the arches of a railway bridge, in an empty plain of office car parks, the building has the air of something out of place, even occult. There is a feeling of suspense and unease in its efforts to lure; the candy-coloured glow below the awning, the jewelled glass and the lit entrance. It winks across the wind-blown dark tarmac like a gypsy caravan with one light burning, a haunted carousel; a witch's house, made from sweets.

Kaya gets to the door and explains who she is to the doormen, two black men in their forties or fifties, who nod and wave her through without curiosity. Having got used to the sting of ice in the night air as she walked to the club, she finds its interior abruptly too hot, the fog of it clinging to her skin like tar. Apart from a couple of girls sitting at the bar talking to the barman, who raises his hand and smiles at her, the club is empty; empty but ready, the interior lit by its various chandeliers, the previously dark corners trembling with the intimate, arterial thump of the music.

One of the girls leaves the bar and comes over to Kaya. Unlike the other girl, who is wearing perspex heels like glass slippers and a translucent baby-doll dress through which her breasts are almost visible, she is wearing jeans and a shirt.

'I'm Annie,' she says. 'I'm the house mum. Chloe explained that, right? I look after everyone and make sure you have anything you need . . . underwear, tampons, make-up: you come to me. If you have any sort of problem, you tell me about it. All right? This way is the changing room. I say changing room, really it's a corridor with a couple of mirrors.'

'Like school,' Kaya says, not really meaning to say it aloud, but startled by the white-painted corridor, with clothes hanging on pegs and a row of lockers, a fire door at one end, two girls standing naked, heads together, looking at something on one of their phones.

'Dunno what sort of school you went to, darling,' Annie says, and laughs. 'What did you bring with you to wear?'

Annie approves of Kaya's (Chloe's) choice; a pair of stilettos, a short black lace dress, and black lingerie ('Black'll suit you. You a natural blonde? Lucky girl.'), and leaves her to get changed. Without looking at her, the two other girls dress themselves – suspenders, garters and negligees – then leave, their bodies piled somewhat awkwardly on top of their stacked heels, as if on the verge of a landslide. The door bangs shut behind them and Kaya is alone in the empty corridor, which smells not of perfume so much as hundreds of different perfumes, merged into a brackish pool of decaying spirituous flowers, with a faint undertow of cigarettes. A draught cuts through from the fire doors. Standing there suddenly nauseous and near tears, she really does feel as if it is her first day at school. She blinks, blinks again, and begins undressing, concentrating on remembering the advice Chloe gave her yesterday.

'Don't try and climb up on the fucking pole. That's my first tip. Just hold on to it and grind up against it.'

'Like how?' Kaya asked.

'What do you mean, like how?' Chloe looked confused. Her face without make-up was childish and pretty, the unfolded, wide-eyed kind of face, holding no secrets. 'You know how you grind in front of the mirror at home like you're Beyoncé or Rihanna or one of them lot?'

'No.'

'You never done that?'

Kaya thought of herself, back at Louise's flat, of Carl interrupting her while she was grinding her hips in the mirror. 'No.'

'Fuck's sake, Kaya,' Chloe said, not without kindliness. She put her cigarette down. 'There's something not right with you. Look, just grind your hips like this. Round and round. Or side to side . . . yeah? Then pop your arse out. Bam. That's it.'

They were interrupted by the arrival of Dave, fresh out of the newsagent's, newly endowed with a cigarette and a lager, putting his head around the kitchen door and raising his eyebrows: 'Making a slag out of her and all, are you?'

Kaya was about to answer but Chloe caught her eye and shook her head. She went out after Dave and after a while the noises of their argument behind the bedroom door dissolved into simple, primitive sounds, as if broken down into the basic components of human language: a yes, a cry, a moan.

Once Kaya is dressed, she forces her eyes to her reflection, making them stare when they would rather drop. She thinks she may as well get used to being watched. Looking at herself, she thinks of dreams she has had where she finds herself walking down a road or at a party in her underwear, or naked; the plummeting sickness of the realisation. But this will be usual now; she meets the predefined criteria of a specific category of female (albeit one that exists only in the male imagination); sitting open-mouthed on a top shelf or waiting eagerly to talk dirty in a CALL NOW ad, a girl who sees nothing strange in see-through platform stilettoes and make-up so weighty her lashes tremble under the burden of it like exhausted moths, like the wings of seabirds after an oil spill.

She goes to the door and looks out, waiting for Annie to come back for her. From here the stage is visible, with its single dancing girl. Her head drops so low that her hair brushes the floor; her fingers move over herself slowly and deliberately, as if teaching an instrument. Her lips are as slick as PVC, her eyes ecstatic, like a saint with a divine vision. Kaya squints past the purple stage lights, where she can see tables and men's backs; arranged loosely facing the girl dancing. At most of the tables there are the dim outlines of other girls, perching, fussing with their hair, sipping stagily at their drinks.

She becomes conscious that Annie has arrived and is standing behind her.

'That's some body you've got there,' Annie says. Her wording, implying that the body isn't anything to do with Kaya herself, takes Kaya a moment to detangle. She blinks, struggles to raise her eyelashes, and says, 'Thank you.'

'So what's your name?' Annie says, after running through the house rules. 'Did Chloe not tell you that? Nobody here uses their actual name, out *there*.' She gestures at the plum-coloured shadows beyond the door.

'Oh,' Kaya says. 'I hadn't thought of one.'

Annie looks at her for a moment. 'Well, my love, you look like a celebrity, so why not go with Star.'

'Star?'

'Yep. There's already a Venus and we used to have a Luna, so it's pretty intergalactic around here. You like it?'

'OK,' Kaya says.

'Good.' Annie holds open the door for her, looking suddenly and sharply ironic. 'Now go out there and twinkle.'

Kaya had been relieved to find out that her taking A levels would not affect Louise's benefits, as they both had feared. Her mother received the good news, brought to the sofa, with her usual gestures of gratitude and guilt; always with a slight delay, as if she were underwater. Kaya supposed she was, in a way: swimming up through a weight of alcohol. What always struck her about Louise was how delicately she

managed her drinking: never reaching the point of true catas-
trophe – a hospital trip or arrest – but never cutting back
either. She had been in a kind of stasis for years. Perhaps her
body had become attuned to its high-octane fuel, and sometimes it did seem that she existed in a more rarefied physical
state, all her limbs light and translucent, apparently without
fat or muscle, as insubstantial as tissue paper.

Kaya got a job while she studied, working in a local factory
on Wednesdays, Saturdays and Sundays assembling burglar
alarms. 'I wish you didn't have to work so much,' Louise said
often, but the truth was that they were in debt: benefits
payments couldn't cover the cost of Louise's alcohol and
Kaya's books. 'You should be going out, going to parties,
kissing boys. Not more than kissing, though. You don't want
to get knocked up at this age.'

This advice sounded like something someone else's mother
would say, to a different teenage daughter; a generic girl with
posters in her room and selfies on Facebook and sneaky alcopops
at parties. It sounded to her like a transmission from space.
Between her A levels, her job at the factory and the daily routines
of looking after Louise – coaching her through what to say to
social workers, dealing with the times when she had drunk too
much, frightened for her mother but frightened to call an ambu-
lance because Louise might never be brought back, helping her
dress, levering one wayward leg after another into her tracksuit
bottoms, brushing her fine blond hair – Kaya had no time for
going to parties or kissing boys.

When Kaya did get time on her own, she liked to move
away from her own life, find a clear space above it, looking

down on the tiny flat blocks and the Spartan road home from school; herself and Chloe and Satvinder walking aimlessly, smoke threading back behind them like a jet stream. She liked to read. She moved from the set texts of A level English to borrowed Kafkas and Murakamis, and in these Kaya found something that excited her; wide, spacious endings, unanswerable questions. Sometimes she thought about her own existence, asking herself: did the universe begin, or has it always existed? How did it do such a thing as *begin*, but then, how could it not? She pushed her mind towards the question until she felt herself leave the edge of possible reasoning. The free fall was what she liked: the high, the jolt at the end, feeling both lost and delighted. She never came to any conclusion, but then a conclusion would have spoilt the game.

Yet, if she had been asked why, at that particular time in her life, she was so preoccupied with philosophical conundrums, why she ran so fast and so intently towards the abstract, Kaya would not have been able to say. Nor would she have been able to explain why, though there were plenty of unanswerable questions in her everyday life – what she would do once A levels were over, what would happen to Louise if Kaya left home to go to university, where the money for university would come from – she avoided thinking about these sorts of puzzles almost as determinedly.

Kaya's first night shift passes as quickly and surreally as a dream; a silent film in different shades of purple, dark below and dark above, pinpricked by the artificial stars of the stage lights. Her first dance on stage is restrained but successful; she finds that, after watching the other girls, she slips, somehow, into the same place as them, beyond all ideas of her usual self, not that she had very many to begin with. She throws her head back and a man near the stage makes a stifled noise, longing, almost fearful. Before she realises it, the song is over, and she walks down the steps towards the men waiting for her, their faces almost invisible with the lights behind them, as if they are only one man repeated any number of times, only one thing being thought.

She barely has to make small talk, and is glad of it. She takes her clothes off once, and then many times, in the small curtained cubicles past the bar; is winked at each time she passes by the barman, who collects the money for the dances. Her first dance is for a man more awkward than she is, a small man with large, sorrowful eyes and thinning hair irradiated by the single bulb of the cubicle. He asks her where she planned to go for her holidays, a question that makes her smile, so that she has to turn away.

Aside from Annie, she speaks to only one of the girls; Alisha, a black girl with her hair in long braids, half coiled, the rest heavy against her bare back. The other girls seem indifferent to her presence, aside from one or two assessing, sidelong looks, in which they appear to gather all they need to know.

'What it comes down to is competition,' Alisha explains. 'You and I aren't in the same market. That's why I'm the only one being friendly. The other girls aren't going to be too impressed with you right now, obviously, but don't worry.

They'll get over it. They didn't like Chloe either when she first showed up. Girls come and go so quickly you start not bothering keeping track.'

Other things happen that night. A man, his hands straying drunkenly and irrepressibly away from his sides, is escorted out by the bouncers. Another man, part of a group, puts his head on a table and falls asleep, his friends and two amused girls drawing obscene pictures on his cheek before he, too, is taken away. One of the strippers, a blonde with a tan sitting oddly, unfixed, on her skin and eyes trickling blackly down her face – a girl Kaya doesn't know and never sees again – leaves the club after an argument in the corridor with Annie. She is denying something, her voice threading back through the lit space of the doors, until she disappears into the no-man's land of the car park, and Annie closes the doors again.

When the night is over, Kaya leaves with a feeling of sticki-ness on her skin – sweat and breath and vaporised alcohol in the crooks of her arms and knees – and her pay: six hundred pounds. The money dizzies her so she divides it, then assigns jobs to each portion. She will pay the rent she owes, making sure she puts the money into Chloe's hands, and not Dave's (Dave calls himself a mechanic and a dealer but fails, in Kaya's eyes, at both, smoking more weed than he sells and never having been seen actually working on a car). Another share of the money will be laid aside for the hope – quieter, shyer, but not relinquished – that she will go to university. She thinks for a moment, that she could buy something for Louise, before remembering how pointless that would be.

In the taxi back to Chloe's flat the driver tells her, 'Some of the girls, we have an arrangement, we take them to the men afterwards. We don't tell management. You get me?'

It takes her a moment to get him.

'Oh,' she says. 'No, I don't think I'll do that. Thanks anyway.' Afterwards she thinks that prostitution, as an industry, makes much more sense than what she is doing. She has no idea what the men who come to the club are getting in exchange for their money. Nothing they can touch, and certainly nothing they couldn't see, in more variety and detail, on the Internet. She wonders what they are thinking on the way home from the Purple Tiger – thoroughly mauled – with a subsiding erection, a hangover in waiting, and hundreds of pounds gone for ever. She can't see the point, but then, perhaps, it will become clear once she has been working for longer. For now, it remains another unanswerable question.

Over the next weeks, Kaya discovers that the Purple Tiger – though it touts itself as a secret pleasure garden of unimaginable bacchanalia – operates, like any other business, under a strict set of regulations. Photocopies are taken of the girls' IDs, contracts issued, waivers signed. The building's fluorescent-lit back rooms are peppered with fire extinguishers and health and safety notices; stickers on the kettle, the hand dryer, even Annie's curling tongs, announce their compliance with electrical standards. Kaya is surprised at how routine it all comes to feel; sitting on a plastic chair eating a cheese and pickle sandwich, listening to complaints about the dodgy flush in the women's loos. The dynamics between the girls are similarly prosaic: small rivalries and resentments, squabbles over girls being late onstage or hogging the mirror. The management – represented by Paul – are not sinister but tedious, issuing only an occasional reprimand about a rise in incidences of laddered tights, or the importance of not chewing gum. The only thing that really distinguishes her tea breaks from those of her old job at the factory is that the girls are wearing lingerie and not hair nets and tabards. Neither can she remember, at the factory, seeing one girl with her leg in the air in front of the mirror, cutting off the string of her tampon.

Over the last few weeks, Kaya has got to know most of the girls at the club. Alisha, she has found out, is a dental nurse. There are two other medical students, a receptionist, a couple of shop assistants, some students from the university, whom she watches with a shy fascination, and a couple of unfriendly career strippers, who never talk about anything but how the money gets worse every year, and how they ought to get out and go to London. Aside from Alisha the girls are white. Two are Eastern European, sitting slightly apart and talking to each other in their own language, clacking and mysterious. They both have high cheekbones and angular mouths, and she wonders if they are sisters.

'I wouldn't like to see any of my family in here,' Chloe says. 'Bit weird.'

Kaya thinks but doesn't say that it is weird to see Chloe dancing here, with her own jaunty kind of movement, lifting her arms and shrugging her breasts with a cheerful eyebrow raise, as if to say, 'what have we here, then?' She is a popular dancer. If she was the highest earner before Kaya's arrival, she doesn't mention it.

'I saw my uncle in here once,' one of the students says. '*That* was weird. Annie let me hide out the back for a while.'

'*Gross*,' Chloe hisses, delightedly.

Kaya spends the most time talking to Laura, a friendly history student with an expensive accent, dove-coloured skin and breasts that swing gently under her sheer dress like heavy bells. Laura is one of the least self-conscious girls at the Purple Tiger; appearing to genuinely abandon herself, artlessly open-mouthed, enjoying the sight of her body in the mirrors. The other girls say she isn't *serious*, and while Kaya thinks this is ridiculous – Laura works as hard as any of them – she can also see what they mean. There is something almost exaggerated, play-acted, about Laura's performance, like a tipsy tourist invited onto a Turkish stage to take part in a belly dance.

Kaya would not have revealed her university savings account – growing every day – to Laura, in case Laura answered her with a smile, quickly hidden, or with surprise, or even with a 'Good for you!', or a 'Great plan!' ringing unmistakeably with insincerity. But in the end it is Laura who brings the subject up, after rummaging in Kaya's bag for eyeliner and finding an Italo Calvino.

'Are you studying, then?' she asks, with every appearance of seriousness. And so Kaya, all the while watching Laura's face like a wary magpie, one eye on flight, tells her about the university fund, and her plans to study English, or classics, or possibly both, becoming in the end so vehement that the two Eastern European girls break off their murmured conversation, and look over at her in surprise.

'I have to wait until next year, though,' Kaya says, 'to get the money. So all I can do in the meantime is read.'

'If you're that desperate, why don't you come to campus and just go to a lecture?'

'I can't do that.'

'Sure you can. You couldn't get away with it in a seminar because they take a register. But most of the lectures you can just walk into and sit at the back. No one would notice. They wouldn't expect someone to try to study voluntarily.'

'I can steal an education?'

'Sure you can,' Laura says again. 'I'll tell you where to go.'

And this is how Kaya ends up looking for a Modernist Literature lecture at the university, a red-brick cluster of buildings bedded in a rainy soft pillowing of green hills and lakes, its paths and small squares criss-crossed by students wrapped in the same sort of coats, wool hats and boots as herself. Laura has helpfully provided her with a translation of the names of each building – the HUMS, the DARC, the Arthur Plackett theatre – which seem designed for only students to understand. When, after a long search that takes her to almost the hour of the lecture, Kaya finds the humanities building, she sees a crowd of students filing into a theatre and – blank with panic – walks straight in after them.

She has no idea if this is the lecture she's been looking for, and can't ask. She finds a corner where she sits edgily on a fold-down chair and tries to breathe more regularly. Nobody pays her any attention, and she wonders what she expected: for them all to turn and identify her as an interloper, for a low hiss to go up? Pointing fingers, herself rushed out into the hallway? But she sits undisturbed in the stodgy warmth, taking photocopied notes when they are passed to her (the lecture, apparently, is on Kant), smiled at briefly, by a boy in a baseball cap. Someone nearby has a coffee in a paper cup. The smell of it reminds her of Louise, sitting in the wan light of the large window and making one of her periodic efforts to sober up.

'I'm sorry, Kaya,' she would say at these times, 'I'm a fuck-up. I'm a shit mother. You should hate me. You can hate me, if you like. I'd understand.' And Kaya, inhaling the dark scent of it, the smell of distant jungles, her mother's face veiled with steam, would always shake her head.

The lecturer is a small man who frightens her for a moment with his resemblance to the first customer she danced for, the one who asked her about her holidays. Not long after he starts speaking she realises with relief that it is not the same man, and not long after that the Purple Tiger itself and all its habitués are completely forgotten, driven like alarmed birds out of her head by the arrival of a bush fire, a great blaze of surprise and towering beauty.

Kaya, while enjoying her own amateur existential meditations, has never encountered a genuine philosopher before, or not in any real intimacy. She gets the impression early on that Kant – a notoriously tricky customer, as the lecturer puts it, his theories endlessly disputed – may not be the easiest introduction to philosophy; yet his theory of phenomena and noumena appeals to something in Kaya, as yet only in the very earliest of stages: a question she hadn't got around to asking, a thought she might have been about to think.

The lecturer gives them the example of a hat. The hat is

both phenomenon – an object that can be experienced – and noumenon – an object we cannot know. Kant claims that nothing is knowable to thought alone: we know things only by experience. So, while we experience something of the hat, its true nature is a mystery. Thus noumena only exist in a negative sense: representing the limit of our knowledge. It is that blank beyond experiential knowledge – the feel of it – that Kaya likes: the utter limitlessness of it. She is inclined to leave it as it is, a sparkling unbounded secret.

On the way out of the theatre she spots and steals the lecture timetable off the wall; unnoticed, first strolling, then – when she reaches the door – nearly running out into the gentle rain, shoulder to wet shoulder with the oblivious students, feeling suddenly euphoric: not just at her small crime, but at the sudden and incomprehensible openness of the whole wide world.

Kaya turned eighteen not only on the same day that sixth form ended, but also the day the factory she worked at gave her two weeks' notice, having outsourced production to India. She supposed it would make it easier to revise, after which she could look for another job. Her teachers urged her to consider university, but though she wanted it badly, she could see no way of making it work. Louise, money and university were three large and contrary puzzle pieces: trying to fit them into the same picture was impossible, no matter how she shuffled them.

When Kaya got back to the flat, she found it filled with a

lemony light, sparkling in a hung fog of cigarette smoke and vanilla fragrances. Louise was in the small kitchen, her eyes burning with a near-sober glow of production. Her mother was a rare but preternaturally accomplished cook. On her less befuddled days she would go out to the shops with a list of esoteric ingredients – gelatine, bicarbonate of soda, chocolate ganache – then create extravagant cakes, towering sundaes, delicate cloudy soufflés. She did all this in one extended burst of activity, like a mayfly, then, flagging by the evening, could rarely summon the energy to eat any of it. She would go back to the sofa to watch Kaya eat, tenderly following each spoonful of cake from fork to mouth, as if this sight had been her dying wish.

'Happy birthday, sugar melon,' she said now, putting her head round the door. Apparently, at the zenith of her high spirits, she was wearing a sequinned top, dusted with flour. 'Don't come in here. It's a surprise.'

'Why does it smell of smoke?' Kaya asked.

'Oh, that's Carl! He's in the lounge. He came to fix the gas meter and I invited him to stay. He's been such a good laugh today. Went out and got me some vanilla essence when I ran out. Go in and say hello.'

Kaya went into the sitting room, where it took her a moment to make sense of the room, the sofa having been moved to a position in front of the window with the sun streaming in behind it, so that the figure on the sofa was only a glowing black shape of a man, smoking faintly at the edges.

'Oh,' she said, without thinking. She squinted at Carl.

'Had to move the sofa to get to the gas meter and your mum said she preferred it this way,' Carl said, as if understanding her confusion. He got up, putting down the cigarette and his can of beer, holding his emptied hands up in a gesture of celebration. 'Happy eighteenth birthday! I'm Carl.'

The rest of the evening passed strangely and slowly, though Kaya was apparently the only one who thought so. Carl's box of tools and branded fleece lay in the corner, apparently cast off at 2 p.m., which is when he and Louise hit it off and decided to spend an afternoon drinking beer. Carl was a tall man, his legs folded politely under him, knees skewing out at a wide angle. He was good-looking, or at least Kaya supposed Louise would think so. Something in his heavy lower lip, slackened with drink, his experienced blue eyes, set off a small answer of dislike in her, though not in a place she could easily communicate with. She felt it physically; in her stomach, in her hands, set neatly on the table like a Victorian schoolgirl's.

Louise, ironically, seemed less drunk than usual, presumably because she had been drinking the beer Carl popped out to buy, rather than her usual spirits. She had dusted the flour off her top and sat laughing at Carl's stories, all her sequins catching the light, splashing their three faces.

'This is a lovely place you've got,' Carl said.

Kaya looked dubiously at the sitting room; the pile of washing in the corner, the black wires of the television, the DVD player and the stereo colliding in a sudden skirmish, the damp-stained ceiling. The porcelain lady had her eyes raised to some far horizon, as if genteelly affecting not to notice.

'Oh, it's shit,' Louise said modestly.

'It's got a nice atmosphere.' Carl leaned back and smiled at them both. His hands rose irrepressibly outward – apparently a favourite gesture of his – to indicate the room, the table, the two women sitting watching him. 'My place isn't like this. It feels unloved. Lonely.'

At this Louise looked at him with mingled pity and lust, and before she could even say, 'You should come here and visit us, shouldn't he, Kaya?' Kaya saw it all unfold: the evenings with her arriving home to find the two of them half cut and giggling over some football match, in which Louise would pretend to have an interest despite having said on many occasions that she can't bear it, football being the sort of thing her dad, 'that arsehole', used to love; the smoking in the flat, another thing Louise used not to be able to bear; the gradual decline in Carl's gas engineering work, so that by the time Kaya's exams came round he would be mostly at their flat, his long legs having uncurled more and more day by day, finally making their way up onto the sofa arm (shoes on: another of Louise's cast-off hatreds); the days Kaya would get the bus and study at the library in order to avoid the two of them, and, more particularly, to avoid passing Carl in the kitchen or the hallway, him standing aside exaggeratedly, the very theatre of his movements conveying the possibility of him not being so gentlemanly, as if containing their own shadow.

And, though it gave her no pleasure to be proved right, this was exactly how it turned out.

On days when it isn't raining, Kaya stands outside the Purple Tiger's back door with the girls who smoke; preferring the distant drone of traffic from the underpass, the wheelie bins, the moths dizzied by the light of the doorway, the bite of the clouded air and the sugaring of broken glass at intervals along the road to the club's interior, which she knows too well, like the inside of her own shoe. Like a shoe, the Purple Tiger has become too comfortable; worn in and warm; something that bothers her almost as much as the queasy nervousness of her first nights. She doesn't want to get used to it; to wake up one day and realise that she is one of the old girls, stripping at thirty-five.

Cameron, one of the two regular doormen, is standing with them, smiling along when they all laugh. Kaya likes the doormen, neither of whom demonstrates any interest in the strippers; rather, they remind her of eunuchs, stoically guarding the gates to the harem. When faced with naked breasts they neither look nor pointedly look away; neutral as gynaecologists. She imagines them going home, swinging their arms and whistling, relieved of the tedium of sex.

'It'll be quiet tonight,' Chanel says. Her real name is Chanel: she strips under the name Rachel. 'Days like this I think I might go to London. There's more money there. You can make thousands in a night.'

'But you got to be naked in the floor shows,' Alisha says. 'And they pack the girls in, so you end up fighting like rats. It's fucking ruthless in London.' The girls tell their horror stories of London: clubs openly dealing coke, places run by East End gangsters, sharp practices over pay, broken CCTV, veiled threats.

'It's decent enough here,' Alisha says. 'Give me a quiet life.'

'*She* should go to London.' Chanel indicates Kaya. Her tone is not unfriendly. 'Make a bloody fortune. Get noticed by a businessman or something. An actor. A *sheikh*. Get bought a flat in South Ken. Do the food shop at Fortnum and Mason. Tell 'em their caviar's not up to spec.'

For a moment, the girls' eyes are wide and naked, stripped of their usual clothes; the dreaminess, the longing underneath exposed.

'I don't think so,' Kaya says. She smiles, placatingly. She is conscious of the disparity in their earnings. Sometimes she feels like she is back at school; top of the class. Paul stops to chat to her, solicitous, slightly anxious – 'Everything OK, Kaya? How's the family? Great work this week. Really fantastic' – as if, with these moments of small talk, he himself might prevent Kaya from leaving the Purple Tiger and shacking up with a sheikh.

And just as at school, Kaya does her homework. In the daytimes, when she isn't at lectures or working through her own ersatz version of the other students' recommended reading lists using public library books or the small screen of her smartphone, she puts on MTV and copies the women dancing in the videos, rolling her hips and arching her back. She has her body hair waxed. She uses sunbeds, because white skin under the club's purplish light looks unearthly, but she keeps her thong on when she tans, wanting to keep track of her real colour, fearful of forgetting where she started and getting lost in the woods of self-perception, the trickeries of her own unreliable gaze. Some of the other girls have no memory of what their skin used to look like; knowing only their current state of deep and artificial brown, heading down the sunbeds every other day.

She makes the effort, too, not to succumb to self-hatred. The other girls mostly do it by drinking: a few glasses of vodka, lime and water to keep the weight off and provide a soft cushioning, a numb fuzz between their delicate hearts and the being looked up and down, the shake of the head or – at worst – the explanation: 'No, love, I don't want a dance, I'm going to wait for that girl over there with the tits.'

Alisha, ever confident, doesn't drink. 'You can't please all of the people all of the time,' Alisha says. 'If one man thinks your tits are too small the next will love them. Small breasts are classier anyway. That's your brand, by the way: classy.'

'Isn't Laura classy?'

'Nah,' Alisha says authoritatively. 'She's good girl gone bad.'

'So why are small breasts classier?'

'Dunno. But high fashion models have small ones and glamour models have big ones. I think it's that men are fucking idiots. They see a big boob and they think it must be for their benefit. A small boob maintains its mystique. It stays quiet and haughty. It's like, "Oy, men, *you* make the effort".'

Kaya seeks out Alisha's advice: randomly given, often interrupted. Alisha tells Kaya that it is scientifically proven that blonde girls have an advantage over dark-haired girls: if several girls walk into a room it's the pale head that men notice first. She tells her to wear red, black or white: nature's warning colours. They raise a man's heart rate, making him think something exciting will happen. She says no compliment is too insincere, no lie too obvious ('I'm single but I'm looking', 'Nobody's ever asked me that before', 'If I didn't have to earn money, I'd stay here and talk to you all night'): that all the men want to believe you could fall in love with them, or at least have sex with them for free.

And so here is Star: smiling, lying and wearing white; a translucency, a pane coloured by her surroundings. Sometimes Kaya wonders whether she has kept a part of her original self untouched – like the pale triangle above her pubic hair – to compare her present self to, or if it is too late: if she is lost in the woods.

The girls finish their cigarettes and Kaya follows them inside. She dances first; her white negligee glowing a pale lavender in the lights. At the right of the stage she becomes aware of a man watching her, sitting with a couple of other men, though the other men – one bald, one red in the nose – look like coarser creatures beside him; a finished picture between two discarded attempts. This man, who must be about forty, looks as hard and refined as a statue. He has thick dark hair, a long mouth, a sharp, slightly piratical look. His shirt is as crisp as a sheet of paper. He watches her without looking away, ignoring the efforts of the sweating man on his left to engage him in conversation.

Kaya knows without understanding why – or being able to stop herself – that she is avoiding his eye. When she steps down, she goes over to another table, out of his sight. After a while Luca, the barman, comes over to speak to her.

'There's a guy who wants to talk to you. Asked when you were free.'

A narrow-bodied, black-irised boy, Luca was hired by Paul on the rationale that he was gay and thus less likely to give the girls free drinks: an assumption that has turned out to be incorrect. He lives close by Kaya and Chloe and has joined them for takeaways on nights when Dave is out.

'Who?' Kaya asks, knowing who. She doesn't look around – not wanting to squint and gape, to be at any sort of loss – but, nonetheless, she is unsettled. As with boxers or tennis players, nervousness in a stripper is a fault line; a crack that travels across the yards of artificial hair and tan and nails, opening up fatal crevasses and chasms. A stripper with her nerve broken may as well go home for the night.

'The film star in the corner,' Luca says, with envy. 'Lucky you, eh?'

'Lucky me,' says Kaya. 'Hey, give me a shot of something, will you?'

Luca looks at her with surprise, and she responds with her emptiest face, all readable traces scoured out of its clean bowl, leaving him no other option but to shrug and hand her a vodka. With the cold metal taste of it hissing in her mouth and throat she turns and walks towards the corner table, where (and only here in the club) the purple light falters and gives up without really touching the booth's occupants, creating an imbalance of exposure, so that she is forced to approach as if under a spotlight, hardly able to see the man who waits for her.

PART TWO

ALICE

Over the next weeks, Alice watches Jasper more closely, and less obviously. She finds out nothing. He doesn't welcome sexual overtures, claiming to be tired, but he has wanted sex less and less often each year, and the slight acceleration of this decline could be statistically insignificant. (Alice, in turn, becomes more reluctant to ask him – to pester or beg – in the awareness of her own longing, vast and vulnerable. She takes an enjoyment in sex that is almost shameful, because it is so grateful.) He plays tennis and keeps in shape, but this is not a recent development. He comes home clean and sweet smelling as if he has showered, but then he never has been a hot, damp person, prone to odours and secretions; his skin is as smooth and hard as soap. He is absent more often but there is always a reason – a colleague or an old friend – none of whom she knows well enough to call. His mobile phone is protected by a code, and he has always kept his accounts and credit cards separate to hers, his statements all stored in a secret chamber of the Internet, beyond several sets of locked and passworded doors.

All Alice has is the awareness that he is different with her; less tolerant of their unequal partnership, less gracious. He answers her shortly if she asks him something he thinks ought to be obvious. Their conversation – previously alive and darkly glittering with criticism of mutual friends, politics, television, the neighbours – has sighed out and their interactions now are those of the shop queue; the train station. They talk about whether Jasper's suit should go to the dry cleaner's this evening or tomorrow morning, when the window in the upstairs guest bedroom should be replaced – the fog of the outside world having sneaked inside the panes, freezing there – and why they often get two copies of the local newspaper, one on Friday morning, one in the evening, as if there are two delivery rounds, or just one round, carried out by a forgetful boy.

She tries not to start fights, but then does anyway. The way he picks up the argument, as if grateful – as if he's been waiting for it – bothers her. It reminds her absurdly of walking a neighbour's dog when she was young. All the way along the path it would shadow her side, watching the ball in her hand, waiting for that moment when she would throw the ball across the fields, and it could run after it into the flat grass horizon. At least the dog ran back to her just as eagerly. Jasper does return, but with reluctance, or resentment; vanishing for longer and longer each time.

On Saturday morning, Alice cleans the house. She picks up the clothes that both Ben and Jasper discard onto the floor (where, once they have landed, they seem to drop out of all memory). She cleans the chrome of the kitchen until it burns with mirrored light, removes, washes and replaces the crystal drops from the large chandelier in the sitting room. Moving into the hall, with the intention of dusting the picture rail, Alice is drawn towards a mysterious red light blinking behind a pot plant and an artfully arranged heap of books on the chiffonier. Investigating, she discovers their house phone, edged into the corner to while away its twilight years, as disconcerted as she is by the new answer phone message worrying at its memory.

'Hello, this is Nicky, from Laud Park Surgery. I'm sorry to call the home telephone but we have Dr Rooke down as working today and he hasn't arrived yet. I tried his mobile but it was switched off, so I'm just trying this number to check that everything is OK. If Dr Rooke could call back, that would be much appreciated. Thank you.'

As Alice is listening to the message, the telephone rings again.

'Oh, hello. This is Nicky again.'

'Hello, Nicky,' says Alice.

'I'm so sorry, I know I already left a message, but I've now realised we've had a mix-up here today . . . there is a Dr Rooke and a Dr Hook here at the practice and the two of them got muddled, somebody put the wrong name in the computer for today's rota. Dr Hook is here today but obviously not Dr Rooke. So there is no need for him to call. I'm so sorry to have disturbed you at home. There are only two of us in reception this morning, and we're both new . . .'

'Well,' Alice says kindly, hearing the girl is flustered. 'I won't say anything if you don't.'

After that she and the grateful Nicky go back to their own days, as if this chance intersection is nothing much – and it could have been nothing much, if Jasper hadn't come home and told her that he'd seen a succession of more than usually tedious patients that morning, and that he was so tired after a busy week that he was going to head straight upstairs for a nap.

And there it is: the reflexive shudder, the sudden, comprehensive chill, the dead silence in her interior. She has felt it a few times over the years, each time with the sense that it is something that has never really left, not since it began in Greece over ten years ago, in a villa owned by their friends at the time.

Their hosts had thrown a party on the terrace overlooking a blue velvet sea, lanterns hanging from the olive trees, their ghosts scattered across the surface of the pool. The party came at the end of a week in which Alice had gradually unclenched, getting browner and calmer, until, finally, she felt as new and open as a child, walking barefoot with her glass of wine, dancing with absolute strangers. At about three she realised she hadn't seen Jasper for a while and went to look for him, wandering away from the terrace towards the landscaped gardens, squinting at the shadows under the blazing trees, where – in the deepest patch of darkness – she saw the prettiest wife of the night lighting a cigarette. Her face and Jasper's glowed ember colour for a moment only, before the dark came back, darker than before.

Alice turned away and went to bed and thought various confused, noisy things – past dropped phone calls, missing nights, sidelong glimpses – before she was delivered from her unhappiness into a welcome alcohol blackout. The next day, she said nothing, as she and Jasper walked around the nearest town with their map and camera, each enfolded in their own particular reveries, holding them apart like a soundproof window, or the black panes of their sunglasses.

After an hour or so, Alice came out of a shop selling ceramics and found that Jasper wasn't in the street outside. Assuming he had got bored and wandered away, she looked into shop windows and down the streets and alleys, before turning back to wait for him. After a while – the protracted drag of time reserved for people who stand still to wait, with nothing else to do – she was overcome with a sudden, comprehensive feeling of rage. In front of a window of fake antiquities she felt the heavy door of her anger swing closed, the clang of it, blocking out the light. She left the street, moving quickly into the unfamiliar old quarter, finding a road that led up a steep hill and walking up it, teeth set, as if pitting herself against its hostility. The people she passed glanced at her, a lone Englishwoman sweating under her sunhat, guidebook swinging unheeded in her fingers. The shops disappeared as if on a downward conveyor belt, replaced by houses with wrought-iron balconies and leprous paint, gates opening on to battered cars or strung washing, under the blur of bougainvillea.

Near the top she ran out of energy and sat down on the uneven pavement, looking down at the town below her and the sea beyond it, all her anger evaporated, or burnt off, condensed into tiny crystals. She knew Jasper was probably lost, waiting furiously in the heat, if he hadn't already given up and caught a taxi back to the villa. She didn't really care what had happened to Jasper. She felt herself lighter and brighter, almost transcendently untied. It was a kind of satisfaction, and relief, to be alone now – with the thought that she could have always been alone, living at the top of a hill in the sun, doing something, nothing, anything at all.

She didn't know, yet, that she was pregnant.

The next day Alice rents a small hatchback and waits outside Jasper's surgery for him to leave work. She sits in the car squinting through the windscreen in the low winter sunlight, which is hard and bright and without warmth, turning the passers-by into dark shapes only, like cut-outs, their voices moving close then fading as they walk by her open window. She begins to worry that Jasper will slip by, another black shape, when she sees him standing by the door. Alone for a moment, Jasper blinks in the sunlight and shifts in his coat, pulling it around his shoulders. He takes out his phone and looks at it. It is a moment before Alice, with fascination and dread, realises what she is watching: a new hesitancy, an uncertainty he as well as she must be unaccustomed to, stopping and starting him like a bad recording.

She starts her car before he gets to his own, guessing, correctly, that he will move quickly once behind the wheel, leaping like a fish through the shoal and out into the current; and indeed he is already a few cars in front of her by the time she manages to get back onto the road. They move together through the town, passing through the unlovely concrete valleys at its heart, below the cranes and scaffolding of developments delayed by the recession, the near-empty Lego apartment blocks. From the centre they travel west, into the long, shabby streets of high

Victorian houses long since divided into flats, watched by unblinking CCTV cameras. The names of the roads are familiar to her from the local newspaper; the spare, uninterested coverage of drugs and prostitution. The town can, in fact, be neatly divided according to its criminal geography. In the centre: violence, surrounded by a halo of muggings. To the west are the prostitutes, shifting from street to street as new cameras are installed, pushed further each year from the cleaned-up centre of town. To the east are the shootings of young men, the finales to stories she doesn't know, though their elements are the same: gangs, feuds, allegiances. Her own world, the hilly land of the north, is the preserve of the burglars, drawn in by the glut of goods, the rich pickings of the lazy middle class. They enter without even the need to break: a hand through the letter box, car keys lifted from an open window.

It is, appropriately, in a road known for soliciting that Jasper stops. Alice takes her own space in the steep, narrowly car-lined street further down: far enough so that she can't be seen, close enough for her to see, holding herself rigid and wincing; an eye held painfully open, waiting for the shock of the cold drops. As she expected, a door opens, and a girl comes out, but this is not quite the girl she might have pictured, pausing at the top of the steps with an odd little wave, serious-looking, wrapped in a thick quilted coat like a pupa. Her face isn't visible, but her hair, which is blond, streams and billows over the top of her swaddling in the wind. Alice finds herself leaning forward, as if she might be able to see better, find a way through the turned-up collar and the hair in flux, but it isn't necessary, because halfway down the steps the girl turns, as if feeling the weight of an unknown gaze, and looks in Alice's direction.

Surprised, Alice looks down quickly, but not before she sees the girl's radiance; an illumination not of any particular emotion but the simple flare of youth, the finality of beauty. The road is seedy, the coat is ugly, the hair looks cheap, but the girl is something precious; like Cleopatra half hidden in her rolled carpet. Alice looks back up to see her getting into the car, which gives a sudden groan as Jasper spurs it on, climbing the hill, heading up towards the roundabout at the top of the road.

When Alice and Jasper had been dating for a little while, in the final year of university (a time when Alice was still claiming to be undecided about Jasper), they went to the theatre to see *Cat on a Hot Tin Roof*. On the way home – the two of them sitting in a nearly empty train carriage, sharing a bottle of wine – Jasper told her, 'You know they changed the ending for the film version. They got rid of most of the references to homosexuality and gave them a happy ending.' (Alice was impressed by Jasper's general knowledge. Whatever they did together, he was always able to tell her a few interesting and relevant things. At the zoo she learned that polar bears sometimes turn green in warmer climates because each hair of their fur is hollow, and algae can form inside it; on a picnic she was shown the pressure an unshelled egg can withstand before it cracks.)

'That's so stupid,' she said.

'That was how it was back then.'

'But even if they didn't make him gay, they didn't have to give them a happy ending too. They could just have left it out but everybody would really know that's what it was about. It would just be a secret, rather than a lie.'

'Everybody loves a happy ending,' said Jasper, who had been looking at the programme again.

'I don't know why.' Alice looked around to see who was watching, before putting her feet up on the seat opposite. Nothing was visible beyond the window: a current of darkness hissed by as if they were inside a submarine, or space capsule, moving through uncharted atmospheres. There was a long, desolate lowing from the train. She took another sip from the wine, nearly spilling it.

Jasper was curious then. 'What do you mean?'

'I just get bored of these films and TV things where one of the characters is chasing the other, or they both are, and they're kept apart by something, and then finally it ends when they finally do get together. Like there's no more point after that, nothing inter-esting happens –' Alice considered this, and laughed; she was harder then, more testing – 'which, I suppose, is fair enough, because it must all just be an anti-climax after that. True love, I mean.'

'That's a terrible thing to say,' Jasper said, sending an accusing glance at the wine as if it were to blame for Alice's cruelty, which, perhaps, partly it was.

'It's true, though. If you long and long for someone and then get them, it can't be the same. It'll get boring. Housework and children and the commute. The daily routine.'

'No, it's not true.' Jasper was frowning, but had leaned forward, enlivened by the flare of conflict.

'What does happen, then?' Alice asked.

'There is all that, but you love each other, and you're happy.'

Alice must have known even back then that she wanted to be persuaded, because she leaned forward too, tilting her face up as if it might collect more of his gaze, aligned like a satellite receiver. 'Really?' she asked.

'And anyway, I'm going to be rich and there won't be housework or commuting for either of us. We're retiring at thirty.'

They laughed, and he got out of the train first and took her hand, lifting her to the platform as if she were something very valuable, and they walked home under the frozen fireworks of the stars, sharing the rest of the wine, after which she invited him to stay at her house (it being cleaner and sweeter smelling than his own), where they went to bed and had what she still knows – sharp and unmistakeable, even through the fogged window of history – to be the best sex of her life.

Driving behind Jasper now, Alice suspects that what he wants has never been entirely sexual; that it is complicated by his conception of ideal love. His pursuit of this did not end with her; merely transferring itself to other women, other projected futures. He still likes music in which men complain melodically about absent females, watches films or television aimed at a younger demographic, populated by two-dimensional sirens. He has a romantic streak, a longing for the infinitely receding light, the green light of love, or passion. And the girl he is with now certainly has the right credentials: no older than twenty-five, nakedly lovely face, dodgy neighbourhood. Alice realises, heavily, that Jasper probably thinks he is rescuing her.

On the dual carriageway the flow of cars seizes; the van

between her and Jasper ducks suddenly into a faster lane, and she is brought up uncomfortably close to the car containing her husband and the girl. At the same time that the physical distance between them contracts, her sense of detachment – the illusion that she is a detective, or a spy carrying out a routine reconnaissance, hiring the car, changing her hair, wearing sunglasses to hide her face – abruptly vanishes. Her hands squeeze the steering wheel, damp-fingered. Her heart pulses. She wants to get away from the car, the two heads visible through the rear window, turning to talk to each other. But she watches them instead, trying unsuccessfully to fill in the sound, matching their mouths to possible words.

Even when the road opens up again, past the cause of the traffic, a smoking car, crumpled bonnet askew, its silver arteries and organs laid open, Alice doesn't drop back or pull away. She follows them all the rest of the way, along the roads between fields, down narrow green alleys, the trees gathering at either side – the scenic route – and when they stop at their country house hotel she finds her own parking space almost out of sight, from which she watches them walk together, hand in hand, through its pillared entrance.

After that, Alice, left alone, sits in the car without any defined ideas of what she will do next. She becomes gradually aware that she is holding tightly on to the steering wheel as if she were speeding, leaning forward in a strange, arrested Grand Prix. She lets go of her grip and sits back, deliberating. Time passes; though when she looks at the clock, she realises it is not quite as much time as she thinks. She feels as if she has been sitting there for hours, bent into the shape of the car seat, when only half an hour has passed.

The sun has been whisked over by a thick stage curtain of cloud; disappearing as completely as it had arrived, leaving her in a thick, pewter dark. Jasper and the girl will be in a room by now – lamps lit, doors closed and curtains drawn, creating an enchanted space like the forts she used to make with chairs and blankets, except more secret, more secure – and Alice is alone in this unfamiliar car, taking her own warmth back from her as it cools; the lights off, the radio silent, the night seeping in. It suddenly seems unendurable that she would stay there any longer, tormenting herself with Jasper's sexual itinerary, so she switches on the engine and drives back to the hire firm, and then goes home to wait for Ben.

'Did you have a good evening?' Alice asks when Ben arrives at the door. He always holds the doorbell down for a long time, creating a strident clanging that contrasts with the eventual sight of him, uncertain and small-shouldered on the step. 'Did you say thank you to George's mum?'

'Yes,' Ben says, impatiently. They both turn and wave at the estate car idling on the pavement: the window rolls down and a hand emerges to wave back; a white smile, a slice of highlighted hair before the car pulls away.

'So what did you and George do?' Alice asks, trying not to sound strained, or tired, or shocked; keeping her face out of the innermost cone of brightness cast by the overhead light.

She tries for and almost pulls off a playful note, 'Not more computer games?'

'*Actually*, we played a board game,' Ben says haughtily. 'Scategories. With George's mum, and her two brothers, though they weren't very good because they're young, and they kept giving stupid answers. But it was funny. We had milkshakes – George's mum made them in the blender with banana and milk.'

And there it is, a glimpse under the fringe, the quick lift and fall of his eyes, something sweet and bright. Alice tries not to feel pained by it.

'It sounds lovely,' she says. 'We could play board games here too if you enjoy them.' Then, because there is an overly extended moment, in which Ben doesn't answer, she carries on quickly, 'So, is George your friend or your girlfriend?'

'God, *Mum*.' Ben is disapproving. 'She's my friend.' Yet even after this blunder, Alice is still apparently in favour, because, rather than retreat to his room, Ben asks if he can watch the television in the sitting room, and so they spend a while together, Ben absorbed in the posturing and booming of some middle-aged men on a car show, playing out their teenage dreams, while she pretends to read a book.

She is wondering about the girl's age, her origins. Her features could have been Eastern European: the gradient of the cheekbones, the coolly elevated brows. Is she after a green card? Is she an escort? Or is she uneducated and broke and Jasper seems like her entry into a different world – because that's probably what he would let her think, with the splendid hotel, the oversized, over-shiny car (bought last year without warning or consultation). She might be smitten by the trappings. She might – though Alice can hardly bear to allow it – be smitten by him.

Does the girl know who Alice is? Does she blink on occasion to think that there is a wife somewhere beyond her love affair, far behind in the dark hinterlands, yes, but exerting a claim, nonetheless. Does she imagine Alice herself, as Alice is imagining her? As she unrolls herself from that clumsy outer layer – a new, pale body emerging into the amber lamplight – does she shiver when her skin meets the air, not for cold, but because not only Jasper but Alice can see her?

Since the holiday in Greece Alice hasn't looked for anything, and almost nothing has been shown to her. She has accepted this as a peculiar kind of love. If Jasper makes the effort to hide his infidelity, she reasons, it demonstrates a respect for her; a desire to protect their marriage even if he is unable to confine himself completely within it. But his behaviour now is impossible for her to ignore. The lengthening absences, the increasingly flimsy excuses, offered up like balloon animals. When he is with her, Alice can feel his eyes tracking her like CCTV, monitoring her minor offences. If she says something silly, or critical, or needy, it visibly charges him; he crackles with new scorn, bright and exasperated. She can see that he is trying to free himself; struggling against her, as if she is physically holding him, and he must hurt her, to make her let go.

One of her friends asked her once, towards the end of her own marriage, 'What is it with people? Have you noticed how we just keep going in a relationship that doesn't work, pushing on with it, until the whole thing is burnt out and there's absolutely nothing left? When you don't feel anything except contempt for each other, and exhaustion? Why don't we see it coming and leave while there is still the possibility of human kindness?'

'Because then there's still hope that the relationship might work, and we're making a mistake by leaving,' was what Alice said, without even a pause.

'How sad, then, for hope.'

Alice sees herself now, led by hope like a small child being pulled through crowds by her parent – scurrying to keep up with that tall and impassive back, tripping over her loose shoe laces when she turns to look at faces or into the windows that slip briefly by – believing all the time that the hand enclosing hers belongs to a person who knows where they are going.

She spends most of that night wondering about Jasper's state of mind – whether he will leave her, or force her to leave him, or get hurt by the girl or sick of the girl and love Alice more than before – before it occurs to her to consider her own. It's harder to think of what she feels, or what she wants. Her need for him is in parts, or pieces; it is not simple. There is longing, but also fear. There are other things. She peers into her heart like a child outside the overgrown garden of the local witch. She looks over the gate at the ivy blanketing the eaves, the effortful twists of the yew branches, the dark, sticky firs. She could walk inside if she wanted to, but she can't. Not yet.

Wednesdays at the charity shop are the slowest; the store falling into a densely silent snooze, minutes swelling ponderously into hours. Alice leans her elbows on the counter and considers a bag of donations that somebody has brought in. Unpacking the bag and taking it upstairs to steam and price-tag is the only thing she has to do, so she delays it, waiting until the exact midpoint of the day to satisfy her curiosity. Of all the volunteers she takes the most pleasure, as far as she knows, in the donations: their ambiguous revelations, the sudden flare of the unexpected. The stack of pornographic DVDs handed in by the tweed-shouldered matron; the sparkled hotpants and boas brought in by an elderly man. Once a woman gave them a bag containing a perfectly cut dinner suit and an evening dress like a gold cataract, heavy with thousands of tiny bronze beads. Alice – flushed with her sudden need for that life – put the bag under the counter to buy for herself. She only had ten minutes to think about operas and masked balls before the flustered benefactor ran back in, having confused the charity shop bag with the dry cleaning bag, leaving Alice with two golf jumpers and a pink lace dressing gown.

This latest bag, a rope-stringed affair from a London store, has been brought in by a good-looking young woman of twenty-five or so, and as such represents a brief window into the thoughts of the young. Alice has been preoccupied with the thoughts of the young recently: or, more specifically, how different they might be to her own. Would this young woman reject denim cut-offs, slogan T-shirts, short dresses? Would she wear, perhaps, a large and quilted coat?

With this thought Alice forgets to delay the big reveal, and opens the bag. It contains a ski jacket, goggles, salopettes and gloves. It is an anti-climactic moment, and more than a little melancholy. She can't help but feel sad at the disappointment that went into the packing of this bag. She puts the clothes on the shelf of the back room, sniffing at them first to determine whether they ought to be washed or steamed. They are technically meant to use gloves to sort through donations, but Alice trusts the twenty-five-year-old girl, who didn't like skiing as much as she hoped. The two of them share a wordless affinity; the experience of finding out something sad, without knowing whether that makes you wiser, or just sadder.

When the bell above the door emits its broken tinkle, Alice does not expect to see Oliver, and for a moment she sees him with the absolute objectivity of a stranger. His attractiveness becomes even more inescapable; solid and tall, in a dark grey coat and striped scarf.

'Alice! I haven't come in for charitable purposes. I was passing and saw you through the window. I'd forgotten you worked here. Actually, I don't normally go down this road, but I'd walked to the supermarket before I realised I forgot to get my suit from the dry cleaner's, and thought I'd try this as a shortcut.'

'It's not,' Alice says. Feeling somehow supported by the glass-topped counter that stands between them, she leans forward and smiles at him affectionately, 'A shortcut, that is. But I'm glad you didn't realise. I haven't had the most exciting morning. It's good to see a human face.'

Oliver looks around. 'I could imagine someone going slightly mad here after not very long.'

'It's happened to most of us,' Alice says.

'Are you all mad here, then?' he asks with interest.

'Well. No more than anybody else is, I suppose. Most people are crazy in one way or another, aren't they? Sometimes it just takes longer to find it out.'

'That's true. I have an obsessive–compulsive habit of checking crockery for spiders. I cooked one once.'

'That's not so strange.'

'I also check crockery at other people's houses, and if I don't get the opportunity to check I wonder whether there might be spiders in the food.'

'Were you doing that at my house? Wondering?'

'Funnily, yours was the only place I didn't do it.'

'Is that a lie?'

'Yes.'

They laugh, and Alice glances at the door, concerned that Ida, another volunteer due to work today, might arrive to see her laughing irresponsibly with a personal acquaintance. Despite five years of volunteering and only two days off, Ida appears to be convinced that Alice is delicate, girlish and rather flighty. She hints at her opinions by offering Alice first choice of anything pale pink or frilled that comes in, or saying things like, 'You may not believe it, but there was a time when women didn't even think of paying to have their nails done each week, like you girls do', or, regarding taking out the bins, 'It's a grotty job, are you quite sure?'

'We haven't spoken since dinner, have we?' Oliver says. 'That was weeks ago now.'

'Oh, God, it was. What have I been doing since then? I'd feel better about this if I could tell you I had been in some sort of social whirlwind. But it's nothing more than hibernation.'

'It is winter,' Oliver says forgivingly. 'It's a sluggish season. All the best winter activities take place on the sofa.'

'What about skiing?'

'I stand corrected. But I didn't know you skied?'

'Not for years. We took Ben when he was five. Thought we'd get him started early so he could become one of those horrid little children whizzing down the mountain and making adult beginners feel bad about themselves. But he didn't really enjoy it, and Jasper got bored trailing around with the two of us, and it wasn't a great success particularly.'

'Did you enjoy it?'

'Oh, I did. But I'm not great at it. I sort of slither awkwardly down at my own pace and end up holding everyone else back.'

Oliver frowns. 'I've never heard that worry before.'

'I do try to keep my worries interesting.'

'Speaking of that, you never said how you're mad. I told you about my fear of eating a spider, but you didn't offer anything in return.'

'I thought my madness would be taken as read.'

'No . . . you're horribly sane. It would make me feel relieved if you confessed to something. Lifted up the corner of the curtain, sort of thing, a glimpse of the darkness behind it.'

Alice laughs quite immoderately at this, no longer caring if Ida is at the window. 'I don't like how keen you are to hear a confession,' she says, because Oliver, by now, is also leaning on the counter, smiling and intent. 'Your eyes are shining.'

Oliver grins at this, but he stands up straight, and she feels a quick wince in herself for having blundered; gone too far. She is out of practice at this back-and-forth, the understanding of what and what not to say. 'Tell me another time,' he says, and she isn't sure if this is a reprieve, or a reproof.

'So, what's happened for you since the dinner party?' she asks quickly. 'You haven't been hibernating, have you? How's Maya?'

'Oh, that didn't work out. No, no, it's fine. It was a nice enough ending. It was a few weeks ago now. We didn't have that much in common. Not much to talk about. I hoped . . . but it turned out it was more of a sexual thing, maybe.' He smiles as he says it, ironically, but the joke fails to reach the rest of his face, and the smile is quickly discarded.

'Well, I'm sorry to hear it,' Alice says, for a second time.

Really she is feeling uncomfortable at the mention of sex. Alice has never been a prude; she actually enjoys being slightly surprising, dropping an occasional 'cunt' into conversation, and never raising an eyebrow at the graphic whimsies of others. But standing alone in the charity shop with Oliver as he says 'sexual thing' makes her feel lost, and sad, surrounded by the smell of old clothes and so far, herself, from any real sexual things. Unwillingly she thinks of Jasper ushering his coat-blanketed girl through the doors of the hotel, so he can drink from her, warm himself on the fire of her youth and beauty. He came back that night moody but enlivened, the suppressed after-glow of it finding a release in a sudden and vividly felt complaint about her having forgotten to sort out the house insurance.

Alice looks harder and with sudden resentment at Oliver, standing in all his corded, tanned toughness, his evident good looks – unhappy for now, yes, but still redolent with implied love, with sexual things. He could be a romancer of twenty-somethings without even trying. She forgets for a moment that she hasn't seen him with anybody more than a few years younger than himself and allows the pause in the conversation to lengthen into something cooler; more awkward.

The change in mood doesn't go unnoticed, and Oliver shifts on his feet and says he supposes he ought to let her get on, gesturing unconvincingly at the desolate racks. Alice glimpses the here and now, like a bright crack in the doorway of her own darkly cluttered room, and feels abashed.

'I'm sorry if I looked distracted,' she says again. 'I just thought for a second that we might be interrupted. Another volunteer is meant to be here in a second and I feel like she might . . . well, not tell us off, exactly. But look disapproving.'

'Doesn't this remind you of a Saturday job? Maybe not you, but I remember working in an electronics shop when I was a teenager. It was as quiet as the grave but my friends would come in on their way to the shops or the park or whatever and I'd be so grateful to see them.'

'God, yes. Because they smell of the outside world. Where all the fun is. I worked in a gift shop. Weekday mornings sometimes.'

'Christ,' Oliver says.

The talk of Saturday jobs leads pleasantly into reminiscences of their time at university; the night one summer when they both fell asleep outside, in a thick blanket of grass and dandelions. Sophia had lain there with them for a while, a bottle of rose wine tilting delicately in one hand, before she got bored of their speculative, stoned confabulations and went inside. Jasper had run out of patience much earlier and was already indoors, taking firm command of the stereo. The euphoria of the night lingered on the next morning, when they woke up covered in dew and found that a spider had made a web stretching from Oliver's earlobe to the collar of his denim jacket.

Oliver thinks it was the day they first finished their exams; Alice argues that it was the day they got their exam results. The enjoyable disagreement, however, is interrupted by the arrival of Ida, and Oliver makes his exit, leaving Alice with a feeling of unsettlement, both happy and melancholy, sweet and painful to be so nearly, entirely back at university, but to realise that although some elements of the memory are bright and clear, other parts of it have slipped and blurred: because it was twenty years ago. The knowledge that Sophia and Jasper were having sex inside the house arrives, two decades too late. The sweetness fades and she realises Ida is talking to her.

'Do you really think this ski jacket will sell at forty pounds, Alice? When does the "ski season" finish anyway? Do you know about those things?'

'No, I'm afraid not,' Alice says.

Later that night, Alice sits in her dark car and looks at her face in the mean yellow light of the mirror. After she got home from the charity shop she went to some trouble to find her old university photo albums, going from page to page, passing over everything except her own face. She knows now that she was pretty then – maybe beautiful. She didn't have the stark staring beauty of Jasper's mistress-child, but she turned heads in her own way; not that she realised it at the time. She hardly noticed the evidence of her good looks, instead preoccupied by small failures: the times boys ignored her, the wrong angle of her nose, the odd spot, the tiny rim of fat over the top of her ribboned lace thong before she gave up beer. Perhaps if she had seen herself from the outside in, instead of feeling her way, blind and clumsy, from the inside out, her life would be something different. She hears statistics about good-looking people getting more opportunities, more pay, more approval. She could have charmed her way into a good job, a more devoted husband, if she'd only twigged.

Now Alice looks at herself and sees only the ghost of her old prettiness, already lifting away, ready to float off into the ether. She will be left with a face that can only be described as sad, folding in on itself as if it has taken some invisible but terminal blow to its confidence. Her body is still slender – twenty years ago she began the diet she is still on, with grim success – but its firmness is hard won, and only won temporarily. After a week of not walking, her flesh starts to change state, like melting snow; softening, losing its substance.

Today the sadness of Alice's reflection has a new element: she isn't only monitoring the extent of its failure to tempt Jasper; she is also, partly, looking at it with Oliver's eyes. After their talk of university summers she had a stray urge to hide her face, panicked by the sudden appearance of the young Alice; at so obvious a comparison. Will they just get worse and worse, the embarrassments she devises for herself? As if isn't already humiliating enough that she is sitting outside the tall house of Jasper's girl, staring at its impassively peeling front door.

Tonight she is in her own car, reasoning that the girl won't recognise it, especially not in the dark, and she is confident that Jasper actually is where he says he is tonight – at Bloody Robert's birthday party, because she herself had to lie to get out of it.

She claimed she was visiting a friend, something she feels guilty for, because she owes several of her friends a visit, or at least a telephone call, but they have all, through no fault of their own, slipped to the bottom of Alice's to-do list (item no. 1 on the list being: *Stalk Jasper's mistress*). Ben is at a sleepover at the house of George the Scategories-playing siren, celebrating her birthday.

It is three hours before anyone enters or leaves the house. Then, at eight, the door opens, and Alice is startled to see exactly the person she was expecting. The girl is wearing the same coat as before, a knitted hat with ear flaps, and a pair of flat boots. Her pristine face winks out from its utilitarian housing like a pearl. She walks down the road towards Alice's car and straight past it, her hands in her pockets and her face held low against the whip crack of the air, heading for the end of the road.

Alice gets out of her car into the blank, complete cold, where she hesitates, sees the girl about to turn the corner at the bottom of the road, and hurries down the street after her. Once on the main road there is no need to disguise her pursuit: the girl doesn't look back, half lost in the complex paths of other pedestrians, to the extent that Alice begins to worry that she might have muddled her with someone else in a thick coat, another woman, or even a man. But after a while of watching her gait, the light movement under the thick blanket, Alice can tell it is still her – can almost feel, without seeing, the flex and extension of the girl's slender muscles, the beautiful arrangement of her bones. Nobody else on the street – the aimless groups of teenagers, the stoned man swaying on the corner as if hinged at his feet, the unfriendly girls in their tight jeans, the boys looking out from the black windows of their striped and strobed cars – glances more than once at the girl, as if she has the power of not only enchantment but also invisibility; to everyone but Alice, who knows her true nature.

As the two of them near the centre of town, the small shops selling second-hand records and Polish food break up and thin out, replaced by the towers of car parks and chain hotels. The girl, however, doesn't continue on to the pedestrianised high street, that prism of fluorescence and crowded ill-will, but veers at the last minute down a side street of unlit offices and buildings waiting for demolition. It is quieter here, with only a few people on foot, and Alice lets her pace dawdle. She has the superstitious feeling that the girl must know she has been followed and is deliberately leading her off route, towards the abandoned bus station, or a boarded-up row of ivy-clothed terraces. What will happen there – just the two of them – she has no idea.

But the danger passes; they exit the side street and are out into public space again, walking along a main road, passing a block of flats, a car park, a pub, and several other places the girl might plausibly be arriving at, until finally she changes pace and turns off the pavement, towards a place at which Alice almost laughs, because it makes such complete and perfect sense.

The town's only strip club is called – at the moment – the Purple Tiger, as announced by a neon sign featuring a neon tiger reclining improbably on a sofa. On the wall is a mural of scattered diamonds, from when the club was named Diamonds, and the door has a stained-glass panel with an ornate W at its centre like an illuminated letter in a religious text, which dates back to the time several years ago when the club first opened – to mixed reactions from the public, local newspaper and councillors – and was called Whispers.

The minor local storm ('Storm in a D-cup,' according to a delighted local newspaper usually deprived of sexual controversy; forced to subsist on the occasional indecent exposure and soliciting charge) that accompanied the opening of the club soon faded, and predictions of a rash of similar establishments and a rising tide of drugs, rape and prostitution were not borne out. Since then the club has settled into a subdued seediness, closing every few years and reopening under new ownership, its identity shifting with every breach of the law. This is all Alice knows about it.

As the girl walks up to the doorway, one of the men raises a hand to welcome her. 'Star!' he calls. So that is her name. And that is what she is, a star – of a sort – glowing and cold in the clear night sky.

For a few weeks, most of Alice's spare time is spent watching at two doors; that of Star's flat in the shabby west of the town, and, less frequently, at times when Ben is staying over at a friend's house, that of the Purple Tiger, into which the girl usually disappears at around nine, re-emerging at four or five. Alice herself arrives at the club at around three, parking in the dark away from the canopied entrance with its two dispirited potted palms and its pink lamps. She switches off her engine and lets the colours of the night settle in her vision; the chemical yellow of the streetlights, the rose tints of the club, the tiny red lights opening and closing warningly high up on walls and corners, like the winking eyes of bats. Most of the time Alice spends following Star is wasted. She is only able to devote a couple of hours each day to tracking her rival around the lesser-known streets of the town, and often she misses her altogether. But, in the time she does see her, she begins to put together an impression of the girl's life. Star goes to work most nights, and her blinds are drawn most days. She emerges to go to the local corner shop, the library (unexpectedly) and twice (even more unexpectedly) to the university campus, where Alice loses her both times in a cascade of identically muffled students. She doesn't seem to meet friends; she only sees Jasper. He pulls up outside and within a few minutes she is on the step, waving and unsmiling, before the two of them drive away to places where Alice – rigid and adrenalin-filled – can't follow.

Once Alice finds the boldness to tail Star to the supermarket, where she watches her load a basket with fruit, bread, milk, a bottle of good wine (Jasper's taste) and, finally, stingingly, a pack of condoms. The girl's large coat hides most of her body, revealing only the bottoms of her jeans, tucked into scuffed, flat boots. Her large loose-knit scarf has been wound so many times around the collar of her jacket that her head peeps from a mountain of wool. She doesn't look at the other shoppers or interact with them: there is something almost robotic in her unchanging expression, though her body moves fluidly and naturally. She could be an automaton; a Stepford wife of the sink estate. Her face, this close, is more remote than it looked from a distance: cold and hard, like crystal. Surely Star can't wear this poker face at the strip club? No – she must fake it. Sweet smile. Dead eyes. Hard as nails. Et cetera.

The knowledge that Star is a stripper angers Alice. It also intimidates her. She is cowed by not only the girl's beauty but also her credibility; the purity of being tough and poor. She is the real thing, an actual whore in the grand tradition – a Nana, a Becky Sharp, a Moll Flanders – romantically sordid, authentically mercenary. Beside her, Alice is a soft and squeamish thing: over-cultured, over-liberal, an object of derision, like a social worker trying to connect with a teenage gang member.

In all the uneventful hours spent sitting in the car – her back giving its minute sighs and pangs of protest, her head aching and her eyes bored to near closing – two discoveries glitter, like diamonds in a cave wall. They give her surveillance the authority of necessity, and yet she knows – not fooling herself about this, at least – that even without these unearthed secrets she would still follow, still watch.

First: on a couple of occasions, she sees a young man leave the strip club alone at closing time and get into a parked car, where he waits without driving away. He is young and attractive, with the sidelong manner of the wrongdoer. A little later, Star comes out and gets into the car, and the young couple drive away. *Do you know about this, Jasper?* wonders Alice.

Second: Alice is not the only person watching Star. Over the past few days she has been joined by a man; someone new to following Star, she is sure, so sloppy is his stalking compared to Alice's own. He turns up at odd times and simply stands as if bereft on street corners and in the middle of paths, gazing up at whatever building Star is in. He looks like a survivor of a shipwreck, washed up at her shore, still dazed, without any idea of what to do next. Like Star, he doesn't appear to own a car.

Alice inspects this man with curiosity. He has no idea of her own presence; of their strange new partnership. He is a tall man, usually wearing jeans and a parka. In his mid-thirties, if she had to guess. He is not as obviously good-looking as the man who waits for Star to finish her shift (the time when, Alice's research has revealed, strippers traditionally meet the clients to whom they have promised 'extras'), but he has his own charisma, peering through his swagged lower eyelids, his prickly jawline and close-cut hair. He reminds Alice of the louche plumber who arrived last year to inspect some of their more sonorous copper pipework, who drained his tea, leaned easily back, and asked her whether she was lonely. She said she wasn't, and then, later, wished she hadn't, but didn't have the nerve to break something in the cistern and call him back.

Alice's new companion in crime (*Is this a crime?* she wonders suddenly, frightened at the thought of Ben seeing his mother's head being pressed firmly down into the back of a police car) has made life more difficult. Star knows now that she is being followed. She must check the street before she leaves her house, because (though it must inconvenience her) she never comes out until he has given up; casting one last disconsolate look at her house, then turning, moving with his loose, shifting stride like a bear let out of its shackles, back to wherever he has come from. Star's own quick, forward-facing walk has gone to pieces: these days she looks around herself frequently

– once, unexpectedly, meeting Alice's eye. The contact only lasts a second – Star apparently not recognising Alice as a person of significance – but in this moment Alice is thoroughly unnerved. Star's gaze is so flatly neutral, so absolutely incurious, with no wavering towards either warning or welcome, that Alice feels oddly dehumanised under its sights, as if she is a paper bag blowing past a security camera.

Alice wonders about speaking to the newcomer. She could have a quiet word, warn him that he is jeopardising things for both of them. They could compare notes; arrange a rota of shifts, even. They would develop an uneasy respect for each other, like two mismatched detectives in an eighties movie. At the very least she could give him some advice on how to be unobtrusive. For it seems she has the ability of not being noticed: in fact, she has been preparing for invisibility her whole life. God knows why men are favoured by the SAS, she thinks. Just send in an insecure forty-two-year-old woman. Nobody would even glance at her.

Of course, she doesn't introduce herself to him, though she does wonder what his story is. He could be an ex-pimp, devastated that his cash cow has gone freelance. He could be some poor sap who loved her and lost everything and is now reduced to sniffing after her scent through the back streets of the town, following her trail through the gum-studded streets, masked by smoke and petrol and empty cigarette packets. Is this what Jasper will become? What will he think of himself after she finds someone richer and finishes with him? Without his endearingly arrogant graciousness, who will he be? Perhaps the whole thing will teach him to see himself more sceptically, to love his wife, to be a better man. Or perhaps he will divorce

Alice anyway, quit work, and devote himself to waiting on the corner, outside the strip club.

One afternoon, Alice realises that it is almost spring, and she hasn't noticed. The air has changed, the rain is gentle. The artificial winter sunlight, bright without having either heat or life, has been replaced with the real thing. She feels it stir the surface of her skin; a warmth that can only enter her so far. For the last few months she has moved inside her own rigidly cheerful shell, feeling nothing underlying it but packed ice. Her heart presses out its cold beat, her blood runs in glaciers through the Arctic landscape of her body. She is in a state of suspension, like a body cryogenically preserved, waiting for the moment when it is safe to defrost.

She arrives home from work to see Jasper's car unexpectedly present and hurries inside, frightened that she will catch him in the midst of packing up his things. She finds him in the kitchen, making pasta.

'I can do that,' she says.

'I'm almost finished,' Jasper replies. He looks very serious, as he always does when cooking. Even the polka-dotted apron protecting his shirt does not diminish his gravity. He stands with his wooden spoon like the founder of a nation, frowning into the tomato sauce.

'Is there enough for me?' Alice asks.

'I didn't know where you were,' Jasper says. 'You can have some, but there won't be much.'

'No, it's fine. I'll grab something later. I was just being opportunistic.'

She smiles at him and sits down at the table, supporting her chin with her plaited hands.

'Are you watching me?' Jasper asks. 'It's disconcerting.'

'Sorry. I can shut my eyes?'

He makes a face, not willing to join in with her good humour. His hair has curled slightly in the heat and steam of the oven, straying out of its usual lines. It suits him.

'I was looking at our bank statements today,' he says, fixing a stern eye on his pan. 'And I think we need to look at our lifestyle.'

'Our lifestyle?'

'For example. Nearly forty pounds a month on fresh flowers.'

'Does it really add up to that much?'

'Yes. You have to think about that. You need to have a wider sense of what's leaving our pockets.'

'But I don't buy flowers every week. And lilies are ten pounds, unless they're on offer and then they're cheaper. I buy them twice a month maximum and I've bought less lately, because we haven't entertained as much.'

'Entertaining,' Jasper says. 'That's another one. Unnecessary cushions. *I've* given up Sky Sports.'

You're never at home to watch it, thinks Alice.

'What's this about?' she asks instead, then immediately regrets the question, not being ready for a truthful answer. She rushes to derail it, continuing quickly, 'Is there some sort of issue? Are there problems at work?'

'What? No. It's just good sense. We ought to be putting

money aside, not throwing it away.' He looks up from tipping sauce onto his pasta with an expression she recognises – affronted innocence – though she can't work out where it has come from. Only when he demands, 'Why do you ask that? Have you been speaking to your mother again?' does she realise that she has handed him the perfect opener for an argument. He is referring to a conversation between Alice and Tamara the previous week, the latter having called, with her preternatural – almost demonic – instinct for bad timing, on the only evening of the past few months that Alice and Jasper are sitting side by side on the sofa, about to watch a film.

'How is Jasper?' Tamara asked, when she heard he was there, 'Has he got a very heavy workload? Do GPs get promoted if they work extra hours, like management types? Though, I suppose, Jasper would have been promoted by now, if he were to be promoted at all.' She knew perfectly well that Jasper could hear her; her voice could never be channelled into one ear only, instead making itself known to anyone within a few feet, as if the wires and plastic of the receiver were insubstantial, evaporating before the pure sword of her received pronunciation. Alice looked around herself as if she might find some help – a stiff drink or a smoke, neither of which were habits of hers, and were accordingly not to hand – as Jasper got up irritably and left the room.

'Not for a while,' she answers now.

'That's the worst thing she can think of, isn't it? That I might go bankrupt or lose my job. She'd love to see it.'

'I don't listen to her, you know that,' Alice says.

'You think you don't,' Jasper replies. He takes his plate and heads for the doorway. 'But you absorb it anyway. Everyone ends up like their parents. Whether they like it or not.'

That night, Alice lies in bed, her eyes passing gently over the softened linear forms in the darkness, submerged in their blue-black sleep. It seems more restful that way than to attempt to close her eyes – to force them closed – and then feel irritated when, like over-stuffed suitcase lids, they spring back open. The time before Alice goes to sleep is a process of trying not to think about a long succession of things, one after the other. Tonight she is starting by trying not to think about the dog Ben has been asking for lately, a spaniel or a Labrador, which Alice can't yet place in any future. Then she tries not to think about Ben, and how much he absorbs – consciously and unconsciously – of the tension in the house; his father's need for escape, his mother weighting herself down with stubborn unhappiness, like an anchor, preventing Jasper sailing into the sunset. She tries not to think about work: her terror of going back out there, old and soft, to compete for one of the too-few jobs. She tries not to think in the same terms about the dating game.

The larger the thoughts are the harder it is not to think about them. Almost impossible not to brood over the place next to her in the bed, not so much abandoned as untouched, new and pristine. Jasper has always been a graceful and sound-less sleeper, so much so that she sometimes thinks he isn't next to her, then realises he is, or thinks he is next to her, then realises he isn't, and, either way, the realisation is like the start that jolts one out of the beginnings of deep sleep. This uncertainty is heightened by the distance between them. Jasper these days is a man practising astral projection. When he isn't physically with her it seems a mere formality, a relocation of body only. She tries and fails not to think about the flimsiness of his excuse for not coming home tonight: a paper boat sailed brazenly downriver: a dare, surely, willing her to confront him – something she isn't yet ready to do.

Finally, she tries not to think about Star.

Over the course of her and Jasper's marriage Alice has turned being pleasing into an art, an endless refinement of that skill. Without even realising she was doing it she recorded his favourite foods, music, wine; began – without realising – to think that they were her favourites too. She worried about what presents to buy him, playing it safe with cashmere scarves, gloves, wallets. Accessories to trim his edges, lacking the confidence to take ownership of the whole body. However she has tried to please him, she has failed, and this girl has succeeded. Alice feels like she would give nearly anything just to know what Star has done, to differentiate her not only from Alice herself, but also from all the others Jasper has tried and tested over the years. She thinks she could suffer losing Jasper better if she knew for sure how she had lost him.

It can't only be sex, surely, though that must play a role. She returns to the strip club, moving through its pink-lit doors into an interior she can only guess at; clothing it in peeling rococo gilt, reproduction sofas, sometimes upholstered in leopard print, sometimes red velvet. There must be a stage, with poles and perhaps curtains. A stuffed tiger, roaring voicelessly in a corner. She pictures Star dancing for one man, or a group of them. She is wearing some sort of lingerie, lace-cupped: obvious, but successful. The pale dish of her stomach collects the shadows, the convexity of her breasts give back the light. She has a promising look in her eye that Alice has never seen on the real girl's face. She winks. She opens her mouth to show the white teeth. She touches her lips. The men shift in their seats.

This is the sort of thing Alice has to contend with, as she tries to get some sleep.

VIC

When Vic arrives at the Quinta do Rosal for the promised dinner with Michael's lovable hot-house friend Estella, Michael leads her through the dim house and back outside, where he demonstrates with a flourish that he has abandoned the stately dining room, with its plaster-latticed ceiling and reflective tiled floor, in favour of a table in the garden courtyard, under the equally intricate roof of the jacaranda trees. The summer evening is neither light nor dark, hot nor cold. Vic can barely feel the air on her skin, the weather having reached equilibrium with her own temperature and not feeling like weather at all. Its perfect stillness, its lack of difference, reminds her of a dream, that absence of all but the most strange and abstract sensations.

The courtyard is partly enclosed by a stone wall, beyond which the gardens writhe in convoluted shadows. When she and Michael were young they used to sit out in the height of the afternoon, waiting to catch the small bronze and green lizards that emerged to soak up light, poised motionless on the lip of the marble fountain, the cracked flagstones. Michael always lost patience and moved too quickly, diving, scattering lizards in all directions. Vic was more patient but less interested in the outcome. She did not particularly want a lizard as a pet, as Michael did. It was an unpleasant surprise, then, when she did catch one. Her fingers closed on its tail, which came off, horrifyingly, in her hand. The feeling of the nausea of that moment comes back to Vic now, a ghost haunting her stomach, as she stands in the courtyard looking at the wine-glasses on the table, two full, one empty.

'Where's Estella?' she asks.

'Getting dressed,' Michael says. 'She'll be down in a sec. Have a seat. Admire my napkin-folding skills.'

'It's late to dress,' Vic observes, then understands, and blushes. 'Jesus,' Michael says, with affection, 'you really are a woman of the world, aren't you? Wine? Red or white? Don't say you're not drinking. Good.'

He seems more excitable than usual; edgy with high spirits and the responsibility of hosting. He rushes off to get more wine, comes back with olives and no wine, tells a story, forgets the ending, then exits to get wine again. When he comes back, Vic says, trying and failing not to sound accusing: 'You're strange today.' But there is no reply, and when she looks up she sees that it is not Michael in the doorway but Estella.

Michael has always gone for beautiful girls; sirens and vixens and femmes fatales: women who have already had far more than their fair share of attention, and Estella is no exception. She is small-framed; as tall as Vic herself, but more delicately put together. Her long hair is dark brown. (Vic, shy of Estella's eyes, can't say, afterwards, what colour they were. She thinks they might have been blue or green, or grey. Something subtle; oceanic.)

'Excuse me?' Estella says now. She doesn't move forward.

Her voice, though uncertain, is as cool as water, a quiet-flowing stream.

'Oh! I thought you were Michael. Sorry,' Vic says hurriedly. She rushes on: 'I didn't mean that he was really being strange, either. It was just a stupid joke. He's not strange.'

'OK,' says Estella. She looks at Vic for a moment, unsmiling, then – as if she has been hesitating on a stage but has suddenly remembered her cue – she smiles, comes out of the house, and sits down. Vic, for her part, makes an effort to relax the stiff muscles of her face; her tightened fingers.

'This isn't a bad start, is it?' she asks.

'I don't think so,' says Estella. She picks up a glass but doesn't drink from it. 'I've had some bad starts. I should know.'

Vic can't imagine this, and can't think of what to say in response.

'You live close by?' Estella asks. 'I didn't hear a car. I wouldn't have been so slow to come down if I'd realised you'd arrived.'

'Just down the hill. A ten-minute walk. It's less dangerous, walking, too. There are lots of accidents on the cliff road.'

'Dangerous,' Estella says, apparently struck by this. 'I can't imagine anything here being dangerous.'

'Oh yes, there are lots of dangerous things,' Vic says. Finding a subject she can talk about knowledgeably, she talks for far too long. She tells Estella about the precipitous roads winding from the tops of the mountains to the sea, the high cliffs, the mud slides, the shortness of the airport runway. She notes that although levada walking is beautiful and mostly safe, the paths are narrow and the drops are steep. Tourists have tripped and fallen. Some have died. Estella may have noticed the flowers called Angels Trumpets which – though they really do resemble a shower of golden trumpets, descending like heavenly heralds – are a close relative of datura: hallucinogenic in low quantities, fatal in high ones. Three teenagers from Azenhas do Mar died last year after eating it. Every few years, in fact, there is an incident like this in Madeira. It seems to take two or three years for the shock to fade, the dead teenagers to take on the hazy quality of myth, and for curiosity to re-establish itself.

'Apparently the hallucinations are horrible,' Vic says. 'Like a nightmare. Not like the things you apparently get with, er, other sorts of drugs.'

'Mushrooms,' Estella says helpfully. 'Acid.'

'Oh, right. I don't know about them, obviously. But people are still interested. Maybe it even encourages them.'

'A taste for danger.'

'Yes. I suppose I don't have a taste for danger, so maybe I don't understand.'

Estella is smiling. Her manner has changed as Vic talks, going from a mostly submerged wariness to something more relaxed, as if realising that Vic isn't going to be one of the many threats of Madeira. 'It really is like the garden of Eden,' she says. 'Safe, so long as you follow the rules.'

Michael arrives back with a bottle of red and a bottle of white wine ('I got to the kitchen and couldn't remember which one we agreed on') and asks what they are talking about. He doesn't ask casually, but with the vivid, penetrating interest that has both sharpened him and made him error-prone. Vic isn't sure how much she welcomes this change in Michael; his restful charm all burnt away, the man underneath too naked and stark.

'The hazards of Madeira,' Estella says.

'Really?'

'I know all about them now,' she explains. 'Not so much about Vic.'

'Oh, she's perfectly safe,' Michael says, and Estella smiles. Her smiles, like her, are small and cool. Vic smiles too, but without enjoyment. She is used to Michael laughing at her: she *likes* Michael laughing at her, but Michael and Estella laughing at her together now, and perhaps later – more comprehensively – is something different.

'You didn't actually mention people dangers,' Estella says to Vic. 'Rapes and murders and robberies.'

Vic finds the words startling, arriving so suddenly into such a delicate scene; the descending dark of the sky, the stilled leaves of the trees, like arrested confetti. They pierce the evening like a snag in a veil. 'No,' she says. 'Not really anything like that.'

'Though Trinidade may well have murdered her husband,' Michael says. 'According to local gossip.' 'I've never heard that!' Vic protests.

'People don't tell you that sort of gossip,' Michael says. 'I think if the story was true, Trinidade's husband was probably relieved. Like what Winston Churchill said when someone told him that if she was his wife, she'd give him poison. "If you were my wife, I'd take it."'

'That's terrible,' Vic says, trying not to laugh.

Estella doesn't say anything. She watches Michael, with a look that can't be understood.

'Other than that – no people dangers,' Michael continues.

'That's why old people love to come here. Vic's basically managing a retirement home.'

'I like that,' Vic says. 'It's less trouble.'

'Basically, you'd rather deal with heart attacks than people having sex in the swimming pool.'

'I have first aid training,' Vic says, which Michael and Estella seem to find very funny; Michael laughing loudly, Estella quietly, after an initial frown.

'We've made Madeira seem boring,' Michael says to Vic. 'You started so well with landslides and then let us down when it comes to rape and murder.'

'Not boring,' Estella says seriously. 'I like it here. It's heaven to someone like me.'

Michael folds his lips together, as if physically repressing some irreligious joke that has just occurred to him.

'In fact,' Estella says, 'that might be my definition of heaven. No people dangers.' She says this with a glance at Michael that, again, Vic can't interpret. The look doesn't appear to be intended for Michael to see, and he doesn't, having the wine bottle tucked under his arm like an unruly pig as he wrestles with its cork.

'Fuck *me* this is tough,' Michael exclaims, as the cork comes free. 'I wonder if my parents went round the cellar poking all the corks further in.'

'Should we be drinking this?' Vic asks, nervously.

'It's fine. They don't have anything too old. My mother doesn't even drink.' He turns to Estella. 'I wish you could have met them before they left. You'd like them.'

Estella smiles her ambiguous smile.

'So where are you from?' Vic asks her. 'Are your family there?'

'England,' Estella says, then adds, almost unwillingly, 'Berkshire. That's where my family are still.'

'Oh, OK. I don't really know England that well. It's a foreign country to me. Michael knows it better than I do.'

Michael leans back in his chair and smiles at them both. As the evening goes on his earlier intensity fades; he seems more relaxed, more his old self. Easy again, and bold enough to put his hand on Estella's thigh, under the table.

Estella doesn't make a move of her own, perhaps from reserve, or politeness. Vic isn't sure what to make of her; she can't guess at the thoughts sheltering below the drawn-down lashes. She looks closely at her face, its shell colour, a smooth cream like a clam polished down by the sea. And, though Estella is obviously in her twenties, her face has that oddly older quality about it, like something that has taken a long time to pare and perfect, and will not change again. She could have been in the sea for a thousand years, only just brought to shore.

When Estella excuses herself, Michael asks immediately, 'So, what do you think? Do you approve?'

His way of asking – allowing only one answer – makes Vic stubborn. 'I don't see why you ask me,' she says. 'I wouldn't say if I didn't approve, and you wouldn't know if I was lying, if I did. It's a pointless question. Even if it did matter whether I approved or not, which it doesn't.'

'The rules of conversation always flummox you, don't they,' Michael says, not without affection. It occurs to Vic that she is slightly drunk. She puts her wine glass down.

'She's very beautiful,' she says. Michael pauses, as if contemplating Estella, her form called up before him like a vision, and not by any means a holy one. Yet it is the most spiritual, the most transported, that she has seen him look.

'Stunning,' he agrees, and she thinks that he does seem slightly stunned – concussed – as if such beauty could have the impact of a sharp blow to the head.

Later, Vic walks home down the Rua da Madalena, the road she warned Estella about, a steep and tricky route bitten out of the side of the mountain, hardly visible in the soft dark. Her drunkenness moves up from her feet to her head like a rising current that takes her up, floating her from one side of the road to the other, a swimmer carried by the river. She doesn't know how to think about Estella – the suddenness of Estella; her arrival at the side of a man who, perhaps, is in a more fragile, more lonely position than usual. Though he appeared to take the exit of his parents casually at first, Michael couldn't help but feel it eventually; the knowledge of his own aloneness drawing in around him. Left in an empty house, whatever worries or fears he has will occur more piercingly, more comprehensively, than before. Vic hopes he hasn't simply reached out for the nearest available female, to use as a hostage against these attacks.

About Estella herself Vic isn't sure what to think. There is something blank about the girl that bothers her. Not blank, exactly – she corrects herself – and then is unable to think of what word she is looking for. Something to express the sense that Estella is too still, her gestures hemmed in, her hands slow as sedated birds, the unyieldingly perfect symmetry of her face. There was no way of getting a true sense of her that night: Vic's efforts to find out more about Estella having been mainly thwarted; the conversation writhing and twisting out of her hands in unexpected directions, subverted by Michael's tipsy high spirits, so that when she asked Estella what she was doing at Michael's company, they ended up talking about workplace pranks, and when she asked, hesitantly, how long Estella would be in Madeira, Michael interrupted her to show them both a magic trick.

Next time, Vic thinks, she will have a proper conversation with Estella, one that will lay to rest her unease; the odd feeling that comes to her when she looks at the girl's lowered eyes, her restrained smile, barely disturbing the cool, pearly surface of her face.

At home, Vic carries out her usual bedtime routines: brushing her teeth for two minutes, flossing, washing her face, looking at herself unhappily in the mirror, praying for all the people she loves, and for help in loving the ones she doesn't. She puts on a pair of pyjamas: a necessity that has nothing to do with feeling cold, but rather functioning as a screen between Vic and her body, like the wall of a confessional booth, beyond which all sorts of awful things might reveal themselves. Vic would deny anything so dramatic or self-indulgent as *hatred* of her body, but she has to admit that its naked presence in her peripheral vision, awkward and squarish and white with disuse, discomfits – even irritates – her at times, bobbing along persistently beneath her, unwanted and embarrassing; like a piece of loo roll that has attached itself to a shoe.

After dressing, she sets her alarm clock, switches her usually silent phone to silent mode, fills a water glass, and closes the curtains. Then she gets into bed and lies on her back as rigid as a piece of dried meat, eyes fixed wide on the ceiling.

She is drunk, that's the problem. In the hope that it might help her to sleep she begins to masturbate (this, again, is something Vic would rather not see: her preferred method is the invisible hand – thrice hidden, under cover of darkness, under a duvet, under pyjamas) but her drunkenness makes her distractible and strange thoughts and images crowd in on her. She finds herself wondering what Estella looks like naked; what Ana, or Lawrence, or even Father Antonio might look like. She thinks of Michael, but here her imagination baulks and bucks, and she lands far away, at the Quinta Verde, where she wanders in a towel looking endlessly for Kate, to stop her doing what she plans to do.

Vic gives up and turns on her side. She always feels a vague sense of shame about masturbating anyway. The Bible is silent on the subject, but, nonetheless, she has the awkward feeling of exploiting a loophole, of 'getting around' God, who finds so many other acts offensive. This reminds her of sitting on the shaded grass under the lemon trees behind the school, legs tucked under her kilts, while Kate read out a list of sexual misdemeanours.

'Leviticus eighteen,' Kate began. She had plaited her bright hair on each side of her head; the parting pulled so tightly that her scalp seemed divided, neatly halved and only provisionally glued back together. '*Lots* of rules here.'

'When are we doing the New Testament?' Beatriz asked. As usual, she wanted to talk about the crucifixion.

'We haven't got to the New Testament yet,' Kate said impatiently. 'There's some pretty shady stuff in there too, though.'

She ran through the prohibitions – no sex between two men, no sex with a woman during the uncleanness of her monthly period, no sex with animals, no sex with close relatives – but she seemed more distracted than usual. She had dropped the 'case for the prosecution' manner, as Vic had come to think of it, and glanced up at them almost questioningly as she read.

'Sex with animals,' Vic marvelled. 'They must have done that a lot. To have to be told not to do it.'

'It's all disgusting,' Beatriz said.

'Yeah,' said Kate. They watched her expectantly but she seemed disinclined to say anything else, or come up with a conspiracy. She closed her Bible pettishly, with a snap. 'Beatriz is right,' she said. 'We should read about the crucifixion.'

People dangers, thinks Vic now. Kate had been a people danger: not only to others, but also to herself. At the table earlier she'd felt as if she was hiding something by not telling Estella and Michael that, but then, what relevance would it have now? Kate's dead. There is nothing more she could possibly do to anybody.

When Vic calls to thank Michael for dinner and to see if he wants to get coffee one evening, he explains that he sleeps at Estella's apartment in Funchal during the week, but they plan to come back at the weekend.

'We could get coffee then,' he offers.

'Are you moving in together?' Vic asks.

'Christ, no,' Michael says, taken aback. 'I've only known her for a few weeks. It's just closer to the office.'

'Oh, right.'

'I forget how traditional you are . . . let me explain. Modern-day romance takes all sorts of forms. Estella and I are living together because it's convenient and fun. We're not setting up home, and we're not getting married either.'

'You've discussed marriage already?'

'*Vic.*' Michael sounds slightly impatient. 'Of course we haven't. It's too early. These days people don't rush to get married. Mainly because they're allowed to have sex without it.'

'You don't need to patronise me.'

'Well, I'm sorry, but I genuinely have no idea what goes on in your head. The questions you ask! It's like trying to explain dating to Oliver Cromwell.'

'I do *know* about modern dating,' Vic says, after which Michael changes the subject, evidently having decided not to hurt her feelings.

After this conversation Vic decides not to ask Michael about his relationship. He seems to think she disapproves on religious grounds, when the truth is not that, but then not anything else she can pin it down to either. When the weekend comes, bringing with it a late-night call from Michael on Friday, he unexpectedly suggests she and Estella meet up without him.

'I have to go into work tomorrow – one of the engineers has fucked up some measurements and I need to sort it out.

If everything wasn't balanced over a ravine it would be less of an issue. Anyway, I'm basically abandoning Estella at my house tomorrow morning, so – if you're not busy – I thought you might want to drop in for a drink or something. Do whatever it is women do when nobody else is around.'

'I'm not busy,' Vic says, but she is perturbed at the thought of no one else being around, of navigating the cool wide ocean of Estella's company alone, in the absence of Michael's cheery captain.

When Vic arrives at the Quinta do Rosal, she meets Michael in the doorway, on his way out. He looks slightly discomposed, holding a pair of sunglasses as if he has forgotten he has them. 'Oh – good timing!' he says, looking relieved. 'Thanks for this, Vic. I didn't want to leave her with no entertainment.'

'I don't know how entertaining I am,' Vic says dubiously.

'Just don't talk about religion. Or me. Actually, I've changed my mind – you can talk about me. Then you can call me later and tell me what she said.'

'I certainly won't do that.'

'Don't tell her anything embarrassing about me either. Though now I think of it, I can't think of anything I'm that embarrassed by. Which means either I never do anything embarrassing, or I have no shame. You two can discuss that, if you want. I left Estella in the garden reading – you can find your own way through, can't you? I'm in a bit of a rush.'

'Of course I can. You're talking to me like I'm the babysitter.'

He laughs, continues, 'Help yourself to whatever's in the fridge, and you have my number if anything goes wrong', kisses her briefly on the cheek, and gets into his car. She waves as he pulls out of the drive, but the sun is on the windscreen, his face dissolved in the glare, and she isn't sure if he saw it or not.

Vic pushes open the heavy door and – this being the first time in a while that she has been alone at the Quinta – takes the opportunity to wander lightly around its quiet entrance hall, running a finger over the ormulu whorls of a clock, a bronze statuette, until she catches herself in the round eye of a mirror and realises she had better keep moving, in case Estella appears and catches her hanging shiftily around the hall. She goes towards the garden but takes the longest route, delaying the moment when she will see Estella, and have to be entertaining.

From the drawing room a set of doors leads outside into the dimmed light of the empty courtyard in which the approaching sun finds itself barred by stone walls, netted in the branches of the jacarandas. The table Michael set up last weekend is still here, its polished top now snowed with discarded purple petals. Beyond the courtyard is a long lawn, like a green sea, shimmering in the heat, the full sun.

Vic squints at the empty lawn, feeling a stupid moment of relief, at the idea that possibly she won't be able to find Estella, and will have to go back home again. But there is a different side of the garden, hidden by trees but clearly visible from the kitchen and dining room (which Estella would have assumed Vic, taking the most sensible route through the house, would pass through), and when Vic walks around to this other lawn she sees – with a dip of dread that darkly mirrors her earlier relief – Estella lying on a sun lounger, just where Vic would expect her to be.

Vic crosses the grass to Estella, thinking of an explanation for why she has appeared out of the trees, but she realises that behind her sunglasses, Estella is asleep. The book she was reading has fallen out of her hand; the other hand is thrown up by her head, as if she had fainted.

'Hello,' Vic calls cautiously, as she approaches. Estella shifts. Her hand rushes to her face, alarmed; discovers the sunglasses, and relaxes back to her side. This small human moment makes her seem almost ordinary; her beauty is dormant, easy, and for a moment Vic thinks that maybe she isn't as pretty as Vic thought on their last meeting. But she is mistaken: as Estella looks up and waves, the magic jumps into her face, her wakened mouth, like a shower of sparks. She isn't wearing make-up, which surprises Vic, who had – barely consciously – assumed that Estella would be one of those women who never let a man see them without it.

'Don't get up,' Vic says. 'You look so relaxed.'

'Too relaxed,' Estella says, sitting up. Below the precise black and white pattern of her sun dress her legs are brown already, finely narrow. 'Sorry not to be a better hostess. You were so kind to visit.' But something in the way she says it, and her offer to make them both drinks, makes Vic wonder if Estella had actually complained about her solitude, or whether this visit of Vic's was something imposed on her, that she couldn't say no to.

'I'll get the drinks,' Vic says, to hide the fact that she is feeling uncomfortable; not only that, but slightly annoyed with Michael, for setting up this awkward morning, and even

– less reasonably – with Estella herself. Before Estella has a chance to find her flip-flops, Vic goes to the kitchen, where she makes a jug of lemonade and wonders what to say to make conversation. When she gets back outside, still none the wiser, she sees Estella's book and gratefully seizes on that.

'What are you reading?' she asks, her eagerness making her loud, and rather demanding. Estella looks at her with slight surprise.

'Oh, Nietzsche. It's heavy going when you're sunbathing, though. Hence falling asleep.' She offers this with a shrug, depreciating her undoubted ability to read her own book.

Vic tries to think of something she remembers about Nietzsche. 'Isn't he something to do with the Nazis?'

'No,' Estella says, becoming animated. 'He hated anti-Semitism. But his sister, who was anti-Semitic, edited his unpublished work after his death. Then Hitler claimed to be influenced by him but really he barely read him, if he even read him at all. Nietzsche has just been misunderstood.'

'But he is an atheist?' Vic says.

'Yes. He influenced Sartre.'

'What did he believe, if he didn't believe in God?' Vic asks. (She considers this a permissible question, not in contravention of Michael's ban on discussing religion.)

'A lot of things. Have you heard of will to power?'

'I don't know much about philosophy.'

'Well, Nietzsche thought we – people – are driven by will to power. It's not a drive to survive, or be happy, but to succeed. To take power. Happiness is just a by-product of our success in that.'

'Is that what you believe?' Vic asks her.

'Not necessarily.' Estella gives her a small smile, stripped of all meaning by the large, reflective lenses of her sunglasses. 'I do find it interesting.'

Vic sits back with her lemonade and thinks that there is not much evidence of a belief in will to power in Estella. She seems to have shed the people and places of her life like a spider on the move, not making a web but throwing out silk escape lines, parachuting into the unknown.

'What do you do?' she asks her. 'At work, I mean.'

'Payroll. It's not very exciting. I came here for the sun; I didn't really mind what work I was doing. I actually ended up doing some assistant work for Michael too – they still haven't hired someone for him yet. This company's a mess.' Like Michael, she says this with detectible pleasure, conscious of owing her relationship to the messiness of their employer.

'Is that the sort of thing you did before you got here?'

'A couple of times. I've done a lot of different things. There hasn't been much of a *plan*.' She scratches her leg, looking uncertain, as if this is the first time she has really considered her discontinuous existence. 'Michael says you've always worked at the hotel. It must be nice to really love what you do. To know you want to do it.'

Vic searches the black lenses for irony but finds none. 'Well,' she says. This is inadequate, and she searches for something to add. 'It's OK.'

'You don't have to downplay it,' Estella says. 'It's great.'

Vic feels the conversation has strayed somewhat. She isn't a person capable of the subtle mastery of a discussion, guiding it unobtrusively in her chosen direction. On her last meeting with Estella the talk ran wild, laughing and showing off. Now it sneaks away like an unattended child, peering through keyholes and opening closets. If she is going to get a grip on it, she will have to be more firm.

'So what did you do before?' she asks. 'What sort of things? Where did you live?'

'It's rather a lot to tell you about,' Estella says. She moves her arm across herself, as if warding Vic off.

'I don't mind,' says Vic placidly.

Estella looks at her for a moment before continuing. 'Well, I've done office work – admin – I've worked as a personal assistant, a sales girl, a bar manager, a receptionist, and a few other things. Nothing very exciting. I've lived in France, Spain, England, the Netherlands.' She frowns. 'I like to keep travelling. I get bored.'

'Like Michael,' Vic says.

'I guess so.'

'I think I'm the opposite,' Vic says, struck by this. 'I like to be part of a community. Where everyone knows each other and supports each other.'

'You know,' Estella says, 'I think of communities and I think of people being ostracised. Nasty rumours. Informing on each other. Trials of witches and heretics.' Then she laughs – though this is barely a laugh, rather a small, melancholic shrug of the voice – and says, 'I sound very jaundiced, don't I? I'm not really. It's just the first association that comes to my mind. Your view is much nicer.'

Vic is startled, not least by the sudden coldness in Estella's tone, hardly dispelled by her laugh. She wonders at its origins.

'Well, the church here isn't like that,' she offers, rather weakly.

'For now. Or maybe it really is in its retirement years and is content to sit and reminisce about the old days. Appropriate, in Madeira . . .' She looks at Vic. 'Sorry – are you a churchgoer?'

'Yes. Catholic. You aren't, I guess. Michael isn't either.' (Vic reasons here that she no longer needs to observe Michael's ban on discussing religion any longer, as Estella was the one to bring it up.)

'No, but I hope I didn't offend you. Maybe because you didn't grow up here, I assumed you weren't Catholic. Is it something you were brought up with, or did you come to it later?'

'I found God here,' Vic explains. 'Uh, not actually here, in the garden. In Madeira.'

In fact, the circumstances of Vic finding God – while ultimately leading her to a better path – are something she doesn't entirely like to dwell on, and partly out of a disinclination to discuss it and partly out of simple curiosity, she asks Estella, 'Did you ever believe?'

'No,' Estella says. 'I think that's something you need to feel. I don't feel it.'

They sit for a while in silence. Vic looks out over the white-lit lawn. A sprinkler has turned itself on and is revolving in the centre of the grass; a rainbow hovers in the glitter of its spray. Estella is also watching the flung droplets, and Vic's eyes slide sideways over to her, taking the opportunity to conduct a brief, undercover investigation. She notices when Estella leans forward for more lemonade that she isn't naturally brown haired. A pale blond is rising into the darker colour, as if bleached by her pale skin.

'So,' Estella says, and now she sounds as abrupt and uncertain as Vic herself, as if with the same discomfort Vic feels when she breaks a silence, never knowing if the silence is better than her voice. She carries on, playfully, 'You and Michael grew up together. Anything I should know?', but it isn't convincing: Estella is not a playful person, and it's a more serious question than that.

'Michael is great,' Vic says. 'He's . . . he's a nice person. I think you're—' she stops: she can't say *lucky*, it's insulting – 'you're with a nice person.'

'You two look out for each other,' Estella says, and again it is hard to identify her tone.

'Of course! We've known each other for so long. I've always watched out for him. I want him to be happy.'

This is Vic's mistake: one to be turned over and over later, with alternating regret and defiance. She stops talking, then realises what ought to be said, and adds, after too long and final a pause: 'And he seems happy, with you.'

On Sunday, Vic walks back from Mass through the empty white streets of Azenhas do Mar, keeping an eye out for Estella and Michael, whom she does not want to see. She has less luck keeping them out of her mind; remembering in particular the end of her visit to the Quinta do Rosal, brought about by Estella, who said she had forgotten some of her things and needed to go back to Funchal for them.

Vic – scrupulous in her own mind – tries not to believe

that this might have been a lie. But she felt *escaped*, and unfairly so: invited to visit someone who didn't want to be visited, by someone she couldn't refuse. If she bumps into Estella and Michael now, she may well be interrupting Estella saying, 'It was sweet of you to invite Vic over to keep me company, but I really would have preferred to be alone.' Or, depending on how familiar Estella and Michael are, 'Look, I know you're loyal to her. You've known her for years. But she's a pain.'

Funny, thinks Vic, how much it stings: this imaginary rejection from a woman she doesn't know. It's been a long time since she has had a girlfriend, and she looks back on the time when she did – when she was a half of a pair – with relief that she escaped, almost unscathed. Obviously those were unusual circumstances, but she has seen enough of the same dynamic played out in more everyday friendships to want to take on another best friend, re-acquaint herself with the breathless, intimate clutches of sisterly love, its sweetness, its hidden poisons.

What Vic remembers most from the height of her romance with Kate (because it was a romance, fierce and tender) is the uncertainty of it all, never knowing what Kate might say or do next, so that she had begun to get used to living with a low-level feeling of worry, running below her exhilaration. After almost a year of Bible Club – by far the longest-lasting of Kate's clubs – Vic would often feel confused and disturbed after Kate had called an end to their meeting. She didn't discuss Kate with Beatriz, because by this time it had become evident (because Kate said so) that Kate and Vic were best friends, and Beatriz wasn't, quite. It was only with Vic that Kate showed her more secret self; an uncertain and worried Kate at times, or a crying

Kate, capable of sobbing inexplicably for half an hour straight, as Vic patted her hair and tried, ineffectually, to console her. When it was Vic's twelfth birthday, only three days after Kate's, Kate gave her a friendship bracelet and a framed picture of them both, taken with her own birthday camera.

'Your parents got you a camera?' Vic asked, in wonderment.

'Yeah,' Kate said, quellingly. Vic knew better than to ask anything else. Not long after they met, Kate had told Vic and Beatriz that they would never be able to come to her house for Bible Club. She said her mother was ill and her father, who may or may not be her real father, had gone mad, either from the stress of the illness or his questionable paternity, and so her house was not a place for guests. But then, on a different occasion, she told one of the other girls at school she lived alone with her mother and her father was dead, so Vic wasn't sure what to think.

Vic had also found herself in the position of being the only person with any influence over Kate. She wielded it reluctantly, at times when her own fright at Kate's plans overcame her awe of Kate herself; her off-black eyes radiant with illicit excitement, her arms held high as if in a tribal fire dance. She talked Kate into throwing away the pack of cigarettes Kate had mysteriously acquired, and out of meeting up one evening with a fifteen-year-old boy in the Parque de Santa Catarina, who had promised to bring alcohol.

'Why do you need alcohol, anyway?' she said. 'He probably wants something bad.'

Kate laughed. 'Like what?'

'Like sex,' Vic said, in a near whisper.

Kate looked at her, with a suddenly tired expression;

something approaching pity. 'How do you know I don't?' she said.

This was not to say that Kate told Vic about all of her plans: the prank she played on Sister Maria being one such exception. It happened after Sister Maria had objected to Kate's beautifully coloured picture of the Garden of Eden, featuring a startlingly naked Adam and Eve.

'It's before they ate the apple,' Kate explained.

'I know that,' Sister Maria snapped. 'Just draw them after they ate the apple. With the leaves on', and she stood watching as Kate painted dark green leaves over everything pink – nipples, genitals and emission – her blond head bent in what might have been taken as obedience, but Vic recognised as a sulk.

A week later, a stack of pornographic magazines were left on Sister Maria's desk, to her immediate and gratifying horror. '*What* have you awful girls done?' she cried, gathering up the pile hurriedly, so that one naked woman peeped out from above the crook of Sister Maria's arm, licking her lips, and another tumbled and lay spreadeagled on the floor before the schoolgirls in the front row. Sister Maria uttered another cry of outrage, swept up the fallen woman, and rushed out of the room.

That day, the girls were kept behind after school and told that they would be allowed to leave when one of them had owned up to their wicked act. After an hour of silence, the nuns were forced to admit defeat, but not without a severe lecture on what was likely to happen to liars in the afterlife.

'It was you, wasn't it?' Vic said to Kate once the three of them were beyond the school gates.

'I could have done worse,' Kate said. 'I could have taken

pictures of her and put her head on all of the women. She deserved it for being such a hypocrite. And you have to admit, it was pretty funny.'

'It wasn't at all funny,' Beatriz burst out. Vic – who had secretly found it funny, at least up until the telling-off – looked at her in surprise.

'Oh, come on,' Kate said. 'You weren't frightened by all that stuff about people who tell lies burning in lakes of fire and eternal torment, were you?'

At this neither Vic or Beatriz said anything. They had reached Kate's turning, one of the more expensive avenues in Funchal, the houses white behind their frangipani trees, the pavements black and white with neat grass borders. They stood awkwardly on the corner as Kate gave them both a long look of deep disappointment.

'Fine,' she said. 'You don't approve. That's OK. Just don't tell anyone, that's all. We'll forget all about it.'

But though Kate was able to say a lot of things, and make them true, here her powers failed her. After that day Bible Club changed; it was obvious to them all. Kate was more irritable, and more secretive, while Beatriz seemed quiet and troubled. She confided in Vic that sometimes she suspected Kate of not being religious *at all*. Kate, sensing the change in atmosphere, made fun of Beatriz behind her back: her nervous plaiting of her hands, her lazy eye. She said Beatriz had a God eye and a Devil eye, and if the Devil eye ever managed to focus on you, you would immediately die. But Vic – though she laughed guiltily at this – was also experiencing her own private doubts. She remembered, not long after the first meeting of Bible Club, a girl coming over to her in the lavatories with a warning that Vic had dismissed back then, but now was beginning to carry the weight of gathering truth: 'You're friends with Kate Clare now? You should be careful. I mean it. Watch out for her. She's crazy.'

Vic prays more than usual the following week; going to church before and after work, praying before bed and alone in the grottoes of the hotel gardens. Her main goal in prayer is to wrestle with her failure to like Estella. Not that she exactly *dislikes* her. She isn't sure how she feels about Estella because she isn't sure who Estella is. She is as much of a stranger now as the day she arrived. She is not disdainful, but she is cool. She is not sly, exactly, but still – there is something considered about her, as if she is referencing herself against a set of guidelines, some interior template of her own self. It's odd, Vic thinks. It's not usual. She has found herself watching Estella with what can only be described as suspicion.

Vic reminds herself as she prays that it isn't a crime to be aloof, or careful. Heaven knows, Vic herself could do with a bit more forethought when it comes to her own conversational blunders. Her suspicious nature is her own failing; an insidious doubt, like that inspired by the serpent in the Garden of Eden. And so she challenges it: she rolls up her sleeves and marches into the snake's lair and comes out wounded and triumphant, and by the time the weekend comes around, she is able to welcome Michael's suggestion that the three of them meet for coffee in Azenhas do Mar's small botanical gardens on Saturday.

Vic arrives before Michael and Estella and sits down to wait for them on the small terrace overlooking the gardens. The woman minding the small café selling tea and coffee and unidentified cakes glances at her twice, with increasing curiosity, before leaning out and asking, 'Can I help you?' in English: taking her for a solitary tourist, though Vic has been to the botanical gardens several times over the years and knows the woman's son, a gardener at the hotel.

'I'm meeting friends,' Vic explains. 'I'll order when they arrive.' She occupies herself with studying the view until, through the branches below her, she sees Michael and Estella's heads, floating along the alternating light of the path. Michael's hair flashes momentarily in the sun, like a flipped coin.

'Vic,' Michael exclaims when they reach the top of the steps and see her. 'Have you just got here?'

'Yes.'

'No, we're late,' Estella says. 'Sorry, Vic.' She comes forward and gives Vic a kiss. Her hands rest lightly on each of Vic's arms for a moment. She is one of those women with chilly fingers, even on a day like this. Her exposed, tanned shoulders look as if they might be about to shiver.

'I'll get the drinks,' Michael says, but when Vic turns round, he is taking pictures of the two of them sitting at the table, their uncertain chit chat.

'Michael!'

'Thought I'd get you before you started complaining and pulling faces. I've never met anyone who hated being photographed as much as you two. Smile.'

Estella takes off her sunglasses and gives her wary smile. Vic reluctantly joins in.

'Lovely. Now Vic, will you take one of me and Estella? I'll sit here . . . how's that?'

'I think the sun spoilt it.' And it's true, after a moment Michael and Estella's faces appear on the screen, two anonymous dark outlines, the light behind them. They swap chairs and fiddle with the camera settings, but there is no conjuring up a good picture of the two of them, and Estella pleads with Michael to stop.

'Fine,' he says, looking impatient but good humoured. 'Consider this a reprieve.'

'These won't go online, right?' Estella asks. 'I don't trust social networks.'

'Me neither,' Vic says.

'I'm not going to argue with you,' Michael says. 'I'll just put the pictures up on my own page, which neither of you will ever see.'

'I'll know when you do it,' Estella says. 'I'll shudder, like someone's walked over my grave.'

'That's what some tribes are supposed to have thought about the camera when they first saw it. Didn't they believe it stole part of their soul or something?'

'If that's the case, when you die you won't be able to move on to the next place until all the pictures of you are gone. So someone like Michael will basically be spending the afterlife in hundreds of online pictures.'

'How will that work?'

'You'll be divided into pieces.' Estella says this with

confidence. Michael looks at her and she gives him a strange smile, which unsettles Vic: a smile redolent with both warning and promise. Estella seems enlivened today, but it isn't an energy Vic recognises, and nothing like Michael's own sunny transparency. If she has warmth it is a subterranean heat, a light on a dark evening, distant and circuitous as a will-o'-the-wisp.

'This is a strange conversation,' Vic says.

'Estella's fault,' Michael says. 'She doesn't cover the usual topics.'

'What do usual people talk about?' asks Estella.

'I don't know. What their friends have been up to. Money. Problems with their bosses. What they're having for dinner.'

'I don't have any friends or money – and you're my boss. We can talk about dinner, if you like.'

'No friends?' Vic asks, as if she herself has more than she can deal with.

'I move so much, I lose touch with people,' Estella says.

'Don't you mind it?'

'Oh, of course I mind. It's always sad to say goodbye.' She says this by rote, without any attempt at sincerity.

Vic wonders what Estella was like at school. She is curious to track her back through skin after shed social skin, all the way through to that time of primitive friendships, where, she imagines, all truth must be revealed. But in fact, when she thinks about it, the truth is depressingly obvious: Estella, pretty and civilised, would have been part of the popular set. A slightly enigmatic satellite, perhaps. Fitting in, keeping her thoughts to herself.

It is undeniable that Estella is a capable conversationalist. She is polite, picking up on the direction of talk and moving pliantly along with it, offering up information that is always relevant or insightful; opinions that are intelligent yet neutral, like an upmarket newspaper. She says all the right things, but there is something strange about the way she talks. She doesn't exactly sound insincere, but neither does she appear to believe in what she says. She reminds Vic of a television presenter; reciting with expressiveness and emphasis, the occasional brief smile (as if someone has just issued the command to her earpiece), but still: reciting. When she stops talking, her face shuts like a book.

It has been decided that David Berry will be coming to visit the Quinta Verde in a few weeks' time, to 'touch base', as Lawrence puts it, having been the first to see the email. Vic notices that Lawrence seems distracted, his mouth talking as his eyes are drawn back to his computer – where she imagines the announcement must still be displayed – with unconcealed dismay. Out of sight of the tourists, the atmosphere at the hotel is one of edginess, of nervy anticipation. Rumours start: that David Berry is selling the hotel, or closing it down, or that he is – as Vic overhears from two maids – coming to sack Vic at last, to replace her with the despised Lawrence, after which the maids agree they don't know what they will do.

Vic would like to talk to Michael about the whole thing, even if it is only to get a lecture about how she ought to leave the hotel. Any interest from a friend – positive or negative – would be a comfort. But she hasn't seen him for a couple of weeks now. She keeps an eye out for his car, and when she passes Trinidade's café, she squints into the dense shade of the chestnut as if the moving outlines there might resolve themselves into his shape, but he isn't there, only Trinidade, who glances up at her with a strange sort of fellow feeling, as if the two of them have been united in the absence of Michael.

Last weekend she had texted him to see if he was around, but he didn't reply. Then later that same Saturday, she was queuing in the post office and Michael and Estella walked past. She felt them go by before she turned and saw them; their hands knotted, walking with purposeful enjoyment. The other people in the queue watched them too. She supposed the two of them looked almost like a caricature of young lovers: sunglasses aligned, laughing, so used to their good looks that they could forget they even had them; not even noticing their natural advantage, all the extra things they could expect.

Without really considering what she was doing, she left her place in the queue and went outside after them, in time to see their backs turning the corner. They must have been taking the steep steps down to the harbour (a place Vic avoids, having both a mild fear of heights and a healthy mistrust of the water) for a boat ride, or a swim off the rocks. She squinted out over the sea as if she might see them there already, in one of the small boats, glinting like glass beads on its shifting blue satin.

What Vic understood then, as she stood in the street, was her loss. She has been used to not seeing Michael – he has always come and gone unpredictably, living away for months at a time – but she is also used to being the best friend he came back to. Now she sees that she is not his default intimate any more. As is only natural, he and Estella want to spend their weekends wrapped in their discovery of each other. They want to sleep late, then go sailing. They want to drink cocktails overlooking the night sea. They want to share their histories (though Vic can't imagine Estella being keen on that). They want to have sex. And Vic, quite understandably, isn't invited.

She just wishes she could shake off her distrust of Estella. She bows her head in the empty church and feels her failure expand, to fill the available space. (She doesn't want to think that her failure might also be God's failure, but this not wanting is in her head now, a sly negative, confirming the idea that God can't or won't help take her dislike away.) She decides to allow herself one conversation with Michael, in which she will check that everything is definitely OK. She promises herself that, if he is truly happy, she will stop worrying, and if she doesn't stop worrying, she will at least deal with her concerns with a stricter hand, not allowing herself to dwell on her wonderings or doubts again.

In the end, Vic ends up waiting so long for the opportunity to actually talk to Michael alone that when she sees his car parked outside the Quinta do Rosal on a midweek morning – when he ought to be at work in Funchal – she impulsively changes direction and goes up the hill to his house. Halfway there she realises that she will be late for her shift, and that it is too hot to walk so quickly up the steep road, but she carries on, with the thought that she might not see him for weeks otherwise.

The windows of the house are open but there is no answer when she rings the bell. She hears the noise echo sonorously through the large tiled hall, dissolving into the shade within. The sunlight is so strong outside that she can't see in without pressing her face against the glass, and she is frightened that she will be caught if she does. She tries to squint into the hall from where she stands, but the glass is a lit mirror, reflecting only her own moist, harried looking face.

'Michael?' she calls, walking around to the garden. 'It's me! Vic!'

At this side of the house is the stretch of lawn, backed by trees, where Vic had previously found Estella sunbathing. The lawn is empty, glittering in the hiss of the revolving sprinkler, but the kitchen door is open, so Vic goes inside.

'Hello!' she calls again, when she sees a coffee cup on the worktop. She touches the warm side of it as she passes to reassure herself, but of what she has no idea. She wonders for a moment if Estella might be with him, but there is only one cup, recently discarded.

Vic gets as far as the sitting room before she realises her mistake. Estella's handbag is on the sofa, though Estella herself is nowhere to be seen. The handbag is brown leather and box shaped, sitting open with its contents visible. Vic, despite being flustered – not knowing whether to get out while the going is good and risk being seen by Estella as she flees down the drive, or stay and pretend, painfully, that she has come to chat – is drawn over to it, but can't see anything out of the ordinary inside. A leather wallet, tissues, a gold make-up case, a comb, a mirror. As she looks around the room she sees more and more of Estella; another coffee cup on the walnut table – without a coaster – a powder compact on the floor, her watch discarded on the grand old marble-topped chiffonier. There is a silk robe lying over the back of a chair: for all her reserve in person, Estella, it seems, is something of a slob.

Vic is moving towards the robe only half intentionally – just to see what it feels like, what perfume rises up from it – when she hears Estella's voice, travelling from outside to inside, presumably as she crosses the lawn. Vic realises that one of the doors to the garden has been open, unnoticeable in the still, warm day, the curtain hanging motionless beside the empty frame.

'OK. OK . . . I know,' Estella is saying. Her voice is different, in a way Vic can't place exactly: it has lost its usual coolness and carefulness; containing suddenly too many nuances to identify; rises and shifts, almost musical in its sudden variety of meaning. Where previously she had sounded older than her age, now she sounds, abruptly, much younger. Estella continues, 'But I can't help it. After what I did to him, I'm always scared he'll come after me . . .'

Here there is a long pause – Vic frozen and fascinated in the sitting room – before she hears, spoken quickly; 'Don't worry. Of course, of course. Talk soon,' these last words very close, and then Estella herself appears in the doorway to the garden.

Vic has to squint at the burning silhouette, featureless in the light behind her, to gradually make out Estella's sunglasses, the phone still poised in her hand, the lean line of her stomach above the black bikini bottoms, her shoulders glowing brown with the sun. Estella in turn is adjusting to the sudden dim; she pauses, takes off her sunglasses, blinks. Then she sees Vic, and flinches.

'Estella!' Vic says quickly. 'Sorry to surprise you. I rang the bell and I called, and then I saw the door was open so I thought . . . Sorry.'

'No, it's fine,' Estella says. She looks both formal and nervy, as if she is appearing in court. She looks around herself and picks up the robe, saying unnecessarily, 'I was just sunbathing.'

There is a pause in which it becomes apparent that neither of them are going to mention the telephone conversation, though Estella must be trying to guess how much Vic has heard. The most immediate question, of course, is why Vic is actually here. She tries to think of a reason while Estella, having wrapped herself in the robe, watches her and waits. 'I was just on my way to work – I saw the car was here so I stopped in,' Vic says.

'I was going to see if . . .' she falters, then hurries – 'we could have dinner this weekend. Saturday? It's been a while and I thought it might be nice. To have dinner. Or a drink, or something.'

'Oh, OK,' Estella says. She looks for a moment like she might be trying to think of an excuse not to. 'That sounds lovely.'

Once she has accounted for her own presence – her heart rate ticking back down to normal, the rush of panic no longer hissing in her ears – Vic starts to wonder what Estella is doing here alone, with Michael's car. Estella doesn't look as if she intends to explain; smiling politely now that dinner has been settled, moving forward with minute, oblique steps in order to usher Vic neatly in the direction of the door, but Vic – considering that she may as well put her talent for being awkward to good use – stands obstinately where she is and says, 'Michael isn't here?'

'I had the day off and he didn't,' Estella says. 'I thought I'd come here and lie in the garden. We don't have a garden at the flat, and the air conditioning is erratic. It's nicer here.'

'Oh,' says Vic, 'that makes sense.'

'I'd offer you a drink,' Estella says, 'but you said you were on the way to work?'

Vic considers her options for only a moment before giving up. 'Yes, yes I am,' she says, allowing Estella – who is smiling more sincerely than usual, perhaps in genuine relief, having decided that Vic can't have overheard her – to accompany her to the door.

'See you at the weekend,' Estella says, as unreadable as ever. Vic is beginning to wonder whether she might have been mistaken about the telephone conversation, but when she turns back to wave goodbye, Estella is standing in the doorway looking both taut and uncertain; a slender figure in her glimmering silk, arms wrapped around herself, hardly managing a smile.

Later that night Vic dreams about Kate. Though the details of the dream are largely nonsensical – Kate having stolen a tiger from a pet shop and it being Vic's responsibility to hide it and feed it, trying to poke inappropriate foods (sandwiches, crisps) through the bars of its cage as the tiger howled and swiped at her with its claws – the feel of it is unmistakeable; the particular unease she associates with their friendship following the prank on Sister Maria.

Kate, while still unpredictably affectionate, seemed to trust

Vic and Beatriz less: when she spoke of the secret plans and conspiracies of the nuns and Father Blanca (a mild, milky man wholly unsuitably cast as an evil genius), she would look at the two of them as if considering whether they, too, might be in on it. Vic found herself trying not to act suspiciously. Friendship with Kate by now was not exciting so much as exhausting, to the point where at times Vic would feel like crying, without really knowing why.

Around that time Jim and Bernie Robinson – at first amused, then exasperated, then concerned by Vic's apparently earnest interest in Catholicism – suggested to Vic that she invite her friends ('Bible Gang' as Bernie persisted in calling it) over to the Quinta Verde for a day, where they could, Bernie suggested brightly, 'just play in the pool and have fun'. Jim would collect the girls from Funchal in the morning and drop them back home again. Bernie would make a lunch with Vic's favourite foods: Battenberg cake, crisps, cheese and pineapple on sticks.

The day was, at first, idyllic. Even Beatriz shrieked and laughed in the water billowing around the wavering outlines of their arms and legs, a turquoise blue as improbable and glittering as stained glass. Kate, always boldest, swam under the water open-eyed, finding Vic and Beatriz where they splashed at the surface, tugging suddenly at their ankles. Vic's body can still remember the intense fright of it, the cold hand reaching up below her, the surprising strength of Kate's delicate-looking fingers.

They showered afterwards in the stone-tiled spa, which, off-season, was a quiet and echoing sequence of chambers, like the interior of a pyramid. Kate was first out of the shower, disappearing along with – as Beatriz and Vic discovered when they finished their own showers – all the towels, the swimsuits, and the neat piles of their clothes.

'I can't go out there like this!' Beatriz said in despair from behind her frosted glass.

'It's fine,' Vic said, realising that, for once, she had a certain authority. 'The guests walk around with no clothes on all the time. It's a five-star spa: that's what you do. I'll go out and find our stuff.'

She got out of the shower and went naked into the room where the towels were stacked, then, re-wrapped, followed her own wet footprints back and gave another towel to Beatriz. Kate was nowhere to be seen. In the end Vic brought Beatriz some of her own clothes to wear; jeans rolled up and hanging at the waist, Beatriz's small dark head peering from the over-sized shirt, like a querulous cat dressed up by a child.

At the lunch table, which was laid prettily on the terrace under the palms, with a white tablecloth and a single orchid, they found Kate waiting for them, sipping orange juice as if she were an adult, talking to Bernie.

'What were you two up to?' Bernie asked gaily, passing them as she left. 'Dressing up?'

'You look hilarious,' Kate said to Beatriz. 'Where are my own clothes?' Beatriz demanded. 'I put them back in the changing room. Oh, come on, you both look so fed up! It was a joke. It was funny.'

'I'm not fed up,' Vic said.

'It wasn't funny,' Beatriz snapped.

'Well, it was a bit funny, but not that funny,' Vic said, trying to be neutral. 'It was probably more silly than funny.'

At this Kate became cold. She bit disdainfully into a celery stick and informed them that they were the silly ones. Not only silly: they had become boring, and annoying. In fact, she was considering finding new members of Bible Club; girls who wouldn't complain about a little bit of fun.

'I don't care,' Beatriz said, startling both Kate and Vic. 'I don't like Bible Club. It's not nice. I only wanted to talk about parables and collect money in tins for earthquake victims.'

There was a long silence. Kate put down her celery stick. 'Is that what you think too?' she asked Vic.

Vic looked away. 'Um. I don't know. But perhaps we *could* change Bible Club? Just a little bit?'

'*We?*' Kate demanded. 'There isn't any "we". *I* started Bible Club, and I'm revoking your membership. Both of you. But most especially you –' she turned to a startled Vic – '*Judas.*'

The rest of the meal passed in a dark, turbid silence, with Kate gazing out at the sea balancing her celery stick in her fingers like a cigarette, and Beatriz aiming her face just as stubbornly plate-wards, so that in the end Vic was relieved when her dad arrived – jolly and oblivious so the tension at the table, the Battenberg that nobody had touched – to take both the girls home.

After that day the three of them, without further discussion, went their separate ways. Beatriz took up an interest in hockey, and made friends with the girls on her team. Nobody came forward to claim Vic, and she didn't particularly want to be claimed, preferring to spend her breaks indoors, volunteering to pin up the wall displays, or carry out any odd jobs the nuns might have. She also started helping Father Blanca in the school chapel; grateful that he, unlike the nuns, didn't ask her any questions. He simply allowed her to help chip away the hardened stalagmites of candle wax and to lay out prayer books; and sometimes, standing outside in the sun, beating sighs of dust out of the cassocks, she detected the presence of happiness. It was not quite something she *felt*, but she could tell it was there: in a tremor of the light, a note in the air; something almost within her reach.

Kate became friendly with a couple of girls from the year above, who had already been suspended for smoking. She didn't, however, forget about Vic. If they passed each other in the corridors she would give Vic a stare like wind blown off a wide Arctic waste, stripping her quickly down to the bone, or one of her new friends would elbow Vic as they passed, then all of them would quietly laugh.

While Vic recognised the behaviour of Kate's friends as the mostly bored, intermittent malice of young cats, batting at something inanimate – a pine cone or a ball – before losing interest, she could tell that Kate's dislike of her was something committed and passionate. She found notes in her locker that said *Betrayer*, or *Fat Bitch*; sketches of Vic swollen far beyond her usual chubbiness; a porn magazine was slipped into her bag, though she managed to throw it away before anyone saw. She didn't tell anybody, hoping that Kate's fury would after time exhaust itself, or find a new focus, such as Sister Cecilia, who recently had made Kate stand outside for the duration of a lesson when Kate asked her why God had put the tree in the Garden of Eden, if not as a joke.

But Kate did not get tired, and she did not get distracted, and then the day arrived when school finished, the bell rang, the girls seethed out of their classrooms like wildebeest, and it was quickly discovered that on the door of each classroom and on the gates (and, as it turned out, on the lamp posts all along the street outside, and even on the doors of the boys' school a block away) were black and white photocopied pictures of Vic naked, standing in a pale, stone-walled room, looking like pale stone herself; a lumpen early man carving, with crudely prominent stomach and thighs, and the obvious beginnings of breasts.

After that Vic – knowing her parents, if called, would recognise the spa from the picture – was forced to tell the nuns who was responsible. Her parents were called anyway, despite Vic's protestations; Jim quite clearly squeamish, Bernie expressing surprise that the charming Kate had turned out to be such a bad egg. 'I suppose you never know,' she said. 'Thank goodness she's been expelled. Let's hope it's a lesson to her and she doesn't carry on causing trouble at her new school.'

Vic nodded, though she was less optimistic. After the incident Vic's classmates regarded her with pleasantly disgusted fascination, as they would a dead dog or a drunk tramp, while the boys at the neighbouring school – who had seen the pictures before they were taken down – spent the last days before the summer holidays shouting 'Big Tits' or (less logically) 'Lesbian' at her on the rare occasions she passed their school. She was grateful when the holidays finally came, and she could be permitted to retract like a snail; curl back into the safety of Azenhas do Mar.

Michael was back for the summer too, and she told him about Kate's final prank the next time she was over at the Quinta do Rosal with her parents. The two of them were sitting in the shade of the ornamental garden playing cards; Michael having got bored of chasing lizards by now. At twelve he had overgrown blond hair, a sudden height advantage, and an air of being difficult to impress. 'I can't wait to hear what sort of pranks you convent schoolgirls play,' he said at first, one eyebrow irritatingly high, but in the end he whistled and said – respectfully, as if assessing the work of a fellow professional – 'OK, that friend of yours has balls.'

'She's not my friend,' Vic said.

'Oh yeah, right. You upset about it?'

Vic shook her head. 'Aw, Vic, you are. Don't be. It's stupid. What's wrong with being naked? Nothing.' He picked up his cards again. '*I* wouldn't care,' he said, and she saw that this, as far as he was concerned, was an end to it.

Vic makes her next trip to church on an unusually hot day. The steps down from her house give her the strange feeling of walking uphill, shimmering under her feet, the orange flowers waving like flames on each step. The naked colours of the village – the red roofs, the fiery blue sky, the white buildings, the welter of bougainvillea and the green of the trees – seem no longer lovely but too stark, as if they have lost all but their most elemental substance. When she gets into the empty church, dark and gravely cool, all her sweat condenses on her skin at once; forming droplets under her breasts, her back and stomach. She sits in a pew and hears the sound of her disordered breathing fill the high space.

Vic isn't even sure what to pray for. She doesn't see the point in asking to be released from her dislike of Estella – a shameful and precious antipathy – when it seems she was right to mistrust her in the first place. In a way, she is relieved to have some confirmation of her suspicions; not to have to fight them any more. But still, she is unhappy. She has been left with the responsibility of deciding whether Michael might already know about the existence of a man who might be looking for Estella, after what she did to him; and if not, whether to tell Michael about what she heard. She has been watching the two of them, trying to guess whether anything has changed, but they both appear exactly the same: all Estella's former edginess and hesitancy gone, wrapped up and refrigerated once more, to the point that Vic feels slightly annoyed, watching Estella accept Michael's compliments and plays for her attention in her usual way, as if she barely notices it.

Vic bows her head but instead of peace a dark swell of misery rises to meet her, swirling low like floodwater. She looks up and meets the painted eyes of the Apostles, arrayed on the wall opposite her, their faces blank and pure, as if they have been emptied out. Nobody she has ever met has a face like that, besides – ironically – Estella.

After leaving the church, Vic walks to the café in the village square to buy a coffee – in the hope the caffeine will sting her sluggish brain into producing some sort of plan of action – and is unexpectedly hailed by Trinidade. She hadn't intended to sit down, but Trinidade's enthusiasm flusters her, and she ends up taking a table under the chestnut tree.

'How do you like the coffee?' Trinidade asks. 'You like whipped cream?'

Vic, who didn't even know that such a thing was available, nods. She waits for her coffee, watching as the flower market is unpacked from the backs of vans at the opposite side of the square; the colours being ladled out; blues, scarlets, stinging yellow. The slightly obscene-looking calla lilies and anthurium; a large sheaf of bird of paradise flowers like origami dragons, stately and awkward. As she sits there, several people she knows pass by, giving her a nod or a wave without breaking stride. She realises that after twenty or so years of making the acquaintance of most people in the village, she doesn't know anybody well enough to invite them to join her. This seems to her something she can understand fully only now that she is not on the move herself: now that she has come to rest, her true nature is physically realised; the tourist, the spectator. Sitting half asleep with her face supported by her palms, forcibly preventing it from sliding down onto the table, Vic watches the life of Azenhas do Mar turn itself out of doors and thinks she may as well be looking at a postcard.

Trinidade, without being light footed or subtle, still manages to surprise Vic when she appears at her elbow with the coffee. Vic accepts it warily. A powdering of chocolate dusts its frothed top. She decides not to question it.

'Thank you very much.'

Trinidade glances at the other unoccupied tables and pulls up a chair next to Vic. She leans her head back and gives a great sigh, as if she has been waiting for Vic to come so that she can finally relax.

'I don't see you so much these days,' she says, 'you and Michael. You still like it here?'

'Of course,' Vic says. 'I just haven't done much of anything recently except work. And Michael . . . is busy.'

'I know what busy is,' Trinidade says. 'I've seen his new girl. I've heard about her.' She looks up with an intimate slyness. 'Estella.' The name becomes odd, foreign, the way she pronounces it.

Vic is taken aback. 'You've heard about Estella? How do you mean?' Realising she has spoken too quickly, and with too much interest, she takes a casual sip of the coffee, covering her top lip with foam.

'My cousin's daughter Maria works at Michael's company. Her friend Theresa was his assistant until Estella arrived. Michael is important, you know, everyone wanted to be his assistant. So this strange girl, Estella, was meant to be something very small, very low down in some other department. Then all of a sudden she is Michael's assistant and Theresa is pushed down to some nothing job. Then Estella is doing other things too, making herself very important. Nobody can say anything to her because she's with Michael now. She knows what she did to Theresa but she ignores her. Every day she ignores her. She goes around like that Angelina after she stole Brad Pitt. He was married to such a pretty girl. She thinks she's as beautiful as Angelina too. Too high to talk to anybody. Not a nice girl.'

'Couldn't Theresa have complained, or something, though?' Vic asks. 'There must be official channels . . .'

'No, like I say, she could be fired if she complains about Estella now,' Trinidade says, with slight impatience. 'That company is a shifty business. Many secrets. Estella has a lot of secrets. One day the police come to the office. They were there for nothing much, or nothing bad, but Theresa said when Estella saw them come in the door she is panicked – her face is white, she is shocked. She thinks they are there for *her*. She is only calm again when she realises it isn't for her.'

'Really?' Vic asks, forgetting her coffee. 'Does Michael know that?'

'I worry about Michael,' Trinidade says, becoming suddenly mournful. She smoothes out her apron and looks sadly at the flower stalls opposite. 'Such a beautiful young man. His hair. So much energy. Always friendly. I don't see him now, except walking by with that girl, her nose like –' she thrusts her own nose into the air – 'holding on to him like he might run away. And so he should. No parents here any more to guard him, and this is the first thing that happens. She'll get his house – she will, and all his money.'

'No,' Vic says, not in disagreement with Trinidade, but as a weak protestation, against the unfairness of the world.

Vic finishes her coffee and lets Trinidade withdraw reluctantly back behind her counter without telling her how stingingly, unwittingly close their suspicions are. This is more out of a simple, long-standing wariness of Trinidade than anything else: an aversion to the woman herself; wiping her hands on her red-stained apron, drawing Vic into a partnership she isn't sure she is ready for. But there are details she knows to be authentic. The sloppy management of the engineering firm. The arbitrary nature of its jobs. Estella's coldness. Michael's money. The mysterious wronged man, who might – it now seems – have the law on his side. Without jumping to conclusions, Vic decides she will make her own investigations. As quietly and as carefully as she can, she'll find out what Estella wants. Then she'll decide what to do.

STAR

Once Kaya crosses the border between the lavender-tinted light and the dark of the booth, she sees that the good-looking man sits alone; hands resting on his thighs, fingers tidily woven, his drink brimming on the table before him, as if forgotten. The two other men are occupied with Venus, who is putting up a good show of wanting to talk to them and not their friend, stroking her hair as if soothing a kitten, flashing her frozen-toothed smile.

'I hear you want to talk to me,' she says, sitting down. For the first time in a while, she feels underdressed. The way he is looking at her – soberly, with a distinct note of assessment – makes her feel as if she is at a job interview. She folds her legs at the ankle; makes an effort to smile.

'I'm Jasper,' he says. 'Do we shake hands, in here? I'm afraid I don't know the rules. I didn't know if I was allowed to take up so much of your time.' The admission – not a genuine question, true, but sincere in its way – takes some of the force out of his openly well-bred voice. She looks him in the eye, which is a perusing, dry blue. His eye says: I am intelligent. I am making my decisions. But beyond this she thinks she can see other, less civilised impulses.

'Star. We can shake hands if you like,' she says, slowly. She extends her hand and watches it disappear, his fingers (cool, long, confident) drawing over the hand before retreating with the same deliberateness; as if he is a magician performing a trick – stepping back with a look of restrained victory, returning her own hand to her, significantly changed.

'I'm glad you wanted to take up my time,' she says, smiling. The smile is a stab in the dark – a guess at the sort of smile he might want. She puts various things into it, shyness, promise, reserve. An idea of things being withheld, for now. It is the first in a series of guesses and adaptations she will make as they talk, realigning herself to become the sort of girl he expects. As starts go, it is a good one. He smiles back at her, with a flare of approval, and says, 'You're not the kind of girl I expected to see in here.'

At this she relaxes a little, finding herself on familiar conversational ground. Men often say this; then they ask – after she has finished dancing – why she is doing this job. Some tell her to go to college. Others ask her to marry them. Mostly the men she meets talk about themselves; though this is not entirely their fault, as Star has become quite adept at avoiding discussion of her own life. (Sometimes she feels the skills of conversational parrying and dodging ought to be recognised as a sport: a swordless fencing; a strange, unmoving martial art.) Often men want to talk about sex, which she allows, up to a point. On occasion they say something mocking, or insulting, their bodies lordly, their eyes peering out half frightened and half excited, like children throwing eggs from behind the bushes. By the end of each shift her face has hardened with the effort of it all; a wall with a smile painted on it.

The rest of Star's and Jasper's preliminary small talk follows the usual templates of the strip club. No money is mentioned: the men with money never discuss it, and she can tell that he is of that type. (No shirt could be so beautiful, so unwrinkled, without money.) He tells her he has come tonight with some old friends. They were all celebrating a birthday at a restaurant, moving on to a bar. Most of them went home when the bar closed, but one of the party, as is tradition, suggested a casino or a strip club. Nobody had the correct ID to join the casino and so they ended up at the Purple Tiger. Jasper came along mainly to keep an eye on the birthday boy, who is minute by minute inching down the back of his seat, his body pooling towards the floor.

After a while there is a long pause. Star intends to ask him something innocuous, to break the silence, but his eyes have got a grip on hers and she has the strange feeling of being subdued; of being physically held. She looks away, realises she is losing her nerve and, furthermore, that she is giving away that fact, and looks back with an effort. 'Would you like a dance?' she asks. She hears how the question sounds: not sweet, or seductive. It sounds like a challenge.

'No,' he says. There is a short pause; a dark well of suspension. Then he says, 'I just want to talk to you.'

'Talk to me? All night?'

'That surprises you?'

'Not many people come here for a chat.'

At this Jasper shrugs. Then he asks her, 'What does this place do to your idea of men?' and she understands that, conversationally, they are to be going off-road; looking at each other suddenly with the consciousness of it, of being subversive together – a strange delight; a thrill of recognition.

'You want my honest opinion?' she asks, and he nods, and leans forward, arranging his body as if he can more perfectly attune it to her answer, careful not to miss a thing.

An hour later, Jasper's companion's chin has finally made the drop to his chest and Cameron – in deference to Jasper's relative sobriety and the amount of money he has already handed over – comes over to warn Jasper politely that his friend will have to be removed. It seems to Kaya that in a very short time it is all over. Jasper stretches, blinks and laughs, as if he has woken up from a rather amusing dream. He thanks her, too chivalrously, for her company and wishes her well. Then he leaves, the surface of his untouched drink rippling gently on the table behind him.

Kaya tells Annie she is taking a break and goes to the loo; a dank cavern with a dripping ceiling and a blinking light, shared by the dancers and the few female customers. She is alone in the room and is glad of it. On impulse, she stands on tiptoe to look out of one of the long high windows. The glass is so smogged that it is impossible to make out the people passing by on the road outside, tiny and silent, as if bottled in the prison of the panes. There is a commotion at the door: Chloe and Venus arriving in haste at the same time, each refusing to give way to the other, and being forced to squeeze inside together, pressed against their own sides of the doorframe.

'Well, well, well,' Chloe says with pleasure. She comes over to Kaya and strokes her back, tenderly rearranging a few locks of her hair. 'You excelled yourself tonight. Luca said that guy paid five hundred quid!' She turns to Venus, alight with insolence. 'You ever get paid that, Venus?'

Venus, fiddling with a false eyelash in the submarine light of the mirror, affects not to hear. A former ballet dancer ('about a hundred years ago,' says Alisha), and having the most experience, she considers herself the head dancer at Purple Tiger despite there being no such title, and maintains a suitable distance from the rest of the girls, none of whom know her real name or her age.

'He was fit as *fuck*, too,' Chloe exults. She performs a victory dance. 'You need a fucking savings account, man. You're in the money! You're in the money!'

The victory dance loses its initial focus and becomes a full-scale striptease performance; exaggerated for the mirror. Chloe bends over and wiggles her bottom at Kaya, who laughs. She kicks her legs up in a half-mast cancan ('Oof!'). Finally, she undoes her sequinned bra and whirls it around her head. The end of the strap catches Venus on the ear.

'Watch it,' Venus warns.

'Sorry.'

'*You two*,' Venus says, bringing her body – an impressively muscular body, as if hewn into its present improbable structure from something elemental and mighty, like a figurehead carved out of an oak – around to face them. Chloe and Kaya, faced with the fact of Venus's cleavage: older, wiser, and significantly more expensive, are subdued. Chloe puts her bra back on. Kaya looks at her shoes. 'You think you're in a musical? It doesn't take much to turn *your* heads. One lecherous old man.' She luxuriates in the word lecherous, its swampy depths, its expressiveness; recalling other words: retch, leech, leprous. Kaya can almost feel it on her skin.

'What does lecherous mean?' asks Chloe.

'Dirty,' says Venus.

'Well, how could he be that, then, if he didn't even ask her for a dance?' Chloe says, becoming defiant. 'He didn't, did he? He just paid Kaya a shitload of money for the pleasure of her fucking company. For chit chat. I call that a result.'

Venus laughs. 'Oh, *right*. Excuse me! I didn't realise I was insulting Prince Charming. What is it, then – love? He's going to drive back here in a carriage to meet you at four a.m., is he? Little kids, the pair of you. I don't know why I'm wasting my time.'

She exits, stately as a queen, trailing curls and ribbons and floating particles of glitter. Once the door is closed Chloe rolls her eyes and says, 'Silly cow', but she is deflated, and when she asks Kaya what they did talk about, Kaya isn't in the mood to tell her.

'We talked about him and his job and stuff,' she says.

'Oh,' Chloe says, and now she does look disappointed. 'The usual.'

Kaya isn't sure why she feels the need to keep any of it secret; as if it is something both special and vulnerable. She ended up telling Jasper about how she sneaked into a lecture and he laughed, apparently captivated, and said that took guts. He told her a few other philosophers she ought to sneak in to hear about, if she could. He said his favourite was Plato, and when she asked him what Plato had said, he smiled, almost wistfully, and said half the pleasure was discovering someone for yourself, without anyone else's understanding of it spoiling it. He told her he was a doctor and when she couldn't find anything to say to this (he was so obviously a doctor), he said that normally when he told people about his job they would promptly tell him about their ailments. She said; 'Better than telling them you're a stripper', and he laughed.

'You are different, aren't you?' he said. 'A rare creature.'

That was the extent of his comment on her; either her looks or her conversation. She wasn't sure whether the entire thing was a failure on a grand scale or a strange, beautiful success, and for this reason, she won't give it up to the other girls for analysis.

When they get home, Chloe and Luca insist on a couple of drinks to celebrate her windfall. Kaya joins them but her sociability is put on; beneath it she feels a sigh waiting in her, a suppressed pocket of air under her ribs. She is imagining the sort of life Jasper might go back to: that of a sofa commercial; Jasper's crisp shirt sleeves rolled up to the elbow, a coffee cup, a blonde wife and a blonde Labrador gazing at him. His car will smell like leather. His television will be paid for outright, his newspapers will be pushed through the door by a sleepy schoolboy. There will be flowers she can't name in his garden, watered by someone else, or perhaps Jasper, at the weekends. He will eat muesli. She realises that she has, without meaning to, applied a classical soundtrack to Jasper's life: piano notes, dropping spare and elegant. Her own creation oppresses her: each additional detail laid down between them like a fence paling, until she can't see beyond it, loitering on the dusty pavement; a child who has thrown its ball over the fence, and is too frightened to ask for it back.

As a distraction she gets drunk. She doesn't do it often; having only recently been forced to overcome her hatred for it since moving in with Chloe (for whom there is no fun, no celebration, without bottles of something in virulent blue or orange), but in terms of not thinking about things alcohol is strictly a last resort. Drinking brings its own problems; it reminds her of Louise, sitting on the floor with a bottle tilted in her hand, her legs having collapsed midway to taking her to bed, surprising Louise with their sudden betrayal. She waits, ashamed, for Kaya to help her up, her beautiful, oceanic eyes sorry again, submerged in contrition. 'Sorry, Kaya,' she whispers. 'Sorry, my angel.'

One of life's many small fillips and ironies – sometimes examined by Kaya, sometimes not – is that, though she has written down the date and time of the lecture on Plato and Socrates, and made sure that she is free to sneak in that day, once she is actually waiting for the lecturer to begin her thoughts are not on the subject ahead, but on Jasper. Though she wouldn't say she is thinking about him, exactly, he has a tendency to appear randomly in her thoughts, clinging on to the end of another thought, like a man towed by a boat, appearing suddenly in its wake. The things he said appear at times, like large floating letters, usually apropos of nothing. She woke up one night and he may as well have been at the end of her bed, saying, 'A rare creature' with that peculiar look that had arrived in his eye at that moment; the results of a brief and half-hearted scuffle between regret and admiration, with neither emerging as a clear winner. In the grey din of the morning – bin wheels towed across the pavements, shop shutters rattling up; one frenzied night owl, having found himself adrift in the morning, calling out, 'What's it all about? What's it all about?' – she remembered this expression and felt something small and anxious stir inside her, a mouse or a bird; the quick fibrillation of its heart.

A night meeting with Jasper, however, is a rarity. More usual are the bad dreams. She isn't sure when they started. They arrived like dark gulls; one landed, discovering her, then the others followed. Some nights she is picked over by a whole flock of them, circling and returning. She has heard that bad dreams ought to be considered and analysed – but what would be the point? What will she discover that isn't already painfully obvious? (In the lecture theatre, now that the dreams have dwindled in the daylight like spilt water, she can dismiss them.)

Kaya likes Socrates' allegory of the cave: the idea that reality is not something that is at the disposal of the senses; everything in life being only a temporary, reflected version of an ideal or perfect form. People, for Socrates, are prisoners in this cave, facing a wall on which shadows are cast by a fire behind them, imagining that the shadows are the truth. The allegory strikes her like something she used to know and has suddenly remembered, arriving with a weight of association; the powdery taste of icing, the late autumn sun briefly lighting a window, a perfectly round pebble in the palm of her hand. Sitting in her seat at the end of the lecture, while students squeeze past her legs, she is moved at the idea of Jasper being similarly struck by the beauty of the idea; and rather than have the pleasure of telling her about it, generously holding off, so that she could have the discovery to herself. But then it was Plato who told the world about Socrates – now 'Plato's Socrates' – leaving Kaya with the sense of a missing man, removed from common experience, like one of his own forms. She wonders whether it really would have spoilt it for her if Jasper had told her about him: Jasper's Plato's Socrates. She thinks she might have liked to hear it from him; his face serious, his words underlined with a few gestures of his long, noble hands.

On the journey home, however, Kaya's initial exhilaration gives way to a slow and comprehensive unhappiness. The bus coalesces gradually around her, becoming a bus again, not a shadow. She sits in the damply rising smells of the wet coats around her, the world tinted melancholic by the fogged window. She gets off several stops early, with the intention of walking quickly until the action of walking itself strips away her thoughts layer by layer, taking her back to an animal state, sweaty and exhausted. The rain has stopped and the traffic hisses through the long slicks of water on the road; the sky is grey and close, breathing down her neck.

Kaya is nearly at her mother's road before she realises how far she has strayed. Her feet must have relapsed into an old route: the hour-long walk from the town centre she used to make, to save on the bus fare. She stops at the road sign, garlanded with cans and cigarettes like tokens left at a graveside. In front of her is the block of flats; its ungiving, squat outline. It is not a living shape; it would never occur naturally.

It is not a place for people to live inside. It is a disturbing thought to imagine Louise herself in there, floating within her own small cell, her eyes ranging far beyond it, roaming over strange, wild lands.

The club that night is unusually busy; drawing Paul out of his office to vacillate anxiously behind the bar like a new housewife hosting a Tupperware party, watching Luca measure out shots and take money until Luca tells him irritably that he can load the dishwasher if he's at a loose end. The frantic gloom is woven with the clothed shapes of men and the bare shoulders and legs of the girls. Chloe and Laura are kissing each other on stage when Kaya arrives: Laura the more showy of the two, ostentatious of tongue. Her silky dress falls knowingly about her breasts like a stage curtain. There is sweat on the walls; the pole is slick with it.

Kaya spends most of the night dealing with a stag party; though she doesn't join the girls on the stage for the usual rituals; stripping off the groom, putting ice down his trousers, whipping him with his own belt before riding him triumphantly around the pole. His friends cheer and knock their drinks over. She has no idea why the grooms put themselves through it. They seem to think they deserve it; humbly accepting their treatment, as if knowing it is a fair punishment for getting married, for going to a strip club, perhaps just for being a man.

'Hey, Kaya,' Alisha taps her elbow. 'The doctor's in the house.'

She turns around and there is Jasper at the bar, looking

like a man who has just arrived from some 1930s film noir, as if he has just removed a fedora from his undisturbed hair. He looks at the stag party – the hooting, howling boys, enjoying a dirty joke – with forgiving irony. This is a man, she thinks; eyes narrowed in the gloom, the precise and composed outline of him. She doesn't wonder that she seems different to him, because he is totally alien to her. She has never met anybody like him. He appears to have arrived alone.

'You look terrified,' Alisha observes. 'Go on. Get your best smile on and get over there', and with that she gives her a little push, so that when Jasper turns he sees her starting quickly forward, before approaching in her own stroll, hoping that what she has on her face is a reasonable approximation of her best smile.

He doesn't say hello. Instead, they stand and look at each other for a moment.

'I had to see you,' he says. His expression is blazed out on the one side by a light hanging above the bar, vanished into darkness on the other; neither side readable. She doesn't say anything. Her breath seems suddenly short and inadequate; it scurries back and forth, like a trapped animal.

'I don't know what to do,' he continues. 'I've been thinking about you. I want to talk to you more. Is that something you would want?'

She nods.

'But I mean outside, with your clothes on, on an equal footing. Can we do that?'

She nods again.

'How do we do it? Do you give me your number?'

'Luca will give it to you,' she says. Luca, who had initially slid tactfully across to the other side of the bar, before becoming curious and gradually moving back into her peripheral vision, hurries to oblige.

'Star!' one of the stags cries. 'Wherefore art thou?'

'So,' she says, reluctant to give up her place with Jasper. 'I guess you'll call.'

He smiles and inclines his head as if tipping an imaginary hat, and she goes back to the stag party, who want her to officiate over a drinking game. She plays with affection; suddenly feeling forgiving towards these boys, some of whom can barely get their words out, picking up the rules of their game and administering them with stern benevolence, almost beginning to imagine herself as a mother, watching over her children – rascally, noisy, but ultimately innocent – until one suggests that the winner of the game should get a free flash of tit, and the illusion is over.

Jasper calls Kaya a few days after taking her number. The day after that he arrives outside her flat in a car as sleek and clean as a porpoise, its interior closeted in camel-coloured leather and polished burred wood. She sits inside, feeling her chipped fingernails and bruised knees intensely, and they drive without saying much to a small pub several miles outside of the town. The pub is hidden at the end of a long, potholed single track road, so that for a moment – as they bump along under a tunnel of leafless trees – she wonders whether he might be planning to kill her. It seems the most plausible explanation for her presence here, next to his stern profile, one hand effortless on the steering wheel, his shirt more pristine than ever, its collar like the finest origami. But instead he leads her into the cloistered space of the pub, into a panelled side room densely heated by a log fire.

Once inside she feels more capable, and after a couple of glasses of champagne, finds herself able to tell him her thoughts about Plato. Having been used to men casually reaching her conclusions for her, Kaya is surprised when Jasper replies delicately, without attempting to interpret or take hold of the conversation. They talk about his home life: he is married but separated, living with his wife while they try to sell their house. He says they are both civilised about it: neither one finishing the milk, meeting in the hallways with polite hellos, like two gentlemen bowing to each other on the street. He hints at a vast sexual desert, at separate beds. While he talks he watches her; as if wondering what her reaction to him might be, as if her reaction is something that matters. Finally, he tells an anecdote, but the story itself is barely connected to the point he had begun to make. He seems to be reaching for something that his words are replacing, erasing. When he finishes, there is a silence. She decides to say nothing. They look at each other for what feels like a long time, until the fire makes a loud cracking noise and they both flinch, then laugh. The moment passes, and he asks her about her family, whereupon she tells him a shameless pack of lies.

He takes her home and, the road being blocked by two

Rastafarians trying to fit a sofa into a van, lets her out at the bottom of the street. He doesn't try to kiss her. She wasn't sure if she wanted to be kissed, but now the possibility has been withheld she is disappointed. She walks up the street, feeling the sting of it, wondering which of the many ways in which she isn't good enough had finally made his mind up against her. She has never met anyone as self-possessed as him. In the bar he spoke just enough to the bar staff, neither haughty nor ingratiating; his tip casual but generous, his smile friendly but seeming to fall from a high place, like a piece of gold thrown from a carriage. She supposes this is what is meant when people talk about natural authority.

Kaya is halfway up her street when she is startled by the sight of Carl. He is leaning against a wall opposite her flat, smoking a cigarette. He looks surprisingly like himself, though what she might have expected him to look like, she couldn't say. He doesn't see her approaching; being too absorbed in the closed doors and windows of Chloe's building. Her feet carry her a few paces more, out of habit, then falter in the absence of further instructions. There is a long, sticky moment of stillness and fright. Then she gets herself together, and flees.

After finding a coffee shop in which she could wait for Carl to get fed up with his surveillance of her house, Kaya sits with her cold fingers tight around her burning cup; returned abruptly and without warning, like a teleportation, to the weeks after she got her A-level results (three As: abstract, and seeming to have nothing to do with her); the days when she lay in her bedroom and thought she wouldn't particularly mind if she died. It didn't seem like such a significant adjustment to her. Nothing tied her to the world too tightly; it seemed sometimes like nothing more than a starting point from which her thoughts made their frustrating reconnaissances, trying to find a way out. If it weren't for Louise, she thought. But the need to watch out for Louise seemed both ever more pressing, and less and less possible.

Kaya had been able to delay the question of university for another year in which she planned to work, save money, and see Louise through the current situation (Kaya refused to see it as anything more than a situation, temporary and fixable), before it came around again to face her next summer. Work had not been as easy as it sounded, however; she was competing with the middle-class girls from the leafy part of town, all recently released from their own exams and flooding the shop floors, bars and restaurants of the town centre. Kaya had taken a job in a local takeaway on the understanding that she would be there only temporarily until it was sold, knocked down, and turned into a supermarket; at which point she hoped she'd find a job that would better fill her savings account. She worked peacefully enough in a perpetual, dense cloud of oil with the owner's mother, an elderly Chinese lady who watched her with unvoiced suspicion. So long as the suspicion was silent Kaya didn't mind it.

Louise's situation, as Kaya saw it, was Carl's fault. Carl was the one who lost his job on the (flimsy, according to him) grounds that he wasn't doing his job; Carl was the one who used to have a drug problem, before he got himself clean. It was Carl who has decided to take his drug problem back up again, Carl who brought this rediscovered drug problem home, and introduced it to Louise, so that Kaya arrived home from the takeaway one night and found them lost on the sofa together, floating across a calm sea on their velvety green boat; a smell of burning, an inky sweetness.

Kaya's temper, never lost before, now made its own maiden voyage. 'What the fuck are you doing?' she shouted.

Louise looked startled. Her arms made swimming motions but her body stayed where it was, hopelessly beached. Then, as if deciding to remove herself from an unseemly situation, she closed her eyes, becoming immediately and beatifically absent. Kaya tried to grab the wrap but Carl fended her off, laughing. He stood up; held it above his head.

'Jump,' he suggested. His smile, always slow to catch on, lay slovenly over the new expression making its way into his face; a canny, greedy look.

Not wanting him to see that he had intimidated her, she banged out of the room. The noise she made slamming her bedroom door came too late to cut off Carl's closing observances, made to a comatose Louise. 'What's up with her? Must be all that work at the chinky. She smells like spring rolls. Maybe that's why she's in such a shit mood, eh? She ain't going to get laid smelling like that.'

On the few occasions Kaya managed to get her mother alone to talk to her, Louise retreated from her; elusive, at times crying behind her hands like a child. 'It makes me feel better,' she said.

'They won't give me proper medication. I stopped drinking. It's pain relief. Carl wouldn't let me do too much. He's very careful.' At times she was defiant, 'We're all adults, aren't we? It's my business,' at others agonised and guilty: 'I know I've fucked you up, my baby, my beautiful cherub, my Chelsea bun.'

Kaya sat up on the bed and looked out of her window at the wall, on which last week's graffiti was still in place. *Fuck You*, it said. She wondered what was going to happen to them. The odd shabby peace of their lives was flapping now like torn paper, as if paper were all it ever was, a picture of happiness rather than the real thing. Perhaps their life – Louise's tenderness, her infrequent fits of motherhood, the more sober evenings in which she and Kaya played card games or watched films together, mock-puking over the most offensively romantic scenes – wasn't much of a picture to begin with. But it was better than this. The last time they watched a film – hopefully initiated by Kaya, with popcorn and Coca Cola, on a night Carl was out – Louise began yawning after five minutes, her head tilted back onto the motley cushions of the sofa. Outside the window was black; their own two faces reflected. Yellow light from the moving cars of the street slid over them, lighting in turn Kaya's hands, the sofa, Louise's tucked-up feet, her sideways face, suddenly asleep.

It wasn't long before the china lady disappeared. Kaya noticed it the moment she came into the lounge. She clocked the familiar elements of the room: the density of the air (she cut through it without inhaling; opened the window), Louise asleep on the sofa, the television muttering away to itself. Then the little absence on the shelf.

Kaya shook Louise awake.

'Where's your china lady?'

'Oh, hello, star kitten.' Louise smiled beyond her, dreamy and sweet. 'What china lady? Oh yes. She was broken. Carl knocked her off the shelf by accident. I was so sad. But, you know, these things happen.'

'Did you see him do it?'

'I was asleep. Why? These are funny questions.'

'Never mind,' Kaya said. She put her hands on Louise's shoulders, relieving her of the need to speak, to struggle herself up from the cushions. Louise carried on smiling, a serene, transported smile that didn't strictly belong to her, having arrived by accident, as if it had fallen off the *Mona Lisa* or the Botticelli *Venus* and ended up here somehow, only half fixed on.

Kaya walked to the building site where Carl had found some temporary work as a hod carrier, where she rattled at the chain-link fence until he looked over, fluorescent-coated and startled, and came to meet her.

'You sold her, didn't you?'

'What the fuck are you talking about?' Carl asked. There was something childish about his face; like a small round boy's, comically touched up with sun-lines and dirt and a capped tooth, whiter than the rest. It wasn't a face for hiding its feelings and she could see them all there then: connivance, mild fright, guilt, quickly manufactured hurt, at being falsely accused.

'I hate you,' she said. 'Why did you come? We were happy before you arrived. You're going to kill her.'

'Oi, now,' Carl said, shocked. 'Don't be like that. It won't kill anyone. It's not your business what your ma gets up to. You're a grown-up. Right.' He warmed to his theme, building his own confidence as he went, 'What's she going to do instead – drink? What, like, you two had a perfect life? She was out of her fucking head all day. Booze'll kill you. Smack don't.'

'I want you to leave her alone.'

He stood back, chin up, as if he considered himself to be playing his trump card. 'Maybe *you* ought to leave her alone. You haven't done so well up till now. Maybe you ought to get your own place.'

'If you don't go, I'll tell your boss and the police about you. I'll do it right now.'

'You little cunt.' He moved forward suddenly, reaching his hand through the fence as if to get hold of her, but she had already seen the idea arrive in his face and had jumped back. By the time he had run around to the gate she had got to the end of the road, where she checked back over her shoulder to see him come to a halt far behind her, apparently giving the chase up as a bad job. 'You want fucking *sorting out*, you do,' he called. 'One of these days . . .'

When Kaya got back, Louise was where she had left her. She shook her and talked loudly and janglingly into her face until most of the chemical haze was shaken off her, knocked away like snow; Louise exposed numb, blue, and with the beginnings of irritation.

'What on God's earth are you doing, Kaya? I was having a nap.'

'Mum, you've got to stop this. We've got to get you some

sort of help. We can go to a clinic or something. Carl's not nice. He doesn't care about you. He sold the china lady.'

'Oh, well, so what if he did,' Louise said. 'It's only a bloody *thing*. What's that china lady ever going to do besides look smug and get dusty.'

Realisation arrived. 'You *knew* about it?'

'Kaya. My love. It's just a china lady.'

'It's not just that.' Kaya felt the weight of everything then like a wall held up only by her hands. Behind the wall were her mother and Carl and the world. Behind Kaya was nothing. A darkness; a drop. She felt panicked, not knowing how long she had to convince her mother before Carl came home.

'It's not right what you're doing. I'm going to tell someone so they can get you help. And make Carl go away. He's . . . I don't like the way he looks at me.'

'Carl?' Louise cried, affrighted. 'You don't mean that. I know what's up – your nose is a bit out of joint because Carl's come along. I know you don't approve of . . . stuff, but it's only occasional. It's pain relief. Listen, love, you can't decide things for me.'

'I can't stay if he's here,' Kaya said. 'He's bad for you. He's bad for us. He's going to ruin everything.'

Louise blinked. 'Kaya . . . what is this? You're not usually like this.'

Kaya was stubborn: 'You have to choose.'

'I'm not bloody choosing! You're acting like a kid.'

'If you don't choose, I'll leave.'

There was a long silence. Louise turned her face mulishly away, to the blanched flowers of the wallpaper. Great overblown long-dead roses; a memory of pink. Kaya stood over her and willed her to say something. She fixed her eyes on Louise as if her mother might feel them; some of the heat, some of the sting.

She couldn't even tell how long she stood there silently compelling Louise before she gave up and went to her own room. Probably more time than it took her to pack all her things. She thought distantly that there was a black comedy about the whole thing; her big exit: half an hour to put all her possessions in five carrier bags. Finally, she stood and looked around the room, which showed no sign of having been vacated, having shown no sign of ever being lived in, in the first place. Only Kaya could know that the melamine wardrobe and chest of drawers were empty, or that there would usually be a book and a pair of ear plugs on the night stand.

The windows of the flat all faced away from the sunset, so that dusk came early. In Kaya's room she had pinned up a square of voile behind the curtains. It faded the detail of the road so that only colour could be seen: a tender lilac sky soaking into grey, grey soaking into black; hung with the hazy orange globes of the street lights. By the time she finished and passed the sitting room, carrying her things, Louise had sunk back into her fathomless sleep. The cold air pouring through the open window had scoured the flat of its familiar perfumes, leaving an icy absence of scent.

Kaya closed the window, then went to the sofa and looked down at Louise. One of her mother's hands had slid off the sofa, hanging as if discarded. The other curled by her cheek. Her hair was dirty. She still had a ransacked sort of beauty;

the nobility of her cheekbones, the high brows still apparent under her bruised, dinted skin. Kaya touched her fingers to Louise's forehead, stroking her mother without waking her. She noticed that Louise was wearing one of Carl's old T-shirts; the logo rising and falling over her heart as she breathed.

Kaya held herself upright as if withstanding a great wave; feelings risen and repressed over the last months, now larger than before, occupying all the space inside her. She felt the pressure of it as if her own skin couldn't contain it. It cried at the back of her eyes, in her aching throat. She took her hand away.

'I'm sorry,' Kaya said. 'Goodbye, Mum.'

Over the next weeks, Jasper takes Kaya out again, to pubs and hotel bars out of town. He never touches her aside from a gentle steering hand between her shoulder blades, a brush of the fingers when giving her a glass, but she thinks she can see something there, well hidden beneath his urbane manner. She glimpsed it for a moment, back in the Purple Tiger: and it *is* like the stripes of a tiger, passing through trees. She can only see it when it moves; a rippling of gold and black, a heavy, muscular movement. When she takes off her coat or stands up his eyes move quickly over her, returning to their usual place, before she can catch them at it. Sex is on his mind; it is on hers too. *What are you waiting for?* she wonders. For the first time she wants to do it; to find out, finally, what all the fuss is about.

The more Kaya sees of Jasper, the more she sees of Carl,

waiting outside her flat and, on occasion, at the strip club, slightly out of range of the doormen – until finally the two men's trajectories intersect and Carl happens to choose an afternoon when Jasper is meant to be picking her up to enact his own smoke-shrouded vigil outside Chloe's flat.

Kaya, edgy, gets dressed and puts on her make-up, repeatedly returning to the window to check if Carl has moved. She isn't sure how he found her. She didn't have a mobile phone when she left. She had asked Satvinder to keep an eye on Louise for her, and Satvinder duly reported back each week. Carl was still coming and going, Louise still housebound, emerging only infrequently – usually, these days, to ask to borrow a twenty from her neighbours. The idea of Louise reduced to this pains Kaya even while she knows the impossibility of giving her money: any cash, any gifts transmuted quickly and irreversibly into dingy brown rock.

'Fuck *off*,' she hisses now, standing at the window ten minutes before Jasper is due to arrive. 'What's he doing here?'

Chloe looks up from her daytime TV programme, concerning a woman about to have plastic surgery. The woman's future breasts have been brought out to her so she can feel them before they are put inside her. They sit on a platter before her like jellyfish, trembling under her blank gaze. Kaya is reminded of the pictures of Saint Agatha in her religious education textbook, painted holding her own severed breasts on a plate. The doctor picks one up in his gloved hand; gives it a reassuring squeeze.

'Want me to go out there and see him off?' Chloe offers.

'No. No. I don't know what to do. Maybe he'll go away before Jasper gets here.'

'Why don't you ask him what he wants? It's got to be better than this. Look at the state of you. You're *pacing*, man. You're starting to freak me out.'

Kaya considers it. She isn't sure how to explain her thoughts to Chloe. On her mind is the fact that after she left Louise's flat she called the police and Louise's community liaison officer to tell them about Carl's and Louise's heroin problem. She didn't see the point, in the end, of telling Carl's work, but Carl might be looking to pay her back anyway. She remembers the way he said, *'You want fucking sorting out'*, each word emerging hard and substantial, as if pressed under a great force.

Though Chloe is sympathetic, she doesn't quite understand what might panic Kaya about the arrival of Carl, and Kaya doesn't know how to explain it. It was not only the time he lost his temper and punched a door after she took some money from his wallet to buy food, or the casual way he told anyone who called at the door – the postman, the council, Louise's and Kaya's neighbours ('nosy cunts') – to fuck off. It was a tone of voice, an expression that was gone almost as soon as it arrived. His nicknames for her, as varied and imaginative as her mother's (yet never said in the presence of her mother), dwelling mainly on her vagina's frostiness, its snobbery, its lack of use. The gradual disappearance of Louise into her dream state, until Kaya and Carl were the only two left, facing off uneasily in the sitting room. Early night after early night. Putting a chair up against the door of her bedroom, after a night when his shape blocked the hall light.

'We could throw a jug of water over him,' Chloe suggests,

sympathetically. Kaya is standing with one eye to the gap in the blind. *Go away*, she wills. *Go away*.

As if in response, Carl takes a cigarette packet out of his pocket and peers inside, before dropping it on the ground. He shifts off the wall and stands as if uncertain, passing his weight from one foot to another. The wind, which has been stirring litter and leaves in small hurricanes all day, catches his hair and presses his head down into his parka. Then, miraculously, with a long, final stare up at the flat, he turns and walks away down the road. A moment later, Jasper's silver car rounds the corner.

'You shagged Jasper yet?' Chloe asks. Unlike the other girls at the Purple Tiger, who are taken with the idea of Jasper as an old-school gentleman, of a type none of them have ever encountered but are inclined to believe in anyway, Chloe is impatient for sexual detail. 'You better fuck him this time,' she warns, as Kaya goes out of the door. 'Cos this is getting ridiculous.'

Full of loosened feeling, relief throbbing in her body like excitement, Kaya is flushed when she gets into Jasper's car. She sits in the heated interior, which smells of his own distinctive aftershave, darkly sweet, powdery edged, an undertow of clear pine resin, the amber teardrops she used to dig her fingernails into when she was a child. He looks at her with the attentiveness – almost sharpness – she has begun to get used to.

'Are you OK?' he asks her. 'You look . . . I don't know. You look different.'

'Do I?' She puts her hands up to her face and feels the sting of her cheeks. She is lightheaded. She sees his concern and it makes her laugh; an unpractised sound, like a squeaky bedspring. On impulse, she puts her hand into his.

When Kaya gives a private dance – trying to remove her clothes under the single light of a booth not much bigger than a large wardrobe without jabbing an elbow or a toe against its walls, the curtain trapping their breath and a round blackbird's eye in the ceiling – there is a particular noise a customer makes; something halfway between a sigh and a groan: an almost exasperated sound, as if they have realised they left their keys at home. The first time it happened she stopped, knickers arrested in mid-descent, to check that the man, a tipsy solicitor, was OK. It is this sigh that Jasper makes now, after a long intake of breath; as if, after so long, the sound has lodged deep in his lungs, and he is struggling to retrieve it. Then he moves across the car seat and kisses her, holding her shoulders with both hands; kissing her hard, as if he is looking for something. She kisses him back, willing to allow him anything; whatever he can find of value.

When Jasper moves back he begins an urgent string of confidences, rushed out as he grips her hand. She is beautiful, he tells her, with a radiant beauty, her own particular, rare beauty; he hasn't felt this way in a long time – didn't think he could or would, in fact, since his marriage – until he met her. He thinks about her all the time. He can't concentrate. He wants to take her to a hotel, if she wants to. He waits for her to answer. For the first time he looks hesitant.

When it comes to it, Kaya is surprised by her own capacity for sexual excitement. The hundreds of times she has shown herself to strangers only make the difference of this encounter sharper, more distinct. She feels keenly the significance of another's fingers rather than her own, pulling fabric up, down, off and apart, until she is unpeeled, for the first time, by someone else. She even takes pleasure in the inhuman luxury of the hotel room – with its heavy silver pen arranged at an exact angle on the leather-bound blotter (an item she has read about but never seen), its filigree chairs standing so precisely she can't bring herself to sit on one – they are lit only by tilted, silk-shaded lamps, bestowing only the most select of lights onto their suddenly naked bodies. There is something perfect in the contrast; the barbarism of sex in such a civilised room; the sweat, the cries and the shocking pains; the final, exhausting delight.

Afterwards, Jasper goes over to the window and pulls the curtain back and she is surprised to remember that it is daylight outside. The sun has dropped below the line of the trees that ring the hotel, a large Georgian manor reached by strange and twisting roads. She has had little experience of the countryside, and goes over to the window to look at the gently grassed slopes, studded with oak trees and horse chestnuts.

'It's so pretty,' she says.

'It's all landscaped,' Jasper says, coming to stand behind her. He picks up her hair and coils it neatly over one shoulder, before kissing the other shoulder. 'If it was left to itself the grass would grow up, more trees would appear, and the whole thing would turn into a wood.'

'Oh, I wish it would!' she cries, struck by this, and he laughs.

When they turn round it is impossible not to see – in the centre of the disordered sheets – the Rorschach pattern of blood in the centre of the bed.

'Your period?' he asks, not horrified as a customer would be, but with doctorly matter-of-factness.

She shakes her head.

'You're not..?'

Now he does look unsettled; at a loss in a way she hasn't seen, certainly not in the past few hours, when he was guiding her from one thing to another, a gentle, firm hand moving her leg up, or her shoulders down, smiling, but watching her with absolute composure.

'Not now,' she says.

'Good lord,' he says. He sits down on the edge of the bed and forcibly rubs his forehead with both hands, so that she can't see his expression. 'I didn't realise,' he says. 'You should have told me.'

She guesses at disappointment – even worry – but when he looks up she realises that he is moved. 'But it's nothing. It's stupid.' She knows she sounds defensive. Her arms itch to cross themselves over her body.

'Come here,' he says. She sits beside him and he holds her hand. Then, in an odd, medieval gesture quite different from his usual suavity, he brings it to his mouth and presses his lips to it, quite hard, as if wanting to get through their skin, to put teeth against bone.

'I didn't know . . . I didn't know,' he says. He keeps hold of her hand.

'You're such a rare girl. I don't want you ever to worry about anything. I'll always look after you.'

'So, I finish here in a month,' Laura tells Kaya. 'Just handed my notice in.'

They are standing in the back corridor of the Purple Tiger under the crackle and fizz of the dying fluorescent light. The night is about halfway through and music seeps through the walls, made vague by the layers of paint and plaster and brick; bricks over a hundred years old, dreaming of their past lives.

'Really?' Kaya stares at her in dismay.

'Yep. I'm graduating in the summer and I need to revise. I always planned to do Christmas and then quit. Plus I've got an internship thing in the Foreign Office when I'm finished. Three of us were picked from, like, over two hundred people. How awesome is that?'

'Congratulations,' Kaya says, trying to sound pleased.

'I think I'm done with it here anyway. Mentally, I mean. The money would still be handy. But I'm not really enjoying it these days. I don't know . . . I guess I'm a bit sick of the dynamic. It's demeaning for everyone, isn't it? We're objects. We're commodities. Not women. And the men aren't men, they're customers: stupid customers. What the hell are they doing, paying so much money just to see a pussy? I don't respect them and they don't respect me. All we are is a body and all they care about is sex. Nobody has a brain. It's got . . . depressing.'

Laura tails off, noticing a stray pubic hair at the top of her thigh and looking around for some tweezers. She pulls it out with an exclamation of triumph and turns back to Kaya.

'Oh babe. You look sad. I didn't mean to put a downer on the night. This'll be you soon anyway. You're starting uni this year, aren't you?' She pauses, and winks. '*Officially*, I mean.'

'Maybe,' Kaya says, finding a passable smile. She lingers a little behind Laura, watching her go in a haze of perfume, peppermint breath spray and vodka, one last shake of her streaming blond hair.

She is tired. Last night she slept badly, thanks to a recurring bad dream that she had no conception of dreaming, of controlling or creating; a dream that, rather, is dreaming Kaya herself, carrying her, driving her on from one scene to another; a dripping ceiling, a tower, a burnt-out bus, wheels still spinning. She is chased by a man wearing a police uniform, or a hood, carrying a machete, or sometimes a gun. Before he can get hold of her she wakes up, bathed in an acid sweat, her hands up as if to fend him off.

Kaya goes over to the mirror and looks at her face; the uncooked flesh looking anything but appetising in the greenish stutter of the light. Her eyes are half shuttered under the weight of false eyelashes and deferred sleep. She isn't in the mood for the Purple Tiger tonight; not ready to put on her hard face, with its hard smile. She wants to lie in bed with Jasper and unfold for him, new and soft. She wants him to see her properly.

The previous week a man, a young guy, tried to take her arm outside the club as she was arriving. She hadn't seen him, and it made her jump. He held on to her coat while she pushed at him. Both of them were staring at each other wide eyed, as if shocked at themselves. It only lasted a moment before the doormen ran over and pulled him away, sending him off down the street with kicks and blows. He disappeared around the corner at a run; Kaya wanted to cry 'Wait!' She wanted to ask him what he had planned to do.

After that night she makes sure she is escorted to taxis after work on the nights when Luca, who usually gives her a lift, isn't working at the bar. Especially as Carl is still at her periphery, passing in and out of her vision, loitering with intent. She doesn't know what exactly he wants from her either. He might just want to hit her for calling the police; just as the other man might simply have wanted her money or her phone. She isn't afraid of being robbed or hit, though Chloe, who once had her jaw broken by a jealous ex-boyfriend, warns her that being hit by a guy is no laughing matter. ('Even a skinny guy,' says Chloe ominously. 'Even some scrawny little bastard can knock you out. I don't know how they do it. You got to keep your eye on them, man.')

Kaya is afraid of what threatens to happen in her dreams, of Carl *sorting her out*, of the few men who come into the club alone before being identified as 'weirdos' and thrown out, of the complex shadow that passes, sometimes, across a normal man's face. She doesn't tell Jasper about her fears, because he tends to worry about her anyway; turning to her in the hotel bed, where she lies emptied out and languorous on the pillows – something almost obscene about those over-sized, overfilled pillows – and saying 'Why don't you quit that place? I don't like to think of you there.'

'What would I do otherwise?' Kaya asks. 'I need to save up to study. I'm not going to get help from my parents. Anyway, I want my own place, and I can't do that on a supermarket salary.'

'I'll pay rent. I'll get you a flat.'

'Oh, Jasper. No.'

'It'd be more sensible than hotels,' he says reasonably.

'I told you I don't need this. This place is too nice. Too expensive.'

'You're too beautiful for cheap hotels.'

It is a recurring argument, postponed rather than resolved, bought off by sex and conversation, though even the conversations now are more heavily weighted, more questioning; leading like cliff paths to sudden drops.

She and Jasper are visiting the same hotel at least once a week by this time. Now and again they vary the routine: he will have a place to show her; a village with a cricket green across which, in the summer, white figures will move stiffly like dolls; a river bank with a shaded pub garden; a spa, where she gets a massage, lying on the table feeling so loosened and undone that tears come, unwanted, into her eyes. Then there will be a hotel nearby; always expensive, though by now she is beginning to feel more at home in these surroundings. She exchanges her clothes for oversized slippers and heavy white bathrobes, operates climate-control panels, deciphers the chrome dials of the showers, rings confidently for room service. At first she claimed that she preferred room service to eating in the hotel restaurants: Jasper, correctly guessing at the real reasons behind this, bought her a dress and a pair of shoes and discreetly explained the hierarchies of cutlery and glassware. She pointed at dishes and he translated them: a confit, a fondant, a terrine. He was not disappointed by her ignorance, as she had expected him to be; instead appearing to find it charming, becoming more than usually solicitous.

It is when he is driving her home after one of these hotel visits, Jasper watching the night road, Kaya drowsing in the leather-scented heat, that he says to her, 'I wish you wouldn't work as a stripper any more.'

Still wrapped in feathery, suggestive layers of sleep, she doesn't put up her usual resistance to this idea. She smiles and says, 'Mm?'

'I want to get us a flat. I want us to live together. I'd work and you could do whatever you wanted. I'd rent somewhere at first because my wife would make things difficult – financially – if I had property. And if she knew I was with someone else she might get angry.'

'Angry?'

'She doesn't want to be with me, but she'd hate the idea of me being with anyone else. Obviously, after the divorce, we could be open and straightforward.'

Kaya is awake now, and worried. 'What about your son?' she asks.

It had taken Jasper a while to tell her about Ben, and once he did, the way he spoke about his son was strange to her: formal, self-conscious. She wonders if Jasper might be worried that the idea of a son will put her off, or else he may simply be being tactful about the subject of fatherly duties, fatherly love, in the presence of someone less well off than Ben, paternity-wise. But she suspects his discomfort is probably simpler than that; because she shares it herself. How can either of them not feel it: the timeless awkwardness of a teenage son and a teenage girlfriend?

Jasper is vague about what might happen to Ben once he and his wife are divorced. Kaya tries to imagine weekends where Ben comes to stay with them in their flat and they all play middle-class games like Monopoly and eat olives and pretend that this is a civilised arrangement. But the idea of Ben's gaze frightens her; of Kaya emerging from the room she and his father share, closing the door discreetly on the welter of sheets, the faint smell of perfume and sweat, to meet his son's eye over muesli. She'd rather a hundred private dances than one kiss in front of Ben.

'It would – realistically – be a while before you could meet,' Jasper says, and she knows his thoughts have travelled along the same route as her own. 'But after that, I suppose we'd cross that bridge when we came to it.'

'Let's not talk about all this now,' Kaya suggests. She takes the silence that follows this for agreement, but before she gets out of the car he takes her hand and says, with a seriousness that both frightens and delights her, 'Please – think about it. I love you. I can't bear to think of you out there when you could be with me. I'm only human. I can't stand it for much longer.'

Kaya thinks about this again a few nights later, lying in Chloe's and Dave's spare room (a room she will never – despite Chloe's fond protestations – think of as her own), watching the revolutions of tiny star shapes across the walls and ceiling, cast by her lamp, the yellow light cut out by the paper shade. The stars do not warm the room, in which a thick chill has settled. The heating has been cut off because Dave borrowed Chloe's bank card to buy a car to fix up. The car has since been passed to a friend of his, the money vanishing into some other shady exchange, the endless trail of swap and loan, ending with a small bag of something or other for Dave, and nothing, as usual, for Chloe. Kaya turns over in the sludgy bed and wonders if the motionlessness of the cold inside the flat is really much more preferable than the wind outside, when set against the intermittent laughter of Dave and a couple of his friends; beerish lowings, underscored by the wilfully moronic bass line of the stereo. Earlier she arrived home and walked, before she realised her mistake, into the sitting room where he sat resplendent in billowing smoke, flanked by his marble-eyed courtiers. He looked at her with both hostility and appraisal: 'Do a private dance for us then, Star.'

Kaya understands that men and women can both dislike someone and want to have sex with them, but there seems to her a greater danger when it is a man who can't decide between the two. It may simply be down to the basic mechanics of sex itself; in which, rather like a play fight, you have to trust that the more powerful of the two will play fair.

The next morning, she calls Jasper, then brings Chloe a conciliatory cup of tea and plate of biscuits, over which she tells her that she will be moving out and leaving the Purple Tiger. Chloe blinks – once, twice – then cries, the tears appearing so quickly that Kaya wonders if she had been about to cry over something else.

'I'm just happy for you,' Chloe sobs. A whole-hearted crier, she has managed to smear both her lipstick mouth and mascara eyes, so it looks as if another, blurred, face is slipping off her own. 'I really am. I knew you'd do something special. You're going to be looked after by a rich man just like we always said.'

Kaya fetches a tissue and wipes Chloe's face. 'I'm not going to sit around all day,' she says.

'Why not?' Chloe asks. 'I'll come over and we can watch MTV. You won't ditch me, will you?'

'Of course not,' Kaya says. 'Don't be stupid.'

Chloe, content with this, puts her head on Kaya's shoulder and Kaya rests her nose in the coconut-scented nest of Chloe's hair. She is aware that by attaching herself to Chloe – hopelessly open, painfully ready to love – she has found herself another Louise. Of Louise herself she has had no recent news. She hasn't spoken to Satvinder in a couple of weeks but expects that the next update will be the same as the last. Louise rarely seen outside the flat. Requests for a twenty – a tenner, a fiver – to see her through the weekend. Bailiffs at the door. Carl, still. She sighs, and Chloe lifts her head and gives her a sympathetic kiss, only slightly sticky.

The reactions at the Purple Tiger to her departure were predictably mixed. Paul was sincerely moved by the loss of his biggest-earning employee, while the other girls were mostly excited at the prospect of riches, of transformation.

'It's just like *Pretty Woman*,' cries Annie.

'I haven't seen it,' Kaya admits.

'More like *My Fair Lady*,' Venus says.

'I haven't seen that, either.'

'You've got to wonder – what's he up to?' Venus says, though – when pressed – she is unable to think of exactly what Jasper might be up to, settling instead for a raise of her eyebrows, and an ominous silence.

It is this look of Venus's that comes to Kaya's mind as she

and Jasper walk around his new apartment overlooking the river and the other brand-new buildings of the town centre. The inside of the apartment is composed of whiteness and metal and cool, fake air. Hundreds of glass windows stare back at her when she looks out of her own. She is annoyed that Venus is in her head, the cool portentous stare below the broom-like eyelashes, the glistening gold lids. She is bothered, too, that Alisha said nothing when she heard, turning her face down to the screen of her phone; an unexpected disappointment from someone she admired, whose opinion she would usually seek out. She tries to listen to Jasper now, talking about stone composites harder than stone, concealed handles, the property market.

'I got the essentials,' he tells her, meaning the leather sofa – the cold black hide of which shocks the back of her thighs when she sits on it – and the oversized television, marooned in the polar waste of glossy floor and wall. He has also picked out a feature radiator and a piece of modern art for the walls, without explaining which is which. She plans to investigate them when he is gone, back to his first home. 'We'll obviously need to decorate. Make it perfect.'

'It's perfect already,' Kaya says uncertainly.

'You won't be lonely?' he asks. He brushes a loose streak of hair out of her eyes. 'I'll be here as much as I can. Soon I can move in properly. I'm hoping there won't be too much of a fuss about my leaving . . . the situation at home really is intolerable. I think it will be better for everyone. But not everybody sees it that way.'

He always speaks about his wife that way, as if she is several women.

'What's her name?' Kaya asks.

He looks surprised. 'Alice. We don't need to talk about her, though. I'm sorry I brought her up. I don't want her to spoil this moment.'

Kaya, not having realised that this was a moment, tries to look as she imagines he would want her to look, during a moment. He smiles and kisses her. 'Will you be happy here?'

'So happy,' she says quickly. 'Thank you. I'm going to get a job as soon as I can. And go back to lectures. Then go to university properly next year.'

She hasn't been to any philosophy lectures in several weeks. Her initial delight at sneaking an hour's worth of learning, swiping an education from under the noses of the establishment, has seemed thinner, less substantial, when compared with the many splendours of Jasper's love. She knows, too – guiltily – that her time with Jasper demands less of her; less concentration, less thought. She can be simple and quiet and still be lavished with affection. Sometimes it makes her wonder if perhaps this is what life ought to be.

'There's no rush to think of something to do,' Jasper says now, as if answering her. 'Just enjoy yourself.' High spirited with largesse, he goes over to the fridge and brings out a bottle of champagne, which they barely start drinking before they discard the glasses and go to the bedroom; their two bodies making barely a dent in the white expanse of the new bed, clasping each other to create a cocoon of warmth, like a shelter dug in a snow slope; two survivors of an avalanche.

A few weeks later, in the rainy spring, Kaya is lying on the floor of the flat typing up lecture notes when Jasper arrives and smiles at her. 'Getting good use out of that?' he asks, indicating the laptop. It was paid for by him, though Kaya has a second interview at a book store in town, and intends to pay him back. These things – the laptop, the clothes, the champagne – sit weightily on her shoulders. When she lies down in bed they rearrange themselves, shifting onto her chest, ready for another uncomfortable night.

'It's great,' she says. 'Thank you.'

'What are you working on? Not more CVs? I told you not to worry about all that.'

'Actually it's those lectures on structuralism and post-structuralism. And deconstruction.'

Kaya likes this crowd: Saussure, Lacan, Derrida; the way they seek to uncouple what had been previously assumed to naturally follow, lifting meaning away from words, to reveal the spaces between. This isn't necessarily this; that isn't necessarily that. Her own instincts run towards the fluid, the ambiguous and the possible. If a line is drawn, she would like to see it rubbed out; if a statement is made, she would argue against it. She had the same sort of admiration for Plato and Kant; their insistence on the inaccessible essence of things: the fire that casts the shadows, the mysterious noumena.

'I'm writing about Saussure at the moment. You know his work?'

'At one time, probably,' Jasper says. 'But I've forgotten it. I'm going to make a coffee. Would you like one?'

'I really like the idea that words can't really capture the

essence of something. If you try to do it, something is lost. Like, Derrida got criticised – but I don't think that was fair. He was trying to protect meaning, not take it away.'

She looks up and is disappointed to see that Jasper has his back turned, apparently absorbed in the coffee machine, which he is feeding with beans. When he turns back around it is with an amused expression.

'Sorry, darling . . . I tuned out, I'm afraid. It's all just pretension really, isn't it?' he says, smiling.

Kaya sees how things are, and is quiet. But unobserved, she looks at the coffee machine with dislike.

She isn't sure quite how reasonable it is to pin her sense of things beginning to change on this object, a handsome silver-spouted steam engine of a machine, pretending to be of another, more authentic era, but she has done it anyway. It seems that after the day Jasper arrived to unpack the boxed machine ('What do you drink?' he asked, 'Cappuccino? Macchiato?' and because he expects her not to recognise the words, she pretended she didn't), she has watched the familiar territory of her happiness being eroded; its land conceded, stolen in night ambushes, or – more rarely – battled over, and lost.

She isn't sure if Jasper has the same sense of what is happening. She isn't sure of him at all, or of herself. She can't tell if he has changed, or if it is her perception of him that is different. Did he always, for example, look at her so quellingly when she mentioned university – or refer to, with an expression of contempt, the sweaty little undergraduates who would grope her, the jaded lecturers who would fail her? Did he always used to make quite so many references to his own wealth of experience: the foreign holidays, the encounters with minor gentry and local MPs, the dinner parties at the houses of his friends? He was angry when he heard that she was still meeting up with Chloe. He said that was part of her old life.

'She's a burden,' he said. 'I know that type.'

'She's been helping me. She's been teaching me to drive.'

He frowned, then appeared to decide against arguing with her. He put his hands out forgivingly.

'Come here.'

Kaya almost didn't make it to the Sartre lecture: Jasper had stayed overnight and was in the mood to lie in bed, lazily playing with her hair and hands, drawing circles around her nipples with his finger.

'Do you have to go?' he asked, rolling back in the bed. The sheet had dropped away from him and she looked at him for a moment as if he were a stranger: a shocking, fully grown man sleeping with her, Kaya, who should, in the natural order of things, be experimenting with boys right now, someone her own age; without this twenty-year-old scar on one arm from falling off a motorbike in the eighties, the dark density of chest and stomach hair, the hard, cured shoulder muscles, toughened by years of squash and tennis.

'I do want to,' she said apologetically, dodging his approaching hand and getting out of bed.

He looked at her with a great sternness, giving his

annoyance the appearance of something more substantial. 'We don't get much time like this.'

'I'm sorry,' she said, gathering her clothes and leaving the room.

When she was dressed she came back into the bedroom to say goodbye, but he was pretending to be asleep, and she left relieved that she wouldn't have to find out if she was capable of fighting for this lecture, of stealing it not only surreptitiously from the university but at gunpoint from Jasper. They have only argued outright once, when she went out with Chloe and Luca. He had warned her not to; she – thinking he was advising her rather than commanding her – had gone out anyway. The ensuing fight surprised her with its scale: a great, bombastic storm, threatening to capsize them both. She apologised just to put an end to it.

It is this lecture – the one that almost didn't happen – that changes pretty much everything for her, from the moment the lecturer dispenses with biographical detail and opens with the example of the voyeur peering through a keyhole at a couple. Only when the voyeur hears the noise of another person's footsteps behind him – and knows he has been caught out – is he ashamed. Before the other person approaches him he has not considered himself to be a voyeur: he simply *is* a voyeur. But afterwards he knows himself to be a voyeur: he has been forced to consciousness.

Sartre said that individual human consciousness consists of the 'in itself' and the 'for itself'. The 'in itself' is what we are before we think about what we are, the voyeur who has not yet been caught. The 'for itself' is the voyeur a few moments later, the consciousness that thinks about itself. Sartre said that our efforts to close the gap between the 'in itself' and the 'for itself' are impossible, because the two cannot be made to be the same thing: there is no essential human nature and, furthermore, no God.

'Sartre acknowledged that this gap, and the futility of trying to close it, can cause us great pain,' the lecturer, a young woman with red hair and a bright red mouth moving sharply in her indistinct white face, says. 'But it also means that we have freedom in that we are not predefined. We can determine ourselves and our own existence, creating our own meaning.'

At the end of the hour the lecturer says over the noise of students unzipping bags and folding their papers away, 'Listen, I have requested that Simone de Beauvoir be given her own lecture, but the powers that be say we don't have enough time for it, so all I can say is: make sure you actually *read* some of the recommended texts. De Beauvoir took what Sartre said and explicitly applied it to women. She said that there is no essential femininity. It is a social construct, and as such, it can be taken apart.'

As the lecturer is saying, 'One is not born a woman, one becomes one', the girl next to Kaya leans across and rolls her eyes and says, 'She's always got to get feminism in there somehow, hasn't she?' so that Kaya hears both at the same time and can't quite make sense of either.

Sitting on the bus home she feels almost relieved: the lecture seeming, somehow, to approve certain things that she has been up to lately, reassuring her that she has not done anything wrong, which is ridiculous because it wasn't wrong to begin with. Only her keeping it secret ever implied any sort of wrongness. But the reasons for her secretiveness are shifting, and hard to keep track of, and so she hasn't examined them.

It started when Jasper said he wanted to take her away on holiday, to the Maldives, or the Bahamas. He said he wanted her to see the sea for the first time, and she didn't correct him, not being entirely sure if she has already seen it. He had an idea of her lying on white sand. This idea necessitated Kaya travelling up to London on the train to apply for a passport, her first. On the way there, however, she had the idea that if she was going to be committed to an identity in this way, she might like to choose her own. She was not attached to Doherty, or even sure why Louise, hating her father as she often said she did, had inexplicably decided to pass his name on to their daughter without keeping it herself. Perhaps she had thought it was the proper thing to do. And then, she didn't see herself as a Kaya any more than she saw herself as Star, and Jasper always said it didn't suit her. So she decided to change the lot by deed poll.

Technically, the girl on the bus is now Estella White, though it is not yet a name she feels comfortable claiming. Neither has she told Jasper about her decision. He wasn't there when she thought of it, then later she thought it would be a nice surprise. But since then moments in which she might have told him have been and gone, and something keeps her from revealing it. The train doors open, and she refuses to board. This is a dream of hers: that she is waiting at a station as dusk falls and train after train passes. After a while, it is so dark at the platform that the people in the lit train can't see her; the doors open and close without them having any idea that someone might have got on, and didn't. She experiences the feeling of her body fading, becoming a ghost in the usual world. Without looking around she knows that if she leaves the station there will be no town, nothing but a wide, rustling forest. Somewhere out there is Estella. If Kaya hurries along the path she might see her, waiting there in the night wood, for Kaya to catch her up.

After the lecture, Kaya goes to the chemist in town to collect her prescription for the pill; also picking up – while she is there – waxing strips, panty liners and cystitis medication: the unspeakable tools of the sexually active woman. She emerges from the syrupy heat of the mall into a thinly cold day; the rain ebbing and storming with fitful malevolence, agitating the threadbare trees, blowing in sprays under her umbrella, so that she puts it back into her bag and gives herself up to the weather, letting her hair plaster itself in darkening strips over her forehead and cheeks.

As she is turning onto the path near the graveyard she sees Carl, walking in through another gate. She doesn't think he has seen her, so she puts her head down and walks faster, hoping to become only a small, vague figure by the time he has looked up. She skirts the few people making their desultory way along the path: weekday people, an old couple, a family watching their toddler teeter before them, a middle-aged woman. It is only once she is out of the graveyard and has started to breathe more regularly that she hears Carl call out, and – sick, finally, of being pursued – decides that if this meeting is going to happen it may as well happen now, in daylight and in a public space and with passers-by within shouting distance.

She stops under the awning of a coffee shop to allow him to catch her up. As she waits, the rain beating now onto the reflective pewter of the pavements, she has the opportunity to assess Carl as he approaches; hurried and flustered and wet, his stubble turning into a patchy beard and his face thinner than she remembers. The soaking of his head has revealed a thinning crown. She feels less afraid of him, seeing him so visibly fucked over by life, the weather, his own body hair.

'Kaya,' he says when he arrives. He looks for a moment as if he might be about to take her hands, so she stares at him hard until the impulse appears to leave him.

'What the fuck have you been doing, following me?' she asks. 'I've seen you. You're lucky I didn't call the police.'

'I had to talk to you. But you never gave me a chance, Kaya. It's not like I could call you, and I didn't know which flat you was living in. You working at that strip club?'

'None of your fucking business.'

'Look, I'm not judging. I can't judge nobody, can I? I just needed to talk to you. Not on the street though, Kaya. Come back with me. Just for a bit. Just to talk.'

She shakes her head, hoping she isn't going to have to fight him off. The woman she passed earlier has appeared again and is ambling past them, making for the coffee shop. Kaya wonders if a woman like her, carefully attractive, nicely clothed in coat and boots, would stop and help if Carl got hold of her. Probably she'd hurry into the coffee shop to pass the problem on to the uninterested girl behind the counter. Or, once inside, she might call the police. Then, when her friend arrived to meet her for coffee, she would tell her about it: the underclasses, brawling in the streets again. Town going downhill. Et cetera.

'Then I'll say it here, but I didn't want to do it like this,' Carl says. 'OK. You won't come back? OK. I won't argue with you. I know what you look like when you won't be swayed.'

He says this last gently enough, almost lovingly, which doesn't reassure her. 'Kaya, your mum's in the hospital. Since last week. She's got cancer – liver cancer. They reckon it was the drinking.'

'What?'

'I'm sorry. This is why I didn't fucking want to say it, on the street. She ain't got long left. They were surprised she went on this long without no treatment. She was told about it a couple of months ago but she said she didn't want treatment. Thought it would be better that way, you know, at least she had a laugh at home for a while, without dealing with all them doctors and shit, you know what I mean? I thought you'd want to know though.'

Tears have come into his eyes, 'I wanted to say sorry to you, Kaya; I know you left because of me and that weren't fair. I know I was a cunt. Your mother misses you and I don't want to be the reason you're worried about coming to see her. You got to see her. You will, won't you?'

She nods dumbly. Her body is absorbing the words; rolling into her ears before dropping, cold and hard as boulders, falling silently through her empty chest and coming to rest in her stomach. She accepts them with a sense of inevitability that is also of the body, felt as it is all through her, with the heaviness of the obvious. Of course. Of course this is what would happen, once she left Louise.

'Now?'

She nods again. He does take her hands then, and kisses them, his mouth cold against her own cold skin, in an odd echo of the kiss given to her by Jasper, which now seems much longer ago.

After that they go to the hospital, where Louise is sitting in a chair facing the window, wearing a robe, with her hair loosely pinned back, like a resident in an old people's home. There is something of old age, a soft giving up, in the position of her shoulders, her round back. It startles Kaya, this transformation, as if it erases and overwrites her own history; her images of both Louise and herself. Then Louise turns around and smiles and, despite the darkness around her eyes, the pale, drooping skin, she is her mother again, and Kaya goes to her like she used to and puts her face in her neck, inhaling a scent that is not alcohol but a sharp, thin medicinal odour that is almost the same.

Kaya spends the rest of the afternoon with Louise, arriving back at the flat only a few minutes before Jasper is due to meet her there. Mindful of her rained-on and dried-out hair, describing strange arcs and angles around her face, and her smell – or her imagined smell – of hospitals, green witch hazel and chlorine, she gets straight into the shower. She doesn't want Jasper to look at her with the distant, considering look he gets at times, and say, 'You look ruffled. I hope everything's all right?', by which he means that everything *is* all right, and so she has no business being ruffled.

But today she can't win, because she has forgotten their dinner plans, and when she gets out of the shower Jasper is waiting for her with an air of unfriendly forbearance. 'I called and delayed dinner by an hour to give you time to get ready,' he says, as she apologises.

'I got rained on,' she says. 'Sorry. I looked a mess. I shouldn't have forgotten.'

'Where were you?' he asks.

'I went into town to get some stuff,' she says, pushing the explanation at him too quickly, so that he looks at her with the beginnings of suspicion. Another thing that she didn't predict: his jealousy. He asks her who she sits with in lectures, who she has met. He wonders what she does in the flat all day – if she has people over. He calls her at odd times, with a challenging note in his voice, as if he expects to catch her somewhere she isn't meant to be.

Kaya doesn't even consider telling Jasper the truth. She feels the same about her mother's illness as she did when she changed her name: a need to stow the information away, as if – in the same way that married people preparing to leave a relationship begin siphoning off assets or hiding antiques – she is setting aside parts of herself, ready for her eventual departure. Though this departure is, as yet, too stark and abrupt to believe in, she continues to approach it tentatively: she circles it, nibbles at the edges of it. Like a bedroom light switched on suddenly in the darkness she views it through her fingers, preparing herself for the full glare.

The rain has stopped but manages to give the impression that its retreat is only temporary, so that Kaya and Jasper walk into the restaurant under a heaviness of grey, a sullen, swollen sky. It takes two doormen to usher them inside, as if they are going to prison, and might turn and run. The sound of their feet as they walk to the table vanishes oddly quickly, as if swallowed up by the thick drapes and silk-covered walls; a strange effect, as if someone has stolen their echoes. A waiter lists the specials in the monophonic style of a Gregorian chant and Kaya chooses the most rational of these without feeling any appetite. Jasper orders cocktails, amber cones glowing like stained glass, too strong for her. She sips hers and smiles and listens to him talk.

'I told him, I don't want the price that you give to everybody. I want the real price,' Jasper is saying. 'Once you let them know you understand what they're doing, they respect you.'

'Yes,' she says.

She remembers Alisha telling her that research shows men cheat for the sex and women for the conversation, but she thinks now that men can be just as susceptible to talk: their own talk, which has to be heard and admired if it is to mean anything at all. She has noticed that Jasper is a consummate bluffer: if he doesn't know an answer he makes it up; if he is told something new he nods, as if he knew it already. He becomes cold if he senses his words haven't been accorded all due respect, which, in most cases, means Kaya becoming silent and wide-eyed and generally appearing bowled over by what-ever comment he might have made on the weather, the nature of capitalism, or the failure of the increasingly unpredictable coffee machine to make a decent espresso. She absents herself from the present conversation (which has segued into a run-down of the various crimes of Robert, his fat and incompetent colleague) and returns to the time she spent with her mother. When she put her face against Louise's, even the bone of her mother's skull felt delicate under the lax, silky skin, though surely it couldn't have been affected by her illness. Can bones waste away? Her head felt like porcelain, like an eggshell.

'I'm sorry,' Louise said. 'I'm so sorry, Kaya. I wasn't thinking straight. You were right about everything.'

'I don't care about being right.'

They didn't talk about the illness. They talked about the past. Having finally learned the art of absence, Carl went out to get them drinks from the machine. When he came back to find them still talking about Kaya's year 3 art project, Satvinder's cut lip from falling off a swing, and the pigeon that got into the flat, he sat in a corner chair and fell easily to sleep. Kaya turned her polystyrene cup around in her hands, marking it in an elaborate, nervous pattern with her nails.

'You talk very nicely now, love,' Louise observed, without suspicion or reproof. 'And don't you look lovely? You were always beautiful, I know, the most beautiful girl in your class. Now you look . . . expensive. You look like you're making money.'

Kaya glanced at Carl, his eyes closed, his mouth peaceably agape, wondering if he had told Louise about her new line of work, but Louise asks next; 'Have you got a job, sugar cloud?'

'Yes. Um, it's sort of admin.'

'Oh, that's good. It doesn't matter what it is, does it? So

long as it's your own money. It's your freedom in this horrible world. It's the only freedom you get.'

Kaya realises that Jasper has paused and is looking at her with annoyance, Kaya having presumably missed a cue to agree with him.

'You seem tired,' he says, accusingly.

'I'm sorry,' she says. 'I was just thinking how unfair it is, that you have to work with someone like Robert. It's beneath you.'

He is gratified; the uncomfortable moment, scratchy in the air between them, passes. She thinks that was a cheap thing for her to do: reverting to the conversational tricks of the strip club; tricks she had at first thought he would see through immediately. But it turns out he isn't so different from the other, less well-put-together men, the crude and wrinkled and fat and unruly. He is not so rare, in the end.

The food arrives and she picks up her cutlery to start, not without a quick internal check, making sure she has the right ones. Jasper watches her with a small smile; a complicated smile. He leans his head back and examines the view from the window; the hard shapes of the town. The rain starts to fall again. She eats, her hands moving with the knife and fork like trained animals, following the correct routine.

It all comes to an end with Kaya and Jasper, of course, but not in the way that she expects. She spends the next week visiting her mother in hospital every day. She has been told that the doctors can't do anything but manage Louise's pain.

She is to be moved, soon, to a hospice, so that her hospital bed can be given to someone more promising. Kaya looks up the particulars of her mother's illness when she gets home. Liver cancer. Usually discovered after it is too late to cure. Linked, unsurprisingly, to alcoholism. A rare condition in a relatively young woman.

'Rare,' she says aloud. The word dissolves into the impassive silence of the flat.

Sometimes she is home when Jasper arrives, sometimes she isn't. She has continued to lie to him about her whereabouts, becoming increasingly careless with her excuses. A good lie takes thought, and she doesn't have the energy to construct something realistic.

'You're going for a lot of walks lately,' he observed yesterday, frowning.

'I told you, I can't stay here all day. I'm going to go mad,' she said; adding, to distract him, 'What I need is a job.'

When did she stop loving Jasper? She wonders this vaguely, not interested enough to pursue it to a conclusion. She knows she is going to leave him, but right now she can't summon up the energy for it; the necessary impetus to pull free. She hopes that he will get tired of her – her silences, her lame excuses – and let her slip out of the relationship like someone excusing themselves from a lecture early, mouthing apologies and sidling towards the door, provoking raised eyebrows, but no outright opposition. She knows that it isn't going to happen that way. It won't be easy, it won't be clean, and so she holds off. She stops sleeping. She feels an old despair untying itself inside her; in her room at night she pulls her hair, silently, feeling the electrical pain penetrating her numbness.

On Saturday morning, while Jasper is at his other home, she gets a call from the hospital: Louise has taken a turn for the worse. The tone of the voice on the phone is gently urgent. She isn't sure, later, if they actually said it, or if it was simply understood that she would be saying goodbye. When she arrives, Carl is there too, sitting rumpled and dismantled in a chair next to the bed, and she finds she doesn't mind him being there. The room is dim; spring soaking palely through the windows. One of the fluorescent lights has broken, unnoticed.

Louise isn't conscious when Kaya arrives. Her face is folded in between stiff white sheets as if to demonstrate how far from white her skin is now; yellowed like parchment, like an old book. Her hair is damp and lies on the pillow in pale ribbons. Her eyes open from time to time, revealing the discoloured whites like stained china. Her lips move: the involuntary discourse of deep sleep. Kaya wonders what her mother is dreaming about. It occurs to her that maybe she could influence Louise's dream, soothing her, the way hypnosis tapes are supposed to. She leans down and murmurs into Louise's ear.

'Hello, Mum. It's me, Kaya. We're at the beach in the sun. We have ice creams. Remember that day? You always said you didn't, but you can now. See it? I'm looking through the pebbles. You're wearing your white sunglasses, and you're looking out to sea.'

There is no sign that Louise has heard her. The hand lying in her own, lightly curled, is as motionless as before. She straightens up.

'She's going to heaven,' Carl said hoarsely. She looks at him: his eyes are closed hard, crunched deep into the sockets with a child's strenuous resistance, tears struggling through the crevasses and ravines of the crumpled lids.

Time passes. Kaya sits beside her mother without moving, as if moving might do some mysterious and irreparable damage. She shakes her head when a voice asks her if she wants to take a break, to have a walk. She takes the water that is handed to her with no idea who has brought it.

It is evening when Louise opens her eyes next, to stare up through the ceiling. Kaya and Carl start and lean over. Both of them are expecting something – last words, perhaps, a moment of recognition – but, without turning her eyes to either side, Louise dies. Her lips sag, her eyes become flat. The horrified look vanishes from them, but Kaya knows it was there, and that Carl is wrong; because wherever her mother was going, whatever she was seeing, it was not heaven.

Carl takes longer than Kaya to understand the situation. When he does he sobs. The loud noise of his crying passes back and forth between the pale green walls of the room; it fills her head, leaving no room for her own thoughts. She can only sit numbly, wide eyed and dry eyed, patting his arm.

After Kaya leaves the hospital, she does not feel the expected weight of grief but a lightness and emptiness that is more terrible; as if she were a helium balloon no longer held by anybody's hand, cut loose, sailing upwards into the edgeless, soundless void. She stands outside the flat, which she does not want to go back to, looking up at the tall front appearing to be from another century, the gleaming yellow bricks and black railings outside the brand-new windows. She finds her own window, without really considering it to be her own. It is just a window, beyond which Jasper might be waiting, or perhaps not. There is a light on, which indicates that he is probably inside.

She walks in through the underground car park and notes the presence of his car, its muscular silver curves occupying every inch of the allotted space. Out of habit, she starts thinking of an excuse to present to him. Then she understands that she isn't going to give him an explanation today. She will go inside and tell him she loved him once, but she doesn't any more. Then she will pack her clothes, scrupulously separating the things he has bought her from those she has bought herself, and go to a hotel for the night.

Strange how it is her mother's death that has, finally, brought an end to her inertia. It is as if Louise's departure, the soul abruptly decanted from its casing, has hollowed Kaya out too, leaving a wide, clear, inhuman space inside her, her body arranged around this central vacuum like a suit of armour. There is a kind of will there; not an active force, but something still and cold and infinitely capable. It has suspended her exhaustion, her guilt at upsetting him, her loyalty to his love if not her own. It will allow her to clear everything away, after which time she can sit down, alone, and try to puzzle it all out.

PART THREE

c

ALICE

When Alice gets home from an unsuccessful stake-out of Star's street, the sun is out, sparkling in a sky sluiced clean by rain, its cheery light kaleidoscoped by the dropleted windows of the house. The pebbles of the driveway glisten like a river bed. When she gets inside and closes the door the colours of its stained-glass panels are painted across the wall, casting their lovely ghosts over her hands and face. She stands for a moment before hanging up her coat, listening to the faint noises of the empty house: the subterranean music of its antique pipes, the plink and sigh of the cast-iron radiators, the hum of the dimmer switches, the occasional yawn of a floorboard.

Alice isn't sure whether it is quite right, morally, to take so much sustenance from a house; to walk in and look it over with such an enjoyable sense of possession. Jasper barely notices it until it demands his attention with a sudden, decisive failure: a leak in the guttering, a smoking chimney, a central-heating crisis. Then he says they ought to move to a modern place, with an energy efficiency rating and right-angled ceilings. At first when he said it she felt panicked, and would argue the side of their own house in terms he could appreciate:

its accumulating value, the original features that can only be more prized as time goes on, the unique character that will always impress their visitors. Then she realised that Jasper has no real intention of moving, beyond these occasional outbursts, which she has learned to sympathetically ignore.

The past few months have taken some of her pleasure in the house away, it having been the site of so many silences, broken only by the quick violence of an argument. She has wondered if the house will somehow absorb this tension, cooling and petrifying in its bones, but now, alone together in the sun, the two of them can share a sigh and a raised eyebrow, and their intimacy is re-established.

By the time Ben gets home from school Alice is almost happy again, blending fruit into a mulch-coloured smoothie which Ben eyes sceptically, reminding her suddenly of Jasper.

'Honestly, it's really good,' she says. 'You shouldn't judge on appearances.'

'Why not? Everyone else does,' Ben says, sounding much older.

'That's not true,' lies Alice. 'Oh, that North Pole documentary is on tonight. We can watch it if you don't have computer game commitments.'

'It's funny how you say "computer game",' Ben says, tolerantly. 'I do want to watch the documentary.'

Alice aims her face at the fruit peelings, feeling painfully grateful. Ben is the love of her life, but she doesn't want to weigh him down with it; trying to be light and make jokes, occasionally giving in and hugging him too long or too tightly, or gazing at him with a tear in her eye when he's asleep or absorbed in his homework, vulnerable neck bent over his diagram of the human heart. She has to make sure he doesn't find out the extent of her dependency on him, and become worried, or prematurely tough, under the new responsibility.

Less than a week later, Ben arrives home from school, ebullient and shy, to ask if George can come for dinner at their house. 'You have to make something nice, Mum. Make burgers and chips. Why don't we have a deep-fat fryer? Mark's family have a deep-fat fryer.'

'Mark's family do a lot of things we don't do,' Alice says, thinking of Mark's mother at the school gates in her pyjamas, the ever-changing but always broken cars parked on their front lawn. She catches herself, hearing the coolness of her tone, and issues a stern warning: don't turn into your mother, Alice.

'Have you invited her already?'

'Yes, and she said yes. She said why's it been so long. I said Dad's often grumpy, but he hasn't even been here much, so we wouldn't be eating dinner with him anyway.'

Alice looks startled at Ben but he has no idea of it, slinging his schoolbag triumphantly onto the stairs and heading down the hallway, calling back to her, 'And chocolate sundae for pudding.'

Alice picks up the schoolbag and takes it to the cupboard. She thinks about the love breaking out around her, flaring in the dreams of the people living in her house. Ben, planning his American diner-style romance. And – less endearingly – Jasper, for whom love is blooming behind high walls, in a late garden of nightingales, the scent of lilies, the unblinking moon. Alice doesn't stop herself imagining Jasper and Star together, trying to guess at whether he carries out his usual routines (but with more passion, and more tenderness, than she has seen in a while) or whether he has thrown away the map altogether and gone into the wilderness. The worst thing is the idea of him going down on Star: an image that comes to her mind at odd times – over the potato peelings, while driving, when plucking her eyebrows – in careful detail. The intimacy of it is too much: she looks, turns her eyes away, looks back again, at the raised thighs of Star, clasped tightly in his arms; watching with a mixture of pain, envy, and – at times – uneasy arousal.

The problem is that Star is designed to preoccupy the mind. She means to be watched and wanted. She could have been a model, but she is a stripper. She could have dated someone her own age – gone to the cinema, held hands in parks, played spin the bottle – but she prefers a life slipping in and out of hotel rooms with Jasper. She has rejected the easy equality of her peers for the older man's heavy love, his grave declarations of intent. Star is not an ordinary creature; she is a woman seen often in film and fiction but rarely in life (though which came first, the art or the living woman, Alice doesn't know): a femme fatale. Alice thinks about her own cinematic self and finds it depressingly simple to identify. A deceived wife. A *hausfrau* on the edge. An ordinary woman, with moments of desperation.

Unfortunately for Alice and her increasingly wild-looking stalking companion (who she had, for no real reason, begun to think of as John – latterly softening into Johnny, as her sympathy for him increased), Star has gone. Neither of them know where. Johnny stands on his corner, fiddling boredly with his phone or the crotch of his jeans; she sits in her car, and they wait. But Star hasn't come out of her flat or the Purple Tiger for nearly a fortnight, and each day Alice and Johnny have to give up, moving away in their different directions, he to the west and she to the north, under the same cloud of bafflement and sadness. She almost wants to exchange a look with him – maybe a disbelieving 'What the hell?' or a more rueful 'Ain't life a bitch' – because he doesn't know that he isn't alone, whereas Alice at least has the comfort of their strange solidarity.

Jasper's behaviour hasn't changed – his bags packed upstairs for a golfing weekend in Scotland – so she assumes the affair isn't over yet. Finally, she gives in, hires a car again and follows him from work, her wet palms sliding on the steering wheel, shrinking behind her large sunglasses and wool hat whenever their cars end up too close together.

Jasper's car starts off impatiently – hastening through orange lights, refusing to wave old ladies across the road – before getting trapped in the traffic of the town centre, the cars that turn, here, into a mindless herd, pushing their noses forward, crowding each other. He appears to be heading for the turn-off to the motorway, and she thinks for a moment that he might be going to Scotland after all, but then he extricates himself from the snarled anarchy of a roundabout and slips off down a road that leads to the canal, and a newly built enclave of luxury apartments. It is a while before she can get off the roundabout herself, and all she sees when she does is the tail end of his car, disappearing into the underground car park below one of the flat blocks, the gates closing behind him. This is the moment Alice knows she is about to be left.

After that day, she exists in a state of fright, watching the clock and watching Jasper. The most likely times for a confession, she believes, are the lull between Jasper getting home from work and having dinner, and the hour or so after Ben has gone to bed, once he is left to face another night with his wife. During dinner would be cruel, after dinner would be crass. Late night might be when he feels most ready to speak, but then the practical issues – of sleeping in the spare room, of the possibility of being discovered there by Ben in the morning – would deter him. The moment of arriving in the house seems like the most likely, after a day away from her in which he can gather up all his objections to their marriage, to practise aloneness, ready to push it all at her when she calls a greeting from the kitchen. But then Ben is usually around, with a slightly uncertain, 'Hello, Dad', almost as if he, too, is waiting for the big announcement. Alice doubts Jasper would tell her when Ben is home, though he might be tempted to use Ben's presence to enforce reasonableness – or at least volume control – in Alice; to rein in what he perceives as her extravagancy of emotion.

The days pass; every evening that goes by without him leaving making the next more unbearable. She wonders what is delaying him. He has bought his executive home, and installed a suitably upgraded female within it. All he has to do now is break the news to Alice, and make the twenty-minute journey to his new life. In the meantime, she watches with interest the changes in Jasper's behaviour towards Ben. Previously, Jasper had only paid occasional, heavily overdone attention to his son, which often ended in confusion and misunderstanding. The time, for example, that he decided to help Ben with his biology homework ('the only benefit of having a doctor dad, eh?'), but wasn't familiar enough with the curriculum or Ben's level of comprehension, and spoke too complicatedly about the heart, until he realised that Ben was doodling in the margins, and snapped, 'You'll never get it if you don't bloody listen', so that Ben flushed and dropped the pen.

But now Jasper makes more frequent efforts, with an awkward obsequiousness that Ben detects and is as wary of as his father's previous impatience; retracting, turning silent, becoming ever more frustrating, as Jasper presents him with a new football or a pair of trainers. Alice isn't sure how much of Jasper's attentiveness is guilt and how much is prudence; an awareness that these efforts might be remembered when Ben's home is cracked messily in two like an egg, and it will be up to him to decide which is the good half, and which is the bad. But no – Alice corrects her thoughts here – this isn't really the truth of the analogy. The truth is that when an egg breaks a chick will be spilled out; too soon to hatch into the new, harshly bright world, too early to cope with its coldness.

With this comes the memory of her own broken home; of the seven-year-old Alice sitting outside in the garden watching starlings quarrel over the crusts of her sandwich, unbothered by the velvety drizzle of rain that misted her face, fogging her vision into a grey wash, pierced by the sharp heads and wings of the birds, quick as bronze darts. The door to the kitchen had several steps down to the garden. Alice, sitting at the bottom of these, must have been out of the sightline of her parents standing at the table, facing each other in a long-since calcified stalemate. They were quiet but audible, allowing her a developing sense of their conversation: from her first assumption that they were arguing about what to do with dinner ('Who do you think puts the food on the table?') to the realisation that they were talking about divorce, and, more specifically, custody of her ('She's not exactly difficult') to the final understanding that they were batting her back and forth between each other, trying to keep her in the air, in a protracted, panicked rally ('How do you expect me to look after her?').

That night young Alice lay awake until four o'clock in the morning, according to the smiling face of her cat-shaped alarm clock, when she decided to get up and walk around the house. She was pretending that she was still asleep, and probably was still partly asleep, because her memories of this circuit have both the oddly coloured, slow-motion precision of a dream, and its lack of sense or connection. She remembers seeing the sun in one window and the moon in another. She remembers pouring herself a glass of squash to hold up as an explanation if she were to be caught out of bed, but they never had squash in the house; she didn't taste its poisonous sweetness until a later party at a friend's house, when it gave her a headache.

Alice ended up in the dining room, holding a decanter of port. The curtains were drawn and it was very dark, the air still and soundless, smelling faintly of cigarette smoke from after dinner. She could see her hands only in outline, the bottle a dulled silver, like lead. She took out the stopper and tipped the decanter so that it lay on its side, standing back and holding her nightdress out of the way as the port rushed out, gulping loudly for air like a dying red fish. It occurred to her that someone in the quiet house might hear it, but by that time it was all over; only a trickle left in the bottle. Port all over the beautiful Persian carpet; blood everywhere. Dizzy and elated, she crept back upstairs to bed.

In the morning, as her parents argued over whether an animal could have got in, or whether there was such a thing as ghosts, or whether Tamara resented Edward so much that she would tip away his 1950 vintage Taylor's just to spite him, or whether Edward did it himself in order to blame Tamara and have even more to bitch about, Alice reassessed her career as a madwoman. She remembered the old woman at her tap recital, saying 'blood and bandages', and the thought frightened her. Hearing the scratch of the wild at the door, she resolved to make it fast; to turn back to the known, whether it welcomed her or not.

Alice doesn't follow Star any more. She can't. Parking in the town centre is an impossibility, and there is nowhere to sit unobserved in the sparse, newly implanted landscaping around the small square of yellow brick faux-Georgian flats. And it appears that Star is no longer working at the Purple Tiger; Jasper obviously having had enough of sharing her graceful body with the drooling masses. But though Alice doesn't see Star, she isn't without her. The girl has moved from her foreign world of closed doors and night streets into the more intimate confines of Alice's head. Asleep and awake, Star's face is her

mind's screensaver. Her beauty like contained energy; the absolutely flat loveliness of her eyes, her blank pale radiance, as if
she really is a star – not a blazing star of the night, but a cool
star, a star underwater, or suspended in ice. Alice has given up
trying not to think about her at night and falls asleep with the
girl the last thing on her mind. She imagines Star making her
own preparations for bed; what she might do with Jasper, what
she might do in his absence. Call someone else up; change the
sheets afterwards, on her brand-new bed.

It is ironic that Alice, consciously quitting her pursuit of
Star, runs into her by chance outside the mall, where she has
been buying a tea-cup to replace one that got broken. She
wonders why she is bothering to locate the same type of
tea-cup, to make up a more pleasingly even set of eight, when
realistically she has no idea when in the future she will be
pouring tea for eight people again. Jasper could even claim
the tea-cups, or half of them, in the divorce. Star might express
an idle appreciation for this sort of charmingly hand-painted
crockery, and her wish will be his command.

She walks back through one of the town's graveyards,
following the paved path through the cenotaphs and grave-
stones, leaning rakishly in different directions. Dense rain has
been forecast for today but the weak grey sky manages only
a peevish drizzle, swirled and swept up by the wind into her
downturned face. She hurries her pace and glances up only
occasionally to check she isn't about to walk into someone,
when, on her second or third check, she realises that she has
been overtaken by Star, also umbrella-less, her own face turned
down, and apparently in more of a hurry.

Alice automatically switches focus and sets off after Star, who has abandoned her large coat on the worst of all possible days and is now wearing a denim jacket rapidly spotted with rain-drops. Her long legs are apparent now; exactly as perfect as Alice has imagined them to be. When they are almost out of the graveyard, the reason for Star's haste becomes apparent: Johnny is running after her, his hair disordered, parka flapping.

'Wait!' he shouts as he passes Alice, nearly knocking her over.

Star has got too far down the next street for Alice to see her expression, but when she hears the call she looks around, and stops still for a moment, like a cat hesitating on the road as a car approaches, deciding which way to run. Then she appears to abandon the idea and simply stands there, her hands loose at her sides, as if resigned to the inevitability of their meeting. When Johnny reaches her, he stands directly between her and Alice, almost proprietary; almost in conscious-ness of having won the strange competition between the two hunters, claiming his victory by blocking Star from view.

Alice approaches the two hurriedly now, but the rain blown into her eyes by the sly wind, the noise of traffic and sudden pigeon flights, their wings clattering like flapping tarpaulin, and the way the two are talking – closely and quietly, as if discussing something of grave importance – mean that she can't make out anything of their conversation until she is within a couple of feet of them.

'Come back with me,' Johnny is saying as she passes them, as slow-paced as she can plausibly be. 'Just for a bit. Just to talk.' He sounds anguished; his voice emerges like the groan of an injured wildebeest, staggering under the weight of a lion.

Now she is near the two of them Star's eclipsed face reappears, as expressionless as usual. She doesn't glance at Alice, though Alice herself must be staring at her; her nerves alive with proximity, her heart quickened with the edgy flare of adrenalin.

Star doesn't answer Johnny: she only shakes her head. It seems Alice won't hear her voice after all, though she longs to know, finally, where Star comes from; to find out whether she has a feline, sexy voice, to match her job, or a hard, cool one, to match her face. But Star isn't tempted to add anything more to her decisive head shake, and Alice is forced to carry on her slow passing-by, entering the coffee shop Star and Johnny have conveniently stopped beside, overlooked by its large glass window. As she does she hears the man say; 'Then I'll say it here, but I didn't want to do it like this. OK. You won't come back? OK. I won't argue with you. I know what you look like when you won't be swayed', and in that short time managing to cram in various different tones, from distressed to cajoling to finally, maudlinly affectionate.

Alice, inside the coffee shop, watches them through the window. Johnny, who is facing Alice, takes Star's hands and kisses them. He looks like he might be crying, though it is hard to tell, his face already dropleted with rain.

'Are you all right there?' the pink-aproned woman behind the counter asks Alice – smiling even though Alice has turned around irritably, with what must be flustered and fiery-eyed avidity – and, as there is no queue and Alice can't stand stubbornly in the doorway as if holding a bus, she has to smile back and order a latte, and by the time she makes it back to the window, Star and Johnny have both gone.

Alice knows she ought to end their marriage before Jasper does; out of self-respect, or pride, or something (she has lost sight of exactly what it is she would be saving or protecting, and what the point of that might be), but she can't do it. She had been hopeful, before, that Jasper would get over this latest infatuation. His buying Star a new flat was a blow, yes, but it didn't take Alice long to make up a new hope: that once Star got more settled – more *herself* – Jasper would realise that she was after his money all along. Alice glimpses a future in which she gets him back in the end and it is all for the best: his crisis will turn out to be life changing, he will be sorry, and appreciate her more, their marriage will be stronger – maybe even stronger than that of a happy couple, who haven't had to work for their happiness. She thinks: what's love if it isn't tested? What's wisdom if it isn't experienced? She thinks she might be able to say to people: 'It made us realise how much we meant to each other.' It will be something they went through together.

At times she hates herself for manufacturing these happy endings, but she can't help it. She still believes that he will realise he is making a mistake, and that if she delays for long enough, he might realise before he asks her for a divorce. She would like to make it harder for him by being sweet, but the distance between them is now so wide and impassable that her presenting him with some freshly baked biscuits, or even saying 'I love you', would seem almost surreal, and it is far more natural for Jasper to come downstairs and say, as he does a week later, 'Alice, I think we both know we can't go on like this.'

It is a Saturday morning and she is sitting in the kitchen in front of an uncooked chicken and a recipe book. Ben is out, kayaking with George. Alice's first thought is how carefully timed Jasper's announcement must have been. The chicken can go back in the fridge, and he'll have his things together and himself out of the door before Ben gets home. 'I feel awful being the one to say it,' Jasper continues, 'but I can't imagine you've been happy, either.'

'Well, no,' Alice says, 'but I don't want a divorce. Is that what you want?'

Without answering immediately, Jasper sits down opposite her. He reaches for her hands. He looks both noble and careworn. In the early sunlight his face blurs slightly with brightness, as if he has been beatified by his many sacrifices, in the name of selfless love. He is still handsome, painfully so.

'I just don't feel the same any more, Alice. I've really tried to give it time but I have to be honest. It's not your fault. I still respect and love you. But not in the way that you deserve.'

'OK,' says Alice.

'I think we've turned into friends, haven't we, really?' he says, his tone gently marvelling, at the unpredictability of life. Then he continues without waiting for her to reply; 'And we can deal with this like adults. Have one of those civilised divorces. We can be friends and it will be better for Ben – you can, of course, have custody. I wouldn't challenge that.'

'Right.'

'And you can have the house. I'll move out.' He looks at her expectantly, presumably wondering if she is going to cause a fuss.

'To a flat?'

Jasper looks slightly thrown by this. 'Yes, probably.'

'Then, after a decent period, I suppose we'll both start dating again,' Alice says. Jasper is starting to frown now. 'And then, when it seems appropriate, Ben will be introduced to your stripper girlfriend.'

Jasper drops her hands as if they are rats. 'What are you talking about?'

'Oh, for God's sake, Jasper, don't bother lying.'

Jasper pauses, as if making a series of minute calculations, then complies. 'So you found out, I suppose, and kept it to yourself. What were you planning? To take me to the cleaners? Have you been amassing evidence?'

Alice looks at him silently. It occurs to her that she isn't crying: outrage has suspended usual production at her tear-ducts. She sees his face lit up by the sun, shining on his holy mid-life crisis, and she wants to strike a blow.

'She's the one who'll take you to the cleaners. She's a *child*. What do you think she sees in you besides money? You look good for your age but to a twenty-something you're just a bag of bones. Over forty is like another world to her. You're making a fool of yourself.'

He stands up angrily, not to leave, but to move a few steps back, giving them both space to throw their verbal projectiles.

'You have no idea what she's like. Not everyone judges people by age and looks.'

'Says the man who's fucking a beautiful young girl.'

At this Jasper opens his mouth, then closes it again, with a look that she recognises as both pitying and – unbearably

– distinctly smug. Alice stands up, pushing her chair back so hard it gives a startled squeal.

'You're not her only lover. Do you know that? If "lover" is the right word. You're not her only john.'

'What?' Jasper says, the unbearable expression sliding abruptly off his face, leaving a blank, confused screen, like the static of a television between channels.

'I followed her. I wanted to know who you were leaving me for. I saw her with another man and he very obviously wasn't a family member. Not unless she has a seriously fucked-up family.'

'Who? When?' Jasper recovers himself, and accuses: 'You're lying to spite me. You can't bear to see me finally in love.'

The accuracy of this makes Alice even angrier. Her fingers curl up; her mouth twitches. She can't allow him to find his smug expression again: she has to run him out of his known territory, send him panicked into the woods.

'Ask her about her afternoon clinch with a sexy rough-and-ready type by the graveyard. He isn't even the only one, you know. Yours wasn't the only car I saw her hopping into at night after she'd finished her shift.'

Jasper is looking at her now with the beginnings of disruption in his face, the capsizing of its embattled dignity, like a galleon running into rocks, breaking up, swallowed by the roar of the sea. She continues, 'Just ask her about it. I'm not going to try to convince you. I don't particularly care if you believe me. I just think it's so perfect – it's so *fitting*. My not believing that our marriage was over, you not believing that you're one of many. What a sorry bloody pair.'

Jasper turns away from her. He doesn't move. She can tell he is thinking about everything that has happened between him and Star in the last few months; looking for the small time slips, the delays and silences. Because he believes Alice, who has never lied about anything in her life. Jasper is the liar; Alice is the predictably moral one, sticking doggedly to the straight and narrow, the boring old truth. He really loves this girl, and now Alice has – without really believing it could be done – broken his heart, which she had wanted so much to win back.

She sees herself as Pyrrhus looking over the long grey wasteland of his triumph, breathing smoke. She stands over the end of a man; the strips of tissue like streamers, attached to the bones, flapping loose. There is a small thing in the wreckage, a smouldering black lump of coal. If she were to pick it up, it would burn her. If she ate it, it would taste of ashes. Funny how this epic fuck-up seems to inspire epic imagery. Perhaps it is the only appropriate way to consider the downfall of a tragic hero like Jasper. A beautifully shaped head to survey a battlefield; cannon fire and bayonets in the stern line of his shoulders, still facing away from her.

'Jasper?' she ventures. Her anger has gone, as quickly and unpredictably as it arrived.

Jasper doesn't answer, or even allow her a glimpse of his expression. He walks so quickly to the door that by the time he is out of it she has only just understood the fact of his leaving. There doesn't seem any point in going after him. He is a master of the hurried reverse out of the drive, the gravel-scattering exit. She hears it now, followed by the receding roar of his engine, descending the hill towards the centre of town. She pushes her stray chair back under the table, closes the recipe book, and puts the chicken back into the fridge.

What Alice has forgotten is that this is the date of George's visit, ringed by Ben on the calendar she hasn't thought to consult, so that the first reminder she has of the plans for the day are the faint sounds of Ben's enthusiasm on the front step. 'Home!' he cries, happily unaware of how *unheimlich* his home has become in his absence. Alice stands up quickly, as if caught napping on sentry duty, and stares panicked around herself for evidence of things not being as they should be. But the kitchen is clean, the house tidy, and the blanketing numbness that settled over her like a dust sheet after Jasper bolted has left her in the same pristine condition; dressed, hair combed, unspotted by tears.

The afternoon passes in a strange, slow-moving stupor for her, as if they are all underwater. She watches the movements of mouths and hands with a mindless clarity, finding it hard to harness any meaning to them beyond the most basic sense. Her impressions are sluggish to arrive and to leave, something that is most apparent when meeting George; a friendly girl with hair the dark ember colour of a red panda and round, dark eyes, so that Alice is ready to think of her as a shy tree-creature, and is startled at the racket of her shoes on the floorboards, her sudden raucous laugh.

Neither George nor Ben appear to find anything unusual in Alice herself, and it occurs to her to be grateful for the basic law of the young: one new child and the adults are wallpaper. Ben, who might have noticed her mood if he were alone, looks at her today with fond indifference, and George absorbs it as if Ben's mother is always like this, a knackered virago, burnt out by some mysterious conflict; making only wan attempts to join the conversation. When Alice tells them she forgot to prepare lunch and will order pizza, they are delighted. As soon as Ben has prised a promise of biscuits out of her he is on his way out of the kitchen, pulling George upstairs to play Call of Duty with unseemly haste.

Once the bedroom door is closed on the strafing and sniping of the video game, Alice sits down and allows herself ten minutes of crying. Afterwards she holds her hands against her eyes, soothing the inflamed lids with the chill of her fingers. She wonders whether, across town, Jasper or Star might be crying, in argument or reconciliation. She can't really believe it of either of them. She has never seen Jasper cry, not even last year when he told her his father had been diagnosed with a slow-burning form of cancer, and nor can she imagine Star's affectless Noh mask buckling or leaking, disrupted by the arrival of emotion.

Jasper doesn't come back that day. Alice eats pizza with Ben and George, drops George back to her mother's, harries Ben to do his homework, goes up to check on him, finds him asleep surrounded by books, tidies the room, pulls the duvet over him and switches off the light. Then she pours herself a glass of wine and sits staring through the television until midnight comes, when she tips her untouched wine back into the bottle, and goes to bed.

At about six in the morning, she is woken by the sound of Jasper coming home. Her first feeling is a near-nauseous delight, an unhealthy lurch of hope, echoing in her empty stomach like a heavy bell tolling. When the bedroom door opens she switches on the lamp, which reveals that Jasper is a mess. His hair is a forgotten garden, his eyes hide in dark pools. His shirt is tucked in but creased so extensively it could only have been slept in. He looks at her, for possibly the first time, with open grief.

Thinking blurrily that this devastation might have some relevance to her, Alice sits up and says, 'Jasper,' with all the compassion with which the two syllables can be invested, 'what are you doing?'

Jasper raises his hands. Distress, which has made his face older, has had the opposite effect on his body, now fallen into the awkward honesty of a boy. His gesture reminds her for a moment of Ben.

'I don't know,' he says.

'It doesn't have to be like this,' she says, rushing into the silence. 'Jasper . . . can't we make it work?'

When he looks at her with a comprehensive, absolute blankness, as wide as it is deep, she realises her mistake. He is confused by an offer that is irrelevant to the point of surreal, appearing to him like a stuffed flamingo on a golf course, or a shit placed neatly in the middle of a desk. She understands finally that he has no love for her any more. He isn't divided or conflicted, pushed and pulled helplessly between two women, only one prod away from settling back into his marriage. All he wants is Star; all he can think about is her betrayal.

'I only came to get some things,' he says.

She pulls the sheets up to her neck and watches as he takes

down a holdall and puts in clothes hurriedly. There is no method in his packing, which is unusual. His haste makes him clumsy: something else she hasn't seen before. He stubs his toe on the bed and hardly notices.

'Where are you staying?' she asks.

'I don't know. A hotel. In town.'

Alice lowers her voice, in case Ben has woken up. 'What are we going to tell Ben?'

Jasper doesn't look up, taking handfuls of socks and putting them in the holdall. He answers distractedly, 'You can tell him.'

Alice looks at him in disbelief.

'You shit,' she says, quietly.

Jasper doesn't even appear to hear her, such is his hurry. Once he finishes filling the bag he leaves the room, still without looking at her. She turns out the light and listens to the noise of his packing things in his study, the thin light of his presence greying the darkness under the door. As the room refills with silence she becomes aware that there is a car engine running outside. She moves the curtains aside and sees a taxi waiting, its headlights cutting out incandescent shapes in the rain. Jasper comes out of the house with his holdall, two coats draped over one arm and his laptop under the other, bowed by the weight, or the rain, or loss; she can't tell. He gets into the taxi and it pulls away.

Alice, focussing on the wrong thing to the very last, finds the brain space to wonder why Jasper hasn't driven his own car. He didn't look drunk. Abandoned, gutted, eviscerated like a church awaiting demolition – but not drunk. Perhaps he has been tricked or robbed by Star and her shady small-hours friends. Or he has had an accident, led off the road by love.

Of course, it is more likely that the car simply has a mechanical fault and wouldn't start. She wonders if he will take it to their usual garage, owned by a friend of Alice's, which could cause awkwardness. Then at last the main thing – the end of her marriage – stands before her, stark naked and staring, and she puts her head deep into the pillows and cries.

'So when are you going to tell Ben?' Tamara asks.

She and Alice are sitting facing each other across a flat plain of oak, in the unsettling chill of Tamara's kitchen. (Alice suspects her mother of turning the heating off before her arrival, so that Alice will say, 'Aren't you cold?' and Tamara can reply, 'Oh dear, you aren't very hardy, are you?' or 'Some of us live frugally, darling.')

It has been five days since Jasper left. His phone rings out when she calls it, the perky bell tones dying in empty space, and he hasn't replied to the messages she has left. Alice hasn't told Ben about what she has come to think of as 'the situation' yet; wanting to do it properly, which means Jasper being present for the big announcement. She has read up on divorce and the professional consensus – in terms of limiting the damage to the inevitably fucked-up kids – seems to be that they both sit down with their child and tell him all the usual lines about it not being his fault and them both still loving him very, very much and so on.

Alice wouldn't have told her mother either, but over the last few weeks Tamara has become impatient with Alice avoiding her calls and finding reasons not to visit, and finally left a message on her phone warning her that if she didn't visit Tamara soon, she might, for all she knew, never be able to speak to her again, as Tamara is of an age where she might have *serious* medical issues, and Alice ought to be mindful of that.

These unexpected dramatics from her mother, who has no medical issues at all except for the usual undiagnosed sociopathy, surprised Alice. She realises that she has simply never forced Tamara to this point before, and the discovery that Tamara would go to such obvious and – yes – childish lengths to keep her daughter close is an odd one. Alice always assumed that Tamara kept in contact partly out of habit, partly out of a desire to flex the old muscles of her control, which otherwise might atrophy in retirement, and partly as a simple checking up to make sure that Alice, adult and loose in the world, isn't embarrassing her. Now it is apparent that there is a strange need there too; a sad, cold sort of love.

So here is Alice, trying to warm her stonily cold fingers on a delicate tea-cup, being stared out by a poodle. Behind her mother is the window, and beyond that the countryside, which is almost outlandishly beautiful. It is difficult not to be moved by the stark blue of the sky, the late sun blazoning the hedgerow, the snowdrops below the apple trees, the scattering of small birds on the long green lawn. Tamara doesn't appear to notice it: for her, nature is a job. Perhaps it is only townies who can take this innocent delight in the country. Maybe nothing can be innocent or delightful once it starts writing your pay cheques; once the usual struggle of mastery and resentment begins.

Alice realises that she hasn't answered Tamara, whose eyebrows are rising up her forehead with each tick of the reclaimed station clock that hangs large on the wall like the inescapability of time.

'I think I'll probably tell him tonight. I wanted to tell him together, but I don't think Jasper will be around for that.' At the moment Ben thinks Jasper is at the funeral of a great-aunt Mabel, the decline and fall of whom he accepted unblinkingly, not even asking when his father might be back.

'I expect Jasper won't want to take the responsibility,' Tamara says. 'He never has.'

'No,' Alice agrees, wondering if this is really it: a turning point. Perhaps this divorce will be the making of her mother, into something resembling a mother.

'You know, I foresaw this the day you two married,' Tamara continues. 'It was a sunny day, darling, do you remember? We had just arrived with you at the church and I was standing in the graveyard having a quick cigarette, back when I smoked' – Alice blinks at this: Tamara still smokes – 'and I was looking up at the sky, which was such a beautiful shade of periwinkle. Then at once the sun vanished behind such a thick, dark cloud. I was quite cold standing there in all the graves. I became aware – because you don't, often, do you – that under my feet was death. And I had this awful feeling that Jasper wouldn't be coming. I had a very strong sense that he would jilt you. Even after he arrived I couldn't shake the feeling of unease. Now I know what that was – it was a premonition. I knew you would be abandoned and now –' she opens her hands dramatically wide – 'here you are.'

Alice, herself beginning to feel slightly under a dark cloud, says mildly, 'Well, even if it didn't turn out well, at least I have Ben.'

'And now you're a single mother! No, darling, don't make excuses for him. This was cruel, to wait until you were this age and in these circumstances, before he left.'

Tamara then tells a story about a friend of hers whose husband left her and remarried three women, one after the other, while she ended up dying alone, as Alice watches the little birds hopping out beyond the window and marvels at her own capacity for hoping for the best. The unexpected compassion she felt for her mother when she made her needy, querulous call has led her into confiding too much; which has only allowed Tamara a more accurate aim. Perhaps it is also that Tamara, conscious of having exposed herself, is more than usually dangerous. It reminds Alice – too late – of a story she read when she was young which warned against the inaccurate shooting of panthers, because if a panther is only wounded, it is likely to hide in a nearby tree, wait until its attacker passes underneath, and then drop on him.

Tamara finishes her story and looks at Alice with an expression that is hard to read: part satisfaction and part disappointment. She appears to be hovering between frustration at Alice's failure – both her failure in marrying Jasper to begin with, and her failure at keeping him – and her own rightness. In the end the latter wins out and she says: 'I just wish you could have listened to me in the first place.'

'Oh, fuck off,' says Alice.

They both stare at each other, startled. The poodles under the table shift and resettle, as if sensing the change in atmosphere.

Tamara puts down her cup and opens her mouth. Then she closes it again firmly, to demonstrate her own speechlessness. Then, after a long moment, she says. 'I'll put that down to the severe emotional strain you're under.'

Alice is also thinking about what she has just said. It wasn't, admittedly, particularly eloquent, but it did what needed to be done. It had its own economical charm. She considers adding something witty about calling her mother back in a few months and reiterating her wish that she fuck off, but she isn't practised in retorts, and, in any case, her hands are already trembling at her own defiance, so she decides to quit while she's ahead, gathers up her bag, and exits, pursued by two poodles.

When Alice gets home she finds a politely pissed-off letter from Jasper's surgery, confirming the decision to grant him a leave of absence. It is implied that the surgery had no choice. Alice knows that there will be no other post to explain her husband to her, Jasper being a devotee of online statements. She wonders whether she ought to go to the police and tell them that her husband is missing.

'Did he tell you he was leaving?' she will be asked over a Styrofoam cup of scalding tea, by a sympathetic policewoman about a hundred years younger than Alice. After a few more questions the policewoman will say: 'So, Mrs Rooke, your husband has left you, has taken time off work, and isn't returning your calls, while the woman you believe to be his new partner is also missing. It's been five days. Have you considered the possibility that they might have gone on holiday?'

'But I told him she was cheating on him.'

'Might it be possible that he didn't believe you?'

'I knew he believed me.'

'How was that?'

'I saw it in his eyes.'

Saw it in his eyes, the policewoman writes, and there is a silence as both she and Alice look at it, the stern boxes of the official paperwork, the flimsy filigree of the biro. *Mrs Rooke claims she saw it in his eyes.*

Instead, Alice calls a school friend of hers who once used a private detective to check if her husband was cheating (he was). She takes the number from her friend, before spending the rest of her afternoon prevaricating, considering her situation; moving ceaselessly back and forth, navigating the darkness by the sparks of illumination that hang above her; the dull glow of the light in Jasper's study, the louche blink and flicker of a neon tiger, the candles on a crystal-decked dinner table. Then she calls the number, and a few days later Maura arrives at her house.

Maura is a short and compactly built woman, so neatly hemmed by her wool suit that it is difficult to tell whether she is mainly composed of fat or muscle. Though Maura must be only a year or so older than Alice herself, Alice notices (it seems her capacity for comparing the length and depth of wrinkles is not something that vanishes at times of trouble) the firm, straight division in the centre of Maura's eyebrows, the business-like lines from nose to mouth. The wrinkles of a serious individual. Her near-black eyes move comprehensively over the hallway and Alice herself with a directness Alice finds she appreciates. Then her hand pops out to shake Alice's own and she accepts a cup of tea.

'It's best if you give me an accurate idea of the situation here,' Maura says, early on. 'Do you want him back?'

'No,' Alice says. 'Not at all.' Maura nods, with no discernible change of expression.

'So your end goal in finding him is . . .?'

'To get a divorce. And so I can tell Ben what on earth's going on. He needs some sort of plan – he needs to know if he'll be spending holidays or weekends with Jasper or whatever. For God's sake, he should know that he hasn't just been abandoned. Though that does seem to be what Jasper's done.

'I'll put up with a lot from someone – too much, I know. But I can't see Ben hurt. I hate Jasper for leaving him to wonder.'

Maura, unreactive, continues writing in her notepad. 'Are you under financial pressure at the moment?'

'No. Though I imagine this girl plans to bleed him dry. Another good reason to get a divorce organised quickly. If she's going to take all his money I need to separate our finances.' Alice hears herself speaking for a moment, wondering at the way her voice, hard and new, is finally slicing everything away – all the mess and grief of the previous months, to leave only absolute sense – though Maura simply nods again, because, as far as she knows, Alice might always have been like this.

'Obviously you'll need a solicitor too,' Maura says. 'In Jasper's absence, will you have enough money to pay bills over the coming months? The mortgage?'

'Oh, the house is paid for. I got some money after my father died. Jasper paid all the other bills. I'll need to get a job soon, though.'

'Maybe you could go into interior design,' Maura says.

Alice is startled. 'What?'

Maura, expressionless, indicates the room. 'This house is beautiful. Will you keep it?'

'I do want to,' Alice says. 'It's mine, really. Not just because of the money. It's more my home than it ever was Jasper's.'

After that Maura takes as many details as Alice can give her about Jasper, down to his clothes size and passport number. She takes a photograph of him, and one of Star, which Alice had found on a memory stick that had slid unnoticed down the back of Jasper's desk. In the photograph Star is standing by the banks of an unidentified river, flickering silver behind her. Her hair is one long horizontal stripe in the wind, her mouth is slightly open, as if she is talking. Her face – though it could be the effect of the sunlight – appears less opaque than usual. In this picture she almost looks uncertain.

After another week, Maura comes back. She tells Alice that the lease Jasper had taken on the flat has now been cancelled and the flat is on the market once more as a rental. She gives Alice a brochure with pictures of the flat's interior, though Alice already knew how it would be: stainless steel and black granite. Hardwood floors and soft-close loo seats. A black leather sofa, in the shape of a Tetris block. Maura also – though she won't explain how she did it – found out that Jasper bought one plane ticket to Dublin the day after he left Alice.

'He has some family there,' Alice explained, confused. 'Though he barely knows them. I'm not sure why he'd leave the country.'

Maura couldn't discover what had happened to his car. It wasn't parked at the flat, reported as abandoned, or advertised for resale. 'Perhaps he gave it to the girl?' she suggests.

'I'm not sure he'd have been so generous in the circumstances.'

Maura had asked after Star at the Purple Tiger, but the manager, a thin middle-aged man in a golf sweater, wouldn't tell her anything. ('Come back with a warrant,' he said, revealing an ignorance both of the remit of private investigators and of police procedure, before theatrically shutting and bolting the door.) Maura explains that caginess is to be expected in this outpost of the sex industry. 'It's a delicate business. They aren't allowed to sell drugs, or give extras, or cheat employment law, but if they don't they might not survive.'

Neither could Maura find out anything about Star's whereabouts. There is nobody of her name at any of the flats in the once-genteel Victorian house, and no Star on the electoral roll. 'I assumed she was staying with a friend or family member, so I spoke to the residents. It seemed most likely that she was staying with another girl called Chloe, especially as Chloe was unusually defensive and insisted she didn't know anybody called Star.'

'Why would she be so secretive?'

'The simplest explanation would be because she had been illegally subletting a room.' Maura pauses and looks at Alice, with understanding. 'I know it's a frustrating process. Unfortunately, Star's world isn't one of mortgages and council tax. She and her friends don't want to be traceable and transparent. She doesn't vote, she probably doesn't use social media. It's unlikely that Star is her real name. Really she's a creature from another era.'

'From *Oliver Twist*?'

'She may as well be. You aren't likely to find out more unless you get the police involved.'

'Do you think I should?'

Maura stops here, visibly in the midst of deciding her next words. It occurs to Alice that Maura might suspect that Alice has simply made Star up. Alice is starting to wonder about this herself.

'This isn't going to be an easy thing to hear, particularly after all you've already been through,' Maura says. 'But there are possibilities we haven't considered. The absence of Jasper's car, his buying a plane ticket and leaving his job so suddenly, plus Star's disappearance . . . there might be a crime here.'

'Oh,' Alice is almost relieved. 'I see what you mean. No. No, I don't think so. Jasper's a philanderer, not a murderer.'

'A lover not a fighter?' said Maura. 'You'd be surprised how rarely the two things are mutually exclusive.'

'All the same, I think I'll give it a bit longer.'

Maura nods. Before she leaves she says, 'I wish you all the best' and, honest woman that she is, isn't quite able to remove all the traces of scepticism and sympathy from her expression.

Alice sits now in the kitchen, looking from the window to her watch, waiting for the doorbell to fill the house with its sonorous metal ripple, announcing the arrival of Ben, back from his kayaking expedition with George. A noise at the window – the sly scratch of the overgrown wisteria – startles her. The garden is on the move again: the new shoots of the bay bush extending their antennae, the climbing rose snaking onto the apple tree. The passionflower has, quite appropriately, died, and will need to be replaced with something that can stand the snow. This week she might take Ben to the garden centre, which sells snakes, lizards and tortoises, allowing parents to pick out perennials as their children gaze into the tiny tropical worlds of the unmoving reptiles.

Funny, she thinks, how the idea of this enlivens her; of trowelling around in the dirt of the garden she will fight to keep, planting things whose only purpose is to please her in the future. It seems she is already making preparations for future happiness. Yesterday she thought of a friend who had invited them to stay at her place in Cornwall, and wondered if the offer would still be valid without all its original invitees. She has remembered friends of hers Jasper hates, whom she might now invite to dinner. She might cook fish, after it went so well last time. Even this morning she caught herself looking acquisitively at his study. It surprises her how soon after a crisis – in this case the smoking, demolished wreck of her marriage – she is able to imagine her recovery.

Now the doorbell rings and she goes to it, with the usual wave to the other mother in the car outside, the hug for Ben, before she shuts the door and fills herself with a long breath and says, 'Come into the kitchen with me, sweetie. I need to talk to you about something.'

VIC

Across the tables of the cafés and restaurants of Azenhas do Mar, in Michael's garden, along the scorched white streets, Vic tries to find out more about Estella. She has the feeling when she talks to her now – peering into the girl's indeterminate-colour eyes, trying to read the minute quirks and crumples of her mouth – of being in pursuit: chasing Estella through the back roads of her history, through the dark woods and valleys. She can't tell if Estella herself senses it; if she suspects that Vic overheard her phone call; or has recognised that Vic might be a threat to her. Estella answers all Vic's questions with the same tone: politeness, but a lack of enthusiasm, as if her own life is a subject she studied years ago at school, and found boring. But at times this careful indifference breaks up, and Vic sees something beneath it, moving quick and flustered. Three times, altogether. Like a bird she can repeat each conversation from memory, without knowing what it means.

The first time was when she asked Estella who she was named for and Estella said she didn't know; she never really asked why. She looked at Vic then with real, stark wariness. Unfortunately for Vic, she had no idea why this question out of all her questions might bother Estella, and couldn't follow it up with anything more penetrating.

The second (and more significant, in Vic's opinion) time was when she asked Estella where in England her parents lived.

'Berkshire,' Estella said. She answered so unhesitatingly, as if prepped for the question, that Vic was sure she was lying. She decided to test her theory with a lie of her own.

'How funny – my dad's family were from Berkshire. Whereabouts are yours? Which town?'

'Windsor,' Estella said. She was looking more than usually guarded. Her hands lay in front of her, unmoving. 'But they moved there. I didn't grow up there. I don't actually know where they are exactly.'

'No?'

'There's sort of a rift,' Estella said. 'That's why. Sorry – this isn't ideal afternoon chat, is it?' She apologised as though she were the one to bring it up; abruptly waved her hand, dismissing it with careful brightness: 'That's enough ancient history for now!'

Vic supposes that this is the reason that Estella doesn't like to talk about the origins of her name, having fallen out with the parents who gave it to her. She isn't sure what more she could ask about the family fracture, especially after being so firmly cut off. She wishes Michael had been there for that conversation, because she doesn't know if Estella has even told him about it. He has never mentioned it, but then he doesn't discuss Estella except in the most vague and passionate terms ('Isn't she incredible?' 'Look how quickly she picked up Portuguese, Vic. I really think she might be a sort of linguistic genius.'):

observations that are final, allowing no further discussion. While Estella was looking profoundly uncomfortable talking about her parents, Michael was cooking: one of the many pastas, curries or salads he brings out, with an air of expectancy and hope, so obviously trying to charm Estella with his skill.

The last time Vic managed to visibly *bother* Estella was when she asked Estella about Manchester University, where Estella studied philosophy. (Vic actually thought she did rather a good job here, pretending to be artlessly envious of Estella's student years.) Intrigued by Estella's increasing rigidity as the conversation went on – the flush rising up from her clavicle to her satiny neck, ending in her cheeks – Vic pressed her on small details: halls, friends, boyfriends, until eventually she was playing for time and asked, merely to keep the subject alive, what year Estella graduated. Then she answered in that unhesitating, precise way she had sometimes: times when Vic suspected she was probably lying.

Possibly out of tactfulness, Estella doesn't often ask Vic about her own life, but there are times when Vic feels as if it's Estella who has her on the run, harried and secretive. On one such occasion it is late evening; the three of them sitting in the garden. The sun has dropped below the top line of the jacaranda trees; their upper branches blazing as if they have caught fire, streaming lilac and white. The courtyard below is left submerged in an odd evening light, still and cool and weighted with green.

Michael and Estella are talking about a disciplinary in their office concerning a prank, the details of which nobody has been told.

'The problem is that there wasn't any friendship there,' Michael says. 'You have to like the person you're pranking. Otherwise it's bullying.'

'I've never played a prank,' Estella says thoughtfully, 'or been the victim of one.'

'I went to a boys' school,' Michael says. 'It was a way of life. I still don't get into bed without wanting to pull the covers back, looking for a puddle of water – or worse – or nettles, or jam, or live toads.'

'That's terrible,' Estella says. 'Bed ought to be a place of safety.'

Vic is keeping quiet: worried that Kate will be brought out, smiling and malicious, into the light of conversation. But Michael is looking at Estella with absorbed affection, presumably at the idea of her safe in bed, and she is relieved.

Then he looks up and says, 'One of Vic's friends got expelled over a prank. She was pretty crazy, though, wasn't she, Vic?'

In a sudden calm moment, a near out-of-body experience, floating on absolute panic, Vic decides that Estella's eyes aren't blue, or grey, but a salty, cool green, the colour of the sea when you are under the surface, something she remembers only vaguely, from her own childhood, before she was scared of the water.

'What?' asks Estella.

'She wasn't my friend,' is all Vic can think to say.

'Oh yeah – it was a friend Vic had fallen out with. What was her name? Kate? She put up naked pictures of Vic all over the school. On the street as well. What a little bitch, eh?'

'This might not be something Vic wants to talk about,' Estella says, glancing at Vic, who squirms afresh in the irony of it: Estella protecting Vic's privacy.

'You don't mind it, do you?' Michael appeals to Vic, who can't meet his eye, knowing that if she does it will be with intensity: bright-eyed and betrayed. 'Vic!' he cries. He leans forward, suddenly solicitous, making it worse. 'You do mind! I'm sorry. I had no idea.'

'I don't mind,' Vic says, though she knows it is obvious to both of them that she does.

'Did you ever see her again – that girl?' Michael asks, and she realises that he has completely forgotten. She told him when he was drunk, and then neither of them ever mentioned it again, which suited Vic. She had thought Michael was being sensitive, but the truth was that he had no idea.

'She died.'

'Shit! Really? Christ, sorry, Vic. I think I remember this . . . or maybe I thought that was a different girl . . .'

'It's OK. It really isn't a big deal,' Vic says hurriedly, to prevent Michael – now frowning at the sky in an effort to marshal his memories – unspooling the whole story. 'I'm not traumatised or anything. And it was just a schoolgirl prank.'

'But you were good friends?' Estella asks. 'Before, I mean.'

'I suppose so,' Vic says. 'But afterwards, when she died, we hadn't seen each other in years. We weren't on speaking terms.'

'This might seem like a strange question,' Estella begins. It is apparent she is choosing her words even more delicately, more carefully than usual; hovering for a second over each word like a maiden aunt selecting a candied almond. She continues, 'And please stop me if you'd rather we change the subject, but I was wondering – did you ever visit her grave?'

'I don't even know where she's buried,' Vic lies.

'Oh, OK. I only asked because I feel that would be important for me. I mean, if it were me and she had been my friend once I would probably want to visit, just on account of that. Even if she was cruel afterwards. Because she isn't here any more being cruel, and I'd feel like, I don't know, that all she is now is a collection of memories, and if I had a memory of caring about her then I'd want to say goodbye to that, if that makes sense.'

Estella pauses here, and Vic and Michael briefly exchange a glance of surprise. Then she continues; 'I know that probably wouldn't feel emotionally necessary to everyone. I'm only thinking of what I'd do in the situation. If someone died and I didn't get to visit their grave I'd feel like it wasn't quite . . . done. I don't think it would be a really strong feeling. More like when you go out somewhere and you feel like you've forgotten something, but you aren't sure what it is. Or leaving someone and knowing you had meant to tell them something but you can't remember it. Just that little feeling, picking away at you, all the time.'

Michael sends Vic an email with the pictures he took of her and Estella in the botanical gardens. When she sees them she understands why he felt the need to photograph them: two women sitting before a railed-off view, the light crashing down behind them over all kinds of trees, a fountain falling in a glittering curtain; beyond that, the softened blue of the sea. As a composition it is stunning. As a picture of two friends it doesn't work. She and Estella sit as if forced into each other's company; Estella facing slightly away, towards the view, Vic angled back, towards the place where the photographer is standing. Estella looks aloof, as usual. Vic doesn't look for long at herself; in one picture bowed over as if trying to cover her entire body with her arms and shoulders, in another open-mouthed, mid-sentence. Her expression is more nervous than she realised at the time. Eyes wide, mouth stubbornly agape; as if conscious of not being wanted, but determined to press on regardless. She closes the email.

She tries to remember what it is she and Estella talked about while Michael was pretending to buy ice creams. Her past conversations with Estella tend to fall into two types: the interrogation, with its unsubtle and blundering stratagems, or a loose, untargeted kind of small talk that has always been more nerve-wracking. She can come away sweating and depleted from a discussion of whether it will be cloudy in the afternoon, or of the benefits of tea as opposed to coffee.

Yet she feels like she's making progress. Vic has seen Estella's disquiet, her nerves when the conversation approaches certain areas. As with her thoughts on visiting graves (Vic still has no idea what to make of that), these moments when Estella behaves like a real girl only highlight the artifice of her usual persona. Estella may have perfected the poker face, but she never builds relationships, or stays in one place long enough for it to be truly challenged. A poker face can't cover every situation: sooner or later it would be realised that Estella has parts missing. Or perhaps not missing; rather, it's as if she has hidden everything – her history, her plans, her feelings – and hasn't bothered to come up with anything to replace them.

Not that Michael seems to notice. He is deeply and publicly fascinated by her; paying an almost comically sincere attention to everything she says, and hailing its cleverness once she has finished. He is always trying to make her laugh, but without the teasing he directs at everybody else – his parents, whom he teases with love, his friends, with energy and skill, Vic herself with affection and the occasional eye roll – and when he succeeds in provoking one of her sudden, sunny laughs he is visibly delighted. Everyone else laughs like that, yet it only seems special when she does it. How has she managed to reinvent the laugh? He is still recognisably himself – entertaining, easily amused – but there is something more serious in him these days. He is making an effort. He seems weighted by it, the gravity of his love.

Estella herself is reserved around Michael. She rarely gives him affection – an infrequent, charming smile, a restrained touch of the fingers, but never a kiss. It strikes Vic that this might be it: that Estella, shrewdly realising that Michael is used to being loved, has played it cool. If so – depressingly – it seems to have worked. Vic thinks of Anne Boleyn's captivation of Henry VIII, on what must have been nothing more than her refusal to sleep with him. She couldn't have been more beautiful, more clever or witty than anyone else around her – and God knows Estella isn't – rather, it is the rejection that was extraordinary to Henry, and to Michael after him.

The young prince of Azenhas do Mar, its golden-haired, grey-eyed pride – trying and failing to win Estella's approval, waiting on her when they are alone, rushing to make sure she is happy. Vic is dismayed that Michael could fall for it so stupidly and completely. An unimpressed shrug, a turned shoulder, a cool, sceptical stare: are these really the true secrets of the famous femmes fatales, the seduction techniques Vic has imagined with mingled disapproval and unease. Is that all Helen of Troy was? A pretty girl with an attitude problem?

Vic has to admit that Michael was right when he accused her of not understanding modern dating. For such a supposedly important area of life, it slipped past her as quickly and unnoticeably as a moth outside a moving-car window. The initial commotion the pictures of her naked had caused did die down during the summer holidays, replaced by other scandals (a year 10 girl's pregnancy, a year 7 wetting herself spectacularly while on stage dressed as Moses) and other preoccupations (Vic no longer being the only girl with breasts). But while nobody would make a special effort to seek Vic out for mockery, any entry of hers into the other pupils' line of vision would still always remind them of who she was. *That's the naked girl*, they said to each other when she passed. The year she turned thirteen, she was not so much concerned with her transformation into a teenager – supposedly hormonal, party-loving, and boy mad – but with avoiding the girls at her school, the boys from the neighbouring school, and Kate herself, still at large in Funchal; a potential risk at the park, the marina, the cafés and ice-cream stands.

After Kate was expelled she was sent to a boarding school in

Portugal, but her terms were slightly out of step with Vic's, and for about five weeks a year Vic was aware that she and Kate were both in Funchal at the same time. During those periods Vic stayed in at lunch (not that she had anyone to roam the streets with; she had formed a vague association with some other misfits of her year, but they all seemed to understand it for what it was: a friendship of subsistence and necessity, not a true meeting of minds) and took the bus straight home from school.

Even so, she still saw Kate once or twice. A blonde thirteen-year-old, walking with a cigarette in one hand and a boy's hand in the other. Still blonde at fourteen, drinking on the beach with some other teenagers. A fifteen-year-old red-head sitting on the harbour wall, legs swinging. Kate's face paired with the unexpected hair took Vic by surprise: she squinted at her for so long, trying to work out whether it was Kate or not, that Kate looked up and saw her. The awareness of recognition passed between them, stinging and immediate. Then Kate turned away. Vic was relieved; she was also obscurely hurt. Kate hadn't looked angry, as she had expected: she didn't look anything much. 'I don't hate you – I nothing you', was what the girls said at Vic's school when they wanted to cut each other deeply. That was what she saw in Kate's eyes: that – despite the friendship bracelet, the framed picture, her betrayal of Vic and Vic's betrayal of her – Kate now nothinged her.

Wary of running into Estella again, Vic texts rather than calls on Michael after seeing his car parked outside the Quinta do

Rosal several nights running. He replies with a jauntily abbreviated message to say that he and Estella are going to live at his parents' house because the apartment in Funchal is too small and too hot. He estimates that it only takes forty-five minutes to commute between Azenhas do Mar and Funchal if he drives along the cliff roads. He says they all ought to have a drink to celebrate his and Estella's move.

Vic thinks of Paula Worth, who wrote to her from Boston a week ago and asked how everything was 'back home'. She hasn't replied, not simply because she doesn't know how everything is, but also because the thought of describing even part of it makes her feel almost panicked, overcome with a sense of impending tragedy; the same panic she feels when she thinks of Estella throwing her silk dressing gown into the bedroom of the Quinta do Rosal, that elegant old house, a place that seems always to be dreaming gently of the past, when she and Michael used to play hide and seek barefoot, hearing the muted slap of each other's feet on the cool marble tiles.

'What's Estella's career plan?' she asked Michael, to which Michael said he had absolutely no idea.

'Do you think she plans to have a family, then? To get married?'

'I don't think she has a plan at all,' he said. 'I like that about her. It's refreshing.'

Vic thought then: everyone has a plan. Everyone wants something. All this means is that Estella has decided against telling Michael about her plan. She can't fail to understand the power she has over him – but she won't say what she intends to do with it.

Vic sits down and prays, and then she stops praying and turns on the computer. She types *Estella White* into social networks and search engines. She looks up the name in Berkshire news-papers, in directory enquiries, and on the electoral roll. When nothing comes up, she goes to the website of the University of Manchester. She does all this in a kind of suspended daze, carried along by something that doesn't seem to come from her own mind. She feels as if she is an actor in a thriller, and when she calls the main switchboard of Estella's Alma Mater, it is the actor who tells and asks the woman answering that she is an HR employee at the engineering firm Cooper Erdinger Shaw, and would like to check the details of Estella's CV. When, finally, Vic has been passed along to the correct department and a person there has searched their records, and searched again, and eventually reported, sounding confused, that no Estella White – no Estella of any surname, in fact – has ever enrolled at the university, she experiences the sensation of waking from her dream-state, breaking out of the ambiguous grey-blue water into a daylight so knifelike and bright she can only wince at it, shocked and disbelieving.

'Well, I'm sorry about that. You're sure that's the correct first name?' the woman asks. 'People do change their names.'

'Her parents called her Estella,' Vic said. 'She said she didn't know why.'

'Sorry,' the woman says again, with more impatience, and Vic thanks her and ends the conversation.

She hadn't really expected to be right, that was the thing. She thought things would carry on the way they always do, without real reversal or revelation, just the dimly lit marshes of civility and compromise; a twilight, becoming slowly darker, the drift of life and friendship. She thought she would dislike Estella for a while, and feel guilty for it, and then the three of them would lose contact and eventually Michael and Estella would finish their work in Madeira and leave together.

And now she has a sudden answer. Not a complete answer, but enough of one. She still doesn't know who Estella is, but she knows what she isn't. The knowledge is as tangible in her hands, as electric and real and heavy as a gun – or how she imagines a gun to feel, never having held one. It is a weight and at the same time a relief: to know that her instincts were right. Michael himself is fond of saying: 'The simplest explanation is usually correct', and it is, after all, a pretty simple explanation: the beautiful, untruthful opportunist meets a naive (*innocent*, she corrects herself, feeling bad) heir to a family fortune. The rest is obvious.

Vic doesn't sleep that night. Her bedroom always traps the last heat of the day – she is habituated to it – but tonight she rolls and welters uncomfortably in the close darkness, her sheets pushed back and her arms outspread as if in supplication. Now that she has both concrete information and a moral duty to report it, the idea of actually doing so makes her intensely anxious. She is frightened of telling Michael, though not as frightened as she is of confronting Estella, the idea of which makes her palms wet. She can't tell if speaking to Michael privately is the most appropriate thing to do, or the most cowardly, or both.

Finding all this weight suddenly coming to rest on her – Vic, who has avoided moral dilemmas since a date she can exactly pinpoint, it being engraved on her as if she were Kate's last memorial, and not the stern black rectangle of granite in the graveyard just outside Funchal – she is paralysed. She wants to do the right thing, but she feels acutely that she is alone in her unlovable task: that of the planning officer, ordering the disman-tling of Michael's happiness, to be rebuilt on a more stable foundation. She can't feel God. She thinks suddenly that it is as if she left Him behind when she finished school; that if she went back she'd find Him there, the same as always, at the school chapel with Father Blanca; the white walls, the muted sounds of the outside world, the dust floating on the radiant air.

By half past six, the sun already saturating the room through the pale curtains, Vic – still wretchedly awake – has decided that Father Blanca is the only person who could possibly help her now. She gets up and moves in a strange crystalline daze through her morning routines – tired but fixated, all her energy concentrated on one small point; her former school – and by half past eight she is in Funchal, without even knowing if he is still a chaplain, or how to find him if he isn't.

Vic never feels comfortable wandering the broad-patterned avenues and squares of the city; watched by an unfamiliar audience gazing from under the long awnings of coffee shops, or lined up on benches or on steps like spectators at the Colosseum. The beauty of the trees meeting neatly in arches overhead; the blue and white azulejo tiles of the buildings; the stir and whip of the sea beyond the esplanade is made distant by her own anxiety; like a view beyond cracked glass.

It is not only her tiredness and her nervousness of the decision she has to make that alienates her from the city. Even now, long after the time that she might run into Kate, she is alert for the possibility. Several years of scanning passers-by – glancing up worriedly at the sound of a teenage girl's high laugh, like a seagull's scream – have left her with this unnecessary reflex: evidently old habits really do die hard.

Vic doesn't realise that she is passing by the avenue on which Kate used to live until she is nearly at it, and hurrying by; into the next square, where she finds herself next to a fountain, the scene of her last meeting with Kate. She has the unsettling feeling that she has accidentally joined a guided tour of the places of Kate's life; like one of those macabre days out tourists pay for, to be shown around the sites of famous murders.

The last time Vic saw Kate they were both fifteen. Kate was sitting on the edge of the fountain, flanked by two boys. One lying on his back and laughing softly to himself, smoke floating up from his prone body as if his soul was making its escape; the other talking to Kate, though she was ignoring him, staring out towards the sea. He didn't appear to notice. Vic had seen the group but passed over Kate, who had dyed her hair from purplish red to a flat, ugly black. On high alert for a redhead, Vic didn't realise it was Kate until she jumped with sudden force – startling the boys next to her – off the edge of the fountain and appeared right in front of her, saying, 'Vic, Vic, can we talk?'

Vic's first impulse was fright, but, looking more closely at Kate, the unfocussed sadness in her eyes, her attitude of pleading, she felt her alarm ebb. Having the opportunity to do so for the first time in years, she gazed at Kate close-up. Kate was still pretty – more pretty – even drunk or stoned, even with the dull, artificial look of her hair, the make-up too heavy and slightly askew. She wore a short skirt which had ridden up over her beautifully shaped thighs, one with a large bruise.

'Vic,' Kate said. 'I've been thinking about you. I was actually thinking about you just now and then you appeared. Isn't that weird? I've wanted for so long to say sorry to you. About that thing in school. I know it was awful and I still feel terrible about it. I know you must hate me. And you don't have to ever speak to me again if you don't want to, but I wanted to tell you that you were my best friend. Really. I've never had a proper best friend before or since, and I know I ruined it, but I can only say sorry.'

'It's OK,' Vic said, feeling too surprised to know yet whether it was or not.

Kate took her hand, her eyes, already clouded, filling with tears. 'Oh Vic. Thank you. Do you think we could maybe meet up, or something? If you want to?'

Vic hesitated, then nodded, but afterwards, at home, she wasn't sure whether or not to call the number Kate had pressed on her. She had the idea that the whole thing might be another type of prank, a long con, designed to pay her back for getting Kate expelled. She asked Michael, when she could get a moment with him without his usual crowd of village groupies, what he thought.

'She may well be planning to kill you,' Michael said, 'but you've told me now, so if she does, I'd be able to tell the police who did it.'

'Thanks.'

'Nah, I think you should be her friend again. It's been a

while; she seems remorseful. Give her a second chance. You obviously want to or you wouldn't have asked me about it.'

'I just think even if she wasn't up to anything, we might be too different now,' Vic mused. 'She seems a bit . . . wild. Drinking and smoking and probably drugs. She's got a reputation with boys, but then I suppose so do I, so never mind that. But she'd think I was boring.'

'Wild, you say,' Michael said, with a sharpening of interest. 'Is she hot?'

Vic hesitated. The only thing Michael's girlfriends (if girlfriend was the right word for these transient female associates) seemed to have in common was their hotness; being otherwise so diverse that it was hard for her to tell whether he was shallow or not. A shaven-headed scuba diver, an oil heiress, a sweet French exchange student, a sociopathic waitress, a twenty-something travel agent who appeared to have no idea how old Michael actually was, a dreadlocked hippy backpacker from England; tourists and locals, rich girls and poor girls, clever girls and stupid girls: every one of them beautiful. She wondered whether Michael was genuinely open-minded, or whether he simply didn't care enough to notice such minor things as lifestyle or personality. She suspected the latter from the way his girls came and went, causing barely a ripple in the ocean of Michael's good humour.

'She is,' Vic said now, reluctantly honest. 'But she wears too much make-up and dresses kind of slutty.'

'She sounds great,' Michael said. 'Definitely make friends with her. Then I'll "bump into" you when you're having a girls' night out.'

'Very funny,' Vic said, horrified at the thought. She didn't mention Kate to Michael again, and she didn't call Kate, or – term having ended – go back to Funchal, but then, a month later, Kate called her at the hotel, and Vic's mother, not recognising Kate's voice, put her straight on to Vic.

'Vic! It's me – Kate. God, I'm glad you're still on this number.'

'Hi, Kate,' Vic said warily, wondering if she should apologise for not having called. Kate didn't seem to expect an explanation however; she was rushing to offer her own.

'Look, Vic, I'm really sorry to call you under these circumstances, but I'm in a bit of a messy situation and I was wondering if you could maybe help me.'

'What's the situation?'

'OK – right. It's going to sound bad, but you have to bear with me because it's really not as bad as it sounds. I'm at the police station. Well, just outside. Basically, someone's said to the police that I was selling drugs to these kids. They said a black-haired girl and they described the sort of thing I was wearing. I don't even know this person – some busybody. Maybe one of the kids' parents.'

'Were you? Selling drugs, I mean.'

Kate lowered her voice, so that Vic could barely hear her over the noise of the traffic. 'Yes, but it was only a little bit of weed. To my friend's younger brother and his friend. I don't really see why it's such a big deal but the police want to call my dad –' for the first time her light, amused tone gives way to something like nervousness – 'and I thought maybe if you could come here and say I was with you that evening, just hanging out the two of us, that would really get me off the hook and nobody would have to be called, you know?'

Vic, panicked, asked; 'Don't you have friends who live closer? I mean, it would be more believable if you were with them, wouldn't it?'

'Uh, my friends aren't really the kind of people who would make me look innocent. If you get what I mean. So can you do it? I haven't actually been arrested, they're just questioning me. They don't have anything to go on besides what that one person said. You won't get in any trouble or anything.'

'Maybe you should tell your dad?' Vic asked. 'Wouldn't he help?' As she said it she remembered some sort of problem with Kate's dad, but wasn't sure whether this had simply come from the various and conflicting accounts Kate gave of him, so that in the end there seemed a black vagueness around the very idea of him, something threatening in his unknowability.

At this Kate started crying. 'No, Vic, he wouldn't help. He mustn't know. He . . . really wouldn't like it.'

Vic paused, aware that each moment she waited, the more obvious any lie of hers would be. She hadn't felt so intensely stressed in years – since the days of Bible Club, in fact – and her heart leapt and flailed like an affrighted rabbit. The idea of lying to the police scared her with a near-superstitious dread; neither did she trust Kate's assurance that Vic wouldn't get in trouble. But she knew the largest part of her panic was the simple horror of being involved with Kate again; drawn back into Kate's own peculiar world: a place of dark storm clouds and unpredictable thrills; Kate's smile promising and secretive, redolent of gaps in fences, hastily gulped alcohol, illegal fairground rides. The idea of it would probably have excited Michael, at least for a couple of weeks. It didn't excite Vic.

'The problem is –' Vic said, struggling for excuses like the amateur liar she was – 'the problem is my parents. They won't let me go to Funchal alone, except for school. Since the Alcoforadas' party, I've been sort of grounded. I got back too late. They were really angry.'

'You can't sneak out?' Kate asked plaintively. There was something frightened in her voice, and it frightened Vic even more; made her escape seem more urgent. 'Please?'

'I'm sorry,' Vic said miserably.

There was another small silence, and then Kate said, 'Hey, Vic, don't worry. I'm sorry I had to ask you. Take care, OK', so resignedly that Vic felt abruptly ashamed of her unwillingness to help, a feeling which only worsened, and was joined by others – guilt, grief, regret – when she heard, three days later, that Kate was dead, after taking a mixture of painkillers, Valium and sleeping pills, washed down with whisky. It was reported through the papers and local rumour that Kate's father had been questioned by police about some kind of argument, or incident, involving Kate, after something was overheard by their neighbours, but he was never charged with anything, as far as Vic knew.

By the time Vic reaches the gates of the school – looking with a slow and queasy recognition at the white walls criss-crossed with bougainvillea, the green divisions of the playing field in the distance, the quiet windows of lesson time – she is wondering what she could possibly say to Father Blanca. The idea of coming here, born as it was out of her dawn struggles, dim and feverish, her sleepless castings around for help, now seems at best inappropriate, and at worst unhinged.

The terracotta roof of the chapel itself is visible from the gate. It is smaller than Vic remembers, in the tradition of revisited childhood places. She wonders how much of it would be the same if she were to go inside. Everything, probably. The plaster statue of Mary, the glittering motes floating on the sunlight, the candles with their frozen trickles of wax, the blue azulejo behind the altar.

Not long after Kate's death, Vic was in the chapel helping Father Blanca, the two of them moving in their usual companionable silence, when she said (surprising herself), 'Father, can I ask you something?'

'Of course,' he said, turning and regarding her expectantly, as if he had been waiting for this time to come.

But there Vic stopped. She wanted to ask about Kate, though she wasn't sure what she wanted to know – or how to phrase it beyond a 'Why?' or a 'Did I. . ?'; she wanted to ask about Kate's side of the Bible: the rivers of blood in Revelation, Paul forbidding women to have authority over men, whether gay people could go to Heaven if they didn't repent; but when it came to it, she looked into his mellow, gently concerned face, and started to cry.

Father Blanca, having been the chaplain of a girls' school for the last ten years, wasn't thrown by her tears.

He took her hand.

'Let us pray,' he said.

Afterwards, kneeling in the light softened by the tall dusty windows, Father Blanca smiled and said, 'Jesus will be here for you always'; and for the first time, Vic really felt that he would.

She spent most of her lunchtimes in the chapel after that. She found Father Blanca's vision of Christianity – pray, be good, do good to others – reassuring in its simplicity, in its neat rules. Even the prayers followed a previously decided structure. From not really thinking about God one way or another, to being confused and disturbed by Bible Club, Vic realised she was beginning to feel the emergence of her own faith: something sweet and clean and comforting. It was all so different from Kate's version of faith, which was more like an ongoing tussle, an abusive love affair; and after that first abortive attempt, Vic no longer felt the need to reconcile Kate's ideas with those of Father Blanca. She simply let them go. At the school chapel she knelt and prayed and felt calm. (Praying at home, with her parents raising their eyebrows at each other behind her, didn't have quite the same effect.) She confessed her guilt and said sorry to God and she experienced a new feeling: the possibility of goodness, of absolution.

Vic tries now, unsuccessfully, to remember the exact details of Father Blanca's face, which was never distinctive to begin with. His evenly shaped, multi-purpose features could have belonged to anyone. She isn't sure that she would know him if she saw him in the street, so many years later. It isn't likely that he would recognise her. Even if he did, she doesn't know how she would begin to explain to him why she was at the chapel. She would have to tell him the truth: that she hasn't felt true faith since she left school; that this is her last resort, her attempt to find what she lost – a sense of God's presence – by going back to the last place she found it.

Vic walks away as the bell for the end of classes is setting up its harsh clamour. She gets in her car and drives back to Azenhas do Mar, where – careless with misery – she rounds a corner of the Rua da Madalena a little too fast and nearly runs over Estella.

Vic brakes, bringing her window up to where Estella has pressed herself back against the stone wall, so that for a second she and Vic both stare at each other through the tinted glass, shocked and each one not recognising the other. When Vic realises who she has been brought so suddenly into close contact with, she has the sudden urge, as in a real hit and run, to rev the car and drive away. Instead, she rolls down the window to apologise. Estella, she notices, is pale; Vic's own hands are shaking on the wheel.

'Don't worry – it's not your fault,' Estella says. 'It's fine. I should have been on the other side of the road. I forget sometimes.'

'I was driving too fast.'

'No, no, please.' Estella looks closely at her, so that Vic, penned inside the car, feels immediately like a mouse in a cage. 'Are you OK?'

'Yes.'

'You aren't OK,' Estella observes, accurately; though she doesn't know the true depth of her accuracy.

'Honestly,' Vic says, flustered and longing to get away. 'I'm fine.'

'Maybe you should take a moment,' Estella says gently. 'You seem shaken.'

Vic stares at her: all concern, full colour restored, standing in her effortless loveliness: yellow sun dress, delicate upper arms, expensive watch. Her impulse to escape is carried away in a sudden swell of anger.

'I know about you,' she says, her voice unnaturally pitched, high and flat. 'I know you're not what you say you are.'

Estella blinks for a moment, unravelling the sentence, then looks startled. 'What?'

'You lied. About your past. And I found out.'

After this there is a long moment; stretching out in all directions like a desert, a scorching waste in which Vic finds herself stranded, unable to find her way back or see her way out. Estella is unmoving, her body arrested in its lean towards the window, her face preternaturally still. Only her eyes move, quickly checking the empty road around them with an expression Vic can't read. She can't tell if Estella is looking for a way to escape, looking for help, or checking for potential witnesses. The last thought frightens her. She realises she hasn't thought this through at all. She has visions of Estella, smaller than her but probably stronger than her, talking her out of the car and pushing her over the cliff wall. Then Estella, at last, steps back and says, very coldly, 'I have no idea what you're talking about.'

Vic accepts this with a kind of relief. It seems the most obvious thing to say, and the most obviously untrue. Estella knows it too: she has stepped back, wrapping her arms around herself, as if the wind has risen.

'If you don't tell Michael, I'm going to do it,' Vic says. She sounds almost apologetic, her voice dwindling now that her anger and fright have faded.

Estella smiles – if smile is the right word for this bleak, weary twist of her lips – and says, 'I know.'

Then she turns and walks back up the hill, her yellow dress bright against the rocky path, like a canary in a mine. It is a while before Vic can collect herself enough to start her car and continue on towards her own house, to begin the long wait for the call from Michael.

It is two days before Vic hears anything. Unable to focus on anything else, sleepless and frayed by doubt, she spends the time running and re-running her argument of why it was necessary to confront Estella. If she is wrong – Vic tells herself – then Estella will act to pre-empt her, explaining the situation to Michael, who will be angry at Vic for interfering. He might even end their friendship, but then he and Estella would emigrate anyway, so Vic has nothing to lose in that sense. And if she is right, and Estella has something terrible or illegal to hide, then Vic has saved Michael, Estella will have to leave, and everything will fall back into its natural order. Yet as time passes her argument is less and less able to comfort her. Her worry persists: once talked away it returns at odd times and in odd places; arriving in her throat when she's at work, turning her stomach when she's trying to sleep.

She finds Michael's voicemail on her phone as she is leaving the Quinta Verde one evening. Suddenly she feels so nervous as she waits to hear it that she doesn't hear Rafael saying goodbye, or the little birds chattering at her as she passes under the trees, their shadow patterns slipping unnoticed over her face. Michael sounds flustered, and stilted, as if repressing great feeling. He asks if Vic has spoken to Estella at all, though he supposes she has not. Estella, he says, has disappeared, with no warning or explanation.

Vic hurries her pace, taking the steepest and most direct path to the Quinta do Rosal. As she walks she texts, to tell Michael she is on her way. She understands, somewhat distantly, that she was right. Estella was a fraud, a gold digger and a danger to Michael, who has been saved at the last minute by Vic's timely intervention (though it appears he may not realise yet that an intervention has taken place, or that he has been saved). It is still too early, or too much of a strange story, for Vic to really believe in it. Still, a thin intimation of relief filters through to her, a sense of the possibility of having done the right thing.

The village is quiet at this time in the evening: Vic walks along the Rua da Madalena alone. As she begins the ascent to Michael's house she is reminded of an event consciously forgotten, sunk deep into her memories like a shipwreck, a prow emerging from the gloomy sea bed. It was a night after she had left school, at a time when she had no idea what to do with herself. Her parents wanted her to go to England – to university – and though Vic was resistant to this she had yet to think of a better idea, and so she was whiling away the summer in a mulish panic, hoping that things would resolve themselves.

The year had got around to the anniversary of Kate's death, a time when she usually had trouble sleeping. She had started going for walks at night. At 3 a.m., she was unlikely to run into anybody else, and if she did, the person would inevitably avoid her eye, equally disinclined to explain their own nocturnal perambulations. She would walk quietly through the narrow streets until she exhausted herself, then go home and allow her bodily fatigue to carry her anxious mind away into sleep, rather like a bouncer dispatching a troublesome guest.

That night she was passing close by the Quinta do Rosal. None of its lights were on: the Worths kept regular hours, and Michael wasn't home. It was about six months since she had seen him. She knew from his mother that he had arrived back from university about a week ago, but he was rarely at home, appearing only briefly before disappearing again, attending an apparently endless series of goodbye parties and barbecues and boat trips.

This time a car passed Vic and pulled up at the gates to the house. One of its back doors opened and the noise of music and voices broke into the soft, dense night. After a moment Michael got out; his hair a stark silver in the car lights. Goodbyes were called, neatly cut off as the door closed again and the car moved off, back towards Funchal. As the sound of its engine faded the sound of the sea returned and the night, after an initial hesitation, drifted back down.

Michael, not having seen Vic, had seated himself on the stone wall bordering his garden. Vic hesitated before walking over. She was half pleased to see Michael, but hurt at his failure to call her, and she felt an obscure resentment of his access to the pleasures of the night; alcohol and music, both of which she would have rejected had she been given the opportunity.

A little spot of light appeared in Michael's hands and travelled to his mouth, before he looked up at her and saluted.

'Vic!' She could tell as she got close that he was drunk; his healthy good looks frowsy and debased, eyes squinting against their vagueness. An earthy, leafy scent rose up from his poorly rolled cigarette. 'What are you up to?' he continued, apparently unsurprised by her appearance in the road at four in the morning.

Vic felt suddenly emboldened by this suspension of the usual, and said, in a light, witty voice that was new to her (and slightly startling): 'Burgling. Don't tell anybody.'

'Are you hitting my house?' he asked. 'Take whatever you want but leave the laptop in the third bedroom along. And the magazines under the bed. I need those.'

'You're a state,' Vic said, a little disappointed at his drowsy-eyed complaisance; the failure to notice that she had been any funnier than usual. Michael was rubbing his hand over his face. He took the hand away, looked at it for a moment, and blinked.

'Where have you been?' Vic asked. 'Tonight, I mean.'

'Funchal. A really shit nightclub, actually. I forgot how it was around here.'

Vic, irritated afresh, said, 'I suppose you're too sophisticated for Madeira now.'

'Always was,' Michael said cheerfully. 'Well, I remember you eating ants in your parents' garden.'

'*I* remember you showing me your knickers.'

'I was five.'

'They were blue. And I thought you must be a boy. I was always confused about you after that.'

Vic didn't know what to say to that, and looked down.

(Afterwards, as always, she thought of things someone else might have said – a seductive '*Still confused?*' – but she didn't have the looks, or the balls, for a line like that.)

When she looked up again Michael was blowing a thin stream of smoke and looking at her with curiosity.

'What are you really doing up?' he asked.

'I can't sleep,' Vic said, then, without having intended to, says, 'my friend killed herself. Not recently. It's just that time of year.'

'Oh, fuck. I'm so sorry. Vic, I had no idea. You must be having a shit time,' Michael said. He took her hand and pressed it in his own, so that she could feel the heat of his hands bleeding into her own stony fingers, stinging the skin that had got used to its cold. 'Who was she? How did she die? You never told me about this.'

Vic realised, slightly too late, that she didn't want to tell him about it now. 'She was a girl from school. We weren't even friends by that time. She was the one who got expelled. The photos . . . I don't know why I brought it up.'

'Even if you aren't friends, it's a shock,' Michael said with an effortful sagacity. 'It's always a shock when someone our age dies.' He shook his head. 'Fucking hell, you can't tell me stuff like this when I'm stoned. I'm not at full comfort capacity. My brain is like alphabet soup. Or like a . . . Rubik's cube. Yeah, a Rubik's cube with all the colours muddled up. Let's talk about it tomorrow. I'll come over. I promise I'll be a better friend tomorrow.'

'I don't want to talk about it really,' Vic said. 'There's nothing to talk about.'

'That's a stage of grief,' Michael said. 'I'm sure it is. I remember this when my grandfather died. Denial. Anger.

Bargaining. Depression. Acceptance. Those are the five stages of grief. You must be at denial, or possibly depression.'

'What about guilt? That isn't a stage?'

'No. I don't think so.' Michael looked down at their hands, clasped in Vic's lap.

'Your fingers are cold,' he said.

At this, Vic, self-conscious, tried to take her hand back. 'I wasn't complaining!' Michael cried, holding on. 'Don't be offended.' With Vic protesting and Michael starting to laugh, they commenced a strange, brief grapple that brought their faces close together. Vic found time to be struck by the unusual regularity of Michael's features: straight nosed, symmetrical. Then he kissed her. It lasted a few moments, Vic shocked, opening her mouth obediently as if for the dentist, barely moving; Michael carrying out most of the business of the kiss, with a light, experimental hand on her shoulder. He was the one to pull away, as if thinking better of it, moving back with an uncomfortable smile.

'Sorry,' he said. 'I'm really stoned. And you – you're going through the grieving process. That was really inappropriate of me.'

'I'm not. But that's okay,' Vic said.

She tried not to look too disturbed by this, her first kiss, and Michael made an effort and came up with some near-sober charm, talking about university, and almost smoothing it over, if it hadn't been for Vic's obvious, panicked chatter. She feels the hot lash of embarrassment remembering it, even now; all the nonsensical things she said, frozen a little distance away from him, until finally he finished his joint and said casually that he really ought to go to bed.

'See you soon,' he said, moving unsteadily away across the black grass. 'Sorry again about your school friend. Send my love to your parents.'

After that neither of them referred to the kiss, or to their long-running joke that when they were old they would get married, and Vic decided that it would be better for her not to think about it again, a task at which, over the years, she was almost completely successful.

Now Vic waits outside the Quinta do Rosal, the exterior of which is unlit. It is so dark that she can't see much beyond her own body, though the sky is still a radiant, clouded blue, sustaining its colour long after the disappearance of the sun. She hears Michael's progress across the hall, an irregular footstep, before the lights switch on and he stands in the doorway as if dazzled by them, blinking at her. He is drunk, but without any of his usual affability, his general enthusiasm for the state of drunkenness. He frowns through the brandy-scented fog about him, as if resenting its efforts to soothe.

'Michael, I'm—' Vic begins.

'Let's not talk about it. I absolutely do not want to talk. About. It,' Michael says. 'Let's just all have a brandy.'

But by the time they have got into the sitting room and he has identified the right bottle, he is talking about it, about how he just doesn't understand, why she would leave without saying anything.

'She took all her things – but nothing I'd bought her, like it was fucking contaminated or something – and left a note that said she was sorry but she couldn't stay. Her phone's dead. She was being paid by cheque while she got her new bank account set up, and her pay cheque's just waiting at the office. I don't know her old address or the address of anyone she knows, Vic. I have no idea what's happened.'

'It sounds like she just . . . changed her mind,' Vic ventures, relieved that she won't, after all, have to tell Michael about her own role in events.

The sitting room is dark, Michael being too preoccupied to turn any lights on, or having acclimatised to the gradually declining daylight. The only illumination in the room comes from the strange blue sky beyond the French windows. He hands her a half-full brandy glass and she accepts it nervously.

'Why don't you sit down,' she says, because he is standing holding his own glass, like a man about to march somewhere, bristling with potential energy. The stress rises off him: Michael, who she has never seen look anything more than gently ruffled. The sight of it bothers her; she feels almost frightened, at such a transfiguration.

He sits down but his hands remain tightly curled. 'How could she do it, Vic? I thought she might feel she owed me something more than that.'

Vic drinks some of the brandy and tries to think of what to say, as he continues, 'It must have been that she was about to move in. She said she wasn't sure about it. I talked her into it. It was fucking stupid – it was too quick. She must have felt pressured. You can't confine someone like her. It was a mistake.'

'Maybe it just wasn't the right relationship,' Vic says. Michael doesn't appear to hear her. He leans back in the chair, the glass tilting in his hands, just short of spilling. His profile – clean and regular, as perfectly even as a Renaissance template of a profile – faces the ceiling.

'I've got all the things I bought her. They're just *here*,' he says, and he sounds like he might cry.

Vic, for no real reason, thinks of the gold silk dressing gown.

'We'll put them away,' she says. 'So they can't remind you.'

'Yes,' he says, still staring at the ceiling, then adds, 'Fuck her', after which he appears to descend into a deep and uninterruptible silence, his eyes closed, only his hand still held rigid, around the brandy glass.

Vic sits for a long time in the dark room and watches him until she realises that he has passed out, and she ought to prise the glass out of his hand. When she tries, kneeling next to him, he opens his eyes unexpectedly and looks at her. His eyes are light grey in his upturned, alcohol-softened face; they seem sober suddenly, like two points of lucidity, torches in an indistinct night wood. It is as if his drunkenness, his longing and his sadness have slipped off them; the old Michael looking out, safe and sound. The sharpness of her relief is almost painful: she can't speak, or remove her hand from the brandy glass, where it rests next to his own.

'Thanks for being here,' he says, and smiles.

Vic kisses him. She does it without thinking about it, and it comes naturally after all, like an innate ability, an evolutionary survival trick. He kisses her back and she puts her hands up to the tender skin of his neck, his hair and face, territory she has seen but not crossed. She can't taste alcohol: she must taste of it herself, the interiors of their mouths potent with it. She feels an overwhelming sense of gratitude, like she has escaped something, or got away with something. Under the relief various emotions move: elation, longing, and other, less identifiable feelings.

But after an indeterminate while she realises Michael is drawing back; his hands are on her shoulders, gently increasing the distance between them. She moves her head back, quickly, and they stare at each other, but while she is trying to read his face – examining him – it is as if he doesn't see her at all. He looks through her as if she is a Magic Eye picture, reaching beyond her for something else.

'Vic,' he says.

She shakes her head, as if to forestall him getting hold of the unspoken truth, which she understands very well, now, and hurting her with its loudness, its conversion into harsh, simple sounds.

'Don't,' she says. 'I'm sorry.'

'We're both drunk,' he says, with a brief gesture; excusing them. It seems as if he is already thinking of something else. He leans forward and puts his glass on the table. Then he rubs his face with his hands, pressing hard, as if to effect a transformation. When the hands come away he looks as defeated as before, as dishevelled and as far away.

'Do you think . . . do you think maybe she's in some sort of trouble?' he asks. He doesn't wait for her reply, but carries on passionately, struck by his idea. 'That note was so unlike her. What if someone's done something to her? She could have been abducted.'

Vic is alarmed; 'I don't think it sounded that way. Not at all.'

'I could be sitting here complaining about her when she's out there and she needs my help.'

He sits up and looks about, as if ready to get up and leave, and Vic says hastily, 'You can't make yourself mad, thinking things like this. Coming up with these stories when there is an obvious explanation. Look, you don't know anything about her or what she wanted. It might be better that she left.'

'What do you mean?' He is looking at her now, at last, but it is with a piercing intentness she hasn't seen before, a hard, clarified focus.

'I've heard things. Trinidade—'

'Trinidade? That witch?'

'Not just that . . .' But here Vic falters. She doesn't want to tell Michael that she eavesdropped on a conversation of Estella's – however unwittingly – or that she covertly investigated Estella's CV; not with the kiss still hovering in the recent past, or the way he is staring at her now. She ventures instead, 'Don't you think she was always . . . secretive? She arrived here with nothing and she meets you – her boss – and sees this place and how successful you are, and—'

'*Vic*,' he says, and she sees that he is angry. 'I know you're only saying that because you want to protect me, but you're absolutely wrong. You don't know her.'

'*You* don't know her!' cries Vic, hearing at once how ridiculous she sounds, a wail at the unfairness of it all.

'Yes, I do,' Michael insists.

'Because you slept with her,' Vic says bitterly.

'For a saintly virgin you have a fucking dirty mind,' Michael snaps. There is a brief silence. 'Look. Sorry. That wasn't fair. I've had too much to drink. Vic, I don't know everything, obviously, but I don't need you to enlighten me.' He stands up – not without a hand on the back of the sofa to balance himself – and says, 'I'm going to bed. Thank you for coming,' and Vic realises that she hasn't done anything to undo Estella's spell over him: quite the opposite, because now Estella is gone, without confessing to any crime, and Vic can't say anything now either without making Michael hate her, and will just have to watch him turn his remembered Estella gradually back into Galatea, until the idea of her is as perfect and hard as stone, and no longer comparable to any real woman.

She walks back along the Rua da Madalena, for once not leaning back against its steep slide downhill, but allowing herself to pick up pace, giving in to her own gravity, until she is nearly running. She tries not to cry, but does anyway. She calls it love, for the first time, now that it is over; having bloomed and died, unknown, in only one hour of the night. She understands that it was a childish, dogged sort of love; trained into her by long devotion, and gratitude, and a stubborn refusal to even try to love anything else. And she has acted exactly as a child would; offering herself stupidly, tactlessly; learning she isn't wanted; running home in tears. She sees it all, she thinks, but it turns out that isn't enough; that understanding a pain can't, in the end, make it any less painful.

Two weeks later, Vic is by the pool at the Quinta Verde, wincing in the flat glare of the turquoise water – which has always looked poisonous to her; the colour of a chemistry experiment – trying to calm a woman who is accusing another woman of having stolen her sun lounger.

'What are you going to do?' the woman demands. 'I'll have another lounger brought out to you,' Vic says. 'I hope that will resolve things. I'm very sorry you had this experience.'

'But *she* should be told.' The woman gestures at her adversary, floating lotus-like on the surface of the water, eyes determinedly closed. 'She can't carry on taking loungers.'

'What do you want me to say to her? Do you want her punished?' Vic says.

The woman looks surprised, and wary. 'I didn't say that.'

'OK. Well, I'll go and see about a new lounger now,' Vic says. 'And I'll authorise the bar to bring you a complimentary drink. Whatever you like.' After that she goes to the lavatory, shuts herself in a cubicle, and cries.

The day after she had gone over to Michael's, he came to her house. At the sight of his car pulling up outside she went quietly up the stairs, where she waited, standing at the edge of the window and looking at the top of his head outside, pale in the sun, until he gave up knocking and ringing the bell and drove away. Not long after this he called and left a voicemail, to tell her that he was at the airport. He was leaving Madeira, to look for Estella. He didn't mention her attempt to kiss him, either out of civility, or the plain fact that he had forgotten.

When Vic gets into her office, Ana is waiting for her with

two more complaints. 'I'm looking forward to the winter,' Ana says. 'Fewer Ingleses. Less bitching.'

Vic thinks of the winter: the slow descent of the mist, a clinging grey sinking down from the mountains like a floating, diffuse snow. The heat fading from the landscape; the orchids, the mimosa and the jacaranda packing up their decorations, as at the end of a party. The numbers of tourists will thin: she will look out of the window to see a row of unoccupied sun loungers; one person revolving in the empty blue of the pool. She feels a sudden and enclosing melancholy at the idea of the end of this season, the beginning of the next.

'Vic?' Ana says, looking at her curiously. 'I was meant to tell you – David wants to talk to you.'

David Berry arrived a week ago. His visit has not gone as either Vic or Lawrence expected, since the day he sat in on a staff meeting chaired by Lawrence, with one hand clenching and unclenching on his elegantly clothed thigh and a look of dawning dismay. He has taken to putting Lawrence on the spot about various aspects of the business, watching coolly as Lawrence stumbles and improvises, looking like a small boy who has broken a window.

'Vicky,' says David Berry, when she goes in. He is leaning back in his chair holding a pen like a dart, his sleeves rolled up and his jacket cast over the back of his chair. His large, dark-haired body always appears to be uncomfortably restrained by the suit, which successfully confines him in the morning but has always been partially escaped by midday. With his intelligent dark eyes and profuse ear hair, he often reminds her of a forcibly dressed ape.

'Right, I'm going to be honest with you, Vicky. *Lawrence –*' he thrusts the pen in the direction of the door – 'I did a lot for that boy. I trained him; I thought he had potential. But he's fucking useless. And his suits are too nice. He's been overpaying himself somehow. I'm going over the books at the moment and I'm going to find out what he's been up to.'

'Oh,' Vic says. 'Well. I don't think I'm in a position to comment.'

'Don't be polite. You know and I know you're the one who keeps things going around here, and—'

'Wait, David,' Vic says. She is experiencing a new feeling, one that must be commonplace for people like Michael – just the usual itch – but for her is a revelatory, almost euphoric sensation: the desire to free herself. She rushes on with it, 'Sorry. I'm grateful for what you said, but I can't stay working here. Or living in Madeira, actually. I haven't written anything down but I'll type a letter of resignation today. There's nothing wrong with the hotel, but I think I'm sort of done with it here. I've been here for a long time doing the same thing. I won't explain, but it doesn't really work any more and I think I need to go away and try something else. That's what I believe I need to do now. So . . . yes. I'm leaving. I hope you understand.'

It seems strange to Vic, sitting and watching the runway at Funchal Airport in an attempt to acclimatise herself to the presence of planes – preparing herself for the moment in an hour's time when she will actually have to approach one, beached on the runway like a great blank-eyed white porpoise, and climb inside its belly – that the last time she was here was at the start of the summer, when she was waiting for Michael.

The thought comes to her softly; muffled and velvety and unsurprising. All her ideas have been arriving in this way since she took a Valium. Her previous concerns – the sadness of leaving, the loss of Michael, fear of a plane crash, fear of what she will do if the plane doesn't crash and she makes it to England – poke through the pleasant Valium fog like treetops and pylons in the mountain clouds; distant, and of only minor interest.

Vic can't summon many clear memories of England, and can't separate those she comes up with from things she has heard, or seen on television. She thinks of rain, and cucumber sandwiches. She has a memory of herself feeding ducks, wearing a pair of green wellingtons with frog eyes. The brown sofa was there, but did she ever eat fish and chips on it? She thinks she can recall London, but it is only a stylised skyline, with Big Ben and Nelson's Column standing next to each other.

She doesn't expect that she'll see Michael in England, if that is still where he is. Since he left, she hasn't tried to call him, there being both too much and too little to even begin to talk about. She expects that her next update on his life will come from his parents, passed to hers, and Vic will have to guess from the third-hand news whether he found Estella, or if he is still looking. Even through the Valium, she feels ashamed when she thinks about her role in Michael's and Estella's break-up. She has no idea if she did the right thing for the wrong reasons, or the wrong thing for the wrong reasons. A truth has been outed, without any accompanying sense or meaning, because any possible explanation has disappeared along with Estella. Nobody won anything. The three of them simply got on different planes, and left. The end.

As her taxi left Azenhas do Mar it passed the Quinta do Rosal, now shuttered and empty, its iron gates chained. The white face half hidden in the trees, catching the first light of the dawn, had something newly desolate in its beauty, as if knowing that the last of the Bonifacios had left. She wasn't tempted to stop the car, to slip through the side gate to the garden and put her face up to a window. It seemed the time for all that was done with, more quickly and completely than she could ever have imagined.

Vic did allow herself one look back at Azenhas do Mar as the car turned the corner at the top of the Rua da Madalena. The sun had sunk below the mountains but the water still quivered with light, and the sky was filled with a lingering radiance. The village was a postcard view: terracotta roofs and white houses; red- and purple-flowered trees, a small china model headed by the chequered church tower. She hadn't been to church since the night she tried to kiss Michael. She didn't feel the need to confess either the kiss or her deception; and it was a relief when she decided not to bother. She spent hours in the dense, jewel-coloured darkness of the church, toiling like a miner, feeling anxious when she was meant to feel at peace, frustrated when she ought to have been joyful, and the sad truth was that she never felt as uplifted as when Michael smiled at her, or as happy as when he was sitting next to her in the café under the tree, encouraging her to tell people to fuck off.

When Vic boards the plane she breathes deeply and looks out of the window at the forested heights of the mountains. One hand moves to the friendship bracelet on her other wrist. This is the only ending, Vic thinks: a conclusion she owes, ironically enough, to Estella. On the way to the airport she had asked the taxi driver to stop at the graveyard where Kate was buried. In the early morning chill, grey and radiant, she stood for a while before Kate's gravestone; noticing, without true surprise, that she had been laid to rest next to her mother, Charlotte – who had died when Kate was six – and that her father had yet to join them. She laid down her flowers and knelt down in the grass, still wet with the mist lifting off it, and spoke to Kate. When other people began to arrive for morning prayers she left; not wanting the conversation to be heard by anyone, as is only proper for confession.

As she waits for take-off the late sun crosses the tarmac and hits the plane window, so that she has to turn away. The sights of the island appear to her anyway: Ana leaning on the reception desk, Trinidade sulky with lemonade, Michael waiting at her door to say goodbye, Kate peering over the open Bible with the light on her blond hair, her black eyes containing a night of riches. Madeira, the floating garden, the pearl of the Atlantic, fragrant, sweet with wine and sugar. The great palm leaves like awnings, the patterned village square, the bougainvillea heat haze, the snowy tops of the sea, the white stone of the Quinta do Rosal. Everyone she loved gone, so that it will carry on, for her, only as a dream.

ESTELLA

When Kaya gets into the flat Jasper is sitting on the sofa with his back to her. She notices first that there is no smell of coffee, having come to associate that with his arrival. He doesn't turn around and she has to walk around the sofa and stand in front of him before he will look at her.

'Jasper, what's happened?' she asks, surprised.

He looks at her steadily. Without a single hair being out of place or a crease in his shirt he manages to give the impression of a man who has lost everything. There is a bottle of whisky and a glass on the table next to him, sitting under a lamp so that they glow with their own importance, in what she abstractly thinks would be rather obvious cinematography, if this were a film. His eyes, dark and drunk, appear to drift free of his face, the rigidly held bones of his jaw.

'Who is he?' he asks. His voice is slow and wet and heavy, like poured concrete. 'What is he like? Did he offer you something better than I could, or were you just bored? Or was he in the background all along? How many people are you fucking, anyway?'

'I'm not cheating on you, Jasper. But I am leaving. I'm sorry.'

'You're leaving me for him,' Jasper says, with the same sluggish comprehension, fighting its way up through the weight of alcohol. His eyes, still seeming untethered, stare at her, as if to take hold of her, to make her feel the great hurt and injustice he suffers.

'I'm not cheating on you,' she repeats, aware that she sounds tired and cold and not at all reassuring. 'I'm just not.'

'Don't lie to me.'

'What would be the point in lying, now?'

She can see that he would like to believe her; he hunts in her face for something to comfort him. Apparently without finding it, he stands and takes her arms. Not roughly, but not gently either.

'Don't leave,' he says. 'Not yet. Sleep here with me. Just for one last night.'

'I'm sorry,' she says.

Their faces are too close for their eyes to meet without a level of intensity that she is not up to. Uncomfortable, her gaze falters under the pressure; sliding towards the floor where their feet are awkwardly arranged, as if in the middle of some aborted dance.

'I'm obsessed with you,' he says. He has said this before, but not with this anguish. He hasn't added, as he does now, 'What have you done to me?'

'I'm sorry,' she says again. 'I didn't mean it – I really didn't. I just don't feel the same any more.'

'But why?' he asks.

Kaya ends up going to bed with him for two reasons: to avoid answering, and out of sympathy – or, more precisely, her lack of it. She doesn't feel sorry for him – there is still a great coldness inside her, unmoving and desolate – but she tries to remember what someone else might do in these circumstances; what she might have done once, to show him some compassion.

She lies down next to him in the bed but won't allow him to hold her, or touch her, beyond his grip on her hand. Once he is lying down she can feel his hand slackening, as he is carried away by the tide of his inebriation into a tarry, sticky sleep. Once he is unconscious she thinks she will get up quietly and leave, this seeming like the easiest way to extricate herself. But she hasn't considered her own fatigue, how it will swim up and close over her head, so that she is half asleep by the time she wakes, baffled, to find him on top of her. Things come to her in odd stutters of information, knocked out of their usual order. She realises that her legs won't close; that his legs are in between them, unyielding as sandbags.

'Jasper, no,' she says. 'Jasper! Stop it.'

His face is buried in her neck as if he refuses to hear her, so she hits his shoulder.

'I don't want this,' she says. But this isn't working, and nor are any of the other words. *Stop* and *No* have lost their usual power. She takes hold of his hair and pulls it, aware that it is already too late for this. He catches her hands and holds them together, and when she shouts he puts his other hand over her mouth. He has done this before in bed, playing at restraint, and she wonders, through her fright, if he thinks this is what they are doing now. He doesn't look at her: not once; his face is against her neck, or lifted to stare without any apparent consciousness at the window, the wall behind her head. Tears are crushed, unwillingly, from her eyes in time with his movement. Only when he is finished does his gaze wander over in the direction of hers, as if remembering that she is there.

'Star,' he says, his voice clotted with feeling. 'I'm sorry.' He tips himself off her. By the time his head lands on the pillow beside her he appears to have already passed out.

Kaya lies next to him and pushes his leg slowly off hers. With the same blank stealth she picks up the arm that is slung over her breasts and puts it back onto his side of the bed. She doesn't get up immediately. She is too shocked. She lies flat, her body humming with dispersed energy.

What comes into Kaya's mind then – arriving without any reason to, any connection to the present moment – is a memory of Louise making a cake. It wasn't any particular occasion, just one of those days that she had arrived home from school, coming in out of the rain to find the flat full of the smell of sugar, of flour clouds and heat. Louise was decorating the cake with tiny silver dragées, dropping each one on with unerring precision. She was so preoccupied with it that she had forgotten to drink, and was in a state approaching sober. She brought Kaya up close to the cake (Kaya hushed, as though the cake were an animal that she might startle) and showed her what the hundreds of silver balls spelt out: *Kaya*, surrounded by stars. That night they ate cake and fell asleep together on the sofa. It took Kaya longer to fall asleep because she didn't want the night to be over. She understood that it was special: in its heart a birthday-candle spark, a sweet-wrapper flame or chip of coloured glass; that improbable, temporary happiness.

The scene fades quickly, like a flame lit by the Little Match Girl, and Kaya has to return to the dark room; the scene of collapse in the bed, the whipped-up sheets, the aftermath. But the feeling is returning now to her disarranged arms and legs: her body gathers weight, until it can get up, without looking at Jasper, and go to the door. Once outside the room she stands and listens to the sound of his breathing. It is strained, as if he has been trapped in a landslide. She wonders if he is so drunk that he might die in his sleep. It seems unlikely.

She runs through her options in an abstracted, skittish way, picking up ideas and dropping them without real considera-tion. She doesn't want to speak to him. Nor does she feel the need for immediate, physical retaliation. She doesn't want to touch him again at all, not even to do harm; confirming with her own hands the substance of his body, the irrefutable fact of it. The obvious thing to do is to call the police. But the police and Kaya have never been on the same side, and she knows something of the horror of rape prosecutions, even for women who have the right words said about them in the papers – middle class, student, virgin, mother. She is a girl who fits too many of the wrong words. Council estate. Stripper. Mistress. The police are for people like Jasper. He can call them himself, she thinks, after she is gone.

She doesn't go back into the bedroom to pick up her clothes. Instead she takes whichever possessions of hers are in the bathroom, the sitting room and the hall cupboard, leaving whatever Jasper has bought her, more by way of a statement than from any sense of honour. She takes Sartre, which she had left by the sofa. She goes to the linen cupboard and from under a pile of towels removes her papers and the passport in the name of Estella White. Finally, from the kitchen counter, she takes the things Jasper messily divested himself of before bed. The keys to the expensive car that Jasper had refused to pay anything but the real price for. The limited-edition watch from Switzerland. The Italian leather wallet, with its respectable quantity of notes.

As she walks down the concrete steps to the underground car park, watching the shadows of rats fragment and disappear, she sees herself in the dark windows of the parked cars. Her face looks hard: as hard as it feels; as if she walked into the flat as clay and is walking out as china, as impassive and blank as Louise's long-gone porcelain lady.

In a bed and breakfast not far from Heathrow airport, a 1930s semi she had judged to be suitably 'out of the way' – its swagged chintz curtains and wall-to-wall carpet reminding her of a porn set, the faded flowers on the bed linen like old blood stains – Kaya imagines her mother's funeral. She does this almost as a meditation; conscious of carrying out a rite, a gesture in lieu of the real thing, which she will not be able to attend. She watches Louise being tucked into the ground, the earth pulled over her like a duvet. Carl gives a reading; a piece of paper shaking violently in his hands, the dirt cleaned carefully away from the moons of his nails, the dried out, bark-like cracks of his fingers.

Kaya would have read her own piece for Louise; not a prayer, but a poem. Now, in the absence of any other books, she reads out loud from *Being and Nothingness*. Her voice eddies around the patterned room, seeming to bring the densely filled wall-paper, the low, gilt chandelier and dust-laden pink drapes down on her, until, feeling claustrophobic, she has to open the window and put her head out into the cold night. The wind draws in and draws out like a tide, sweeping over her like sandpaper, until her face is raw and stinging. She finishes the piece this way, the words vanishing the moment they are spoken, as if whirled up to an impassive divine audience. Considering this a decent enough tribute to Louise, or at least the best tribute she is capable of, Kaya closes the window and goes back to the bed, where, once horizontal, her stomach begins to make such desperate and piteous noises of complaint that she has to walk herself backwards through the past twenty-four hours, trying to remember when she last ate. Failing at this, she considers going out to look for a fast-food place nearby, but is deterred by the prospect of running into the proprietor again, a stiff-haired woman who, when she arrived, peered at her suspiciously from behind the artificial plant on her fake wood desk.

'I'd like to stay one night, please,' Kaya asked.

'Is it just you?'

'Yes.'

'Only if it isn't,' she said, looking at Kaya with faded severity, 'there will be an extra charge.'

'No, it's just me.'

The woman shrugged, clearly not believing her, and led her to her room. 'I'm a *very* light sleeper,' was her parting warning.

Kaya sets her alarm for early the next morning, hoping that

nobody will have started looking for her by then. After she left Jasper's she drove to Chloe's and woke her up. (Luck was on her side: Dave wasn't home.) Chloe was eyebrowless and pink with sleep, like a newborn rabbit. When Kaya asked her to help she was tearful ('Babe, what've you done? You haven't killed anyone, have you? Promise? Swear on my life?') but efficient. She called a friend of a friend and he came in half an hour and took everything away for ten thousand pounds in cash, of which Kaya took as much as she could reasonably take through customs, leaving the rest to Chloe, who swore she wouldn't touch it.

'The police won't bother looking for you,' Chloe's friend advised her, shaking his head. 'No need to leave the country. It's an insurance job.'

'Yeah, listen to him. Please don't leave,' Chloe begged.

But Kaya could not be persuaded. Though she didn't explain it to Chloe, the prospect of a plane journey – she has never flown on a plane – and a new country mean something more to her than simple practicality. That night she dreams not of her mother but of the flight. In her dream the plane is dark and hot. She looks out of the window and flames are licking along its body from the nose. 'It's all right,' the stewardess says, 'this always happens.' She continues to look and, eventually, beyond the sheet of flame, she can make it out: a blurred horizon, getting closer and closer, ready to unroll its new, unknown land under her feet.

Estella (Kaya is jettisoned somewhere over the Channel) goes to the south coast of Spain first, where she works for a while at a bar – appropriately named Secrets – run by a cousin of Chloe's. Next she goes to Amsterdam and works as a bar manager, moving on to Berlin, where she produces flyers for a drag club and shares a flat with two transvestites, then Cannes, where she takes a job as a bookkeeper for a bar frequented by Russian prostitutes and their clients. The first time she hands in her fake CV she is terrified; shivering and slippery-palmed until the final sign off. Each time after that it gets easier, until, sitting neatly cross-ankled before the interviewer's desk, she feels only a thin ribbon of fear, curling through her stomach.

In Lisbon she stays long enough to learn Portuguese, and, tired of working in bars, awards herself a degree in Philosophy and applies for office jobs. She is good at what she does – sales, admin, HR – but always quits before she can be promoted. Though she has long since concluded that the UK police aren't interested in looking for her, she is wary of a rise to online prominence, of putting her head too far above the paperwork parapet.

Five years pass: a long time without friends or lovers. She is politely friendly towards her workmates but avoids any intimacy; working through lunch, turning down invitations. This and the middle-class manners she picked up from Jasper, together with the accent she successfully fakes (and eventually comes to find has become her own), sometimes get her the reputation of being a stuck-up bitch, which suits her so long as nobody says it to her face, and they never do.

This isn't the only thing she is accused of by her colleagues. Women note her refusal to join in with wine-drinking sessions or confide in them about heartbreak or sexual misadventure or how she hates her thighs. They begin to suspect her of being a lone predator skirting around their territory; howling to their men. It doesn't seem to matter whether or not she actually speaks to the men in question. She has the aura of sexual misconduct that haloes the unattached woman like a cloud of contagious hormones, dizzying any males who might come within a few feet. She knows, coldly, that her face – refined by adulthood into more minimal curves, lying pearl-like in its newly dark bed of hair – is beautiful, and also that this beauty will not be helpful to her now. It is usually suspected that she is sleeping with the boss.

Sometimes she thinks of her friendships with Chloe, or Laura, or Alisha, and feels sorry for the loss of those days. There was a girl in Berlin who reminded her of Chloe, a kitten-faced waitress with an impressive repertoire of dirty jokes. They had a coffee together after their shift and the girl – Lotte – asked her why she came to Berlin, what her life was like in England, who she fancied, what her relationships had been like, what did she hope them to be, what sort of career did she want? Estella realised then that she couldn't be a friend. Women expect too much; their intimacy involves gradually unpacking and laying out everything about themselves, then asking, eagerly, 'what do you think?' Estella doesn't have enough material for that. She is a mirror, she is one-way glass. If anyone gets around to the side of her, she will disappear.

Sartre's voyeur only understands he is a voyeur because he has been seen by another person: without the other person's gaze there is no consciousness of the self – no 'for itself' – and so, because self-consciousness is dependent on the other, the foundation of the self is outside the self. But when it comes to Estella, the matter is complicated. She knows what the other would have her be and knows, without knowing exactly what she *is*, that she is not what they think.

She watches other people busily defining themselves, marketing their own particular brands, and thinks that, in the end, she has escaped this. She has found Sartre's strange, hard freedom. She never felt like she was a daughter, she never felt like she was a stripper, she never felt like she was a criminal, and now that she is apparently a respectable account manager she can't seriously inhabit that role either. When she dresses in her white shirt and pencil skirt she feels as if she is in fancy dress, or in disguise; a cinematic spy who has stolen a uniform to sneak into the villain's headquarters, and might at any moment be found out.

Estella goes to Madeira in search of some peace and quiet. She had thought that the family-run engineering equipment firm she worked at in Lisbon would be a shelter in the world where she could relax at last into her anonymity, continuing to attend lectures at the university, reading in the park near her flat under the shade of a plane tree she has come to think of as her own. But the owner of the firm, Sandro, has recently been caught having affairs with several of his female employees under the nose of his wife, the finance director, and it is now expected that these conquests – a list generally thought to include Estella – will quietly quit. Not fancying a legal battle in Portuguese, Estella elicits a promise of a good reference from Sandro before packing her box and joining the exodus of scarlet women, taking the lift down in twos and threes, holding pot plants and avoiding each other's eyes.

On the plane to Funchal, Estella is reassured to see that she is the only person under thirty. Her dream of a dull job by the sea where nobody asks her any questions appears to be within her reach. She allows her body to soften into the seat, uncurling her toes and fingers, feeling the pressure drain from her shoulders. When she steps out of the airport with her two suitcases she enters a gentle night, redolent of past heat, pearly and sweet. Even the fuss and blare of the taxis seems as calming as the buzz of crickets in the flood-lit trees, the sound of the sea beyond the runway.

Estella quickly finds herself a place in Funchal, a small apartment with erratic air conditioning but two ceiling-height windows overlooking a black and white paved square with a fountain and a line of jacaranda trees, their branches and trunks twisted as if arrested in some bacchanalian dance, dividing the green grass and white buildings beyond into irregular panes, like a stained-glass window. Each morning two stray dogs trot across the chessboarded paving together, tongues out, following their own mysterious itinerary. On her roof, sea gulls yelp and pigeons croon. She doesn't mind the noise. They quieten down at night, which is when she faces her own problems; waking up from some night-time fight or another, still wrestling with the sheets or pressing the pillow in a death grip, sweating and out of breath.

She finds herself a job in payroll at a civil engineering firm,

Cooper Erdinger Shaw, with offices a short walk from her apartment along the esplanade, the patterns of which pass under her feet like an unrolling etching, grey basalt and white marble, shifting from the geometric to the psychedelic and back again, as the sea rushes onto the rocks below; a gravelly, crystalline sound, like poured sugar. Other days she walks along the Avenida Arriaga under the lines of trees, to see the eighteenth-century mansions tiled with blue azulejo, the coffee drinkers watching her incuriously from under their awnings. In the mornings and early evenings the sun sits lightly on her skin; the shadows are long across the roads. This is enough, she thinks then. This is good.

Work is less peaceful: the company is in utter disarray, something she found endearing at first when she realised it was too disorganised to even ask for her references, let alone process them, but the charm has long since worn off. She has found herself doing the work of her own boss, a chimerical figure who has yet to be named, let alone seen, and yesterday she was asked to take on some assistant duties for one of the head engineers, Michael Worth, in addition to her own job. Though he is rarely in the office, Estella has been aware of Michael, in a vague and second-hand way. He is considered important to the company – too important to answer calls or go to the photocopier, though he has been seen quite cheerfully doing both. He is an immediately good-looking man with a lazily acquired tan, grey eyes managing to appear both colourful and vivid, and hair hovering somewhere between blond and brown, not far from the colour her own natural hair might have been by now. She has noticed his self-assurance; the way he has of looking at everything without surprise. Life seems very easy for him.

Estella avoids conversations at work, but talking about Michael Worth seems to be an office-wide pastime. Standing waiting for a coffee from the machine, eyes fixed determinedly on the large illuminated pictures of coffee beans, she hears that he lives in a village not far away. Sitting on the loo she hears, from the next cubicle, the news that his parents are rich. A woman in the lift says she saw him in a bar with a blonde; two smokers repeat some of his jokes, having apparently memorised the punchlines. It has got to the point where she feels like she is the subject of an aggressive PR campaign and begins to feel irritated by the bombardment, even – unreasonably – resenting the rare appearances of Michael himself, ignoring him when he passes by her desk and smiles. When Carla, who is a sideways step along from Estella's actual boss, asks her to be his assistant, Estella offers up an unusual level of resistance.

'Isn't that girl – Theresa – supposed to be doing that?'

'Not any more,' Carla says. 'It's a case of that English expression of yours: Theresa is (and I say this in confidence) as useless as a teapot made of shit.'

'That's not the expression.'

'What is it, then?'

'A chocolate teapot.'

'Chocolate?! Chocolate is sweet and pleasant. No, she is a teapot of shit.'

'Well, whatever she is, I'm just not sure I have time to take on the extra work.'

Carla is unsympathetic. 'That's what I said when they asked me to be the office manager. I said, "I'm head of HR already." You know what? Nobody cared.'

'OK,' says Estella. 'I take your point.'

The next day she takes a desk near Michael's office and has to acknowledge his 'Good morning!' when he arrives. It is hard to resist a 'Good morning' like this one: radiantly sunny, appearing to contain only the best and most sincere wishes for her – Estella's – morning. But Estella has had a lot of practice at hurting the feelings of well-wishers, and returns only a cool nod before going back to her computer, as if he has wasted valuable working time with his irresponsible greeting.

By the end of the day she hasn't had the opportunity to assist Michael. He has answered his own calls and hasn't asked for anything. He brings her a coffee and a bun when he goes out to get his own lunch: she finds them on her desk, like offerings. By the end of the day she realises with annoyance that she is staring curiously at his door – which has remained closed all day – accompanied by the distracted tarantella of her nails on the desktop.

The next morning she is exiting the lift with a few other colleagues, bitching about Cooper Erdinger Shaw (the astonishingly bad management of which has led Estella to this unprecedented level of intimacy), when she passes a newspaper on a desk. On its front page is a picture of a dead body, left in the position it was thrown violently into, by gunfire or explosives. Not expecting to see it, she flinches. She wonders when it started happening; the sale and publication of corpse shots. She didn't remember it when she was a teenager. Now after every flood or earthquake or terrorist attack there are pictures of the victims. She saw a picture of a man lying face-down, bloody and naked across a bench, after a nightclub in some holiday destination was bombed. He looked like litter; like meat, as inanimate as the rolling bins or the signs hanging blasted from their posts.

'For God's sake,' she says, to the owner of the newspaper. 'We don't all want to see that.'

'Sorry,' he says, stricken. He folds it up, and she regrets being so abrupt.

'I don't mean it's your fault. It's the newspapers. Don't they understand that these people have relatives? A body may not be sacred, fine, but the meaning it has to its former owner's family is sacred.'

A few desks away a man who has been shamelessly eavesdropping turns to his neighbour and says, audibly, 'I'd treat her body as sacred.'

She didn't realise Michael was listening too, standing behind her, until he turns sharply to the other man and says, 'I suppose it's too much to ask for you to treat your work as sacred? Get on with it, why don't you.' Without looking at her, he walks away, going into his own office and closing the door behind him.

Estella sits at her own desk for a while until it becomes apparent that he isn't going to give her any work to do today, either. Then she gets up and knocks on his door. When she is inside he looks at her with faint surprise; the first time she has seen this expression.

'You don't need to defend my honour,' she says, at which his look of surprise deepens.

Making the most of her visit, she glances around at the

office. It is nicer than the others, with its windows (hung with non-standard-issue, wooden-slatted blinds) overlooking the park, several tall and extravagantly leaved plants, a photograph on the large desk: two grey-haired people, presumably his parents.

'It's nothing to do with your honour,' he says. 'I don't like that guy. He's lazy and stupid. I saw an opportunity to embarrass him.'

'So I was just a means to an end.'

'Yes.'

'That's all right, then.'

'Is that all you wanted?' he asks.

'Yes. Unless you have some work for me?'

He looks at her for a while, then says, smiling, 'Have lunch with me today.'

'Is this a work lunch?'

'No.'

'So I don't have to attend?'

'No.' He looks at her frankly.

'But you're my boss. There's a power imbalance. It complicates things like invitations to lunch and it's disingenuous of you not to acknowledge it.'

'I'm not your boss.'

'And yet here I am, working for you.'

'Not by any of the usual definitions. You aren't contracted to work for me. You're not paid to work for me. And – perhaps most importantly – you haven't done any work for me.'

'We both know I'm working for you.'

'Prove it.'

'This is one of the most stupid conversations I've ever had,' she says, exasperated.

He smiles. White teeth, widely offered. The effect is unexpectedly disarming. 'Let's continue it over lunch.'

They go to a park and buy ice creams from a small café; a small hexagonal building with a green and white candy striped dome and delicate wrought-iron curlicues, like a carousel, or Cinderella's carriage. All the tables around it have their own striped parasols. She imagines the whole lot taking flight, opening up wrought-iron and glass wings and lifting off like a family of dragonflies. Beyond their table the grass stretches, divided sharply into light and shade. A rainbow trembles in the plume of a fountain. Small rose-breasted finches hop around their feet, landing on the backs of the chairs.

'Why *are* you doing all my work?' she asks Michael.

'Because you're pay roll, not an assistant.'

'You're an engineer, not an assistant.'

He shrugs. 'So neither of us are supposed to be doing it. But I have a more charming telephone voice. And I make better coffee.' His eyes, this close, have the radiance of simple enjoyment; their grey the colour of a cloud with the sun close behind it. 'Also,' he adds, 'I feel like you despise me.'

'Don't be ridiculous,' she says curtly, without thinking, and he laughs. 'I really don't. What on earth would I despise you for?'

'You want a list?'

'Why not?' She sits back with her ice cream, giving him a

smile she knows, from previous deployment, to be both simple and wholly unreadable.

'OK. I have tried three illegal substances. Magic mushrooms, marijuana, MDMA. Drugs have to begin with M. Meth being the exception to this rule. I am a bad driver, even by Portuguese standards. I cheated on a girlfriend when I was in high school. Not since then. The guilt gave me diarrhoea. I still do not understand the rules of poker; they have been explained to me several times and I always tune out. I have no idea why. I am a rotten cook. I fail to call my parents, whom I love. I am not a good speller. I am sometimes guilty of objectifying women, if that's what staring at women in short skirts is.'

'I don't think it is.'

'Well, in that case, I am ignorant of what does and does not constitute the objectification of women. I have also been to a strip club. It was a friend's birthday party and I didn't approve but I went anyway.'

'That *is* objectification,' Estella says.

'So now you despise me!' he cries, triumphant, ice cream held aloft.

'You look like the Statue of Liberty,' she says. Despite herself, she is laughing. 'I still don't despise you.'

'Well, it was shit,' he says, becoming solemn. 'If I ruled the world I'd ban strip clubs.'

'I wouldn't. So long as there's no coercion, it's a matter of free will. If women want to earn money by taking their clothes off, or even having sex, I'm not inclined to stop them. I'd legalise drugs too. In fact, I would only have laws to stop people interfering with other people's free will.'

'But people make stupid, self-destructive decisions,' Michael says. 'Sometimes free will might not be good for them.'

'You can't ban being self-destructive. You just have to invest in education and support. Look, at first society might be a big mess. But in the end there might emerge some sort of personal responsibility. Where people don't do something because the law or God tells them to do it – because they're scared of getting into trouble – but because they have made an adult decision. It's the only way we can be a society of true adults.'

'So what are you, a libertarian?' He is leaning forward now. 'Or an anarchist? I've never met an anarchist before. Please say you are one.'

'I just think a decision has no value unless you've made it freely.' She becomes self-conscious. 'I don't know what that makes me. Boring to listen to, probably.'

He allows this statement to have its own silence, the weight of consideration. Then he says, looking at her simply and openly, 'You fascinate me.'

And, though she looks at him hard, knowing that if there is flirtation in this statement, or mockery, or condescension, she will find it out – unearth it in whichever eye wrinkle or mouth corner it is hiding – she can't spot it, not anywhere.

Without Estella really meaning it to happen – the relationship having slipped somehow under her radar, smuggled past the security detectors in a foil-lined bag – she and Michael begin eating lunch at the park together every day. She doesn't even realise this has become a highlight of her day until he is off-site one afternoon, visiting a tunnel, and she finds herself sitting at her desk without any food, because she hasn't considered the possibility of having to go out alone to get her own sandwich. She isn't just hungry, she realises: she is disappointed.

She decides not to go for lunch with Michael again; to nip the whole thing, whatever it is, in the bud. She has been feeling too relaxed here, too open, as if lulled by the noise of the sea, intoxicated by the sweet-smelling nectar of the flowers, softened by the sun and the salt in the air. Last week he asked what her parents did and she found herself both flustered by the question and feeling a sudden aversion to the idea of lying to him. She has told everyone else in the office that her mother is a teacher and her father an accountant, but facing Michael's bright grey eyes, his glow of pending delight (a habitual air he has; like a man who suspects that he is on the way to his surprise birthday party), she says instead that she doesn't see them. He nods, respectful and serious, and changes the subject.

But when one o'clock comes around the next day and Michael appears in the door of his office, she doesn't have the heart to tell him she plans to eat alone. It seems like a harmless hour of fun; more fun than she has ever had in her life, because whatever her relationship with Jasper was – exciting, frightening, adoring – it was never *fun*. Her childhood had its moments of beauty, of tenderness, but she doesn't remember much fun there either. She was a child who played Scrabble warily, one eye on her opponent, who might at any moment pass out, and tip over her letters. It would be stupid, she thinks now, to be overly cautious about one more hour of simple enjoyment.

And, in fact, the subject of Estella's personal life rarely arises in her conversations with Michael, which tend towards the abstract. His claim to be fascinated by her philosophy was apparently not an empty one; today he is questioning her about determinism, his forgotten ice cream overspilling its cone. She has just told him that there is no God and no essential human nature. He has taken it well.

'So this is existentialism?' he asks. 'This is Sartre? You've mentioned him before.'

'Yes.'

'Ha!' He points at her. 'This is the first time I've seen you look shy! You love him, don't you? Intellectually speaking. You're like a teenager with a secret boyfriend.'

'I refuse to be embarrassed by a man covered in melting ice cream.'

'Shit.' He licks his hand, and she finds herself averting her eyes, as if his tongue, pink and normal, is an unbearably private sight. 'OK, explain Sartre to me. Tell me why you like him.'

'I like anything that gives us autonomy. And the personal responsibility that goes with that. And freedom. I like the idea of freedom from having to be a certain way . . . freedom from the past –'

He is watching her with curiosity, and she sees something in it that stops her talking; not quite a sharp look but a penetrating one, reminding her that he isn't just the genial Labrador he plays at being: that he is clever, and a stranger, and more than capable of making educated guesses about her.

She goes on, becoming more vague: 'I suppose it's central to Sartre that you create your own self. There is no determinism aside from what he called facticity, which is what we're born with – nationality and so on. The rest is transcendence; the choices our own consciousness makes. He did say that it's impossible to measure how much of us is down to facticity and how much to transcendence. Like I'm not a prime minister, but that might be because I'm too stupid, or because I'm too lazy, or an unknown mixture of the two.'

'Neither,' says Michael loyally. 'It's because you're not a cunt.'

'But anyway, Sartre said our identities are not stable or timeless; we're a work in progress. He called any sort of denial of this "bad faith". Like if we claim we're doing something because "that's the way I am". Or if I have been appointed Prime Minister and I begin to believe I *am* a prime minister. I'm not – it's just something I'm playing at being, and at any moment I could do something different. The goal is to avoid being in bad faith – to live authentically.'

'So how do you live authentically?'

'Well, once you are conscious that you choose to do what you are doing, you have the opportunity to change it or the meaning you give to it. Sartre said we can decide to give our life an overall "Choice" – a meaning or direction, composed of many smaller choices. It's up to the individual what the direction is.'

'I see. So, what's your choice?'

'I don't know.'

He laughs, and she smiles, lowering her eyes as if he has caught her out. As they walk back to the office she wonders what he would say if she had told him the truth, that her choice is simple: not to get caught out. Not to be pinned down, not to be seen. She recognises that his very question is an attempt to see her and she understands the danger of this, without feeling any desire to do anything about it.

He points at the sky, 'Look.' Above them, the clouds arriving from over the mountains are colliding with the clouds sailing in from the sea. 'I don't know why they do that,' he says. 'But it's not something you see that often.'

'I've never seen it before,' she says. She stops walking to watch the sky. Neither battalion appears to be winning. They merge and dissolve, like melting ice cream, as if the blue of the sky is incandescent, pure as a gas flame.

'It's rare,' he says, and for once she doesn't mind the word, coming from him.

A few weeks ago Estella would not have said, if asked, that she and Michael would be walking back to her apartment together after a night out drinking with friends. She wouldn't even have laughed, or scoffed, or said shortly that it was a ridiculous idea, the way people do when plausible but unwanted things are suggested. The scenario would have been so fanciful – so preposterous – that she would probably have just shaken her head blankly, as if someone had come up to her and said 'I have it on good authority that the world is ending tomorrow', or 'Fancy a cup of tea on Mars?'

And yet this is what she is doing, at the end of a night that has been a long train of improbable events; a train picking up speed as it goes, becoming less and less usual. First she was talked (by Michael) into attending the leaving drinks of one of their colleagues, Magda, who has tired of doing four different jobs, none of which were in her contract, and quit. Everyone says, 'You escaped the madness! Congratulations! I should do the same thing', but Estella can tell that by now there is a strange Blitz spirit among the CES employees, and that, running below the congratulations for having escaped, there is an unspoken shared understanding that Magda has broken ranks; deserted, bailed. Every barely raised eyebrow behind its glass of sparkling wine says: Magda is a coward and a quitter.

Perhaps simply by virtue of this peculiar camaraderie, arising in times of chaos and emergency, Estella is treated as a friend by colleagues whom she barely speaks to. She has fun with them. She makes small talk and finds it less small, less mean, than she expected. She tells a joke, her first ever, though nobody seems to realise; laughing as if nothing out of the ordinary has occurred. She drinks two glasses of wine and feels the alcohol diffusing through her, a gentle jangle of her senses, a loosening of her mouth, until finally that mouth, running wild, insists that Michael's plan to stay at a hotel that night is a stupid one, when she has a perfectly good sofa, and is closer to the office than the hotel anyway.

The night they walk through is so perfectly calm the wind feels like a current of water, washing away the packed-in heat of the bar, both sobering her and bearing her up in its radiant cool dark. Music drifts from the occasional doorway, pooling in the street. People pass, talking quietly in Thursday-night voices, though it is true that the weekends are hardly less sedate. On the Avenida Arriaga, the yellow globes of the lamp posts resemble gold cats eyes; the trees are strung with lights, on fire with white stars. The cathedral glows behind them. Below the city the dark water rises and shifts, above it is the black and twinkling mountainside.

'I'd never spoken to Magda until today,' Estella confesses.

'You didn't miss much. Unless you like talking about bed linen and measles.'

'Ha. You know, it's strange. It seems like James will genuinely miss Magda. Carmen seemed to think she was a bitch. You think she's boring. I thought she was nice enough.'

'Everyone's nice when they're at their own party being given presents.'

'I wonder, if you took one person and got an opinion of them from every single person that had ever met them, if all those impressions would add up to the truth about that person.'

'I guess so,' Michael says.

'Actually, I don't know if that would work,' Estella says. 'Because everyone's impression is always biased. Nobody really sees anything objectively. Your own preferences and prejudices compromise you.' They are walking across an empty square, their voices carrying across the wide space like bats.

'So . . . what do you think of me?' Michael asks.

He sounds more serious than usual, which disconcerts her – the idea of him brought suddenly too close – and she replies skittishly, 'It would be silly of me to tell you, because if my theory is right, my opinion would reveal more about me than you', and laughs as if he has been teasing her, then tells him some more of the gossip from the night, until he is back to being his droll and cheery self.

That night she fetches a blanket for him and wishes him a

singsong goodnight, going into her own room quickly so that he won't have to make any decisions about whether to undress in front of her. The idea of him taking off his clothes, the mysterious territory of his body between his arms and ankles exposed behind her bedroom door, at rest on her sofa, is an unsettling one. She has a clue about how he would look from the everyday gape and flex of his clothes; can tell that his back, chest and legs will look much the same as his arms and face: young, tanned, as good as anyone could ask them to be. He has a generous, co-operative body. *You'd like me to be sexy? You want muscle?* it asks. *Anything you say.*

She lies awake in bed and listens to the silence in the next room, feeling tormented. After a while she gets up and goes into the sitting room. Michael is asleep on the sofa, one arm thrown out as if catching an imaginary ball, his face lost in unimaginable peacefulness. The expression strikes her as something central to him: he has an internal equilibrium; he needs nothing, he is profoundly at ease. His own happiness goes out into the world and loops back to him like a Möbius strip. It is not the same as her kind of self-sufficiency, which is a containment only, a lockdown.

It also occurs to her that he is comatose on the sofa; that the familiar smell of alcohol is rising ghostly up from his body, but – strangely – it doesn't bother her, just like it didn't bother her when he said 'rare', giving the word its full wonder and significance. He seems to have the unique ability to over-write old, cold associations, the dark and knotty memories like petrified tree roots, like the tangle of hair in a plughole. He could say, 'Sugar cloud, I'm obsessed with sorting you out', and it would sound like something new and clean and enchanting.

When she kneels next to him he wakes up, staring at her with something like fright until his consciousness, floating slightly loose, settles back into his body and he recognises her and says:

'I was dreaming about you.'

'Yes?'

'It was a good dream.'

'You have good dreams . . .' she says. Then she laughs. 'Of course you do.'

Not understanding, he smiles at her. Then she climbs onto the sofa next to him and puts her mouth up to his, her hair falling onto his cheek and her own as if drawing them together, kissing him like she could take all the good dreams from him that way, by mouth, and live in them herself.

As Estella and Michael drive along the viaducts and tunnels of the Madeiran interior, the car wending its route familiarly around and through the mountains, he tells her about the island with a marvelling eagerness, as if both of them were tourists and Michael, having arrived a week earlier than her, is keen to pass on some tips.

'These are banana plantations,' he says, pointing to terraced hills like great mossed steps. 'They stop at a certain point up the mountains; it's too cold for them higher up.'

Estella gives the hills the solemn contemplation they appear to be due. From Funchal, looking up, it was difficult to believe the mountains could be so cold, steaming with cloud high above them. Now she is here she can't remember how warm it was by the sea that morning; turning up the heating in the car as they travel up through the steep, cool valleys and waterfalls, the mountain peaks towering through the mist. When they get out – parked confidently on the edge of a sheer precipice – so that Michael can show her the view, the air closes on her immediately, foggy like waterlogged velvet, pillowy and cold. The view is of white cloud, parting to reveal endless graduations of green. Not one type of green has been left out: grass to emerald to olive, chartreuse, teal, bottle green. She sniffs: even the air smells green.

The two of them have been spending most nights in her apartment lately, staying up talking and having sex, exhausted yet awake, humming with wide-eyed tiredness. They walk to work separately, Estella starting the day earlier than Michael. Nobody at the office officially knows that they are sleeping together, though everyone thought they were sleeping together anyway, so in a way nothing has changed. Michael continues to do his own work, refusing to delegate to her, refusing to admit he is her boss. When the subject comes up, he deflects her with light – but firm – mockery ('What are you after, a pay rise?').

Now they are on the way to the Quinta do Rosal, his family home, from which his parents have thankfully already departed. Estella is grateful not to have to meet them. She is nervous enough about meeting his childhood friend Vic, who has not been particularly well sold by Michael.

'You have to get past certain things before you can "get" Vic,' he explains. 'I do because I've known her for years. But I can see how everyone else would just be confused by her. Or annoyed. She's very religious, though I don't know where she got that from – not her parents, anyway. And socially she's quite awkward. You'll see what I mean. I think she is dimly aware of these concepts like small talk and tact and politeness, but she doesn't think they apply to her. I blame Jesus. He forgot to leave instructions on that stuff. If there had been a parable about the importance of not asking someone how much they earn or why they were at the doctor's, Vic would have been all over it.'

'I can't wait to meet her,' Estella says, uncertainly.

'Honestly, she's a really good person. Too good. She has one of the most well-developed senses of guilt I've ever seen. It's her biggest problem. It holds her back, I mean.'

'Well, as we've already established, you *would* think she's good, because you're good yourself.'

'So what would you be? Suspicious?'

'I'm not falling for that. Anyway, I don't mean to cast any doubt on Vic. I'm just being argumentative for the fun of it.'

This isn't strictly true: because Estella is not having fun; something that once would not have seemed unusual, but is a rarity in these post-Michael times. She is worried about the expectations that have been appearing lately: the basic social requirements she has, as a determined loner, previously been exempt from. She is used to avoiding contact, not seeking it out. She never needed to get further than the initial stages of 'getting to know' anybody, beyond finding out their name and then avoiding the use of it in favour of a cursory nod in passing. But now she has been for several drinks and dinners with friends of Michael: a well-rounded collection of friends, healthily diverse, but all funny, all *good* (through Michael it seems she has unprecedented access to the good people of the world). If his family were here it would be assumed that she would meet them. As it is, she is expected to meet Vic, and to learn to love her.

She is comforted once they get onto the steep road on Michael's side of the mountain and she sees Azenhas do Mar below her; the white buildings with their terracotta roofs and deep green or red shutters, vivid under the heavy sun. And then she is enchanted, too, by Michael's house; the cool shadowy rooms filled with the smooth purple scent of lilies; the garden lit almost white, a bright lake; the hushing of the lemon and jacaranda trees. At the end of the garden they stand at a low wall of smooth white stones, worn and voluptuous as the palms of hands, and look out at the hazy rim of the Atlantic, the impression it gives of its own disappearance, as if it is pouring over the edge of the world.

Before Vic arrives, Estella and Michael are already slightly drunk, having spent the afternoon sitting in the courtyard half watching the little lizards that gather in a sunny patch under the table, serious-faced and motionless. When one of them moves the lizards all disappear, like little trickles of melted copper. After a while of talking it seems unbearable that she and Michael aren't having sex, and so they go to his room, the voile full at the windows like a sail, blowing in apparently one minute to show a blue sky, the next to show the purple of the evening.

She falls asleep with Michael next to her and dreams about the apartment she used to live in with Jasper. Jasper is not there; she is standing alone in the evening light looking around at the tidiness of the flat, the leather sofa, the blank floor, the untouched marble and chrome of the kitchen, all cut into abstract night shapes by the town lights outside. The air is heavy with something just gone, or something about to arrive. She realises that Jasper's cast off shoes are on the floor, his keys and wallet on the side; that it won't be long before Jasper himself walks in. When she wakes up, with a sharp gasp of air as if she has been choking, she is startled first by the unfamiliar room, and then by Michael, not lying next to her but standing beside the bed.

'Are you OK?' he asks. She nods, too shocked to speak. 'I thought I'd leave you to sleep while I got dinner ready. Vic'll be here soon. Don't worry, she'll probably be late. It's very rude to be on time for dinner here, because it won't be ready, and an early arrival would draw attention to it.'

Estella, feeling the bitter sweat in the meeting points of her arms and knees, under her breasts, asks if she has time for a shower.

'All the time in the world,' says Michael cheerfully; something she later realises, as she hurries down the stairs to join their guest (never having believed before that the words 'their guest' would ever be used by her), to have been total bullshit.

When it comes to it, meeting Vic is not quite as awful as she had begun to expect. Estella finds it hard to talk to her; partly out of her own inexperience at chatting, partly because she feels a painful sympathy with the girl's awkwardness; her uncertainty. Vic's eyes land only every now and again on Estella's, like flies, taking off again almost as abruptly. She doesn't seem at ease in her own body; fidgeting in her chair, generally giving the impression of someone much younger and less attractive than she really is. Vic asks once about her parents, but the moment quickly passes, barely unsettling Estella, and no other moments follow it.

Once Vic has gone home, she and Michael sit in the garden again, talking lazily; the candle flames waving like ribbons in the blue dark; the music pulled this way and that by the low breeze.

'Vic was nice,' she says.

'She loved you, I could tell,' Michael says. 'Though that was a foregone conclusion.'

'Is it? I don't think I'm particularly lovable.'

She isn't looking for a compliment but making a statement, and Michael considers it seriously.

'I suppose when I met you I thought you wouldn't be friendly,' he says. 'You looked . . . guarded. Now I realise it's just that your expressions don't show all that much. Your resting face is . . .' he searches for a word – 'closed. In a nice way. You look like a Holbein noblewoman.'

'Or a broken television,' she says.

'Not at all. It makes your smile stand out. It's momentous when you smile. I love . . . I love it when you smile.'

The night hangs over them both suddenly as a candle flickers out. In the spaces between their voices there is a silence that radiates out for miles. Overhead the last traces of unearthly pale blue that had streaked the sky have vanished, leaving a uniform darkness that presses down between the jacaranda branches.

'Thank you,' she says, knowing, without even seeing it in his eyes, that this isn't enough.

The two of them carry on for a while in the same way, dividing their time between Funchal and Azenhas do Mar; agreeing that the latter has become their favourite. Estella likes to lie in the garden of the Quinta do Rosal sunbathing, absorbing the heat as if it alone sustains her. She learns the names of the flowers, like Noah getting to know his ark. Protea flowers are the primitive ones, visceral-looking, a heart on fire. The stiff, vivid green spines are aloes. Night-flowering jasmine, arum lilies, hibiscus, azaleas, bougainvillea on the white stone wall. Flaring orchids leopard-mouthed, or figured like butterfly wings.

With Michael she gets to know the village better, feeling more comfortable with this sort of intimacy than the human kind. The air feels softer in its narrow, neat streets. They go to the botanical gardens, the town square with its indolent dogs, the cafés. They take the steep path down the cliffs for a boat trip, drifting on the surface of the Atlantic as it gets late and the sun tracks along the sea back towards the sky, the tourists beginning to pass them in their returning boats as Estella leans her chin over the boat rim, watching the water tumble and frill.

They even visit the local graveyard, which – decorated strangely with crosses and monuments, bisected by small cobbled paths – Estella assumed at first to be an ornamental flower garden. It is directly under the sheer vertical cliff face, at a place where the green gives way to bare rock, faceted and complicated like a Braque painting. Michael shows her his ancestors' graves, telling her increasingly preposterous or obscene stories about them ('Great-great-aunt Isabella, contracted syphilis from a wandering pedlar, but managed to conceal it from the family and her husband by claiming her skin was especially sensitive to light and must always be fully clothed and veiled'), until she isn't inclined to believe even the true ones. Becoming silly, they have to quieten themselves as an old woman passes, wearing black.

'The widows here actually do wear black for the rest of their lives,' Michael says. 'Isn't that sad?'

'I don't know,' she says, only half listening.

She is wondering where her mother is buried. Like everything else, she left it to Carl to deal with. More than likely she was cremated, and has no final resting place; no basic square of green in a council-run welfare scheme for the dead. Perhaps Carl still has her ashes, having nowhere to scatter them besides the sofa Louise spent most of her time on. She wishes that she could remember the name of the beach she and Louise went to, now lost in a sun-lit corner of history. That would be where Louise ought to go, flying out over the pebbles, the choppy water.

'Do you believe in life after death?' Michael asks her. 'I have no idea. Tell me your opinion and I'll adopt it and pretend I thought it all along.'

The idea of Louise's soul still being around somewhere unsettles Estella deeply: an image of her mother wandering alone and unprotected through half-lit realms, as if in one of her chemical trances, lost in the woods and unable to get back. Or even worse: a glowing, guardian angel Louise, hovering over Estella's bed at night, looking down on her with her dark, horrified eyes.

'No, I don't,' she says, and changes the subject.

The only less than perfect thing about Azenhas do Mar is Vic. Though Estella doesn't understand her, she doesn't mind her either: earnest and tactless, with her always surprising laugh; ballooning too loud, worried-sounding. She has met Vic alone only on a few occasions. (After the first of these, a morning in the garden that she would have happily spent alone, she told Michael not to worry about arranging entertainment for her while he was away.) Early on, Vic had looked at her shyly – fidgeting as usual, hesitant – and said, unprompted, that Estella and Michael seemed happy together. Estella thought this was touching, particularly for a girl so uncomfortable with any discussion of feeling. Vic prefers to stick to the cold facts of life, as if she is researching a biography. She is interested only in jobs and significant dates: friendship and love leave her at a loss. Estella thinks she is probably autistic.

Early on, Vic gives Estella a fright when she turns up unexpectedly at the Quinta do Rosal and almost overhears a call that Estella has, for the first time in years, decided to make to Chloe. She is lying alone in the garden thinking of her old friend when it occurs to her that she could simply try calling Chloe's old number and see if she answers, which – after a few rings – she does.

'It's Kaya,' she says, hesitantly.

Chloe's voice bursts out into the empty garden, scattering the small birds in the tree above Estella: '*Kaya*? What the fuck!'

After calming Chloe enough for her volume and pitch to subside gradually back into the normal ranges, Estella hears about the life of her old home. Venus slept with a footballer and got pregnant and is set for life. Alisha left the Purple Tiger and now works as a dental hygienist ('Do you know what them fucking hygienists make? Go on, guess. It's mental!'). Chloe left Dave for Mike, a friend of his whom Estella vaguely remembers, a short guy always in the background, hanging back from the roll and crash of the others' banter like a timid swimmer at the edge of a rough sea. Mike is a carpenter, Chloe works as a receptionist, and they have a child named Kaya.

'She's beautiful, like you,' she says fondly. 'Anyway, listen . . . I've still got all your bloody money, Kaya! From the –' she lowers her voice discreetly – 'car, and that other stuff. Plus I did what you said and took all your Purple Tiger money out of your account, a bit at a time. I put it in a savings account for you so Dave wouldn't know about it. There's interest and everything. I didn't touch it – you've got about fifteen fucking grand there.'

'That's for you. You keep it.'

'No way, man, I'm not touching it! It's yours! You gotta come home and spend it. You can buy me a drink, for being so organised with the account and stuff.'

'Has anyone asked about me, since I left? The police?'

'Not a word. I told you, you're worrying about nothing. Nobody came to mine, nobody came to the Purple Tiger. They don't give a shit about you borrowing that doctor-mobile. Actually, a woman did ask about you once. Some old frump. I thought she was from the council. I told her you didn't live with me and she didn't argue with that. She didn't come back, either. Where are you now?'

'Madeira.'

Chloe shrieks with excitement. 'Jet-set lifestyle, man! Just like we always said!'

'We said that?'

'I did. I said you'd end up somewhere glamorous –' (Estella, looking with amusement up at the elegant windows of the Quinta do Rosal, has to acknowledge this) – 'You with anyone?'

'Sort of. Well, yes.'

'You're fucking sorted! You guys gonna come back here? Visit little Kaya?'

'I don't know if that's a good idea. You know – I worry about Jasper.'

'The doctor? Oh, no way. You can't stress about that. What's he gonna do? It's been years. He's got a new car. Probably got a new fucking girlfriend. She's probably stolen the new car. Yeah?! It's her he's after, not you.'

'I know,' Estella says, 'but I can't help it. After what I did to him, I'm always scared he'll come after me –'

'Yeah, I do get it,' says Chloe sympathetically, as there is the sound of a child's cry in the background. 'Fuck! Look, I'd better go. Kaya's woken up. Oh, no, no baby, don't cry, princess. Mummy's here. Kaya – I'm sorry. Can I call you back? Not you, Kaya. Mummy's talking to another Kaya . . . Oops – I didn't think that one through, did I? Let's talk properly soon. Please? Use this number. Love you, man. Fucking good to hear from you. Ahh! I do *try* not to swear around her, I promise. Oh, now, sssh . . .' Chloe's voice shrinks in the billowing wails. Kaya makes out, 'Love you. Bye . . . Bye', before the line cuts out, and she is alone again in the garden, finding herself at the door to the sitting room after what must have been an unconscious circling as she talked; absorbed in the conversation, pacing the lawn like a sleepwalker. Going inside to get some water and to wipe the sudden sweat off her stomach and face, she is shocked to find a stunned-looking Vic, standing in the darkness of the sitting room with her mouth open.

Afterwards, once all the painful explanations and niceties have been done with and Vic has been waved hurriedly off, back on her way to the hotel, Estella sits down with a glass of water (she wandered towards the brandy; veered away) and tries in a slow horror of panic, a drugged fright, to work out if Vic heard. She can't have, she thinks. If she had already heard a voice outside she wouldn't have looked quite so startled when Estella came into the room. And if she had heard what Estella was actually saying she certainly wouldn't have invited her to dinner. Estella watches Vic more closely after that to check for any signs of suspicion, or anything at all different in her, but can't detect a change. She is still abrupt, still awkward; still timidly preoccupied with the facts. Estella, with a sense of mingled guilt and compassion, realises that Vic is trying, in her own ham-fisted way, to get to know her.

What concerns Estella about the time they spend with Vic is not really the girl's interrogations – her dogged pursuit of a single line of conversation like a children's toy tractor that has been wound up and set off, rolling clumsily in only one direction – but that Michael will notice that Estella's replies to these questions are slightly off; that she is more than a little cagey. She isn't prepared for a situation like this; in her life as Estella nobody has been close enough – or boring enough – to ask what year she left university, or what her parents' favourite colour was.

'Vic's very interested in small details,' she says to Michael. They are walking through the botanical gardens along a cobbled path submerged in green, a bowered tunnel, fronded leaves knitted over their heads. The light is slow and dim as if they are on the seabed, moving through an underwater kingdom, the blue heads of hydrangeas like anemones, spiny aloes coiling like kraken, the tall cacti trees with their branches like coral. The real sea is visible only in glimpses, through clearings in the leaves.

She watches Michael carefully, but she needn't have worried. 'It's that village mentality,' he says, dismissively. 'It's a strange and narrow way of looking at things. But she'll go from worrying about the minutiae of local life to contemplating God without stopping anywhere in between. Like walking along, staring at the tiny stones on the path, or straight up at the sky, without actually looking at the road ahead.'

'You've given this some thought.'

'She exasperates me. She needs to get out of here, go and do something different. She doesn't even like travelling to Funchal, for fuck's sake.'

Estella's relief – having taken its first tentative steps out of hiding – stops dead, sighting a new trouble on the horizon.

'You want to travel a lot, don't you?' she says.

'I want to go everywhere. That's one thing I love about you; that you never stay in one place too long. That's how I want to be.'

He becomes enthusiastic. He tells her he wants them to go together to Japan and sing a karaoke duet. He wants to go to the Valdivian forests of Chile to see the deer as small as a cat, to visit the Intihuatana stone at Machu Picchu, to get drunk on Cachaca in Rio. He tells her about being robbed in South Africa by a group of men with machetes. He thought, for a few minutes, that he was about to die. He remembers his outrage, lying face down in the dust glittering in the sun, as the men talked about him in a language he didn't understand. 'I thought of all the things I wanted to do, before they let me go. I was making a list of things I was angry about not having done,' he says. 'Hey – that must be my "Choice". To see everything.'

Later he asks her, 'Why don't you have a Choice? How can you believe everything that leads up to it and not the conclusion? You need a project. What is it you want?'

She puts him off: 'I want to fuck you.' And Michael, always won over by a joke, drops the subject and obliges.

Afterwards, she lies next to him watching the drapes breathing at the window and trying to work out how she has changed. She feels as if she has taken off a heavy raincoat. She lets the sun onto her skin, eyes onto her face; close up, without ducking away. She is forgetting what it's like to feel cold. One night a few weeks ago it was unexpectedly cooler; the rain in the day sweeping all the heat off the coast. There was a sharpness to it, a sudden kick of memory. She thought of rain on traffic, water-spotted parkas, the grey sky above a knotweed-wound chain-link fence.

'How can you leave here?' she asks Michael, waking him up. 'Won't you miss it?'

'I always come back,' he says.

'And you always will?'

'It's like when you're little and you're out with your parents in a big place. Like a mall or a town centre. And they tell you that if you get lost or separated from them you'll all meet again, under the clock tower or by the fountain, or whatever –' (Estella smiles here, as if she, too, had that sort of childhood) – 'well, that's Madeira.'

'Meet you in Madeira,' she says lightly.

'Exactly.'

The next morning, Michael is out and back before she wakes up, arrested mid-stretch by the sight of him standing over the bed.

'You keep doing that. What are you doing? What time is it?'

'Too goddamn early, that's what time it is. I want a lot of credit and appreciation for this. My grand gesture.'

He has brought her flowers with diaphanous, layered petals, fresh bread for breakfast, small sticky cakes. 'Thank.you,' she says. She sits up in bed and he sits down next to her. The sun, undiscouraged by the thin drapes at the window, drops brightly onto him; dissolving his edges in white light. He looks extremely good; gold haired, grey eyed, warm skinned.

'Tell me a joke,' she says, to cover her unsettlement, the disorienting, sharp rise of tenderness.

'A woman gets out of her bath just as the doorbell rings. She's naked, so she doesn't answer it, but the doorbell keeps ringing. Finally, she goes downstairs and shouts through the letter box, "Who is it?" The person outside replies: "The blind man." *That's OK*, thinks the woman and she opens the door.

"Nice tits," says the man. "Where do you want the blinds?"

'Very funny,' she says. 'Kind *and* funny. I don't believe in you. You know that. I'm on to you.'

But after they have sex, once he lies back and she puts her hand on his chest and her head next to his and looks at the side of his nose, the unusual blackness of the lashes bordering the closed eyelid, the cool colours of his body in the shade, she recognises the feeling, running under and close to the shallow breath, the smell of salt, the adrenaline. She knows what it is, with a chill of recognition. Love. The ominous arrival of love.

When Estella tries to express to herself what the problem with loving Michael is, she keeps returning to the idea of a book she had when she was young, about a little girl who felt sick of all the things that were wrong with her life – an irritating younger brother, being bad at spelling, freckles; things like that. Estella can't remember the book in detail but somehow the little girl got to raise her complaint with the man in charge of allocating troubles to people – the Troublemaker – who told her to put all her troubles in a bag and take them to a hill covered in hundreds of bags of other people's troubles. The Troublemaker made her an offer: he would allow her to swap her own bag for another. But after examining the contents of all the other bags, the girl decided to take her own troubles (now appearing more friendly, more lovable than before) home again with her. Fair enough, Estella thinks. But what about the child living in a favela, or a township? The abused child, the child with no hands, the child dying of cancer. Why didn't these children get to take their troubles to the hill and swap them?

The book couldn't answer this. It was a nice book for nice children; children like Michael. She can see that Michael feels sorry for deprivation or injustice or suffering, but those things are alien to him; he can't really imagine them. He has been lucky, and his luck has made him good. He makes no excuses, he is brave, he creates himself at every moment. His happiness is the stronger for never having been called into question: its easy arrival, its facility, is what has made it so unshakeable.

Estella wonders what he would say if he found out that she isn't like that. She intends to create herself at each moment but there are times when it seems too hefty a task. She knows that the creation known as Estella carries smudges from the past, dents and scrapes and joins where, like a cut-and-shut car, she has been divided and re-grafted, becoming a strange, unworkable hybrid. He doesn't ask her about her old life in England and sometimes she wonders if this is out of respect for her reluctance to discuss it, or because he doesn't want to know; in the same way that a healthy animal shies instinctively away from the diseased.

The closest either of them have come to talking about her past was after he offered up (unasked: because Estella never asks questions she wouldn't like to answer) a frank history of his previous relationships, all of which seemed to end in a civilised and friendly manner. He is friends with most of them on Facebook.

'Not Vic?' she asked, laughing.

'God. No. What a weird thought. Actually – I say that, but one time years ago we did kiss. I was drunk. It's a bit hazy, to be honest. I'd been out somewhere and ran into her when I got back. She must have been out too, with other friends. It was like French-kissing my aunt. I think we both realised it was a silly idea. So, what about you?'

'I haven't kissed Vic.'

'I mean, what about your love life? I don't need numbers or anything. I don't care about any of that. Just tell me I'm better than they were in bed.'

She thought of Jasper in bed, holding her hands and staring at the wall.

'You are,' she said. 'Don't worry.'

Now Estella is wondering where this will all end. At customs, probably. At some point Michael will want to travel somewhere that carries out proper background checks, and if she tries to go with him it will end in her being ushered into a small room with plastic chairs and pale green paint, to wait for the arrival of the police. She knew this from the beginning, but didn't stop herself from getting emotionally attached. And it *does* feel like a near-physical attachment: her heart putting out its tiny shoots, to find him and curl around him, extending themselves, unfurling leaves and flowers. She finds she still doesn't want to stop herself. She wants to carry on, without thinking about the future. She has never had the kind of existence where it is appropriate to play relationship outcomes through in her head – the way she sees other women do, trying every direction and seeing what is at the end – and so she doesn't have to make an effort not to consider where she and Michael might end up. The only provision she makes for their future selves is this: If anything goes wrong, she tells herself, she can always just disappear.

Estella and Michael only argue once, walking along the seafront in Funchal arm in arm, until the conversation reaches the point where it feels strange to be in such apparently amicable contact, and they mutually draw away. A colleague of theirs had been in tears earlier that day: she had a brother who had been arrested, accused of rape. The colleague insisted the woman was cheating on her husband. When she was found out, she said she had been raped.

'That's awful,' Michael says now. 'How unfair. If it's true.'

'Who knows,' Estella says. 'And anyway, it could be more complicated than he did or he didn't.'

'What do you mean?'

'Well, are rape and sex two poles, or is it a sliding scale?'

'You can't be serious? Surely they're two poles.'

'You haven't ever wanted to rape somebody? Even just a momentary impulse?'

'Oh sure, yeah, my first girlfriend. My English teacher. Some girl I saw yesterday. Jesus, Estella, of course I haven't.'

'OK, well, let's say that's true,' she says quickly, noticing that he is irritated, ringing his keys in his hand like a bell, an alarm, 'what about those situations where the girl puts up a token protest that she doesn't mean? Or if she's too drunk to give consent but the guy is too drunk to know how drunk she is?'

'"Let's say that's true"? Can we go back to that? Are you saying you think I'm capable of it?'

'I think anyone is capable of nearly anything. Sartre said—'

'Fuck Sartre. Answer the question. Do *you* think *I'm* capable of it?'

Having already disentangled their arms, the two of them have now – with the same silent agreement – stopped walking, facing each other so that the joggers and the tourists moving along the promenade have to divide and detour around them. They stand like this for some time; Estella saying nothing, staring at the sea, until Michael turns and walks away. She watches him go; a straight-backed figure with its quick, clean stride, his hands tight in his pockets, not looking back.

When she goes back to the apartment and finds he isn't there she calls him. His phone rings out, twice. Estella goes from room to room looking for the things that are missing: his shoes, his wallet and his keys, in an odd inversion of her last night in Jasper's flat. When it gets dark and she is still sitting on the sofa with her phone blank in her hand, she realises he must have gone back to Azenhas do Mar. They were meant to drive down together in the morning, but he has left without her.

At midnight, lying stiff and staring in the bed, she realises she has lost the knack of sleeping alone. Not just that; she is in the grip of an unfamiliar emotion – arising from a situation she has never experienced – the feeling of having said something unfair to a lover, and refusing to take it back. Her fingers pinch and worry the sheets; regret burns at her corneas. She gets up, dresses and orders a taxi to take her to Azenhas do Mar; driving unbearably slowly down the mountain, her face against the window for the first sight of the Quinta do Rosal below them, its lights on, casting long shapes of yellow across the darkness of the gardens.

Estella lets herself in at the kitchen door, which Michael always leaves open, and finds him half-folded over at a table in the sitting room, his head resting on his hands. He looks up at her without saying anything, neither welcoming nor unwelcoming. He looks tired.

'I'm sorry,' she says. 'I'm sorry. I know rape isn't to do with sex. It's anger and control and punishment. I know you aren't like that.'

She puts her arms around him and rests her cheek on his back, until he sighs and unbends himself.

'You worried me,' he says.

'I'm sorry.'

'No need to apologise. What time is it? You must be tired.' He rubs his face and puts his arms out, stretching expansively. 'I for one am bloody exhausted. Let's go to bed.'

Estella watches him uncertainly as he gets up and pours two glasses of water, with his back to her, saying, 'Oh, remind me, tomorrow morning I need to go out and buy some coffee.'

'What?'

'Yeah, I looked in the tin and we're out.' To her surprise, he is smiling when he turns around; handing her the water with a joke about remembering to lock the back door in future, and by the time he is in the shower ('I smell like a dog's armpit, if dogs have arms . . . do they?') singing the chorus of a particularly bombastic eighties hit, she understands the argument is genuinely over.

In the morning, Estella, waking first, takes the opportunity to look at Michael; almost every part of his body laid and overlaid with muscle, burnt brown skin, rough blond hair. She finds the unprotected places: the sleeping eyelids, his newly vulnerable mouth. She strokes the pulse at his throat, which is silky and fragile. She fits her body into his, angling around his knee and shoulder, breathing his grassy, cool smell.

Her mind, unattended, leaks time. What comes back to her then is the ending to her memory of her day at the seaside with Louise. She – Kaya – is sitting on a train with her socks wet from running to the sea one last time: the water, rising suddenly, had lapped over her feet. Louise has started to doze off, rocked into sleep by the genial chug of the train. Kaya sits next to her, running her tongue over her lips to get the last sweetness of the ice cream, utterly content.

Michael wakes up not long after her; exiting sleep as messily as always, with nonsensical mutterings and a roll like a crocodile drowning an antelope.

'Good morning,' he says eventually, focussing on her. 'How long have you been awake? What are you pondering?'

Estella feels a strong urge to share the good news: that she has landed a memory, reeled in silvery fresh, a fish from a dark and unfriendly sea. But she isn't sure how to convey the importance of it without telling him that she has been lying about her parents – supposedly alive and well and estranged in Berkshire – after which he might guess that there are more lies, holding her together like stitching. One thread can't be pulled without the whole thing coming apart.

'I love you,' she says instead, surprising them both. Never

mind, she thinks, that it feels like an evasion. He is delighted, and she feels something of that delight too, holding him tightly, her face in his neck so that he can't meet her eye.

The day of discovery comes, of course. It isn't a surprise to Estella, who begins every encounter warily, with a flare of trepidation. Finally, a conversation has turned out the way she expected. Even the timing of it, so soon after Michael has asked her to move in with him ('It's ridiculous that we live in two homes. My parents would be annoyed if I sold their place, so we should get rid of the flat.'), seems appropriate. When she said yes to him she had the feeling of over-reaching, taking too much. People who get away with something always go too far: gamblers who lose more than they just won; party crashers who aren't content with standing at the fringes and must move, emboldened, into the centre of the dance floor. Robbers who get too reckless, swindlers who get too greedy. She has been dawdling with her hand in the monkey trap, clutching her treasure, and now she has been caught.

The hows and whys of how she has been found out seem almost irrelevant to her; it is simply the natural tipping back of the universe, restoring balance. This counter-reaction to her deception could have been a letter, a summons, a knock on the door, a call into an office. It just happens to take the form of Vic peering up at her through her open car window, looking both terrified and self-righteous, her hands still clamped on the wheel. She isn't sure how much Vic knows but that doesn't seem to matter either: if one thing is revealed the rest will inevitably follow.

Walking back to the Quinta do Rosal with the backs of her legs stinging from her jump against the wall and her hands clenched against her fluttering dress, Estella finds the capacity to be blackly amused at how she had previously judged Vic. She had thought Vic a harmless innocent who had the misfortune of sounding like an unfriendly inquisitor, when in reality it was the other way around. Estella can't find the energy to guess at how Vic found out; to wonder whether it was the telephone call or not. It's all over, she thinks. The fire has come and gone and taken everything with it, and there is no point in poking around the smouldering remains, looking for evidence of faulty wiring or unstubbed cigarettes.

Estella gets back to the Quinta do Rosal, packs her things – scattered thoughtlessly across the bed, bathroom and sitting room as a further reminder of her fatal complacency – and calls a taxi to take her to the apartment in Funchal. She leaves the silent house without looking back, not wanting to see the paintings of Michael's ancestors, or the view through to the sunny gardens, or anything else that might make her dwell on the nature of happiness or loss, the sharpness of the line between one and the other, and in this she is almost entirely successful, at least until she is in the car climbing the cliff road for the last time, when she looks back to see it all disappearing behind her like a brief and colourful dream; like nothing substantial, which – she supposes – it wasn't.

Estella goes into her apartment the back way, through a quadrangle with a dusty fountain at its centre, its mermaids half covered with flowered vines; mimosa and eucalyptus trees leaning over the walls from the gardens backing on to it. The square is empty but for a cat watching her from a wall. The sky is motionless. There is a feeling, in the silent, thinned heat, of the end of the summer.

She tries to remember what she and Michael said and did that morning as she climbs the stairs to the apartment. His face – its straight, short nose and grey eyes – takes a few moments to turn and rearrange in her memory, as if there is already something of the stranger about him. He was leaving the Quinta do Rosal for work, getting into his car. She had leaned out of the bedroom window to wave.

'Bye, Juliet,' he called, and she blew him a kiss, not knowing that this was her last sight of him, gazing up with his hand shading his eyes and the sun erasing the rest of his face, turning it back into a dazzling emptiness, a blank white space.

In the flat the air conditioning has broken again, and Estella packs in a solid, muggy heat, pushing her way through it as if wading through marshy water. The heat doesn't penetrate the chill of her body; the hairs on her arms standing up as if unsure whether to fight the warmth or the cold. She doesn't have much to pack; old habits have kept her from accumulating possessions – even here – and after only an hour she finds that everything she owns has fitted back into the suitcase she arrived with. She has never cared much about the weight of her own existence, but now, standing in the doorway, she finds it a bleak thought: coming and going like a dead leaf, neither adding anything, nor taking anything away.

She goes back into the flat and picks up each of Michael's

things, holding them for a little while, as if determining how much of him each one retains. A toothbrush, a watch, a jumper, a book. The jumper is soft and limp with wear, smelling slightly of cinnamon and grass. She puts it to her face and breathes it in, before worrying that she will inhale all its stored scent, when she ought to be saving it for the future. She rolls it up tightly and puts it into her bag. It will be the first thing she has ever had that can be called a memento. She took nothing of Louise's before she left: she didn't have a chance, and wouldn't have known what to take anyway. She wonders whether she would even have wanted the china lady now, if it could somehow be got back. It seems to her that there is an inherent sadness to an object once its original owner no longer exists. All it can signify is absence; it becomes an abandoned thing; negative space. She takes the jumper out of her bag and puts it back on the bed. Then she lets herself out of the flat, posts the key back through the door, and takes a taxi to the airport.

EPILOGUE I

Maura is sitting with a cup of tea and a client in her new office in London. She moved two weeks ago and most of her files are currently stacked in a cupboard, still in their labelled brown boxes. The temporary emptiness has given the office an air of efficiency and minimalism; her desk bare of anything except a computer and a peace lily, her newly painted walls staring at each other's empty faces.

The new location is decent enough. It has a good view of the London Eye, which Maura considers to be rather pointless, but everyone who comes in comments on it, apparently impressed. There are ten other people working for her firm, all of whom would probably appreciate this view more than she, but Maura sits here anyway, like a dog in the manger, knowing how much importance the world places on small signs of authority. Who gets the view. Who makes the tea. She did not make this cup, steaming in front of her. She looks at it assessingly before reaching for it, as if daring it to be too hot. It is, however, a perfectly pleasant temperature, and she sips it with a minute nod of approval.

Michael Worth, the man sitting opposite her, is young and

– though she has come to think of good looks as at best distracting and at worst actively duplicitous – extremely good-looking. Dark blond and broad shouldered; grey eyes and a straightforwardly disarming smile. She finds herself smiling back at him. 'Well, well,' she says, slightly flustered.

Michael has got her details from the large and expensive ads that she has been told now dominate most online searches for private detectives, insinuating themselves into the Internet's suspicious and hopeful hearts. He has turned down a cup of tea. He wants her to find a former girlfriend of his called Estella White, absconded under strange circumstances.

'I know something isn't right about the way she left,' he says. 'My friend Vic thought she might have been a gold digger or something sinister, but she didn't take anything of mine. She didn't even collect her pay before she left. She didn't give any sign at all that she was going to leave. She'd said she was going to move in with me. I thought she was excited about it.'

'When did you see her last?'

'I went to work in the morning and she stayed at the house. She had the day off. She was gone when I got back.'

'Take a tissue,' Maura says. She offers no more comfort, usually, than a box of tissues pushed gently across the desk.

When Michael gives her his photographs of Estella she looks at them with the sense of a far-off bell ringing, an insistent chime, echoed in distant reaches of her memory. After he has gone she goes to the cupboard and starts opening the boxes – scattering them, regrettably, all over the clear floor of her office – until she finds the picture of a girl named Star, given to her by Alice Rooke, several years before.

It is obvious that this is the same woman, changed by just a few years into a dark-haired, stony-faced siren. Only in a couple of Michael's pictures does her expression relent, revealing something younger and sweeter, a smile, or a look of worry. She remembers how elusive the girl was. Living in someone's spare bedroom, moving through the low lights of the strip club, the night road home. A girl like that slips through some cracks but stands out in other ways; none of which are good for her. At the time she made no judgements concerning Star: accordingly, it does not surprise her now that Star has turned into Estella, or that Estella has vanished.

She remembers Alice. She had quite liked her, as much as it was practical to do so: an attractive woman, with the artificial composure that overlies intense nervous stress. She was numb, polite, cocooned with misery. Maura had suspected her husband Jasper, who had fled the country, of some sort of violence. She still wouldn't rule it out. Jasper had, in fact, turned up again after a month, and they had divorced. Later, she checked up on Alice, out of interest rather than professional necessity, and found out that Alice got the house and custody of their son. She became an interior designer, acquired a rescue greyhound, a boyfriend named Oliver. Jasper remarried and moved to Canada, where his teenage son found excuses not to visit him.

Maura, calling around various companies across Europe, discovers Estella White's CV to be a strange mix of fact and fiction. She genuinely did work for an office supplies firm in Germany, and was fondly remembered as a quiet and diligent employee. A bar she spent a year managing in Amsterdam never existed. The woman she speaks to at Manchester University says, 'Not this again.'

'What do you mean?' Maura asks blandly.

'This is the second call we've had about Estella White lately. There was no Estella White here. I'm sorry, but there's obviously some misunderstanding.'

'Oh, my colleague has already called, has she?'

'Yes, but as I said to her, we have never had a student of that name. You must have it wrong.'

'Clearly,' Maura says. 'I'll pass that on to her.'

Maura calls Michael and asks him for Vic's details. She doesn't explain why, and she doesn't tell him about Star. Though she would never admit to anything so vulgar as *showmanship*, she favours a grand unveiling, presenting her information only at the conclusion of a case. Michael himself does not press her for explanations or a progress report; he answers her obediently, like a child who has put all his faith in his parent to sort things out. He seems relieved simply to be asked questions, comforted by the idea that something is happening.

Maura tracks down Vic, who has been managing a restaurant in Brighton for the past couple of months. It takes her a while to realise that the woman bringing her cucumber and ginger mocktails is the Vic of Michael's description. She has evidently lost weight, at least six inches of hair, and a few hang-ups. This Vic has a professional glittering smile and an air of capable assurance. Her cleavage peeks discreetly between the buttons of her neat black shirt. She isn't inclined to linger and chat to Maura, but then the restaurant seems both busy and understaffed, presumably the reason why Vic is serving food herself. Maura waits patiently for other customers to leave, then, once it is quiet, she asks Vic if she might speak to her.

Maura finds that if difficult questions are to be asked it is usually better to be direct. She has a neutral, matter-of-fact manner and the knack of prying without it seeming intrusive. Her questions are those of a diagnosing doctor, measured and detached; like them, she is often delving into places of shame and sickness. She explains now to Vic that she knows Vic was investigating Estella. 'I haven't told my client yet,' she adds, 'I thought I'd speak to you first.'

Vic stares at her for a moment, before her mouth trembles. She asks if they can talk outside. Maura notices with interest that she seems almost immediately like a younger, more awkward woman. Her hands plait around each other. Her eyes move about quickly, stopping nowhere for long. She blinks down on her tears.

'I'm sorry,' Vic says, once outside. 'I'm ashamed of saying anything. I don't know what I was thinking.'

'You feel you were mistaken?'

'I don't know. I don't know what the truth was. I just should have stayed out of it. Or told Michael what I did. I was involved for the wrong reasons.' She sniffles, and Maura hands her a tissue. 'Does Michael know what I said? Is he your client?'

'I'm not able to say.'

'Oh, yeah.' Like Michael, Vic appears to accept the authority of the private detective. 'Of course,' she says in a small voice.

Let me always work with middle-class young people, Maura thinks. It doesn't occur to them to not be polite, to question the wool suit. Star's old friend Chloe, with her monosyllabic hostility, had a lot more sense.

Ultimately, Vic isn't able to tell Maura anything else about Estella: all she knew was that the girl was worried about an unnamed man coming after her, and that she didn't attend university where she said she did. 'Please tell Michael I said sorry, for interfering,' Vic asks her, when she leaves.

Maura nods once, opaquely, but passes Vic's message to Michael when she presents him with her report a couple of weeks later.

'*Vic?*' Michael says incredulously. 'I don't believe it. What the fuck got into her?' He shakes his head. 'Forget it; I don't care. It doesn't matter.' The rest of it – Estella's former incarnation as Star, the Purple Tiger, her involvement with Jasper, her fantastical CV, whoever she was before she became Star – he also dismisses.

'I know who she is now,' he says. 'I never asked her about her past. She didn't want to talk about it and I accepted that was how it would be. She didn't believe that the past changes the present self, because the self is its own creation, every day. And I agree with her.'

Admitting that there is nothing else he can do in the UK, he asks her to keep looking for Estella and call him if she finds anything. In the meantime, he will go back to his parents' house in Madeira.

'I'll certainly do that,' Maura says. She has begun to be curious about Estella herself, moving from one persona to another; different name, appearance, biographical details. The girl has gone through her life as if life is something to be put on and dropped, wrapped temporarily around herself like a cloak. What is inside the cloak is anyone's guess. Perhaps Michael knows most about her, after all. In an indefensible lapse of professional neutrality, she finds herself hoping that they will be reunited.

'Would you do something for me?' he asks her, before he leaves. 'Would you speak to Chloe again? Don't ask her any questions. Just give her a message to pass on to Estella, if she ever speaks to her. Tell her that I'm waiting for her and I don't care about anything from before. I'll go on the run with her if I have to. We can rob banks like Bonnie and Clyde. That's a joke . . . Don't tell her that.'

He stares out of the window at the distant spokes of the London Eye, though his gaze has gone beyond it, out to the fogged grey horizon, as if it might find Estella there.

'I'm hoping she might just . . . come back. We said once that Madeira was our meeting point. I think that's the best place for me to be for now: back in Madeira. Waiting at home.'

EPILOGUE II

Estella spends the next few months in Paris, arriving in time for the start of winter, when everything is darkening and cooling and hardening. The trees shake off their clothing as if to shock with their poverty; their ugly bones. She works in a bar and lives above it with another waitress, sharing the same room. The other girl is from Slovakia and talks in her sleep. 'Nerozumiem,' she exclaims, in a harsh voice unlike her daytime self. The customers come in and drip rain on the floor and occasionally address her in English, with the delight of all English people who encounter one of their own abroad, even someone so blankly unwelcoming.

She walks around the city but can't find her old enthusiasm for visiting libraries or lecture theatres. She walks circuitous routes and goes home again to sleep. She doesn't read. She visits Sartre and De Beauvoir's graves, which are in a cemetery popular with tourists, and tries – in the quiet moments between the driftings up and away of people with cameras and maps – to feel something, but is struck instead by how stupid the whole thing is, seeking out physical remains, valuing only the tangible. As she walks home, she thinks the tangible is the last thing she wants; feeling a sudden disgust for all the surfaces of the city; the chilly burn of the fluorescent lights, the reflective, steely pavement, the spangled glass of shop windows, the dirty train seats, the icy, pollution-coated stone.

One evening, feeling herself goaded beyond her usual tolerance of loneliness, unable to face the horror of her own company in bed, she goes downstairs to the phone in the darkened café and considers calling Michael. She sits among the forest of upturned chair legs and watches people pass below the street light outside, their shadows striping the wall opposite. She realises that while Michael would have wanted to hear from the Estella he knew, he certainly wouldn't want to hear from this one. She hopes he is angry with her, now that Vic has told him the truth. She would rather he be angry or cold than hurt; she can't bear to think of damage to his perfect, inviolable happiness.

It occurs to her that she might ring Chloe, but she reconsiders that call too: it is late, and she might wake the baby. She can call Chloe tomorrow. Having run out of people she might want to speak to, she goes, reluctantly, up to bed.

Estella doesn't dream about Jasper's flat any more, or about being chased. In her sleep she floats over the Atlantic; flying back at night, moving slowly over the tiny mysterious waves, the black, dense cold. Night on water, the same sea she crossed when she left. She looks at it and tries to remember what it looked like in the sun; the blue gullies, the light skittering across its surface, endlessly turning constellations.

That night she dreams about Michael. She must have been struggling in her sleep because she wakes up trussed in the sheets – her arms wide, her pillow desolate and damp – but in the dream she couldn't move. Michael was on a boat and she was under the water, the same night water, dark and airless and deep. She has heard that if you die in a dream you wake up, but in this dream, though she knew she was dead, she did not wake but could only lie there immobile, watching the dream carry on without her. The boat passed over her, and was gone. She floated, for what seemed like a very long time, below the water, until morning came.

She lies in bed, shocked into a cold wakefulness by the dream and the bitter grey dawn outside, gradually making sense of the irregular breathing of the Slovakian waitress. She remembers how she lay in bed once at her mother's flat and thought it wouldn't matter if she died. It seems to matter now, strangely. The idea of it pains her, now that she has absolutely nothing left: cast out of Madeira, the floating garden, giving up her claim on whatever love she might have been entitled to.

She permits herself, for the first time, to imagine how it might be if she went back. She walks through each moment of it as if she has just arrived, allowing herself the immersion, the slow playing out. First the cocooning sanity of the plane; marked neatly with instructions and codes of behaviour. She is glad to conform to it; waiting her turn to grapple with her bag in the overhead locker, shuffling down the aisle with all the other passengers, until they are out on the warm tarmac of the airport, hazy with very early morning, looking out over the wind-whipped Atlantic. The airport's runway (the ninth most dangerous in the world, according to Michael) hovers above the sea on rows of great pillars like the Parthenon. She gets into a taxi ('*Bom Dia*. Not Funchal: Azenhas do Mar. Further along the coast. I'll direct you.') and they pass below it on the old road, watching the pillars slowly rise up around them like a drowned city returning from the sea.

The car slides through the indistinct shapes of the dawn. It has no air conditioning but for the open windows and the air rushes past her face, bringing in the vapour of the sea, the vanished water. It takes an hour and a half to get to Azenhas do Mar, but she doesn't sleep. She watches instead as the trees slowly take on colour; the road brightening as it climbs, up towards the florid fringes of the levadas, dripping with leaves, vined, glossy, plate-leaved, palm-fronded. The sea shows, briefly, through the trees.

When the taxi has navigated the Rua da Madalena and reached the gates of the Quinta do Rosal, she gets out with her case, refusing help, and pays the driver at the window. She watches his car make its gritty progress back down the road, in a white cloud like icing sugar. Then she turns and looks up at the windows of the house, opaque with reflected light. Michael must be sleeping in the bedroom – their bedroom: the gold silk robe he bought her still hanging, perhaps, on the back of the door. She thinks she will go around to the gardens and slip in through the always unlocked back door; wait in the kitchen for him to wake up.

Estella has the peculiar feeling, pushing open the wrought-iron gate and going into the garden, that time has ended in some way. The new sun has something almost transcendental in its splendid opulence, as if it is Plato's sun, shining perpetually on an ideal plain. The lawn burns verdant green and wet, the smooth white stones of the wall glow like deep-sea creatures. The garden is a silent carnival; the camellia, azaleas, the delicately patterned orchids, the lemon trees, the Escheresque branches of the jacaranda. She can smell the nectar of the jasmine; the liquorice scent of fennel.

She stands in the garden and hears Michael in the house; a clatter in the kitchen, a rush of tap water. He is up earlier than she expected. Any moment now he will see her standing outside and come out of the door. She already knows exactly how he looks, before she sees him. She forgot nothing about him after all. He is so clear in the light; every line, every colour and edge defined and radiant. When he comes outside, she will tell him everything.

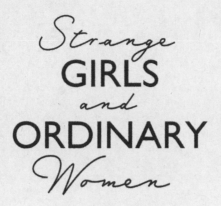

BONUS MATERIAL

The Open Ending
Morgan's Favourite Fictional Females
Q & A with Morgan McCarthy
Reading Group Questions

THE OPEN ENDING

I chose to leave my latest novel, *Strange Girls and Ordinary Women*, without fully playing out the fates of two of the main characters. Michael and Estella's eventual reunion is imagined by both, but has not yet come to pass. Believe it or not, I didn't do this just to annoy readers. My partially open ending is in the spirit of a long tradition of uncertain conclusions in fiction. It can be a risky game, however. Novels which leave unanswered questions or refuse to provide conclusive interpretations of their goings on often divide their audience. Some readers find them frustrating, even tortuous; unable to bear not knowing 'what really happened.' Others delight in the open ending, either welcoming the opportunity to impose their own meaning, considering this type of conclusion more true to life (which is frequently inconclusive), or enjoying the post-modern reminder that a novel, after all, has not really happened.

Open endings range from the gently ambiguous to the sorely challenging. At the lower end of the scale is the ending in which the reader basically knows what is going to happen - and so is not left *too* tormented by curiosity - but the action itself takes place off the page. *Brighton Rock* by Graham Greene is a masterly example of this; leaving the reader with a picture of the unfortunate Rose about to play her record that is far more horrifying for not having been described. I personally enjoy this kind of ending as it leaves me with an increased sense that the characters are real; that they are carrying on their lives off the page, with only the reader's view of them abruptly curtained over. *Strange Girls and Ordinary Women*'s ending falls into this type; though hopefully the implied ending is rather nicer than *Brighton Rock*'s.

More ambiguous is the novel that leaves its characters after a conclusion of sorts, yet with enough of their story untold to leave the reader wondering about them. They may have reached a defining moment, but there is enough hope on the horizon or trouble to come that the reader may find themselves staring with horror and a swelling sense of injustice at the last page. Margaret Atwood's *The Handmaid's Tale*, Margaret Mitchell's *Gone with the Wind*, and Michel Faber's *The Crimson Petal and the White* are all classic examples of this. There is also the 'unanswered question' novel. Who killed *The Little Friend*'s Robin Cleve Dufresnes? What happened in the cave in *A Passage to India*? We'll never know, and while for some readers that's just too much to bear, others find that the apparently central mystery has, as the novel progresses, become less urgent as other elements of the story come to the fore.

Finally there are the most extreme types of open-ended novels. The stakes are high at this end of the spectrum: readers will either never forget these books, or never forget how much they hate them. Here we have the novel that remains obdurately enigmatic, all the way up to and finally beyond its ending, such as Joyce's *Finnegan's Wake* and Ishiguro's dreamlike *The Unconsoled*. Here, too, are the post-modern novels in which the reader is explicitly given a choice of what to believe. Charlotte Brontë, early on, left her readers with a 'little puzzle' of whether the heroine of *Villette*, Lucy Snowe, was rewarded in the final pages with the return of her lover, or whether his ship was lost in a storm at sea. Later John Fowles confounded expectations with his insistence on the fictionality of events in *The French Lieutenant's Woman*, to the point of giving readers multiple endings to choose from. This is perhaps the most confrontational type of open ending: to not only leave the reader to wonder, but to insist on their own role in the narrative; burdening them with the uncomfortable responsibility of drawing their own conclusions.

To return to the disagreement between those who love and those who hate open endings; I myself am (perhaps appropriately) in neither camp and both. Some things, particularly intense love or intense tragedy, can be more powerful imagined than described. And while I may not always enjoy the feelings of frustration or curiosity I am left with after an ambiguous or open ending, at least I am left with it. I love a novel that haunts me, even if that haunting isn't an entirely pleasant experience. With a neatly tied up finale I rarely have the sensation I enjoy most when finishing an open-ended novel: the particular strangeness of the feeling that the life of a novel has sneaked into the everyday world I return to; remaining there long after the book itself has been put aside.

MY FAVOURITE FICTIONAL FEMALES

I didn't realise it before compiling this list, but it seems my favourite portrayals of women in fiction fall broadly into two types.

The first set out to achieve their goals by manipulating male ideas of what women ought to be, rather than remaining obedient to them. They attempt to take control of their lives by performing the hackneyed roles expected of them, while secretly going about something very different. The second type are more open in their efforts to live life their own way. They are the visible leaders of rebellion; women fighting in plain sight against repressive societal convention, knowing they face the consequences of doing so.

Whether these characters covertly or overtly defy the rules of their day; whether they succeed, or find the forces ranged against them are simply too powerful, it is their skill, strength and bravery in trying that is fascinating, and which always brings me back to their stories.

Estella, *Great Expectations*
The adopted daughter of Charles Dickens' mad spinster, Miss Havisham, the young Estella is an unfortunate victim of the Victorian battle of the sexes. Trained by her jilted adoptive mother to become a callous heartbreaker, Estella's adult struggle to assert herself and find her own moral compass is moving and still thought-provoking today. Mercilessly stereotyped by both women and men, Estella is perhaps destroyed, perhaps saved; depending on which of Dickens' two endings you prefer to believe.

Becky Sharp, *Vanity Fair*
William Makepeace Thackeray's unforgettable adventuress has become a template for trickery; exploiting female stereotypes in her rise to the top. She is a complicated character; monstrous in various ways, unexpectedly laudable in others, as when she ultimately frees the hapless Amelia from her own delusions. Though the narrator condemns her he is also clearly fascinated by her; as, inevitably, is the reader. For all her many faults I find myself willing her to succeed.

Grace Marks, *Alias Grace*
Both before and after she is accused of the murder of her employer, Grace learns the hard way that deviation from societal expectations is severely punished. By the end of Margaret Atwood's novel she is an expert in performance art; a master of disguise, leaving not only society but the reader guessing at the truth of not only what really happened, but who she really is.

Nicola Six, *London Fields*
Martin Amis's modern day femme fatale pursues death with the same energy and skill as Becky Sharp pursues life: adopting persona after bewildering persona; utilising the men who have the misfortune to cross her path. As with Becky Sharp, there is always a part of her that remains inscrutable to the reader, adding to her fascination.

Edna Pontellier, *The Awakening*
Kate Chopin's genius gives a haunting power to the story of Edna Pontellier: a thwarted turn of the century trophy wife living in New Orleans. Edna comes to realise that there is more to life than marriage and children, and embarks on a journey of discovery, seeking out creativity, passion and sensuous experience. But society is closing in, intent on bringing her back into line.

Mary Crawford, *Mansfield Park*
Irreverent, cynical and witty, Mary is the life of Jane Austen's novel as well as the party. She shows up the ostensible heroine, Fanny Price, as the dull doormat she is, and for this crime she must be rather jarringly sacrificed; losing her chance to marry Edmund. Really she has had a lucky escape.

Margarita, *The Master and Margarita*
In Mikhail Bulgakov's satirical tale of the fantastical events that ensue when the Devil arrives in 1930s' Moscow, Margarita herself stands out like a dark star: brave, passionate, and kind. Disobeying social convention at every turn (to the point of

presiding over the Devil's ball), she would give up everything to live in penniless happiness with her poet lover.

Janie Crawford, *Their Eyes Were Watching God*
Zora Neale Hurston's Janie is a young black woman growing up in early 20th century Florida. For a woman for whom racism, sexism, rape and violence were daily realities, Janie's determination to find her own voice, independence, and love on her own terms makes for an unexpectedly joyful read. At times her determination to thrive reminded me of another formidably optimistic heroine, Defoe's Moll Flanders.

Fevvers, *Nights at the Circus*
Angela Carter's heroine is a dazzling winged aerialiste, a playful trickster who leaves neither her fellow characters nor the reader in any doubt that she is in absolute control of her narrative. She is covert and overt in her determination to assert herself; both soldier and spy. Switching between virtuoso performance and outrageous authenticity with breakneck speed, Fevvers seduces, manipulates, takes command, and ultimately triumphs.

Q & A WITH MORGAN MCCARTHY

꩜

What was your inspiration for writing such a female driven narrative?

I've always been interested in relationships between women, and how they are affected by their relationships with men. It felt like the right time to write a novel, not so much about love, as about female perception, and how fragile it can be in the face of competition and fear.

Out of your three main characters, who do you most identify with?

Nobody, actually! In terms of both their lives and their personalities – firstly their circumstances, and secondly what these women have become in order to cope – I have no common ground with any of them. There are a few views of theirs that I share, such as Alice's horror of awkward moments or Kaya's interest in philosophy, but on the whole I'm very different to all three.

How difficult was it to write three very different points of view?

Not too hard: I actually wrote them in order and it was only later that I divided them up. This was a good way of doing things as it allowed me to immerse myself in each woman's mindset rather than going to and fro between them and potentially losing the clarity of each.

There are some very sexually aggressive moments in the novel – were these hard to write?

Yes, very much so. My first draft actually was more tentative in terms of the depiction of events; only later did I add more detail. I had planned out these moments, but when it came to actually writing them I did feel slightly squeamish.

Your ending is something of a cliffhanger – do you ever picture what happens after the pages end?

Not always, but in the case of this novel there is an outcome I prefer, and I think that's implicit in the ending itself.

What research did you undertake for the novel?

I went to Madeira to hunt for a location for the fictional village of Azenhas do Mar, which is roughly based on the real village of Sao Vicente. I also interviewed people who had experienced both sides of the strip club industry, and visited a strip club myself. The first research trip was definitely more fun than the second.

Which writers most inspire you?

Too many to list here, but in the context of this novel, I was inspired by Margaret Atwood's *The Robber Bride*, by Alice Munro, and by Jane Austen. In very different ways they all excel at depicting the nuances of female friendship, and how it stands up to the threat of love.

What is your next project?

I'm writing about a man, Oliver, who is renovating an old house when he discovers a manuscript that could hold the key to the unsolved disappearance of a woman in the 1920s. It's a novel about history, and love, and the endless search for meaning in both of these.

READING GROUP QUESTIONS

1. Which of the three women in the novel did you most empathise with and why?

2. Which of the three, if any, do you feel is the driving force in the novel?

3. How did you feel about the development of the characters in the story? Who do you feel grew the most over the course of the novel?

4. Is Kaya's sexuality something she exploits successfully or something she is ultimately abused for?

5. There is a wide variety of depictions of love in the novel. Which, if any, would you consider to represent genuine love?

6. Would you describe Alice as a stereotypical submissive housewife? Is this inverted in any way?

7. Why do you feel the novel was mostly written in the present tense?

8. How did you feel about the slightly open ending? Do you have an opinion about what would happen next?

You are invited to join us behind the scenes at Tinder Press

TINDER
PRESS

To meet our authors, browse our books
and discover exclusive content on our
blog visit us at

www.tinderpress.co.uk

For the latest news and views from the team
Follow us on Twitter

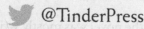 @TinderPress